The
Fifth Season

Patti Dickinson

The
Fifth Season

Patti Dickinson

Bitterroot Mountain
PUBLISHING, LLC.
P.O. Box 3508 Hayden, ID 83815

Bitterroot Mountain Publishing
Hayden, Idaho 83835

Visit our Website www.BitterrootMountainPublishing

Printed in the United States of America

First Edition

10 9 8 7 6 5 4 3 2 1

ISBN: 978-1-940025-15-5

Print layout by eBooks By Barb for booknook.biz

To my husband David

for his love, his humor, and unwavering faith

Acknowledgments

As an observer of people and life, I have come across many women and men who have found the fifth season, and even more who are still striving to find it. They have shared their stories with me and I acknowledge each one and their journey for they have all contributed to this book. A note of gratitude goes to my friend, Diana Johns, Physician and horse-lover extraordinaire, for sharing her knowledge and enthusiasm for these beautiful animals.

Prologue

Late August, Pine Ridge, Montana

Shelby Stamford fastened her seatbelt as the Bell AS350B3 powered upward into Montana's ink-black sky. She donned the headgear to diminish the roar of the copter's giant blades, the pilot's voice sounding firm and in control. "St. Pat's, Life Flight One, we're in the air. Two male patients with gunshot wounds. Patient one: serious condition, patient two critically wounded. Stand ready, ETA fifty-four minutes. Life Flight One signing off."

She glanced back at the two Life Flight nurses, one attending to her husband, Bobby, and the other with a stethoscope monitoring Jack Ketchum. The medical equipment blinking white, green, and red into the dim interior resembled a compact emergency room in the air. The crew's professional demeanor and coordination were assuring, as was the pilot when he helped her into the copter. "It's going to be okay. Your husband and Mr. Ketchum are in excellent hands. St. Pat's is a Level II trauma center and our crew has dealt with gunshot wounds before."

After a few minutes Shelby felt the copter level off and her heartbeat begin to slow. She peered out the window for the lights of a distant town, but seeing only blackness, her thoughts spiraled back to Ellie's Cafe in Troutsprings: *I had a bad feeling the minute those guys walked in the door. Why didn't I say something? I should have tried to stop Jack from going for the gun!* Her heartbeat raced once again as the scene in Ellie's Cafe replayed like the jerky movements of a silent-movie... ...*a grungy thief fanning the gun around at everyone then pointing it straight at Jack... the thief's accomplice staring at her with wild eyes, the hefty hunting knife in his hand quivering, poised to throw... the gunman's shock when Jack lunged and the gun went off... Jack collapsing in a crumpled heap.... blood everywhere.* Shelby tried to turn off the scene, but in vain... *Bobby outside smoking a cigarette; didn't he hear the shot?... rushing outside into the warm night... Bobby sprawled at the bottom of the steps... more blood... sirens, red lights, stretchers... people in white coats running.*

The last thing Shelby remembered was the pilot sprinting toward her, then rushing her onto the helicopter and the roar of the blades drowning out everything else. *My God how did this happen? Six weeks ago, I was going about my life in L.A. running my business, thinking how I could get our marriage back on track and start a family. Montana was supposed to be our chance to get away and spend time together. I wanted Bobby to enjoy the trip but he didn't and made sure to let me know. The farthest thing from my mind about this trip was him getting shot, and Jack—oh my God—he might not make it!*

Tears welled trying to make sense of all that happened; a gracious Montana cowboy now at death's door and the opportunity to see beautiful country for the first time, ending up like this? It seemed inconceivable. *There's no making sense of it. I just have to deal with it.*

When the chopper finally began to descend, she sat up straight and mentally forced a halt to her morbid thoughts. As the pilot's voice in her headgear announced, "prepare for landing" she saw a welcome sight, the hospital's landing pad encircled by a ring of steady blue beacons. Shelby rose and squared her shoulders, trying to gather the strength she would need.

Exiting the copter, she silently vowed to face whatever lay ahead with every ounce of courage she possessed.

Chapter One

Shelby Stamford stretched her arms skyward to loosen sore muscles as the California sun began to show over the mountains. A flock of seagulls, airborne on the coastal updrafts, swooped and dived overhead, their dissonant calls punctuating the morning stillness. Cool for a July morning, the breeze carried pungent, familiar smells: new lumber, hay, and newly-mown grass. Wide flower-filled beds and a vast expanse of manicured lawn separated the Stamford house from the four-stall stable under construction. Behind the unfinished roofed framework was a spacious corral, and behind that stretched the scrub and tree-covered foothills that defined the southern California coastline.

Dressed in worn jeans and her *Born to Build* sweatshirt, Shelby grabbed her thermos and headed toward the corral, stopping at its gate. Out of habit she glanced back at the two-story rambling structure silhouetted against a canopy of giant oaks that birds had unknowingly planted long ago when the world was a simpler place. The sight stirred memories of her remodel of the old Weston house, which as fate would have it turned out to be the catalyst that catapulted her hobby into a successful construction business.

Still marveling how that one event changed her life, she entered the old barn presently housing her three horses. Cherokee, her pregnant mare, greeted her with a nicker. "Good morning, pinto lady." Shelby ran her hand over the horse's swollen belly. "Next spring you're going to have a colt following you around. I can hardly wait. I'm envious. I wish I were having a baby." She fed her three horses then made her way to the unfinished stable and deposited her thermos on her makeshift desk, a sheet of plywood atop two sawhorses. Tacked on a two-by-four above it was a sign: *Skyline Construction, License # CL 909723 Residential Remodeling & New Construction.* Downing the last of her coffee, she heard Enrique Flores drive up in a Skyline pickup.

"Hey, boss, happy Friday." He sidestepped between the studs of an unfinished wall.

"Same to you but I didn't think I would see you until check writing time."

"Well, both crews are where they're supposed to be so I thought I'd lend you a hand on the stables," he said. "I know you're anxious to finish it."

"Any help is appreciated. If we can pull Darryl off the Waterson job for a couple of days, I could call for an inspection and get the horses moved in by the end of the month. Oh, how I would love to do that." They nodded at each other, their signal to "get with it." The day passed quickly as it did when she could physically build as opposed to dashing between job sites, estimating bids, solving problems, or talking on the phone with suppliers. Skyline had one remodel job and two custom four-thousand-square-foot houses under construction, plus a stack of plans waiting. It had been difficult for Shelby to schedule a personal project into Skyline's workload, but Cherokee's impending foal dictated that she didn't have a choice.

By five o'clock when Skyline's two crews showed up for their payroll checks, she and Enrique had the stable's exterior walls enclosed with siding. Shelby liked the guys in both of her crews, ten young, muscular guys. None married and each one a skilled carpenter;

they had come to Skyline from the Coast Hills Junior College Intern Program.

"Okay, it's Friday, why am I not surprised everybody looks ready for some fun. What bar are you off to?" Shelby asked as she handed out checks. "C'mon, at least one of you has a date?"

"Dates are for Saturday nights, not Fridays," Kevin said. "We're headed to Salty's for a few beers and some serious pool." He exchanged his hard hat for a cowboy hat with a snakeskin band. "You and Enrique are welcome to join us." His grin was mischievous.

"Sure we are." Shelby smiled. "I don't think so, Kevin. I'd beat you at pool which would probably ruin your weekend."

Kevin laughed and bowed in mock surrender. "I don't doubt it, boss, not for a minute."

As soon as they left, Shelby and Enrique cleaned up the construction debris then he sprinted off toward the house to see Oscar and Esther, his parents. Hired as housekeepers years ago at the Stamford estate, Shelby now felt closer to them than to either of her distant parents.

Pleased at what had been accomplished, she showered then dressed in a blue, ankle-length skirt and white blouse, something casual she hoped would be perfect for the evening she had planned. Checking her reflection, she could tell that her sad thought was visible on her face. "Fortieth birthday and no children," she said, acknowledging how it hurt to say *no children*.

She turned from the mirror. *I was sure we would at least have two kids by now. I never should have agreed to wait on Bobby's all-important career.* She turned back to the mirror. "Well, forty is the limit. I'm not waiting any—" Her cell phone's song interrupted her pledge, Bobby's smiling image on the screen. "Speak of the devil," she murmured. "Hey, Bobby."

"Hi, babe, how's your day been? I hope as good as mine because it's been fabulous." Her husband sounded every bit like Mr. Successful L.A. Developer.

"Mine was good too and you can tell me about yours when you get home. How soon can you be here? Esther is making her special *carne asada.* I was hoping we could drink a little champagne and have dinner on the patio, just the two of us. Kind of a special even—"

"Dinner is why I'm calling, Shel. I want you to join us for a celebration at the country club. Dad and I just made the arrangements and he said to tell you that you cannot say no."

"Celebrating what and with whom?" Shelby said, unable to mask her disappointment.

"A huge day for Stamford Development, in fact the biggest ever. Covington Square is finally going to happen!" Bobby's excitement was audibly palpable. "It happened so long ago maybe you don't remember the escrow closing on the property we bought from Alice Covington. Believe it or not that was five years ago and we just got a twenty-page fax from Planning and Development with *Project Approved* on it. It's official, Shel! I can't believe it finally happened."

"Wow, that is news," she said, trying to process all that it meant. The Covington Project, a super-elite shopping center and Bobby's dream from the beginning, was the reason he had always given for waiting to start a family. *At least that's the excuse he used when I brought up the subject. Wow, now that Covington is a go, there's no reason for us to wait any longer.*

Encouraged by that thought, she had even more reason to appreciate Bobby's news. There was no denying it was a significant accomplishment but she did wonder if it finally meant an end to years of legal and financial hassle; that answer and her plans would just have to wait.

"I wouldn't ask, Shel, if this weren't such a milestone. It deserves celebrating big and I want you to share it with me. It's going to make your husband famous. Please say yes."

"Of course, Bobby, I wouldn't miss it for the world." Shelby found Esther in the kitchen and explained about Covington. "Bobby is so excited. Can we have the carne asada tomorrow?"

"*Si, señora,* it will be good *mañana* but since you are going out, we must also celebrate." Esther turned toward the dining room. "Oscar, Enrique! *Ven aqui, ahora mismo!*"

Oscar entered followed by Enrique, both sporting big smiles. "*Feliz Cumpleaños!*" Oscar said and hugged her. Enrique had showered and changed into slacks and a dress shirt; he smelled of VSOP, his favorite cologne. He put down a stack of gifts, all colorfully wrapped except for two in shipping paper. "Hey boss, you didn't think we'd forget the big one, did you?"

Shelby grinned. "It would have been okay with me if you'd skipped this particular one. You guys are sneaky, but I love you all."

Oscar retrieved a bottle of champagne from the refrigerator and filled four glasses. They took turns toasting Shelby and then urged her to open her gifts. Shelby opened each package, admiring a beautiful knitted shawl from Esther, and from Oscar and Enrique three hand-hewn redwood signs, each carved with the horse's name. "For their stall in the new barn. We'll do one for the foal when it arrives," Enrique said. They looked so happy that Shelby's disappointment evaporated. She nodded at the nearby chair heaped with colorful ribbons and paper.

"I can't believe we managed to have a great birthday party in thirty minutes. Thank you, dear family. You've made this really special."

"Now go, señora, put on your finest dress and have a wonderful time," Esther said.

"Tough to do with her imperial highness there," Shelby said.

"Do not let Señora Stamford make you feel bad," Esther said. "Promise to hold your head high. Be proud, you are a special lady." Oscar and Enrique chimed in unison, "*Verdad!*"

Thirty minutes later, dressed in her favorite black Céline cocktail dress, Shelby was behind the wheel of her Beamer SUV heading south on the 405 Interstate. Lost in thought she turned off the radio. One of the brown packages, postmarked from Lima, Peru, contained a large handmade copper pot from her father, accompanied by a breezy note wishing her a happy fortieth birthday. He wrote about the artisan who made the pot and lamented that winter in the Andes seemed as though it would never end. David Longren wrote little about himself or how he felt about not having seen his only child in five years. Just a *Love you, Dad,* at the end. "I hate what divorce does to families," she murmured.

The second brown package contained a two-volume set of *Sunset's Basic Gardening Illustrated,* along with a note signed, *Love, Mom and Dennis.* Laura Longren Baxter, president of her Colorado garden club, had for years been a master gardener. "Think how much better the world would be if everyone gardened," she often said.

Shelby entered Bel Air, the city which along with Beverly Hills and Holmby Hills, formed what was locally known as the *Platinum Triangle* of Los Angeles. She turned onto Bellagio Road and then entered Bel Air Country Club's tree-studded grounds. Shelby surrendered her car to the valet and, once inside, paused to look around the elegant room. She spotted her father-in-law, Adam Stamford, recognizing his striking silver hair and tanned face.

She made her way to the table, Miss Telford motioning her forward. Stamford's eldest employee and the only one addressed formally, she had been with Stamford Development since Adam had bought the firm in 1975 from Curtis Weston, his father-in-law. In her late fifties and never married, Miss Telford looked on Bobby like an adoring auntie.

Bobby and Adam rose as Shelby approached. Adam kissed her cheek. "Shelby, you look beautiful. I don't like that Skyline is keeping you so busy we never get to see you."

"Good to see you too and yes, it has been a long time." Shelby returned the kiss.

Bobby hugged her. "Dad's right, Shel, you look stunning. I am so happy you came."

Shelby walked around the table, head held high as promised, first acknowledging Alice Covington who greeted her warmly. Next, Shelby stopped at Martha Stamford's chair. Martha extended her manicured hand. "A kiss, Shelby darling, how are you?"

"Fine, Martha." Shelby grasped her mother-in-law's hand and kissed her on the cheek. The Stamford family matriarch smiled up at her. "My dear, your hands tell me you are indeed a successful builder." Shelby quickly withdrew her hand and shot an I-told-you-so glance at Bobby. He shrugged and returned an apologetic look. "I am proof that construction work and beautiful hands don't go together, Martha, but the offset is that I love what I do."

"Martha, for heaven's sakes!" Adam exclaimed.

"Oh, Shelby, I do apologize. You look absolutely beautiful, darling," Martha said.

The children's arrival dispelled the awkward moment. The two boys, looking grown-up in slacks, dress shirts, and ties, marched in with mischievous expressions, their arms laden with colorfully wrapped gifts. Four-year-old Chloe ran to Shelby and held out her arms to be picked up. She gave Shelby a big kiss on the lips and then shouted, "Happy birthday!" Shelby sat down, the children crowding around her.

Bobby's sister, Karen, and her husband Rick were smiling and laughing; everyone at the table rose.

Bobby led the applause. "Gotcha, babe! You didn't think I'd let you turn forty quietly, did you?" He turned and nodded at the waiter who came forward with a silver bucket, the gold foil top of the bottle visible above the rim. A second waiter delivered a bucket with a bottle of sparkling apple cider and then withdrew. "Serve the kids first," Bobby said. The waiter filled the children's glasses and then poured champagne into the adult's crystal flutes. Bobby raised his glass. "Happy birthday to Shelby Stamford, the beautiful founder and president of Skyline Construction, and the best-looking builder in southern California." Everyone raised their glass.

"I'll second that," Adam said, nodding at Shelby.

Bobby strolled around the table, fussing over everyone, motioning for the waiter to refill a glass or replenish a tray of hors d'oeurves. Sitting close to Shelby, the children barraged her with one question after another about the horses and politely asked to come out and ride. "Of course you can. I would love that," she said as Bobby halted in back of her chair.

He leaned over and tapped a water glass. "Everyone, while you have your glass in hand I want to propose another toast. This is a doubly big day, my wonderful wife's birthday and a huge step in realizing a dream, Covington Square." Bobby nodded at Alice Covington. "Thank you for making possible the most exciting shopping center in California and I hope the crowning achievement of Stamford Development." Bobby raised his glass once more. "Here's to Alice, the wonderful lady who made this dream possible, and to CAPE, the California Alliance for the Protection of the Environment, for giving the project its blessing."

"How about adding that it makes us some serious money," Adam said and grinned at his son. Bobby leaned over Rick Jr., and ruffled his nephew's hair. "Hey, buddy, if I give you a five-spot would you move over by your grandfather so I can sit next to my wife?"

"You don't have to pay me, Uncle Bobby."

"I'll take it!" piped Jason, who turned to his father. "What's a five-spot?"

Everyone around the table laughed. "Talk to me about a job when you grow up, kid," Bobby said. "You've got the right attitude."

Tuxedoed waiters arrived with silver-domed entrees and proceeded to remove the covers with a flourish. "It has been a long time since I've been here, Bobby," Shelby said, eyeing the entrees. "I forgot just how exceptional the food is and every plate is a work of art."

He beamed. "The chef gave me his word this meal would be perfect just for you."

After dinner a steady stream of club members approached the table to congratulate Shelby and to greet Adam, president of the country club's board. Bobby was quick to rise, to shake a hand and kiss a cheek. Shelby observed him memorizing new names and faces. *You love this, Bobby. This is your world.*

"Excuse me, babe, I'll be right back." He sauntered through the room, shaking hands and slapping backs as he went.

Miss Telford came around the table and sat down next to Shelby. "I was so worried you would find out. Were you really surprised?" she asked.

Shelby nodded. "I actually thought Bobby had forgotten. He's been so distracted, now I realize by what. Obviously you two have been overwhelmed with this Covington project."

"Oh, I haven't been involved since March when Bobby hired a new assistant."

"Really?" Shelby caught her breath. "He hasn't mentioned a new assistant."

"Terri Armstrong." A brief flicker of disapproval crossed Miss Telford's face. "These young women, you know, they're so savvy with computers and electronic gadgets. It's amazing how they integrate a new project software the minute it becomes available. They communicate more by smart phones and iPads than by telephone. Ridiculous! I don't like all that techie stuff." Miss Telford sighed and rolled her eyes. "But I do understand she's efficient too."

"What do you mean, efficient *too*?" Shelby said, Miss Telford's dramatic sigh and roll of her eyes bringing back a disturbing memory.

Miss Telford shrugged. "Terri is gorgeous enough to be a model, but I said efficient too because she proposed some promotion ideas for the Covington project that worked well. So well, in fact, that even Adam was impressed. And you know, that is not easily done."

Sitting facing Miss Telford, Shelby felt a familiar dread begin to form as the words sunk in. She fought the urge to tell her to stop, but Miss Telford continued talking. "I assume it was because her promo ideas worked so well that Bobby said okay for her to reorganize his office. Admittedly it needed help but soon as she finished that, without even asking she charged in and revamped his entire filing system. That was something I had asked to do for years, but Bobby would never let me." Miss Telford exhaled another dramatic sigh and rolled her eyes a second time, instantly triggering a scene in Shelby's memory. The two things struck a chord. *I heard her say that before and then roll her eyes just like that!*

Gripped by a pit-of the stomach revelation, Shelby almost felt faint. Two years ago, but indelibly stamped in her memory, Miss Telford had been talking about Bobby's secretary, Brenda Langley. *That's how I found out about the affair. Oh God, he's doing it again.*

Shelby froze, awash with memories of recent evenings at home, Bobby's flurry of activity, his glibness and too-quick laughter suddenly making sense. *Exactly like he acted two years ago!*

Desperately wanting to escape, Shelby rose but paused when she heard a wave of "ohs" and "ahs" sweep across the room. She turned and caught sight of Bobby making his way towards their table, holding aloft a magnificent saddle. Following him, a waiter carried a large candlelit birthday cake. Aware of all eyes on her, Shelby forced a smile but could not stop tears welling at the thought of Bobby orchestrating this grand show while having another affair. She grasped the back of her chair to steady herself. "The saddle, of course, why am I not surprised?"

"Look at that, Chloe, Auntie Shelby's so happy she's crying," Miss Telford said as the youngster climbed onto her lap.

Shelby's thoughts went back to a month ago when Bobby accompanied her to Murdock's *Western Supplies* for feed. This very saddle was displayed on a rail by the front door. She had briefly paused to admire its exquisite workmanship and run her hand over the smooth leather. *The saddle of course—vintage Bobby.* She had often witnessed him picking up on nuances like an alert hunting dog picking up a scent. Bobby absorbed offhand comments; he remembered birthdays and anniversaries. She had seen him mentally note facts that he might need in the future. Shelby thought back to that day at the feed store. She hadn't said a word about the saddle, just smiled at Bobby to show her pleasure. And here it was.

"The saddle at Murdock's," Shelby said. Bobby placed it on the empty chair beside her and insisted she make a wish and blow out the candles on the cake. She closed her eyes and blew out all forty tiny flames. *I have only one wish, but it's too late.*

"I am so glad you like it. Happy birthday, Shel, I love you."

She stared into his eyes. Bobby's smile appeared sincere; his words sounded genuine. He pulled her close and kissed her. She heard whispered comments. "How sweet, he obviously adores her. What a beautiful couple."

Shelby dried her eyes on the handkerchief he offered. "The saddle is beautiful" was all she could say. Bobby bowed slightly, obviously pleased about the evening. Shelby opened the rest of her gifts with the children close by helping to open them. Their gifts were accompanied by hand drawn cards with XXXs and OOOs for hugs and kisses, their affection calming her. After the birthday cake and gift opening, Bobby insisted Shelby stand beside him as country club members came up to greet him and wish her happy birthday. She listened to conversations about real estate deals, charity events, L.A. development, Covington Square, and upcoming golf games. Miss Telford came up and joined the conversations, praising Bobby's work on the Covington project and remarking how he was assuming more of the leadership at Stamford Development. Bobby, appearing a bit embarrassed, joked that Miss Telford was his "office mom" and therefore prejudiced.

Hearing Miss Telford praise Bobby, Shelby's pit-of the stomach reaction returned at the vivid memory of a party at the elder Stamfords' home. *Could it be Miss Telford doesn't remember that conversation? I remember it all too well, that same flicker of disapproval, the dramatic roll of her eyes.* Shelby wanted to dismiss the recollection as coincidence but her gut instinct told her otherwise. As improbable as it seemed, without realizing it Miss Telford had unwittingly revealed Bobby was having another affair.

He gave me his word! How naive of me to believe him. Standing beside him Shelby's anger ignited, causing her to gasp. "You okay, Shel?" Bobby said, squeezing her hand. Unable to speak, she took a deep breath at the recognition that this life she loved was about to drastically change. *I can't trust him*. She remembered confronting Bobby two years ago, shouting at him while he remained infuriatingly calm and then informing her in a quiet voice that when she was willing to talk rationally, he would be happy to listen. And then he walked out the door.

Still silent, Shelby glanced over her shoulder at their table. Karen, a long-haired carbon copy of her mother, was smiling and talking quietly with Rick and the children. A sleepy Chloe, cuddled on her mother's lap, had one hand against Karen's neck, her other hand twisting her own blond curls. The boys were whispering secrets and laughing with their attentive father. *I may never have that, a little Chloe or a son of my own*. What she so desperately wanted suddenly seemed as farfetched as catching a falling star.

Karen and Rick rose and begged off for the evening, saying the children were tired. A club member and Bobby were talking about a condominium project on a piece of prime coast property. Shelby tapped her husband's arm. "I'm ready to leave too." She returned to the table, thanked everyone, and bade them goodnight.

"Don't lose that thought, Hal, be right back," Bobby said. He motioned for a waiter and asked to have Shelby's car brought around. "Wait up for me and we'll have that champagne."

The freeway was less crowded now, Shelby's thoughts skitting back over the evening, the shock of finding out Bobby was having another affair, then minutes later his grand show of affection. *He is the king of duplicity*. She recalled recent evenings at home, him sharing news and stories from the office but not one word about hiring a new assistant. Shelby recalled their most recent chat; *I was estimating plans. Bobby was excited, hoping CAPE would endorse the Covington project. He may have mentioned somebody contacting the L.A. Times, but I don't remember exactly who*. The grain of uncertainty whether or not he had mentioned hiring an assistant lasted a nano-second, erased by her gut certainty and Miss Telford's dramatic account.

I know he's having an affair. The question is what do I do about it. Shelby spent the rest of her drive skipping back and forth between painful memories and the man Bobby portrayed tonight, every inch the attentive husband and dynamic heir apparent to Stamford Development, Inc. Tonight he had been the same exciting, charming man who swept an American Airlines flight attendant off her feet.

Not love at first sight, she remembered, instead a relationship that began with attraction to a handsome man in first class that grew the following year, their relationship blossoming during long walks on the beach, romantic dinners, and wonderful weekends away from L.A.

Love did finally come, she remembered. And despite her politely voiced objections, their love culminated in a high society wedding of gigantic proportions choreographed by none other than Martha Weston Stamford.

Shelby silently admonished herself for her naiveté; until two years ago and now again tonight, she had believed hers was a marriage that would last a lifetime.

"The next step is to find out if my gut instinct is right," she whispered to her reflection.

Chapter Two

Bobby tilted his head to avoid the sun's direct rays in the bathroom mirror. "Hey, babe," he called out to Shelby. "Would you mind getting the newspaper? I'd like to see the real estate section, keep up on what's happening in the commercial market."

"Sure, I'd like to read the paper too. Be right back."

Bobby waited a minute, then called Terri's cell, her only phone. "It's a go. Park where I told you, car facing the ocean, half an hour at the most." Her throaty "I'll be there" made his heart skip a beat. Even after two years he still conjured up memories of sex with Brenda. But Shelby somehow finding out and what followed after, he refused to think about. Shelby made it clear: either their marriage or Brenda. An unpleasant but not a difficult decision, he remembered. *Brenda was a good secretary and the sex was great, but not worth a divorce.* Convincing Shelby of his regret over the affair and then getting her to believe his promise it wouldn't happen again was burned into his memory. He truly meant it and, thankfully, it was on his promise that Shelby called off the divorce.

Bobby turned from the mirror, acknowledging the murky feeling in his gut. *So why the hell am I doing this?* The answer was instant. *Because sometimes crazy, stupid things just happen like Terri Armstrong waltzing into my life at the exact right moment.* Based on her credentials, he could legitimately defend hiring her even to Shelby; Terri was simply too perfect for the job not to hire her. After Brenda's departure and buried in a myriad of legal, Orange County permits, regulations, and construction issues on the Covington project, Bobby allowed Miss Telford to step in temporarily. The trouble was she stayed two years. *Big mistake.* Recognizing his predicament, he finally confessed. "Miss Telford, I simply have to have an assistant who is computer-savvy with solid real estate experience. Man or woman, just find me that person."

Admitting she was actually relieved, Miss Telford put an ad in the *L.A. Times* that same day. Three applicants later, Terri Armstrong's credentials, her letters of recommendation, and her impressive resumé made up Bobby's mind. He remembered genuinely wishing that along with her incredible qualifications, Terri Armstrong had been a man or was fat and happily married. Instead she was twenty-seven and could have been Miss California: long brown hair, a size six dynamite figure, and smoldering hazel eyes he could get lost in.

Bobby also desperately wanted to tell Shelby, maybe even invite her to the office and introduce the two of them. He could recall picking up the phone a dozen times to do just that, but each time fear trumped good intentions and somehow it never happened. Now six months later, it was too late. Terri was indispensable and Shelby would feel betrayed.

Terri quickly adapted to the Covington project like the professional her credentials made her out to be. Since being hired she had brought to the table two high-end clothing stores, both signing a letter of intent, and next a gourmet restaurant to agree in writing to lease "within thirty days of completion of the project." She somehow convinced her ex-boyfriend editor at the *L.A. Times* to write an article about *L.A.'s most successful father-son real estate team.* It appeared in the *L.A. Times Sunday Real Estate* edition, along with a color photo of Adam and Bobby. When he asked her how she got her editor friend to do such a big favor, Terri just flashed her Miss America smile and said, "I owe him."

The article created a flurry of calls from potential lessees, causing even Adam Stamford to admit how great an asset Terri was to the company. By the end of her fourth month, Terri had the files, the plan revisions, and the voluminous Covington correspondence organized enough that Bobby announced, "I think we've got things pretty much under control" to his father.

But the dread Bobby initially experienced at hiring her, however, did materialize. The "sometimes stupid things happen that shouldn't happen" did on a Sunday when he drove to his office to pen a letter to CAPE that his father deemed critically important. Adam had been unwavering that he convince the environmental group to nominate the Covington Project for a National Environmental Award. "Listen, Bobby, construction costs are damned near double to build the shopping center CAPE's green way. We damn sure should try to get it nominated."

So involved in the letter, Bobby didn't hear the main door being unlocked. Startled at a tap on his door he rose, annoyed at being interrupted. Terri Armstrong entered, tanned and gorgeous in a skimpy tank top and mid-thigh skirt. "I was shopping across the street and saw your car in the parking lot. Why are you here on a Sunday?" Approaching his desk she spied the letter. "Oh, the CAPE letter Adam wanted." Terri came around the desk and peered over his shoulder; Bobby inhaled her perfume. "I write great letters," she said and drew up a chair close to his. She crossed her shapely legs, *perfect legs*, and asked if she could help.

After an hour of discussion, editing and then retyping, the polished letter was finished. They laughingly gave each other a high five; Terri did not back away. Instead she looked up at him with a slight smile and an inquisitive look. Every instinct told Bobby to step back or turn away, but her gaze held him. She moved closer and her arms went around him. "Bobby, I've wanted to do this," she said pressing her body against his. "Push me away if you don't," she whispered. Bobby didn't move, couldn't move as she kissed him, her right hand guiding his to her breasts. *No bra.* Red lights flashed in Bobby's mind, every instinct telling him he should pull away, but his body refusing to cooperate as his will evaporated.

Terri's body tight against his and her tongue probing his mouth, her sheer energy took his breath away. After ten minutes and his heart feeling about to explode, Bobby did pull away. Smiling and calm, she kissed his cheek and whispered, "I can see this is not the time or place." Terri retrieved her purse and walked to the door, then turned around. "If you like, we could continue where we left off, but in a more appropriate location." She opened the door and blew a kiss at him over her shoulder. "And I suggest soon, Bobby."

* * *

Remembering that moment as he applied sunscreen, Bobby felt his face flush. Terri's departing comment "soon" left no room for an excuse and it was her gauntlet that resulted in his formulating *The Plan—a Bobby Stamford guaranteed, written-in-stone, one-time-only Sunday morning get-together.* He glanced at Shelby, now sitting cross-legged in the bed in her Snoopy night shirt, coffee mug on one knee as she read the paper. He took a deep breath. *This does not constitute going back on my promise, which technically was not to have another affair. I will absolutely not allow that to happen. Messy things, affairs.* Decision made, he entered the bedroom and asked Shelby what she found so interesting in the newspaper.

"An article about a couple from Laguna Niguel who rented a motor home and toured the northwest for three months. We couldn't be gone that long, but that would be so fun! I'm bored with lounging on a beach in Mexico or Hawaii. We've never been to Idaho or Montana and, according to this article, the scenery is spectacular. Summer is half-over, we need to make vacation plans. Let's do that, Bobby, just the two of us get away together."

"Getting away together sounds great, but in a RV? You're kidding, right?" *No way am I vacationing in a trailer.* "Can we talk about this later then you show me the new stables?"

"Later?" Shelby looked up, obviously surprised. "You said we'd do something together."

"I did and we will, but Doc says I have to get some serious exercise. He recommended bicycling so I'm going to ride until about one o'clock. When I get back you can show me the stables and we'll have the rest of the day together. Tonight we'll have that quiet evening, just the two of us. We can have Esther's carne asada. Does that sound good?"

"I guess so." He could detect the disappointment in her voice.

"You relax and enjoy the paper and when I get back, we'll talk vacation plans or whatever you want, okay?" He observed arched eyebrows above questioning eyes, Shelby's look giving him pause. *She couldn't possibly know.* "I promise we'll talk as long as you like."

He donned a baseball cap and his Porsche sunglasses, then tucked a pack of cigarettes in his shorts pocket. Shelby followed him into the garage, watching as he put a bottle of water in the holder on his bicycle. "I don't get it, Bobby. If you're doing this for your health, why don't you leave those cigarettes behind. It makes no sense to ride then smoke."

"One thing at a time, babe, can't change all my faults at once." He saluted Shelby as he rode out their circle drive onto Canyon Hills

Drive and then breathed a sigh of relief. *Wow, getting out of the house free and clear has to mean Lady Fate just gave me a green light.*

Bobby rode west toward the Coast Highway along the curving road that sloped downward toward the sea, the July morning cool, the sky cloudless. He glanced at his Rolex. *Nine-forty-five, plenty of time.* Two long blocks later he rounded a curve, the asphalt arcing around a giant Oleander bush. Pleasantly surprised, Terri's Lexus SUV sat parked at the vista point overlooking the distant Pacific. *On time and exactly where I said to park.* The windows were down and he heard music as he rode his bike up to her side of the car.

Too late to back out now, even if I wanted to. "Good morning, lady. Could I interest you in a wild morning of sex and depravity?" He leaned over and kissed her tanned arm resting on the window frame. Her skin felt smooth and cool and smelled of a sultry fragrance he vaguely recognized. Inhaling her scent as he continued with brief kisses upward until he reached her bare shoulder, then six inches from her face, he was staring into her gold-flecked hazel eyes.

"Unless you've learned to do it on a bicycle, Bobby, which I wouldn't mind trying, I suggest you hop in." Terri hit the unlock button and, after a moment of apprehension, Robert Stamford, Southern California's star developer, threw his bicycle in the back and hopped in the passenger seat. Terri gunned the Lexus onto the pavement, sending gravel and sand flying.

Bobby glanced over at her, tanned, gorgeous and sexy, a twelve on a scale of ten. "You look incredible," he said.

She smiled. "I am incredible."

* * *

Shelby steered Oscar's Chevy off the asphalt onto the shoulder of Canyon Hills Drive, stopping just short of a giant Oleander bush as tall and wide as the Chevy. Gingerly separating two face-high branches, Shelby peeked through the opening. Her legs nearly gave way at what she saw: Bobby standing beside a Lexus SUV and kissing a slender tanned arm resting on the driver's window frame. Unable to see her face or make out what they were saying, Shelby waited a brief moment and saw the back hatch of the SUV raise and Bobby deposit his bicycle in the back. The hatch closed, then without a backward glance, Bobby hopped in the passenger seat and the Lexus sped away.

Shelby walked back to the Chevy as images she could neither control nor ignore shattered any and all shred of confidence she had in her future.

* * *

Bobby and Terri entered Room 226 at the Spindrift Motel at 10:15 A.M. He had no doubt she would be good in bed; she exuded a sensual energy and aggressiveness that excited him. He had fantasized about stripping Terri's clothes off, but he never got the chance. She was the aggressor, removing first his clothes and then her own. Terri stood naked, tanned to a golden bronze with no bikini lines. She clicked on the radio; Billy Ocean's *Caribbean Queen* pulsed forth as she walked slowly to the mirrored closet and turned to face him.

Bobby lay on the bed and watched her, the smoke from his cigarette curling around his head in lazy, circular wisps. "You are beautiful, you know that?" His voice was husky.

"I know," she said, and closed her eyes.

Terri began to sway to the music, moving slowly and sensually, stimulated by the suggestive song. She opened her eyes and locked her gaze on Bobby's, a half-smile forming on her lips. With a dancer's grace, she swayed her hips to the beat, side to side then forward and back, seemingly lost in the song. Straightening her lithe body, she stretched to her full height, arms in the air. Smiling, she lowered her hands, caressing her breasts then sliding them down over her bronzed stomach, moving to the music and coolly observing the effect she was having on Bobby. Turning to face the mirror, she continued to dance and shot him a sensual smile over her shoulder.

Bobby got up and pulled her into bed.

For two hours she drove him to the brink and he did the same for her, her long hair wet and her tanned body glistening. She couldn't be satisfied; she wouldn't let him stop, demanding, pleading, pulling him into her. He was drenched, her sweat mingling with his own. Bobby looked up at her on top of him and coming again, using him, her eyes closed and her head back, a fierce, desperate expression on her face. Heart hammering, he could only watch and gulp in air.

Finally when Terri's body relaxed, Bobby held up his hands. "Uncle! No more. White flag. You win," he said between gasps. He couldn't move and his arms and legs felt like lead.

Terri planted a kiss on his damp forehead, rolled off and then sprang out of bed. She disappeared into the bathroom and he heard the bathwater being turned on. He closed his eyes, body totally spent, his mind swirling with errant thoughts he couldn't control, one of them that his wife certainly did not have Brenda's or Terri's sexual energy. *Maybe that's a good thing.* Making love with Shelby was satisfying but not particularly exciting, usually over in twenty minutes. Yet despite the unbelievable sex he experienced with Brenda, after she exited his life he was shocked how quickly she faded. *Affair over. Brenda gone. End of story, no big deal.*

As Bobby tried to concentrate on his breathing, a disturbing thought formed despite trying to ignore it. *Will what happened with Brenda happen with Terri – or whoever? Gone, end of story, no big deal?* Not sure of the answer, he found that thought disturbing. Placing

Shelby in that question, however, Bobby's answer was instant. *I cannot imagine my life without her. So that has to be love, but dammit, why is this so complicated! I love Shel, but geez it's hard to resign myself to one woman and one kind of sex experience the rest of my life. Especially when women like Brenda and Terri come on to me.*

Frustrated, Bobby desperately wanted a cigarette but the pack lay inches beyond his reach and he couldn't muster the strength to get up. According to his Rolex, fifteen minutes had passed and he was still sweating. his heartbeat still erratic. He lifted up on one elbow—not good! The room looked to be swaying and he began to feel nauseous. The smoky room felt stifling and devoid of oxygen; he needed air. Apparently in the tub, Terri was humming Billy Ocean's song. He tried to sit up again but fell back on his pillow, certain he was going to throw up. The singing stopped and Bobby opened one eye as Terri emerged from the bathroom, naked except for a towel wrapped around her head, turban style. Her smile instantly vanished. "Bobby, what's wrong? You're white as the sheet!" She looked fearful, her voice uncertain.

"Not a clue. Could you open the slider and bring a cold washcloth?"

Terri quickly pulled open the glass door, Bobby feeling the cool marine air. Caught in the strong breeze the sheer curtains fluttered straight out, waving wildly in the sun, creating a dance of shade and light on the walls. "Stop those waving like that. It's making me dizzier." He closed his eyes and a minute later felt a cold cloth on his forehead.

"Bobby, you are scaring me. Should I call nine-one-one?" He waved her off, wanting only to sleep, but Terri would not let him sleep. She kept changing the washcloth and talking to him. "C'mon, breathe deep." Terri fanned him with the plastic menu from the desk and kept fanning him until he stopped sweating and his heartbeat began to slow. As he was about to thank her, Bobby suddenly felt chilled, cold enveloping him, his body shaking and his teeth chattering.

"Jesus, Bobby, don't die on me," he heard Terri say and opened his eyes as she grabbed the bedspread and blankets off the other bed and piled them on top of him. She looked panicked and, at her mention of the word *die*, it occurred to Bobby that he might possibly be in the process of doing just that. *Crap, not when Covington just got approved!*

The chills lasted half an hour and when they stopped, Bobby managed to sit up in bed. He glanced at the nightstand clock. "Crap, one-fifteen? I need to get going. Can you help me up? I want to shower."

"Are you sure you should get up so soon?"

"No sweat." He managed a weak grin at the pun. Terri helped him to the shower and then into his clothes. She held onto his arm as they made their way slowly across the parking lot. They rode up Canyon Hills Drive in silence, Terri stopping at the same vista point. She hopped out of the Lexus and removed his bicycle from the back. Bobby got out and stood on wobbly legs, his hand on the Lexus to steady himself. Terri tentatively offered to drive him closer. "Not necessary, I'll be okay. I must have a bug or something. Don't worry, you go on home and I'll see you Monday." She rolled the bicycle up close and kissed him on the cheek.

Bobby stood holding onto the bike as Terri turned the Lexus around and drove off. Eyeing the road's upward incline, he took a deep breath. *I'm thinking that was a finger instead of a green light that Lady Fate gave me.* He walked the bicycle up the hill to as close to their driveway as he could without being seen.

As he started to climb on, his foot caught the bottle of water.

"Can't forget that." Bobby dumped some water over his head and shirt then disheveled his hair with his hand. He took a deep breath and climbed on, then struggling mightily and by sheer willpower, he somehow managed to pump the bike the remaining short distance.

Bobby rode into the garage and dismounted. Struggling to breathe but grateful to have made it, he paused at the back door and waited to catch his breath and for his legs to quit trembling.

As soon he felt a measure of control, he closed his eyes and silently willed his body and his mind to summon the strength to enter. *And the courage to face Shelby.*

Chapter Three

Shelby took a deep breath when she heard the garage door open. *Keep your cool.* "Bobby's back," she said to Oscar and Esther. She turned in time to see him stagger in, white as a sheet.

Esther was the first to react. "Madre de Dios!" She jumped up, Oscar following.

"Guess I'm not ready for the Tour de France," Bobby said with a grin.

Esther ran upstairs ahead of them and pulled back the covers. Shelby and Oscar helped Bobby up to the master bedroom, guiding him to the bed. "Thanks," he managed to say.

Imagination in overdrive at Bobby's condition, Shelby helped him undress and get into bed then reached for the phone. "I'm calling Doc Caldwell or nine-one-one… your choice."

"No, please! Don't call anybody, I just need rest."

The phone still in her hand, Shelby counted softly, "One, two three, four," making it to ten and then replaced the receiver. *That's not nearly enough,* she thought, still trying to gain a measure of control. She looked down at Bobby. "Wow that must have been one helluva ride. Did you enjoy it?" She waited for his reaction.

His eyes flew open, followed by a scowl. "Did I enjoy it? Are you freakin' kidding me?"

Hands on her hips, she considered blasting him but held back. "Well, Mr. Jock, you wanted some serious exercise. From the way you look, I'd say you accomplished that in spades. So I just want to know, if beyond total overexertion is your definition of serious exercise, did you freakin' enjoy it? Under the circumstances, I consider that a perfectly legitimate question." Staring down at him, she could hear the fury in her voice. *This is going to be good.*

"What!" Bobby glared at her. "For chrissake, are you nuts or been drinking!"

Of course, the best defense is a good offense. "Don't you chrissake me and I have not been drinking. You're the one who needed help up the stairs. If anybody's crazy, it's you!"

Bobby closed his eyes and sighed, his frown disappearing. "Sorry, I was trying to be a jock. I'm sor..." He began breathing steadily, deflating her anger like a punctured balloon.

Remembering him smiling as he got into Terri's car, and the two of them entering the motel room felt akin to being stabbed in the heart. Shelby plopped down on the bedside chair, rage, disappointment and grief assaulting her system in waves. She tried to think of something positive, anything that would replace the images in her mind. Palms over her eyes, the only thing that came to mind were her three horses and the new barn. Trying desperately to hold onto those images, she closed her eyes and welcomed the blessed quiet.

Shelby had no idea how long she slept, but somewhere in the distance she heard a doorbell then voices and a door closed. She straightened up and glanced at Bobby, still asleep and his breathing sounding regular, the sight bringing fresh anger. *You destroyed every-thing. Last night you said 'I love you.' Was that just for show and the same with our marriage? Is that why you don't want children? You must be in love with her or you wouldn't have gone back on your word. I trusted you—trusted that you were telling the truth. What a huge mistake.*

Shelby made her way downstairs and called their doctor's number; his exchange answered. Evidently reacting to her previous faltering description, Dr. Caldwell himself returned her call. "The exchange said you sounded really scared," he said. After she explained Bobby's condition, this time in control, Caldwell told her that if Bobby's breathing continued steady and without difficulty, she could wait until next morning to bring him in. "But call my pager if it changes and I'll meet you at the hospital."

Shelby went back upstairs and, spying the discarded newspaper, she retrieved it and returned to the article about the Laguna Niguel couple who rented the RV. They were quoted as saying how fun and inspiring it was to see the USA, and "getting away from our demanding jobs made us realize how they affected our marriage. We were leading separate lives." The article ended with their statement that the trip helped them reconnect and how grateful they were.

Rereading their quote hit home. *My God, Bobby and I are leading separate lives. How could I not see that?* Stunned at another disconcerting revelation, Shelby tried to recall a time, an incident, any clue at all that would tell her when that happened to them. Sitting quietly she remembered how Bobby used to praise her "building hobby" and encouraged her to "try new projects." *In my mind it was still just a hobby until...* "Until the Covington Project!"

The truth flashed like mental lightning; the Covington Project was the turning point when their lives changed. *Four years ago or was it five that I first heard Bobby mention the Covington Project? I remember he was so excited at the prospect of building an upscale, green shopping center. That's when he changed—when everything changed, him spending every evening poring over plans, every weekend looking at other shopping centers. That's when he began pursuing Mr. & Mrs. Covington. He wanted that property!*

The truth crystallized; the Covington Project was the catalyst. Relieved at discovering the timeline and the cause, the pieces began to fall into place. The sole focus of Bobby's time and interest became his idea of a Covington shopping center, the effect similar to a divorce: scant private time alone even on weekends, dissimilar interests, less communication. *Covington was all he talked about and I got tired of hearing it. Four years ago is when we started drifting apart. Bobby was either gone or busy so I devoted my time to building—and my hobby became SkyLine Construction!* Another disturbing thought dawned: coincidentally two years ago when their marriage reached its low point, she discovered Bobby's affair with Brenda. Stunned at how the pieces fell into place; Bobby's affair with Brenda was the first sign their marriage was in serious trouble, now two years later he was doing it again probably meant it was doomed.

Silent tears fell unchecked. *So do I give up and throw away ten years?* She envisioned filing for divorce, saying goodbye to Oscar and Ester and Enrique, abandoning Skyline—what would she do? The thought of giving up on the life she and Bobby had built, leaving the home she'd spent a year of her life remodeling was mind-numbing. Then adding in the uncertainty about her horses, Shelby realized she couldn't do it. *I can't. I won't give up yet. I have too much invested in our marriage. Bobby must not feel that way, but I have to at least try.*

Shelby exited their bedroom and went downstairs to her office, the *L.A. Times* clutched in her hand, an idea forming.

* * *

Bobby awoke, the television sounding distant and foggy but clear enough to tell it was the evening news. He waited a few minutes before opening his eyes. A figure in a terry robe with a towel around her head, turban style, was walking toward him. For a moment he was back in the motel with Terri, the image bringing a rush of adrenaline that resulted in full alertness. He blinked several times to focus. It was Shelby. "You're finally awake. How do you feel?"

"Like crap," he said, looking up at her. Shelby did not reply; instead she appeared to be studying him. Bobby put an arm across his eyes to shut out the light and her gaze. "I was doing fairly okay until the last mile up the hill, then wham."

"Whatever. I talked to Doctor Caldwell. We have an appointment tomorrow morning for him to check you out."

"What! Why did you do that?" he demanded, stung by her flippant "whatever."

"Don't even go there, Bobby Stamford. You looked on the brink of a heart attack."

"Okay, sorry," he mumbled. Moving slow and deliberately, he got out of bed and made his way to the bathroom. Bobby took his third shower of the day and then joined Shelby, Oscar, and Esther in the kitchen. "Hey, guys, thank you for your help."

"Con much gusto," Oscar said it first, followed by Esther.

Shelby's sarcastic glance unnerved him as did her curt announcement that they would "finally" get to have Esther's carne asada. They ate on trays in the great room, the television on. He served Shelby Chardonnay; he drank water. Bobby did his best to engage her in conversation but she clearly was not interested. After dinner Bobby removed the trays to the kitchen and complimented Esther on her carne asada. When he returned to the great room and Shelby was absorbed in a TV program, he could no longer ignore her anger. "I'm sorry I messed up, Shel. Tomorrow is all yours. Will you show me the stables in the morning?" Her reply: "Whenever."

Would you like to watch a movie in bed? Her reply, a mumbled "whatever", delivered alarm signals but, too exhausted to deal with them, he rose and calmly announced he was going to bed. She glanced at him but said nothing. "Love you," Bobby whispered over his shoulder.

The following morning, he awoke stiff and sore but grateful to feel half-way normal. Shelby was dressed and reading the paper on the patio when he came down. He kissed her cheek and then slipped into the kitchen. A half-hour later Bobby emerged with plates piled with thick slices of cinnamon-covered French toast and served Shelby with mock fanfare. She was still cool but seemed appreciative being served her favorite breakfast.

They ate at the patio table overlooking the gardens, Shelby finally inquiring how he felt. Bobby used every tool in his charm arsenal: touching her hand, commenting on humorous stories in the paper. Thankfully he was aided by perfect conditions: sunlight, a gentle breeze, the air filled with the fragrance of roses and gardenias profuse in giant terra-cotta pots on the patio.

He refilled their coffee mugs. "How about showing me the new stables?"

"C'mon, you actually want to see it?" She still sounded angry, but not quite as bad.

"Yes, I do, I'm looking forward to it." Bobby let her lead the way as they toured the framed structure. He couldn't help but notice there were no crooked two-by-fours or pieced-together studs. The concrete floor had been swept clean of nails, sawdust, and scraps of lumber. Stacks of paneling were covered with tarps, the whole construction site neat and tidy. He had seen Shelby's other construction sites, all the same. "When do you plan to move the horses in?"

"I'm hoping no more than three or four weeks. Do you like the vertical grooved siding?"

"I do. The lines complement the height. Are you planning a tile roof?" She nodded. "Cool, that'll go with the house. Very pleasing. Those drafting and design classes paid off." Shelby didn't respond but her frown was gone. He followed her to the old stables where she began to feed and water the mares. "Can I help?" Bobby asked. "I haven't seen the horses in a long time."

"Don't give me that bull or pretend to like them. They smell up your patio dinner parties, remember?" Hands on her hips, she was clearly challenging him.

Bobby grinned. "Okay, okay! You got me, but cut me a little slack. From a purely building standpoint I appreciate the job you've done and can see the horses will be better off in the new barn. I've never actually said I don't like them so where did you get that idea?"

Shelby glanced skyward as though looking for divine intervention. He bowed with a flourish, hoping it would salvage their day. He regularly complained about the horses; they were both acknowledging it and, in a roundabout way, she was accepting his apology.

He reached over and patted Cherokee. "After we finish feeding them, we have the whole day. Tell me what you would like to do?"

"How about going to the beach?"

"Sounds like a lot of work."

"Okay, you suggest something"

"What about a drive?" Bobby said.

Shelby continued feeding the mares. "Drive where?"

Bobby filled Cheyenne's water trough. "Down the Coast Highway towards Del Mar. We could have lunch at that restaurant you love on the Pier in San Clemente, near the train station?"

He witnessed a slight smile, her first in two days. "That has potential."

"We won't be far from the Covington property. If we have time I'll show it to you." Seeing her smile instantly vanish, he realized his mistake.

"You just blew it. How stupid of me to think you'd enjoy a day with just your wife."

"No, no, you're not stupid! I'm sorry, really! I want to spend the day with my wife and I want whatever you want. C'mon, babe, puleese?" He gave her a mischievous smile.

A half-hour later, Bobby put the top down on the Porsche, donned a Dodger baseball cap and handed one to Shelby as he drove onto Canyon Hills Drive. "So you look like a native."

Shelby adjusted her sunglasses. "I'm warning you—if you have a client waiting somewhere along the way that you planned to meet, you are a dead man." He recognized her stare.

"Not to worry, babe, today I am solely Shelby Stamford's humble servant."

* * *

Bobby drove south on the Coast Highway, merging with the Sunday traffic on the 405 through Los Angeles, then rejoining Highway One at Newport Beach. There they began one of his favorite drives: through Laguna Beach, Dana Point, Capistrano, and on down to San Clemente. He glanced over at his wife as the wind whipped her long ponytail she had pulled through the back of her cap. She put her head back and bathed in the sun's warmth, a relaxed look on her face. Bobby's tension began to melt.

The sea was spectacular, viridian-tinted waves capped by frothy white plumes crashed over the rocks lining the shore. Their drive took them through picturesque coastal towns with Spanish-style buildings along the drive, many housing expensive boutique shops enclosed by bougainvillea-covered courtyard walls. They rode in silence, comfortable silence, Bobby hoped. He pulled into the Ritz Carlton Hotel in Laguna.

"Let's check out the grounds, then have a mimosa on the terrace. Afterward, we can take a swing through the shops. You never know, you might find something you don't need but can't live without." Shelby cast him an amused glance.

"From death's door to champagne at the Ritz, only Bobby Stamford could pull that off."

They strolled the hotel's manicured grounds, then made their way up to the terrace, noting that wedding preparations had been set up on the lawn below. A white arbor laden with climbing roses had been set against a panoramic view of the Pacific. From their table they watched tuxedoed musicians arrive, followed shortly by guests who sat in white chairs facing the arbor.

Bobby ordered orange juice-champagne mimosas. They toasted "a day off," drinking from crystal flutes as they sat amongst the rich, beautiful people Bobby revered. The warm sun and the music muted by the sound of the ocean made Bobby smile. "God, I love this," he said.

Shelby merely nodded, then said she didn't want to shop so they continued their drive. Bobby's spirits soared, Shelby's hostility seeming to have lessened and he was on his favorite drive. The sea, the lush landscape, the Spanish architecture and all the chic, tanned shoppers reminding him why he loved southern California. "See that parcel?" he said, pointing at an expanse of ocean-front acreage with a sign on it. "I was talking to Hal about that. It's a perfect spot for condos."

"You are certainly in the right business, Bobby." Shelby looked over at him with an amused expression. "You would develop Paradise if you could."

He chuckled. "Well, if I did, Paradise would look exactly like this." Bobby reached over and took Shelby's left hand and pressed it to his lips. She switched on the radio with her free hand, a Billy Ocean song coming on. Bobby dropped her hand and turned off the radio.

"Why did you turn it off? I like Billy Ocean." She sounded annoyed.

"I thought we could talk, Shel. We never get a chance to really talk."

She turned toward him, her demeanor replaced by a look of determination. "Funny you say that. I agree and I have a critical issue we are finally going to discuss—like it or not!"

* * *

Bobby awoke Monday morning, dreading his doctor appointment. After failing to talk Shelby out of going with him, he had to accept that he couldn't discuss with Doc what really brought on his symptoms. Doc greeted them with "From what Shelby told me about your reaction to the bike ride, I feel it's time we thoroughly check you out."

After having blood drawn, getting a chest x-ray and an EKG, followed by Dr. Caldwell probing and poking and checking him over, Bobby heard a tap on the door and the doctor entered for the second time, his brow creased. Not a good sign.

"You don't look like a happy camper, Doc." Bobby grinned.

"Call it concern, Bobby, concern with good reason," Caldwell replied. "Unfortunately it's been over two years since your last complete physical and I—"

"I know and I'm sorry, but the last two years have been extremely busy. To be honest, have been the busiest and most difficult of my career."

Caldwell nodded. "Well, that would account for your test results. Your blood pressure is higher than it should be for a forty-five-year-old male. Your cholesterol and triglycerides tell me you are not following a Mediterranean diet. But most puzzling, Bobby, is your EKG. It points to a man either overweight or under a great deal of stress. But the fact that you are not overweight therefore makes the EKG results even more worrisome."

"Worrisome? I would think not being overweight is a good thing. No?" Bobby said.

"Ordinarily, but…" Caldwell grew quiet, appearing to be thinking how to answer. "It is important you both understand that the results of your EKG better fit a man who is either significantly overweight or several years older. Since you are relatively young and your weight is fine, then to what do I attribute your EKG results?"

"Wow, unfortunately I do understand. You're saying if I were overweight it would explain the bad blips on my EKG. But since I'm not, then what's causing them?" Bobby said.

"Yes, and you couldn't have stated it any better. It's good you understand, Bobby. To find the root cause I would need further in-depth tests and your family's health history."

Bobby glanced at Shelby; she looked as scared as he felt. "So what now, Doc?"

"First, I'm going to prescribe medication to lower your blood pressure. Second, altering your alcohol intake and your diet will help. I'll give you some literature and if you can, Bobby, I strongly urge you to take some time off from your frenetic schedule. I am not referring to a few days. I'm talking about an extended period. You need to significantly reduce your stress level."

Caldwell glanced at Shelby then at Bobby. "I realize this is a lot to absorb. It's good you both came in. Start the blood pressure medicine today and I'll see you in ten days to see how it's working. Do give serious consideration to taking a month off. Totally away from stress if you can, Bobby. That may possibly be the most beneficial."

Neither one spoke as they walked to the car. Shelby looked stunned and Bobby felt sure he looked the same. He took the rest of the day off, mentally wrestling with Caldwell's calmly delivered speech about his health. And he couldn't forget Shelby's proclamation yesterday on their drive home from Laguna that she wanted to get pregnant, and "no more waiting." By evening, he was resigned that he had no choice but follow Caldwell's advice. He told Shelby it would take a few days to wrap up work at the office in order to take a month off.

When Bobby arrived at the office Tuesday morning, Terri's first words were "You look a lot better," then she asked if everything was okay. "Yes, thank you, doing fine now." To his relief, her "that's good" signaled she understood. Bobby confided to his father about his doctor visit and Caldwell's advice. Adam's instant response: "Please, son, you have to take care of yourself."

Ten days later, Bobby and Shelby returned to Caldwell's office. Asked if he had followed the advice he'd been given, Bobby answered, "No booze, not even wine. I smoked half as many cigarettes as I used to. I'm trying, Doc, but I have to admit it's harder than hell."

Bobby was rewarded by Caldwell's affirmative nod, followed by "Your blood pressure is coming down which means the medicine is working. You're on the right track, Bobby, but what about reducing your stress? Any plans to get away from the office?"

Bobby started to reply, but Shelby interrupted. "I'm taking care of that, doctor. You have my word."

Chapter Four

Bobby took note of the changing scenery and the forests on both sides of the road. A thousand miles from home and driving a rig that looked like a yacht on wheels, which Shelby called "thirty-two feet of mobile, luxuriously-furnished, air-conditioned opulence."

Still astounded that, of all people, Bobby Stamford would actually be caught driving a trailer, no matter how luxurious his wife deemed it to be. An even bigger shock, Shelby's explanation why she rented it: "Remember on our Laguna drive when you said we never get a chance to talk? Well, I remember our talk, word for word. I told you I want to get pregnant, no more waiting, and that we always vacation where you want to go!"

You bet I remember that drive. It was the day after the Terri episode with Shelby acting pissed off and sarcastic like maybe she knew. On the drive back she hit me with the baby thing and our vacation. I was so shocked I said okay. What was I thinking!

After Doc Caldwell's advice, Bobby had lobbied hard to spend a month at The Golden Door, eating gourmet diet food, working out in a state-of-the-art gym, swimming laps in a luxurious pool, and getting daily massages. But Shelby stood her ground; she was adamant that she get to choose their vacation and The Eagle trip was something she really wanted to do.

The fact I caved, I have my guilty conscience to thank for that.

They were now entering Montana, the heart of the beautiful

Northwest Shelby so wanted to see. The few overnight stays in California had been okay, a campground in Morro Bay, an artsy coastal village she chose near Hearst's Castle. They sat outside and drank diet cranberry juice from long-stemmed glasses. He remembered her toast: "To good health and great times."

Vivid in Bobby's memory of that evening was that he actually felt relaxed and that, strangely, it was a totally new feeling. Shelby had even noticed, commenting how relaxed he looked and sounded. He also remembered her saying the change was amazing. The fact that his looking and feeling relaxed was rare, Bobby found very disturbing.

He glanced over at Shelby, staring straight ahead, her posture stiff with hands clasped in her lap, her same demeanor since his blowup yesterday about this time. He'd absolutely lost it over the endless driving, the cumbersome Eagle, nothing but healthy food, no booze, this whole stupid idea to see the beautiful Northwest. It made him appreciate Terri dancing naked in front of the mirror for him. She wouldn't go nuts over "beautiful trees," or not let him stop at Arti's Super Burger Stand. Terri would have had him stop and had one with him.

The truth hit him full force. *I've lost control of my life! This isn't me. I love the intrigue, the challenge of multi-million-dollar deals. I dig Armani suits. I like entertaining clients over gourmet lunches and dinners. Instead, I'm driving this dumbass RV on a trip I didn't want to take, to a place I don't give a shit about. This whole dimwit trip is Shel's and Caldwell's fault. It sucks! No wine, no cocktails, just fucking decaf iced tea or lemon water.*

Bobby wanted to scream but he couldn't erase Caldwell's warning: "Get serious about your health or face the potential of suffering a stroke or heart attack." Bobby stomped on the accelerator out of sheer frustration.

"Bobby, you can't drive that way. The Eagle isn't—"

"Oh, great, Shel! The first words you've uttered in a hundred miles, and it's '**you can't!**' Stick to what you know and leave me the hell alone." Bobby floored it, the Eagle engine responding with ominous noises. He gripped the wheel and stared straight ahead.

That night, Shelby again slept so far over in the king-size bed he wasn't aware she was there. Her distancing herself from him created a fair amount of guilt, his ruining the trip she was so excited about. *I feel like a heel but this is too much, too fast. The final on the Covington project, the awesome sex with Terri, then thinking I might be dying. Doc slamming me with the news that if I don't change my life, I'll die of a stroke or heart attack. All that and Shel saying no more waiting to get pregnant! This stupid fucking trip was supposed for my health!*

Bobby, lamenting everything about this trip, wished he could somehow break the ice then had to admit that he didn't have a clue where to start or what to say. So he said nothing at all. He kept his eyes on the road, acknowledging that they had passed the last signs of civilization an hour ago. No more towns now and very few cars; what he saw ahead was the silhouette of massive black mountains dominating the skyline. One minute they were set against a blue sky and the next were hidden by serious-looking black clouds.

The highway suddenly became narrower and steeper as it cut a clean slice through the forest. Out both side windows he saw dark stands of thick-trunked trees that cast shadows across the road in front of the Eagle. Bobby glanced at Shelby, one minute looking down at a map and the next staring out the window, he guessed for a sign of an entrance to Glacier National Park.

Gripping the steering wheel, Bobby drove the Eagle around a curve cresting a lengthy steep climb, the engine clearly straining to pull its heavy load. Finally at the top, the whining noise was followed by grating sounds and then a loud clunk. "What the HELL?" Bobby yelled.

"You surely aren't surprised!" Shelby yelled back. "I told you not to drive like that!"

Bobby glared at her. "Oh sure, blame me. Like it's my fault." Spotting a large dirt lot off to the right, Bobby pulled off the highway, the Eagle bouncing over rain-hardened ruts. "Hang on!" he said as they bounced along, finally lumbering to a halt a few yards in front of an ancient-looking two-story building, a big Ford Diesel Dually pickup parked in front. Before he could turn off the key, the engine clanked a final hollow sound then died.

He threw up his hands. "This is fuckin' all I need!"

Shelby jumped up, hands on her hips, glaring at him. "Typical Bobby Stamford. Why in the hell are you surprised? You destroyed the engine—literally! This whole trip, what a joke! Help get you back in shape, give the two of us a chance to spend time together to save our marriage. You're so self-absorbed, or stupid, you don't even know there is a problem. And if you did, I sure as hell don't get the feeling you care enough to try fixing it."

"Try?" he roared back. "You call a thousand miles of silence try-ing? I thought this goddam trip was for my health. My blood pressure is probably off the charts, thanks to you."

"This trip was for your health," she shouted. "You're the one who turned it into the vacation from hell. I actually thought it would be a chance for us to make things better."

"Better? Better how? For chrissake you have everything you want. You do anything you want. Spend whatever you want. How much better is there?"

"If you think I have everything I want, you couldn't be any more STUPID!" Shelby looked ready to explode. "What about a having a husband who wants to spend time with me, not just show me off like some kind of a prize? 'Superstar Bobby Stamford, look what he's got.' What about kids, Bobby? How many times have I told you I want kids and you keep putting me off—always for one more deal! I've wanted a family more than anything. You promised me! Did you mean it or was that just another lie?"

Bobby jumped up and faced her, "Kids? Is that what this is all about? Then why in the hell didn't you tell me that before you dragged me on this disaster and put me through this shit?"

"Put *you* through shit, that's laughable," Shelby said, her voice laced with contempt. "I did tell you I wanted to get pregnant. Did you forget? I told you that on our drive the day after my birthday party. Do you remember what *you* said, because I sure as hell do. You said you'd have to *think* about it. Who made you God?" So absorbed in their fight, they didn't notice the figure emerge from the building and skirt the Eagle.

* * *

The man stopped a few yards from the RV and leaned against one of the giant maples, his eyes on the couple inside. He could hear them; their argument looked and sounded serious. He shifted his lanky frame from one worn cowboy boot to another, hooked his thumb in his jeans pocket and pushed back his sweat-stained Stetson. "California loonies," he grumbled, noting the license plate. After another ten minutes listening to them holler at each other, he concluded it was a shouting match, not a fight. He walked back to the old building, glancing up at the *Ellie's Café* wooden sign above the door. The letters were nearly illegible. "Got to repaint that thing."

Jack Ketchum took a final glance back at the RV; the couple was still arguing. He also took note of the towering bank of dark cumulus clouds approaching. "That makes two storms." He pulled open the heavy door, his unease over the storms dissolving once he stepped inside.

The café was familiar and comforting, and one he rarely failed to acknowledge as a happy place that helped him get through a dark period in his life. Ellie had loved it, the antique bar, the big mirror in back of it with shelves showcasing an impressive collection of bottles, their contents a rainbow of color. The dozen or so tables in front of the bar still had the blue and white checkered tablecloths she'd sewed. "After all, it is a café too," she reminded him.

Jack poured himself a cup of coffee, removed his Stetson, and sat down at a table by a front window. He lit a cigarette and peered around the neon Bud sign at the RV. He could tell by their posture and gesturing they were giving full vent to their feelings. Hopefully it would remain only words. If not, since they were on his property, he would intervene. Only two or three times did he have to step in when customers looked about to settle things physically.

Ten minutes passed then through the RV's large front windows, he saw the woman sit down in the passenger seat, lower her head, hands covering her face like she was crying. A minute or two later, she got up and disappeared back into the rig. Jack rose, not sure what to do but feeling he at least should go check on the couple. Decision made, he was about to put on his Stetson and head for the door when he spotted a tall, slender woman emerge from the side door of the RV. He dropped his Stetson on the table; she was walking toward the café.

* * *

Shelby squared her shoulders and mounted the wooden steps, noting the *Ellie's Café* sign as she pulled open the heavy door. Beyond exhaustion, she had no anger left, no feelings of any kind; she had screamed them all at Bobby. Uncertain, she paused to adjust to the dim light. A minute later the image of a tall lanky cowboy became clear. She brushed tears from her face in a quick motion. "Do you have a phone I could use? My cell doesn't work."

"Yes, ma'am, and you're welcome to use it."

Shelby focused on him, noticing the imprint of a hat in his silver-streaked hair and the hint of a smile on his face, a handsome face. He looked like a cowboy: worn cowboy boots, faded jeans, a leather vest over his denim shirt. Kind blue eyes were looking at her questioningly.

"I'm sorry," she managed to say. "Our RV broke down."

"Yeah, I saw," he said. "And I couldn't help but notice the dustup you and the fella were having. In fact I was just about to come out and make sure you were okay. Are you?"

The sympathy in his voice, coupled with the genuine concern in his eyes and on his face, dissolved what remained of Shelby's fragile resolve. Her shoulders drooped; she looked down at the floor, tears coming again. "Right now I hate my husband. I actually hate him."

"Why don't you sit down," Jack said and pulled out a chair at the closest table. He retrieved a napkin from the napkin-holder and handed it to her. "Please. You look exhausted. I just made a pot of coffee. Can I get you a cup?"

Shelby took the napkin and sat down. "Yes, thank you," she said and dabbed her eyes.

Jack poured a mug of coffee and brought it to her. He pulled up a chair and straddled it across from her. "Would you like a smoke?" He produced a pack from his shirt pocket.

"No, thanks, I don't... oh, what the hell." Shelby took the cigarette and saw his quick smile as he offered a light. She alternately sipped the coffee and smoked the cigarette until both were gone. "Thank you,

I think I can hold it together now." She tried her best to smile. "You said you had a phone I could use?"

"Sure." He motioned toward the end of the bar. "We have two phones, one digital, one old-fashioned. From the looks of that storm coming, the digital might not work. We're on the fringe for cell reception anyway. Sometimes we get it, other times not. What happened to your rig?"

"I'm not sure but the way it sounded, probably the transmission." Shelby blew her nose and crumpled the napkin. "I can only imagine how I look. Sorry about the hate remark. I didn't mean to dump my troubles on you."

"No need to apologize. All folks get into it at one time or other. My wife and I used to."

"Hopefully it gets better."

"Yeah, as I remember it does."

Shelby noticed his wedding ring. "Evidently it did. You said you and your wife used to. You don't argue anymore?"

"My wife died three years ago last week." He said it softly.

"Oh God, I didn't mean to..." Shelby shook her head. "I'm so sorry."

"No, no, that was my fault. Guess I made it sound like she was still alive." Jack glanced out the window. "Better pull yourself together. I see your husband coming this way."

Chapter Five

The heavy door flew open and Bobby strode in, fists clenched. Eyeing Shelby, he moved toward her. Jack rose and casually stepped around in back of her chair. "I understand you got transmission trouble."

"I don't know what's wrong with it." Bobby barely looked at Jack. "Did you call, Shel?"

Exhausted, she took a deep breath before she replied, "No, I did not."

"Well, why the fuck not? Both cell phones are dead. How're we gonna get out of here?" He shot her an angry glance and the same at Jack. "Hey, I'm in a hurry. Where's the phone?"

"Back there." Jack nodded in the general direction at the end of the bar. "Your wife was just having a cup of coff—"

Halfway to the bar, Bobby hollered over his shoulder, "Where the hell are we anyway?"

Embarrassed, Shelby cast a glance at Jack. "I have no idea, Bobby."

"Why the fuck am I not surprised," he shot back.

Jack swung around and took several steps in Bobby's direction. "You're in Troutsprings, Montana, asshole, in my café!" his forefinger punctuating each word. "And I'd just as soon you quit throwin' around the F bomb. You understand me?" Jack's face was flushed.

"Yeah, yeah, whatever," Bobby grumbled as he picked up the

receiver. He talked for a few minutes then began shouting into the phone, banging his free hand against the wall.

Jack walked back to the table and again straddled the chair across from her. He spoke in a low, even voice. She could see him struggling to control his anger. "Sorry, I don't usually talk like that, but guys who throw their weight around like that rile me up."

"I apologize for all of this. I'll go call. I'm sure I can get some help." She rose.

"No, don't," Jack said his eyes on Bobby. "Until he calms down, I'd just as soon you be where I can keep an eye on you. Under the circumstances, I think we should at least know each other's name. Mine's Jack Ketchum. Your name is Shelley?"

"No, it's Shelby, and thank you, Jack." She gave a nervous smile, her eyes darting back and forth from Jack's face to Bobby, leaning against the wall now as he talked on the phone. "I really appreciate your help and I am sorry to be so much trouble. Bobby is…"

Jack chuckled. "Funny, we've known each other, what all of ten minutes? And I've apologized more than I have in the last couple years. How about you?"

"Same here." Shelby smiled.

"This isn't such a bad place to break down," Jack ventured. "We actually get a lot of folks that come here for vacation. And I like it well enough to call home."

"Sonofabitch!" Bobby slammed down the receiver, then spun around facing them. "The rental company has to check with the manufacturer in Michigan to find the nearest authorized repair shop. Of course, it's after five o'clock in Michigan, so it'll be Monday before they can even check."

Bobby looked and sounded out of control, his voice ricocheting off the walls of the quiet café. Shelby peeked around Jack and saw Bobby striding toward the table, glaring at her as he kicked a chair out of the way. "This is all your goddamn fault."

Not sure what Bobby was going to do, Shelby rose. At the same time Jack stood up. He slung his chair across the wooden floor and it crashed against the wall. Jack placed himself directly in Bobby's path. "Your little tantrum has gone far enough, mister. No more hollering, no more cussing, no more kicking chairs, not if you value living. You got two choices. Either simmer down or take me on." Jack's voice came out low and fierce. Neither man moved.

Shelby took two cautious steps around Jack's right side, intent on trying to calm Bobby. Jack, not taking his eyes off Bobby, raised his right hand in her direction—a silent unmistakable message to stay put. Shelby froze on the spot, staring at the two of them in horrified silence. Bobby was glaring at Jack. *Surely to God, Bobby, you wouldn't be stupid enough to throw a punch. You would be no match for this man.*

She glanced at Jack, his lips pressed into a grim line. At least five years older than Bobby, Jack had a lean powerful body, his stance that of a fighter ready to strike. Shelby held her breath; there was dead silence in the café. She could see Bobby mentally tallying his chances of taking Jack on. She willed her husband to look at her but his eyes remained on Jack.

After what seemed an interminable pause, Bobby's taut features relaxed and his alert posture dissolved into a slouch. He gave Shelby a quick glance then raised his hands chest high, both palms outward in mock surrender then nodded at Jack. "Okay, okay, I'm cool. I simmer down real good," he said. "I've already got enough trouble. I don't need more."

Shelby nodded. "I don't either, Bobby. I think we've caused Mr.

Ketchum enough trouble already." Her throat was so dry it hurt to speak.

Jack's tense stance eased off. His right hand, still up in warning to Shelby, dropped to his side. "I got just the fix for this situation," Jack said evenly, his steady gaze still on Bobby. "I'll buy you a beer. After all, you're in a café in Montana. What do you say about that?" His voice still had an edge to it, a test to find out if Bobby had regained self-control, Shelby thought.

Bobby nodded. "A beer sounds great." His voice and posture signaled exhaustion.

Jack walked behind the bar and returned with three beers. Avoiding Shelby's eyes, Bobby wrapped his hands around the cool wet bottle and took a few deep breaths. He raised the bottle in Jack's direction and downed half the contents, his face slowly beginning to relinquish its redness. Shelby took a drink and for a moment the three sat silently sipping beer.

Jack spoke first. "I can fix you up with power and water to your rig," he said in a matter-of-fact tone. "It might be Tuesday before they get a mechanic or a tow truck up here from Missoula. So, the bad news is you broke down." Jack's voice softened, the beginning of a smile forming. "But the good news is you landed in front of Ellie's Cafe, home of the best steaks in northwest Montana."

Bobby's eyebrows shot upward. "You're kidding me! Steaks? As in prime USDA beef?"

Jack grinned at Bobby's reaction. "I admit I'm bragging, but we grill prime-cut T-bones, New Yorks and Filets to perfection. They come with beans cooked overnight in barbecue sauce that's got a bite to it, and you get a big salad or slaw and lots of garlic bread."

Bobby glanced up and crossed himself. "Maybe there is a heaven after all!" The tension eased. Shelby began to relax, marveling at how Jack handled the situation.

Jack's anger appeared to have been replaced by cordiality though she detected a hint of vigilance or reserve in his voice. Bobby insisted on buying the beers and, to Shelby's relief, asked Jack to start a tab since it looked like they would be around for a few days.

Over another round, Shelby asked, "You certainly don't run this café by yourself?"

"No, I have a lady who comes in at five o'clock to do the waitressing, plus a fellow tends bar for me on Friday and Saturday nights, our busiest. The chef's name is Matt and he came up from Denver for a two-week vacation. He ate here several times and we got to talking. He worked at a restaurant in Denver but said he was tired of living in a big spread-out city and commuting. He married a local gal and he loves Troutsprings. His stepson, who is in high school, does the dishes. We manage to get it done. We serve dinner five days a week, closed Sundays and Mondays."

Bobby took a long draw on his beer. "How big is Troutsprings?"

"Nine hundred, more or less, maybe a thousand by now. This time of year there are a lot of campers and hikers, mostly fishermen. The fishing is great here. Rainbow trout practically jump out of the river at you." He looked at Bobby. "You a fisherman?"

"You bet," Bobby said. Shelby observed his personality returning. "Usually deep sea for tuna and salmon, but I never met a fish sautéed in wine and garlic I didn't like. Although right now that steak dinner you described sounds too good to be true."

"Bobby loves to barbecue. He's a pretty good chef," Shelby said.

"Is that right? Maybe you'd like to try your hand behind the grill at Ellie's. You know how to grill a steak?"

Bobby chuckled. "I've grilled a few. I wouldn't mind trying a turn at being chef."

When Shelby asked about the name, Jack told them Ellie's Cafe had been Ellen Ketchum's haven. "She wasn't fond of Montana winters, so when the old-timers who owned this place said they wanted to move to Arizona, Ellie persuaded me to buy it." Jack gave Shelby a look that hinted Ellie's 'persuasion' had been one of their fights. "Ellen loved this place," Jack said, his voice turning somber. "I think what she loved was being around people, getting to visit with every-body. She sort of held court here. Well, she and her friend, Adele Carson. They're the ones who made this place popular."

Shelby studied Jack as he talked about his wife, a slight smile on his face one minute as he reminisced, followed by a brief flash of pain. *I wonder what happened to her and why does he still wear a wedding ring?* Shelby's first impression of Jack Ketchum was a man of character. He had a temper but also a sense of humor. She had seen flashes of both. He was an intriguing man, a cowboy, and quite differ-ent than the men she came in contact with in her building business.

Bobby had slouched down in his chair, one arm slung over the back. "What do the good people of Troutsprings do?" he asked.

"Tourism mostly, a lot of it related to fishing," answered Jack.

"But what about winter when the snow is ten feet deep, ice fish?"

Knowing Bobby's sarcasm, Shelby shot him a warning look, appalled by his feigned interest. He could care less what the people did around here. He was being charming-Bobby, playing a role she had seen him play a hundred times. 'Disarming the competition,' he called it. His voice and his posture gave it away.

"People actually do ice-fish but not nearly like summer fishing," Jack said. "Troutsprings is a haven for winter sports, snowmobile enthusiasts and cross-country skiers. It started out a mining town but not anymore, a lot of cattle and sheep ranching now. I've got a little spread," Jack said, glancing at Shelby.

"A cattle ranch?" Now it was Shelby who was clearly interested.

He nodded. "About twenty minutes north and east of here and lower in elevation."

"How exciting! But how do you possibly run a cattle ranch and this place too?"

Jack grinned. "Don't spend much time sitting. For a while after Ellie died, I thought about selling everything and moving to Arizona too. But time just slipped by and there were always chores to do. Then I came to my senses and realized I really didn't want to leave, Ellie being buried here and all. There's no better place to be, I know that now. Speaking of chores, we'd better get you hooked up. It'll be five o'clock before you know it and Adele will come through those doors and start barking orders at me."

Jack helped Bobby connect a hose and a heavy power cord to the Eagle. Bobby showered first. Shelby got out clean clothes for both of them, peeking out the windows at the sky every few minutes. Opening the window, she noted bright shafts of light filtering through the gathering black clouds as a rush of air greeted her. Cool and fresh, the air smelled of rain and pines, and then all of a sudden the clouds covered the sun.

"Hey, what happened? It got dark," Bobby called from the shower.

"Clouds. Looks like the storm finally got here," Shelby said, closing the window. She watched the wind kick up the dust in the parking lot as rain began to splat loud drops on the Eagle's roof. There was a knock at the door.

It was Jack. "It'd be a good idea to tie down anything loose and put down that antenna. Don't know how big this storm's gonna be."

"Thanks, we will," Shelby replied.

"And I'd be happy if you and your husband would have dinner inside… on me." Jack nodded and touched the brim of his hat.

Shelby had to smile at the simple, gentlemanly gesture. "Thank you again. That would be very nice. We'll come in after we get cleaned up."

Thirty minutes later, Bobby cranked down the antenna as thunder crashed above them.

"This storm is really something. I like it. We don't see weather like this in L.A."

Bobby rolled his eyes. "Yeah, this is what I call fun."

"Sarcasm noted, Bobby." Shelby took a shower and dressed, then sat in the passenger seat of the Eagle and watched the storm through the giant front windows. The RV faced a creek that Jack described as running perpendicular behind the café. Great streaks of lightning looked as though they touched the ground in the field beyond the creek. Each flash illuminated a kaleidoscope of colors and was followed by a deafening crash. The power of the storm rocked the Eagle with thunder and wind blasts from changing directions, first driving rain against the sides of the RV, then hammering it onto the fiberglass roof, the noise reverberating throughout the compact space.

Bobby walked up and stood behind her chair. "I admit this is quite a show."

Shelby watched the storm in fascination. "What spectacular country."

"Don't get any ideas. I'm not buying property up here. I don't care how spectacular it is."

Disappointed, Shelby looked at Bobby. "Can't we have one conversation without your sarcasm? Or do you enjoy upsetting me?"

"No, ma'am, shore wouldn't want to upset the little wife," he said with a swagger.

"You're not funny," she said in a steely tone. Shelby counted to ten under her breath.

"Okay, okay. I'll try to be a good boy."

"You do that," she snapped. "And instead of a boy? Why don't you try being a man? That would be a refreshing change."

Chapter Six

Shelby and Bobby sprinted toward the café, the wind-driven rain pelting them as they raced up the wooden steps. Behind the bar, Jack looked up as they burst through the doors. "Whoa, looks like the wind carried you in."

"If I'd had an umbrella, I'd be in South Dakota by now," Shelby said. Jack motioned them to the bar and drew a tap for both. About to take a sip, she glanced over her shoulder; someone was struggling with the heavy double doors.

"Damn this wind! I should've used more hair spray." Shelby had to stare at the woman shouldering her way in sideways. "Jack! Oh my gosh—" she said, fighting to balance a pie in each hand with the wind-gust winning.

Shelby jumped down and rushed to her, catching one pie just as it left the woman's hand. "Great catch, thank you. You just saved my Granny Smith with crunch topping."

Shelby lifted the edge of the steamy, rain-splattered plastic cover. "Oh, smell that! It's still warm." She placed the pie on the bar.

The woman set the other pie down, then held out her hand. "Adele Carson." Shelby tried not to stare as she shook the flamboyant lady's hand. Dressed in a University of Montana sweatshirt and skinny jeans tucked into cowboy boots, Adele Carson could have been a former Miss Montana, her makeup perfect, her auburn hair tossed by the wind, her smile genuine. "Thank you again, but leave it to me to make an entrance." After Jack introduced Shelby and Bobby to her, Adele excused herself saying she had to get ready for the Friday night crowd. "Jack, get it in gear, would you? Got the beer locker stocked? Did the bread guy get here? Did you stir the beans like I told you?"

"What'd I tell you?" Jack shot Shelby a knowing look. "Hold on, Adele. I've been busy helping these folks," he called out to her as she disappeared into the room behind the kitchen. "Yes, I did everything you said. Now can I go get cleaned up?"

Adele peeked around the door. "Okay, but no nappin'."

"Yes, ma'am," Jack said.

When Adele reappeared, Shelby offered to help and shot Bobby a questioning look but his expression signaled "no." While he finished his beer, Shelby placed dinner-size paper napkins and silver on the laminated tables. A few minutes later Bobby joined her, helping to transfer beer from a huge refrigerator in the back room into two smaller ones under the bar. "Do you think it will be busy tonight with the storm?" Shelby asked Adele as she worked.

She shook her head. "Hon, in Montana we consider this a gets-the-dust-off-the-truck storm, not enough to keep folks home. When lightning hits the house, the barn or your truck, that's when we take notice." Even as she directed Shelby and Bobby, Adele kept moving about the café like a whirlwind, making sure everything was ready without missing a word. By the time Jack came down from his living quarters, Ellie's Cafe stood ready for a Friday night.

At six-thirty Shelby noted that every barstool was occupied by a jeans-clad man, either wearing a cowboy hat or baseball cap, every one of them drinking beer. Jack introduced Virgil when he arrived to tend bar, then it seemed there was no break in the steady stream of men and women arriving and filling the tables. Every time the doors opened, the customers inside let out a collective whoop and hollered

"Close the doors!" in unison, then everyone laughed. Cigarette smoke hung thick in the air, mixing and swirling each time the doors opened.

Five wagon-wheel light fixtures cast a soft glow over the room from the high ceiling. A red neon Bud sign in the window reflected its light off the rain-washed pane while a muted television above the bar cast the brightest light, Vince Gill and Reba McIntyre on the screen mouthing silent words. The storm disappeared as quickly as it came; the thunder rumbled off into the distance, the flashes of lightning slowly retreating but still illuminating the sky.

Seated at one of the tables near the window, Shelby and Bobby watched the departing storm. Glancing over the room, Shelby saw Jack approaching. "I wanted to make sure you tried our specialty so, hope you don't mind, I ordered for you." Bobby's happy smile spoke volumes. Adele soon delivered each one a New York steak, barbecued beans, salad and garlic bread, Ellie's Cafe style—all at once.

Bobby cleaned his plate and ate what Shelby couldn't finish of her steak. "Man-oh-man, did I ever need that," Bobby said, patting his stomach. Shelby readily agreed.

"Order up!" Jack yelled to Adele.

"Hold on, you old geezer, I'm running as fast as I can."

They heard a customer call out "Hey, Jack, this steak is still talkin' to me."

Smiling, Jack turned from the stove. "Want me to come out and shoot him again, Clyde?"

Clyde laughed. "No sirree, stay behind that stove. I don't want you out here with a gun."

By eight o'clock the bar stools were full again and Shelby and Bobby surrendered their table to an incoming young couple. "I don't want to go back to the Eagle yet," Shelby said.

"Then I think I'll go see how Jack does those beans. They were really good. Beats the hell outta steamed veggies and rice." Shelby didn't know what to think. Bobby acted as if there had never been a fight, whistling happily as he headed behind the bar. *Like Dr. Jekyll and Mr. Hyde, was that fight and this whole miserable trip because he was on a diet? I should have let him go to the damned Golden Door— by himself!*

Shelby watched Adele carrying four plates at once, yell an order to Jack and kid around with the customers at the same time. When Jack yelled "Order up" again and she could see Adele was busy, Shelby grabbed the two plates and Adele pointed with a tilt of her head to the couple who had taken their table.

"Thank you," both said when Shelby placed their dinners in front of them.

Watching and listening to Adele interact with the customers, it was obvious that the majority were Troutsprings locals. Adele knew their names, inquired about their kids, seemed to know their uncles and grandparents and what was going on in their lives. Shelby found it as charming as Jack touching the brim of his cowboy hat. In a way, it reminded her of the camaraderie that evening at the country club, though these people were not elegantly dressed nor spoke in subdued tones. Still, the scenario was similar, people out enjoying dinner, just a different setting.

Shelby smelled Old Spice as she bent to serve Will, who Adele said came in every Friday night with his wife, Wanda. The men talked about work; they told stories about logging, fishing and hunting, and Shelby heard laughter follow. Troutsprings women, most of them also in jeans, some with make-up, some without, joined in the laughter and Shelby overheard snatches of conversations about kids and school and money woes. Adele introduced her when she saw curious looks cast at Shelby.

Easy to identify the tourists; they talked about home, the good fishing, and the area's spectacular scenery. By eleven o'clock the diners were finished. All but a few dishes had been cleared away and most of the customers sat drinking beer. The two gambling machines hummed, a buzzer sounding occasionally, indicating a payoff. Ronnie, the dishwasher finished and then left with friends for pizza in Pine Ridge.

* * *

Bobby swiveled his bar stool, his back to the bar, and lit a cigarette. He'd had fun cooking alongside Jack, and he had to admit the steak was as delicious as Jack said it would be. Bobby noted that the couple Jack said came every Friday night was still there. Standing by their table with a tray in her hand, Shelby was talking and laughing with them as though she had known them forever. *Not in a million years. I don't get how she can be so friendly with these people. Or why she'd bother. This place is another planet.*

Later in the Eagle it was the first night Shelby hadn't been at the opposite edge of the bed with her back to Bobby. On her side as though studying him, she said, "I like Adele and Jack and the people I met tonight. They are nice and friendly, don't you think?"

"They're okay. I wouldn't necessarily pick them as friends. We don't have much in common with them." He spoke cautiously, hoping to avoid an argument.

"I would pick them," Shelby said. "There isn't a phony bone in Jack's or Adele's body and I didn't have trouble finding something in common with any of the customers. They're genuine. I'd pick them as friends over a lot of people I know in L.A."

"You sound ticked off."

"I just said I thought these people are nice. You interpret that as being ticked off?"

"I was referring to the resident phony population of L.A. implication, that interpretation."

Shelby stared at him. "I do not want to fight, okay? I would like to salvage something, anything from this vacation. If it takes a week to get the Eagle fixed, I would like to spend it around here. Jack says the scenery is spectacular. Lots of people come here for their vacation."

Bobby could see her determination, the same determination that ended with him being on this trip. "You really want to? You don't want to leave the Eagle pile of junk here, let the repair place deal with it and hop a flight back to L.A.?"

"No, I would not. I'd like to see this area and go fishing like we planned. Jack said he would show us his favorite fishing spot. We would get a chance to use our fly rods."

"Good old Jack. I'm sure he would."

Shelby's smile vanished. "Try to show me just some of the charm you lavish on the country club set, Bobby. I could really use a break from your sarcasm." With that she switched off her lamp, moved to the far edge of the bed, and turned her back to him.

Bobby reached over and touched her shoulder. "I'm sorry, Shel. You're right. We came all this way so we should stick around and see the place. Okay?"

"Thanks, I'd like that."

"I'm going to read for a little while, do you mind?"

"No, go ahead. Goodnight, Bobby."

Bobby read one chapter of a spy novel until his eyes felt heavy. Shelby's breathing was quiet and steady. He raised up on his elbow and looked over at her sleeping peacefully, her face turned slightly toward him, a pretty face that held a hint of sadness even in slumber.

Memories flooded in: Bobby recalled the years he was struggling to learn the business at the same time Shelby was juggling a hectic schedule working for American Airlines. That was before they moved to the hills above Santa Monica, before Skyline Construction. Before so many things.

Funny Shelby, what happened to us? You used to be so happy. I don't mean to hurt you. Brenda and Terri don't mean anything to me. You do. They're just part of the game. If you could only understand that. Bobby Stamford was born to play the game.

He leaned over and kissed her forehead; she stirred slightly, her sleep undisturbed. He turned off his lamp and tried to remember how his office looked.

* * *

Shelby awoke conscious of a shaft of light streaming through the vertical blinds. She glanced over at Bobby, still asleep. "Hey, it's seven o'clock," she said. He opened one eye. "Darn it, too late to go fishing," she added.

"I can't tell you how disappointed I am," he said in between yawns.

"I know your day must be ruined now," she said with a poke to his shoulder. "My turn to shower first. You have to dry it down."

She called out from the shower, "How about a bike ride instead?"

After breakfast they rode east from Ellie's Café, then turned onto a winding two-lane road, a sign indicating that Pine Ridge was seven miles ahead. Gazing down steep embankments between thick groves of trees, they could see the Flathead River coursing its way along, sparkling in the morning sun like an iridescent ribbon. Ahead, the two-lane highway was a patchwork of shade and sun and quiet. Shelby found the silence delightful, interrupted only occasionally by a chattering squirrel, a blue jay, or a hawk circling above. Two pickup trucks rumbled by. The drivers waved.

She rode easily ahead, thankful the road was fairly flat. Bobby called for her to stop frequently, saying he had to catch his breath. Shelby used the time to drink in the spectacular landscape, green-carpeted mountains as far as the eye could see, everything Jack said it would be. Towering above the lush forest were occasional dead trees, tamarack ghosts bleached by the sun and devoid of foliage, the white trunks appearing like church spires in a city of green.

Shelby slowed and called back to Bobby to look up at the top of a dead pine. "That's an osprey nest up there, see it?"

"Yeah, I see it—big bird," he replied and waved her on. They arrived in Pine Ridge at noon. An old mining town, the highway served as Main Street; it was bustling with people. Shelby stopped and Bobby pulled up beside her. "Can you believe this? It's like going back in time. Talk about charming," Shelby said staring at the red brick buildings lining both sides of the street. The wooden roofs ran the three block length of downtown Pine Ridge. She glanced at Bobby. "I can't believe it, covered sidewalks on both sides of the street!"

"You do remember you're talking to a developer, right?" Bobby was grinning. "Yes, this time you're right on. I didn't think I'd ever see this in my lifetime. It is charming."

An obviously very old Pine Ridge Cinema boasted a glassed-in cashier's booth in the middle of its entrance, a teenage girl inside and a group of youngsters waiting in front to buy tickets for Saturday's matinee. Cars and pickups lined both sides of the street; there were no parking meters. They walked their bicycles to the northern end of Pine Ridge where they found the newer part of town. A modern-looking emergency clinic stood alone and, across Main Street from it, a shopping center housing a pizza parlor and a video rental store.

Shelby found Safeway's deli and wanting to maintain Bobby's good mood, she ordered thick pastrami sandwiches, a bag of chips and two diet Cokes.

They chained their bicycles in front of the store and walked down a steep side street through the grounds of a trailer park to a quiet spot along the river's edge. Granite boulders scattered along the bank protruded into the river, guiding along water so clear that Shelby could count the bright colored rocks on the river bottom. The warm sun and river sound felt like a balm, a welcome respite from anger and tension. They found a large flat boulder and spread out their lunch, then ate without talking, a peaceful silence. Finished eating, Shelby said, "Isn't this beautiful?" She spoke softly, hating to disturb the sound of the river.

Bobby lit a cigarette. "It is that."

"What a different world here, poles apart from L.A," she said, barely above a whisper.

"Tell me something, Shel. Do you actually like it here as much as you make it sound?"

"I can't explain it, but for some reason I do."

"Why? Because of these people you feel are so genuine, the beauty or what?" Bobby gestured at the surroundings.

Shelby reached down, her hand trailing in the water. "The beauty for sure. The people too and maybe because it's the exact opposite of our world. No Spago or Rodeo Drive. You don't see Mercedes or Rolls Royces and none of that matters. I guess I'm beginning to realize just how much where we live influences what kind of people we turn out to be."

"I suppose you think I'm L.A., attitude and all?"

Shelby smiled. "I'm not going to touch that, but wouldn't it be nice if we could take some of this wholesomeness back with us? I think

L.A., the games and everything that goes with them, is why you and I relate to each other the way we do, why we lead separate lives."

Bobby remained silent. "You're not saying a word," Shelby said.

"I think the way we relate to each other is just fine. I like it and, as far as leading separate lives, I thought you loved Skyline and your horses… our life. We're both doing what we love. How many people do you know get to do that?"

Disappointed but not surprised by his reply, Shelby sighed. "Never mind, it doesn't matter. We'd better get back." She gathered up their things without looking at him. Bobby followed silently.

They arrived at Ellie's the same time as Adele. Bobby held one of the doors open for her.

"Thanks, Bobby. Did you two go fishing?"

"No, we slept too late for that. We went biking and had a picnic instead," he replied.

"Beautiful country, isn't it?" Adele smiled at him.

Bobby glanced at Shelby then back at Adele. "You're not a real estate agent, are you?"

Chapter Seven

First thing Monday morning Shelby sent a brief text to Enrique, asking how things were going. His immediate reply: *Just had breakfast with Mom and Dad. Work OK, on schedule. Cherokee & mares fine. Took contractor exam Monday. Tough, not sure I passed. How's trip?*

Shelby answered back. *Be patient, didn't think I passed either. Trip-interesting.* Then catching sight of Bobby emerge from the Eagle, cell phone to his ear, she pocketed her Smart phone and approached. He was talking to Santa Monica RV Sales & Leasing where she rented the Eagle. Bobby touched the amplifier button so she could hear. The manufacturer in Michigan wanted the Eagle hauled to the dealership in Missoula. A RV tow truck would be dispatched ASAP and should arrive in Troutsprings mid-afternoon. Asked his opinion of the problem, Bobby answered, "Clanking sounds, then it went dead. If it does turn out to be the transmission, how long will it take to fix it?"

A gap of silence followed. "I can't say. That would be up to the technician in Missoula."

Not what he wanted to hear, Bobby threw up his free hand and shouted, "You gotta be kidding!" whereupon Shelby turned on her heel and headed to the café. When she repeated the exchange, Jack said "I'm not surprised. Bobby runs on L.A. time. It's going to take at least a week, maybe more. Hey, I have an idea, there's a second bedroom with a private bath upstairs. How 'bout you take a look and if it's okay, it's yours for as long as it takes to get your rig fixed. No charge, except maybe you keep Adele from crabbin' at me." Jack's grin was genuine and his invitation sounded the same.

"Wow, thank you, I will." Shelby hurried upstairs. Jack said the room was at the end of the hall. She opened the door expecting a small room with rustic décor. Totally surprised, it was a spacious room furnished with beautiful antiques and it had large windows on two walls. *I bet this is exactly like Ellen Ketchum left it.* Grateful for Jack's generous offer, Shelby returned downstairs and peeked out the front window; no sign of Bobby. She then found Jack. "The room is wonderful but the beautiful antiques, are you sure you want guests in there?"

"I'm glad you like it, and yes, I'm sure. It would be nice to have some company around after the bar closes. It gets too quiet too quick for me." His voice sounded wistful.

"Okay! Thank you so much." She hurried back to the Eagle and announced her decision.

"You did WHAT!" Bobby looked ready to explode.

"I accepted Jack's invitation. Why are you upset?"

"Because you should've asked me first. I want to go home, Shel. I don't want to stay in some dump and share a bathroom with a stranger for chrissake."

"The room is lovely and it has its own bathroom. As I recall, Mr. Grump, yesterday you said we could explore this area while the Eagle's being fixed. I'm not ready to go home, so it's either the room upstairs or a local motel, which I guarantee won't be nearly as nice."

Bobby stood in the middle of the Eagle's living room, hands on his hips, shoulders drooped, a look of complete bewilderment on his face. "I swear I will never understand you. You keep saying this trip is for my health, then you do things you know I'm going to hate. What are you trying to do, Shel, irritate me to death?"

"You are really a piece of work, Bobby. I hate to break it to you but everything is not about YOU! Is it in Bobby Stamford's DNA to care or even understand what is important to someone else? Like me, for instance, salvaging something from this trip?"

Bobby stepped close, teeth gritted and his pupils dilated. "Well, you wanted a memorable vacation. This sure as hell is one I will never fucking forget. NEVER!"

Shelby recoiled, half-expecting a punch. "You're the reason the Eagle broke down in the first place—the stupid way you drove. But I got news for you. Since you make it a point to let me know every day what a horrible trip this is, why in the hell don't you hop a flight back to L.A.? I don't give a damn what you do! In fact, I'll borrow Adele's car and drive you to the airport. I'm going to wait until the Eagle's fixed, then, with or without you, I'll see to it the Eagle gets back to L.A. one way or another. Make no mistake, Bobby Stamford, I *CAN* do it! So you do whatever the hell you want!"

Jaws clenched and his expression as ugly as she'd ever seen it, Bobby uttered not one word. Instead he began jerking his clothes out of the closet, then stormed out the Eagle and headed toward the café. It took five trips, both hauling clothes and toilet items up the stairs to the guest room. Bobby dumped the last of his clothes on the bed and disappeared without a word. A minute or two later she heard the café's back door slammed hard. Shelby snatched the clothes off the bed one garment at a time, hanging up some and refolding items that went in the empty chest of drawers. By the time she finished, her fury had sufficiently dissipated to appreciate the room and beautiful antiques. A Bible lay on one of the ornate bedside stands. A delicate Lladro statue of a young girl cradling a puppy sat on the Burlwood dresser beside a photograph.

Shelby gingerly picked up the framed picture and studied the couple. They were standing knee-deep in a river, each holding aloft a string of fish. The color had faded but the images were unmistakable, Jack flashing a brilliant smile, his free arm around a slender woman with short blond hair. She was looking up at him with a triumphant expression. *So this was his beloved Ellie. They looked so happy! No wonder he sounds sad when he talks about her.* Shelby clasped the photo to her chest and studied the room with silent appreciation.

That night it was Bobby who slept on the opposite edge of the bed, his back to Shelby.

* * *

The following morning Shelby got up and dressed before dawn, then couldn't believe it when Bobby did the same. He remained silent when they joined Jack downstairs for coffee and a quick bite. Jack then drove them to "my favorite fishing spot," arriving just as the sun came up.

Inexplicably, Bobby's hostility seemed to have given way during the drive. With Jack leading the way, they hauled camp chairs, fishing gear, coolers and bags of groceries from his pickup down the steep embankment to the river.

Bobby immediately plopped down in a camp chair and watched as Jack and Shelby readied their fly rods. "If I see the fish are biting, I'll grab a pole."

Grateful he stayed behind, Shelby could only stare. Now fully visible above the pine-carpeted mountains, the sun splayed golden rays over the waters of the Flathead River. She made her way down to the river's edge, stunned at the incredible beauty and the sound of water rushing over rocks. And except for the three of them, there was not another human in sight.

Jack approached with her rod in hand, complete with fly and ready to cast. "This has to be the most beautiful spot in all of Montana," she whispered.

"It is special. I'm glad you like it. How about it, you ready to catch some fish?"

Shelby renewed her casting skills after twenty minutes of instruction, Jack's strong hands guiding, directing, and correcting her casts. Having spent her teen years fly fishing with her father in Colorado before the divorce, she silently chastised herself for not telling Jack she really didn't need instruction. The truth though, she so enjoyed his closeness that she saw no good reason to refuse his help. Her heartbeat returned to normal when he moved away to fish.

They fished to the sound of the river gliding over rocks, the occasional cry of a hawk, and the hissing sound of their casts. Jack threw a pebble at her to get her attention, then pointed across the river at two white-tail deer grazing near the opposite bank. Smiling at her, he looked exactly like the man in the photograph except for a tinge of gray in his blond hair. Suddenly the source of Jack's brilliant smile in that photo was understandable. It was joy and she felt it too.

Shelby had good results, three rainbow trout in her basket. Observing Shelby's success, Bobby came down and joined them, his casting skills surprising her. It wasn't long before he landed a good-sized trout and a few minutes later Jack reeled in two whoppers.

"That was fun and I am surprised I remembered how to cast. I'm glad we finally got to use our rods," Bobby said when he showed them his catch.

Puzzled at his personality about-face, Shelby could only think to say, "Me too." The sun hadn't quite reached its zenith when Jack put away his rod. Jack cleaned and filleted the trout, then prepared a fire in a pit outlined by river rock and topped by a grate that he said he'd found in a toolshed on the ranch. Bobby said nothing more as he returned to his camp chair, put his head back and placed a hat over his face.

Shelby sat down on a rock and watched Jack coaxing a small pile of twigs, dry needles and pine cones into flame, then added larger wood, poking and stirring until it blazed. He glanced up at Shelby. "If you like dining atmosphere," he nodded at the mountains, "I'd say we have a ten."

"Way beyond a ten," she replied quietly, then got up and asked, "What can I do to help?"

"Nothing quite yet. We'll wait a bit on the fire." Jack pulled out a package of foil-covered corn. "Already buttered and salted," he said, then placed the package on the grate. "You can slice these tomatoes when the fish is about done."

He handed her a sack; she peeked in. "These smell fresh. Are they homegrown?"

Jack nodded. "Adele's. She loves to garden."

"Nothing about that amazing lady surprises me," Shelby said.

Jack retrieved a jug of Inglenook Chenin Blanc from the cooler and held it up, his eyes questioning. Five minutes later they were both sitting on a log facing the river. Jack tipped his paper cup at Shelby. "Here's to pretty ladies and good fishing," he said.

"To Montana cowboys and magnificent scenery," she replied. "You obviously love it here. Have you always lived in Montana?" She spoke quietly, not to wake Bobby.

He nodded. "Except for a stint in the army. My parents were Montana natives too."

"May I ask you something that's kind of personal?" Shelby said.

Jack reached over and poked the fire. "Ask away."

"How long were your parents married?"

"Let me think," He was quiet for a moment. "Fifty one years. Why do you ask?"

"I would have bet it was a long time. You don't know how lucky you are."

"You'll have to explain that to me some—"

"What smells so good?" Bobby called out, sounding sleepy from under his hat.

"Hot buttered corn," Jack said. "You're just in time. Ready to sauté some trout?" He tapped the wood until it turned into glowing hot coals, then placed a large iron skillet on the grate and beside it a metal coffee pot at the edge. Shelby found the "goodies" sack in the cooler: lemons, butter, minced garlic, and parsley from Adele's herb garden. Jack turned the cooking over to Bobby, who quickly became totally engrossed. He added "the goodies" appropriately onto the fish, the aroma making Shelby's mouth water. Jack refilled her wine glass and his, then poured one and handed it to Bobby. He took a big sip, made a face, then sloshed half the wine over the trout.

"Bobby! That was rude!" Shelby said.

He glanced up at them. "Sorry, but it'll be better on the trout. Smell that?" Shelby had to agree; the sizzling fillets created an irresistible aroma of garlic, lemony trout, and corn. Exactly ten minutes later, Bobby loaded their plates. "Now this is what I call a ten."

Shelby shot Bobby a look, acknowledging that she knew he'd heard every word she and Jack exchanged. She mouthed, "I don't care."

"Absolutely a ten." Jack said, refilling Shelby's wine glass then his own.

"Your planning is what made it a fantastic meal, Jack. Thanks for letting me cook." Bobby then said he needed a nap and this time Shelby observed he really was asleep. She and Jack lingered over their coffee, soaking up the sun and surroundings. "This was a wonderful day, Jack," she said quietly as they got ready to leave. "I can't thank you enough. Bobby and I would never have found this spot. I feel like it's a sacred place."

"A person's favorite fishing spot is sacred." He smiled at her. "I'm glad, but for some reason I'm not surprised you recognize that." Shelby woke Bobby up for the trip back.

For the next two days Shelby was surprised that Bobby willingly hiked and bicycled with her. Adele then insisted they borrow her SUV and drive the Going-To-The-Sun Road in Glacier National Park. Bobby seemed to enjoy that too, especially when they spotted mountain goats, elk, and moose. Shelby snapped pictures of the animals and every beautiful vista.

It seemed to Shelby that during their evenings in the café, Bobby seemed happiest when playing chef while Jack tended bar. One evening he tossed vegetables high in the air, everything landing safely back in the skillet to the laughter and applause of the customers. Bobby bought a round of beer for the trio of men at the bar and the four Texas school teachers at a table who witnessed the show.

Shelby dreaded her time alone with him; each time she brought up the subject of children or their marriage, Bobby grew silent or found something to take himself away. Fed up with trying, she switched her approach and ignored him, instead enjoying Jack and Adele's company more and more. That seemed to antagonize Bobby, but Adele treated him with humorous disdain. Jack accepted his friendship when offered and ignored his petulance.

"I've got a surprise for tomorrow," Jack informed them over Friday night's dinner. Bobby listened, his expression indifferent and shot

Shelby a *who cares* glance. Jack was enjoying his steak, unaware. Dinner over, Jack rose and took their dishes to the kitchen. Bobby leaned forward. "I'm not interested in any surprise, okay? I got hold of the RV place. The problem was one of the gear sprockets. They're installing the replacement today and plan to deliver the RV Monday. So we can get the hell out of here as soon as it arrives." Shelby looked at him. The contempt and coldness in his eyes made her shiver. *I don't know him anymore. Did I ever?*

"Everything's done and Adele just left," she said and rose as Jack returned to the table. "I think I'll turn in early tonight. You two enjoy the show," she said, glancing at the television. She shot Bobby what she hoped was *you're an idiot* look.

"Oh, I almost forgot," Jack said. "Your clean towels are on my bed. Adele came by while we were gone and took the laundry home with her. Would you like me to get them for you?"

"That was nice of Adele. No, thanks, I can get them." Shelby said goodnight. Upstairs, she turned the water on in the big claw-foot tub, then went to Jack's room across the hall. The heavy oak furniture looked right for a cowboy, his king-size bed against the far wall. This room also held a surprise, the entire wall between the two bedrooms held three equal sections of floor-to-ceiling bookshelves, each section filled to capacity. Hundreds, maybe a thousand books!

Jack's voice startled her. "The winters can be awfully long here."

"You startled me! I'm sorry, I didn't mean to snoop. I guess I just thought your room would be similar to the one we're in. It's wonderful—and all these books!"

"The furniture in your room used to be in here. Ellie loved that set, but after she died I got rid of the junk in the spare bedroom, moved our set in there and got me a new one."

"Jack, the room is wonderful. I was just surprised at so many books. They're amazing."

"We read, even here in the backwoods of Montana." He smiled.

"Now you are embarrassing me." Shelby felt her face flush; he had misunderstood her. The phone rang and he waved his hand toward the bookshelves, inviting her to take a look. Shelby hurried across the hall, shut off the bathwater and then returned to Jack's room, curious about the books that made up his library. A casual glance did not do it justice; she spotted books on cattle raising, veterinary, weather; there were many on travel, famous cities on almost every continent. The center section contained an extensive collection of biographies, poetry, novels, tattered classics, and newer books by authors she had read. The last section held a set of *Great Books of the Western World*, antique-looking volumes with gold lettering, the edges worn. *This library represents a lifetime of reading. The Great Books were probably his mother's. Were the other books Ellen's or did Jack collect them?*

Shelby spied an open book upside down on the ottoman as though the reader had been interrupted. The book cover was so worn its burgundy color was barely recognizable. Jack was still on the phone. She glanced at him and touched the book. *Favorite Poems*. He nodded his consent. Shelby sat down on the ottoman. The book was opened to *Reflections*.

"When all the fiercer passions cease, (The glory and disgrace of youth) when the deluded soul in peace can listen to the voice of truth. When we are taught in whom to trust, and how to spare, to spend, to give. Our prudence kind, our pity just, tis then we rightly learn to live. When every passing hour we prize, nor rashly on our follies spend, but use it as it quickly flies, with sober aim to serious end. When prudence bounds

*our utmost views, and bids us wrath and wrong forgive. When
we can calmly gain or lose, 'tis then we rightly learn to live."*

The poet's name was Crabbe. Shelby rose and returned the book to
the ottoman like she found it, open to a poem of dying passion, on
wisdom and growing old and truth. The realization hit her. *These
books are a part of Jack Ketchum!* He was still on the phone. Feeling
guilty as though she had invaded his innermost thoughts, Shelby
picked up the towels and slipped out of the room. Bobby's laughter
and the sound of the television floated up the stairwell as she crossed
to the steam-filled bathroom. Shelby slipped into the hot sudsy water,
closed her eyes and quietly tried to remember the words. *What a
beautiful poem.*

After her bath Shelby returned to her room, still processing her
discovery. Jack Ketchum was no simple cowboy; behind that casual
demeanor was a self-educated, poetry-loving man. She gazed around
the antique-filled room, its significance dawning. It stood separate and
complete as a monument to the way his life had been, to the woman
Jack still loved. That he offered to let them stay there humbled her to
the core.

Jack had given no indication of the surprise he had for Saturday
morning, but he left a note on the guest room door suggesting they
dress in jeans, boots (if they had them) and hats. They should be ready
when he returned from the ranch. Excited at the prospect of seeing the
Montana countryside, Shelby dressed as directed. Bobby wore shorts,
a Ralph Lauren golf shirt and tennis shoes. Jack briefly glanced at him
but made no comment.

After breakfast they headed north in Jack's pickup. Pointing out
various sites, Jack turned off the highway onto Stagecoach Road, a
"Montana freeway," he said with a chuckle. Lined with giant shade

trees, steep-roofed houses, dilapidated barns, and yards with rusty equipment, "this gravel road runs through prime ranch land," Jack said. Shelby noted that most of the farm houses had clotheslines with laundry blowing stiff in the breeze. Jack slowed and waved to an overall-clad man on a John Deere tractor waiting to enter the road. The man tipped his hat and Shelby immediately smiled. The lower part of his face was tanned dark from the sun, his forehead glaringly white.

"He always wears a hat?" Shelby said.

Jack nodded. "Lonnie's trademark. Never without it except in bed."

They crossed over a wooden bridge and Jack pulled off the road, pointing north at the distant Rockies. Shelby's intake of breath was involuntary; the mountains filled the eye as far and as wide as she could see. "Magnificent," she said, then noted the dry grass and low hills around them. We must be lower in elevation than in Trout-springs."

"Good observation," Jack said. "We came four miles off the highway and dropped a thousand feet in elevation." Open hay fields ran along the north side of the Stagecoach Road, fenced pastures filled with grazing cattle on the south side. Jack drove another mile or two then turned into a gravel drive under an arch made of whole logs. A weather-beaten carved wooden sign hung from the arch. Broken Arrow Ranch, J.J. Ketchum, Troutsprings, Montana.

Straight ahead at the end of a very long driveway sat a massive two-story log structure, her builder-mind instantly recording its unique construction. "What a gorgeous house!" She felt her heart speed up at the sight of a real cattle ranch and a log house that could have been on the cover of a magazine. Beyond the house, she could see a weathered barn, and to the right of it, a pole barn half-filled with hay. Several sheds of varying sizes Jack said held equipment were scattered about the ranch. As they drew closer, Shelby spotted corrals behind the barn.

"I thought you both might enjoy a horseback tour of my ranch." There was a hint of pride in his voice.

Bobby spoke for the first time since they left the café. "Sorry, Jack, I don't dig horses. They're my wife's thing, not mine."

Jack looked puzzled and a bit embarrassed. "Sorry, partner. Shelby said you had three horses at your place. I figured one of 'em had to be yours."

"That's okay, but thanks for the offer," Shelby said, disappointment tainting her voice.

"Hold on, Bobby, I have an idea," Jack said. "Would you like to check out a new condominium project, a ski resort not far from here? The rumor is it's first class. In fact, it made the cover of a national ski magazine, and now the condos are selling like hot cakes."

"First-class development, are you're kidding? I'd love to see it," Bobby said.

Jack gave him directions, then tossed Bobby the keys to the truck. Shelby couldn't help but notice the look of relief on Bobby's face as he drove away. She and Jack walked to the barn and stopped at the corrals, resting their arms on the top rung of the fence. Half a dozen calves and three horses milled around in the enclosure. Shelby stepped up on the bottom rung and whistled at a bay with black mane and tail. The mare glanced up, ears alert. "Come here, girl," Shelby called. The mare tossed her head, her eyes on Shelby who held out her hand and called again. The bay walked forward and stopped in front of them. "Hello, beauty, you're a pretty lady," Shelby crooned. "What's her name?" She turned to Jack.

"Lolli, as in Lollipop. Would you like to ride her?"

"I would love to! She is beautiful."

Jack swung open the heavy barn door. Bright sun streamed through a row of skylights in each pitch of the roof. He lifted two worn saddles down from a tack-filled wall. "I'll saddle Solitaire and Lolli and be right back." He disappeared out the door, a saddle under each arm.

"Wonderful," she said and walked into the barn, its pungent smells a sharp contrast to the spanking-new stables she had moved her horses into days before they left. This old barn had character: two stories with large stalls along both long walls, a loft that took up the second story, and both antique and modern tack hanging side by side on the weathered wood walls.

The familiarity surrounding her brought thoughts of her own horses, her home in the foothills and her Mayan family. Shelby pictured her patio full of flowers and thought about Skyline Construction and the projects needing her attention. Like water seeking its own path, Shelby's thoughts drifted involuntarily to country club dinners, to the Stamford family holidays, Martha's black-tie Christmas Eve gathering last year and how she had felt like a child, nose against a window, looking in at someone else's family. *It's a good life. I should be happy.*

Shelby glanced around and experienced an inexplicable feeling of closeness to Jack. Fifteen hundred miles from home, standing in somebody else's barn, it seemed okay to quietly admit something in her life was seriously amiss and then it suddenly crystallized with frightening clarity. *I revolve in a Bobby Stamford-only world, one of how many planets orbiting his sun.*

"The Stamfords view me that way and I do too," she whispered. The reality registered, Shelby feeling the sting of tears. The satisfying feeling of loving deeply and being loved the same way did not exist; it had never existed with Bobby. They led separate lives and that's what he wanted. Her building and remodeling began as projects, a personally rewarding activity that evolved into a successful business. But in moments of honest introspection, like now, a feeling of emptiness was acute. Even more acute, the realization came that Skyline Construction filled a space but not the void.

The thought of going back to L.A on Monday suddenly filled her with deep sadness.

Chapter Eight

The sound of Jack and the horses approaching pushed her melancholy thoughts aside. He came through the side door leading the mare and a stallion. "Sorry it took so long. Solitaire was a bit frisky." A mottled brown and white Appaloosa, Solitaire had been given to him, Jack said, because "he didn't like anybody or anything. He bit or kicked anything that got close to him."

At the moment Solitaire stood quietly beside Lolli, not at all looking like the horse Jack described. Shelby held out her hand toward the stallion. The Appaloosa whinnied and shook his giant head. "He's behaving now. We had a little talk, didn't we, fella?" Jack patted the horse's neck. "It took a year but he's finally got some manners." He handed her a cowboy hat. "You'll need this. After the ride would you like to see the ranch house?"

"Absolutely." Shelby put on the hat. "But first, let's see this 'little spread,' as you call it."

They rode west one mile along the edge of rolling hay fields, half-harvested. A breeze blowing from the northwest rippled across the uncut grass, creating golden waves. Giant rolls of hay dotted the harvested portion of the field, while across the road, fat, brown steers with white faces, and speckled longhorns looked up curiously from their grazing as they rode by. Straight ahead across the fields, she could see an adjoining ranch with more rolls of hay, a low ranch house, and several out-buildings.

Jack rode ahead of her, tall and easy in the saddle. He looked back occasionally, smiling and pointing at things he wanted her to see. They rounded a curve now heading north, and followed the fence. Set against a cloud-streaked sky, the endless ocean of gold disappeared into a line of trees at the horizon, the trees appearing to separate the flat earth from the vertical rise of the Rocky Mountains.

"Could we stop for a second?" Shelby called ahead. Solitaire slowed and Shelby caught up. "Jack, do you have any idea just how beautiful this is?" She gestured toward the mountains.

"Guess I forgot but you pointing it out, I'm looking at it with new eyes. It is beautiful."

"Jack Ketchum, I have traveled the world over and I have never seen a more beautiful place. How can you spend your time in that smoky café when you could be out here? That's almost a crime."

Ahead of her and framed against the vista of the mountains, Jack pulled the brim of his Stetson lower and patted Solitaire's neck. When he turned toward her, she caught a glimpse of pain in his eyes, eyes that she couldn't help but notice were the exact color of the Montana sky. Jack's expression signaled hesitancy but Shelby sensed she was about to hear something he had held in. She pulled Lolli up alongside Solitaire. "I loved living on the ranch," he said, looking toward the mountains. "Ellie liked it but didn't really have the chance to enjoy it. She had bad asthma and the hay made it intolerable for her." He gestured at the fields. "I worked outdoors during the day and she was cooped up inside with the air filter machine going. It was lonely—she was lonely."

"So you bought her the café."

He nodded. "It turned out to be more a way of life than just a business."

"How could she tolerate all the cigarette smoke?"

"Ellie's Cafe was no smoking then. People didn't smoke out of respect for her. The café was different then, more of a family kind of place. Ellie liked the bustle and the people coming and going. Folks joked in a nice way that she was the mayor of Troutsprings. It seemed like she knew everybody, and running the café kept her busy while I was out here working. I worked a deal with the neighbor. Jenkins leased some of the ranch—still does—so I could spend more time with her at the café."

Shelby and Jack both dismounted, then began to walk, Solitaire and Lolli stopping to graze. "What happened, Jack? How did Ellen die?" She put her hand on his arm; it felt tense.

He took a deep breath. "It was a Sunday morning. We were rushing around. I was getting ready to take her to church. She went downstairs to bring us some coffee from the café—insisted on doing it. I had one leg in my pants when I heard her get to the top of the stairs and then a big crash. I was trying to pull up my pants and run at the same time. There she was on her knees, her eyes real big and her hands clutching her chest." His anguished expression spoke volumes.

"I carried her into the bedroom and laid her on the bed. She had an asthma box with adrenaline, syringes, and alcohol stuff. I gave her a shot in the thigh like the doctor showed me and called nine-one-one. Ellie's face was already starting to turn blue. She didn't say a word, just looked up at me. I could see the shot wasn't working so I gave her another one and tried CPR. It didn't seem to help either but I kept trying. I tried everything I knew, but it wasn't enough. By the time the paramedics arrived from Pine Ridge, she was gone."

"Oh, Jack," Shelby said, tears filling her eyes. She dropped the reins and put her arms around him. She drew him close and he didn't pull away. "I don't believe there was anything more you could have done," she whispered, holding him tight. Shelby pulled back enough to look up at his face.

"I hope to God that's true. It haunts me that I could have done something else but didn't."

Shelby loosened her hold. "I received basic training for that when I was with American Airlines. Short of having the attack in a hospital or a doctor's office, Jack, I honestly don't believe anyone could have saved her. Ellen loved God. Her life was in His hands, not yours."

Jack took a deep breath and stepped back. "Thank you for saying that." He ran a weathered hand across his cheek. "Terrible feelings I've been holding in for three years, didn't even tell Adele. She keeps saying time cures everything and I'm just taking an extra measure."

"I agree, time does help but Ellen's been gone for three years. Why are you still living in the café? You said you love this place. Why haven't you moved back?"

"I…" Jack shrugged his shoulders and stared down at the ground.

"I'm sorry, Jack. I didn't mean to pry. It's none of my business."

"No, it's a fair question," he said, a thoughtful look on his face. "As long as I live there and run the café, it's like Ellie is still part of my life. At least what she loved is part of my life. That sounds like I need psychiatric help, but because she was happy there, it makes me happy."

Solitaire nudged him and Jack stroked the stallion's neck. "Our marriage wasn't perfect, but we loved each other. Every time I think about leaving, I feel like I'm closing the door on a big part of my life. So instead of selling the café, I bought a new bedroom set and put in some gambling machines. That was about as much change as I could handle." He gave her a crooked grin and Shelby noticed his shoulders relax. Shaded by his hat, his face softened. As he leveled his gaze on her, a smile formed on his lips.

She couldn't help but smile too. "You don't need a psychiatrist. You've got everything you need right here." She gestured around them.

"I'll take your word for it," he said. "But enough about my sad story. How about that tour of the ranch I promised? You ready?"

"Absolutely, but I have to ask how much of this," she gestured at the fields, "is part of your ranch or am I violating some Montana law asking such a question?"

"Well," he drawled, "that's like asking a man the size of his…"

"Jack Ketchum!"

"Bank account!" Jack burst out laughing. Slapping his leg, he bent forward laughing and couldn't seem to stop, which caused Shelby to start. Eyes locked on each other, they kept it up until finally she held up her forefinger, a silent signal that his remark had earned him a *gotcha*.

"Okay, okay," he said, trying to catch his breath. "My place goes a couple of miles down to those trees then wraps around Jenkins' spread next door and continues west on the other side of his property about a half a mile or so. Plus there are a couple hundred acres across the road from the house."

"You're kidding!" Shelby said. "A mile this way, a couple of miles that way—is what you call a little spread?" Jack was still grinning as they mounted up, and this time Shelby rode ahead.

They rode toward the distant line of trees, which turned out to be poplars and giant cottonwoods growing along both sides of a creek that Jack said flowed into the Flathead River. It was cool in the shade, the leaves on the trees shimmering in the breeze.

"This place just gets prettier," Shelby said as they dismounted. She took off her hat and boots, rolled up her jeans and waded into the cool water. "Come on, Jack, get your feet wet." He sat down on a rock, pulled his jeans legs up a bit and removed his boots. Shelby laughed, pointing at his white feet and legs.

"Don't you go laughing at me, lady!" He bent forward, scooped up a handful of water and flung it in her direction. Shelby let out a whoop and did the same. A few feet away, the nervous horses turned to watch them. Jack and Shelby launched into a water fight, laughing, egging each other on until they were both drenched and out of breath.

Giggling, Shelby collapsed on her knees in the creek. "Okay," she said, "You won and I'm a sight. Thanks a lot, cowboy. You look fine and I look like a drowned rat." Shelby rose and pulled the bottom of her soaked T-shirt out of her jeans and tried to wring the water from it.

"You're right about that. You are a sight," Jack said in a quiet voice.

Shelby glanced up. He was staring, an appreciative smile on his handsome face. She felt her face flush. The horses whinnied and moved forward to the water's edge, wanting to drink.

"Would you mind if I rode Solitaire back?" she said, grateful for the diversion.

"Are you sure? He's a real handful," Jack said as they put their socks and boots back on.

"I'd like to try because of your story about taking a year to cure him. That's amazing."

"Alright, if you think you can handle him. But please be careful."

Shelby mounted easily and once in the saddle, Solitaire began prancing around in a circle. She patted his neck. "It's okay, boy."

Jack mounted up, Lolli shaking her head as though ready to run. He glanced at Shelby. "So, city lady, you ride, do you?"

Shelby acknowledged the challenge. She leaned forward, whispered to the big stallion, and patted his neck. A nudge with her heels and Solitaire took off. "Yes, I do!" she shouted over her shoulder. "Do you?" Shelby urged Solitaire first into a canter, then a gallop and finally let the stallion go. Solitaire was a champion and he wanted to run! Shelby and Solitaire flew back over the same trail, past fields, past startled cows, past trees and distant mountains, leaving fear and hurt and emptiness behind. Shelby, aware only of the warmth of the sun and the wind in her face, was on a winged horse whose hooves never seemed to touch the ground.

She wanted to ride forever; the world was perfect and her joy knew no earthly bounds.

* * *

Jack had to spur Lolli on to keep up with Shelby. *That lady can ride!*

She was leaning forward in the saddle, her chin close to the top of Solitaire's neck. Held only by its string, her hat had come off and was bouncing against her back, her long blond hair straight out. Shelby and Solitaire looked to be flying. She didn't glance back as though she'd forgotten he was there. He followed along the fence for a distance until Shelby slowly pulled away and he lost sight of her when she rounded the curve for the last mile to the barn. When he rounded the curve, Shelby and Solitaire were so far ahead he slowed the mare to a trot for the last mile into the yard.

Jack brought Lolli to a stop in front of Solitaire, the stallion lathered and prancing in circles from the excitement of the run. Unable to take his eyes off Shelby, Jack dismounted. Still astride the prancing horse, she had a smile on her face that would melt a glacier. Face flushed and eyes sparkling, she raised her arms in a victory sign, her golden untamed hair flashing in the sun.

Jack could only stare, his heart doing a somersault. His voice failed on his first attempt to speak. Clearing his throat, he tried again.

"Winning agrees with you, Shelby Stamford. When you said you could ride, you weren't kidding."

"Thank you!" Shelby lifted her right leg straight over Solitaire's head and jumped to the ground, landing on both feet at the same time.

"Whoa!" Jack laughed. "Now you're showing off."

"I am, indeed," she said, bowing deeply then coming up with a triumphant smile.

He bowed from the waist. "I defer to you. Never have I lost to such a beautiful opponent," Jack said.

Shelby insisted on removing the stallion's saddle. Jack said nothing, observing that she looked happier than he'd seen her since their arrival, which seemed eons ago.

He removed Lolli's saddle and Shelby helped him rub down both horses, then brush and water them, and give each one handfuls of oats. He watched her murmuring to Solitaire as she groomed him, running her hands over the horse's body and trembling legs, making sure he was all right. Solitaire seemed to enjoy her touch. *You're a fool, Ketchum. You can't have these feelings. Not for her. She is married, and she's leaving in two days.*

* * *

Shelby washed up in an old sink in the barn, then stood aside while Jack did the same. Shaking their hands in the warm air, they rubbed them on their damp jeans. She followed him to the ranch house, pausing to admire it. The two-story main section was built from full-round, saddle-notched logs, with a one-story wing jutting out in the direction of the mountains. A broad covered porch wrapped around the two-story portion. "Old and elegant," she commented.

She glanced over her shoulder at the gravel driveway; it looked to be the length of a football field! A matching lodgepole pine fence lined each side of it from Stagecoach Road. Shelby cast a glance at Jack as they walked past a patch of dead grass adjacent to the porch and a flowerbed full of weeds, silent testimony to the empty, forgotten house.

When he unlocked and pushed open the heavy door, a rush of musty air greeted her. Shelby walked through the entryway into a massive living room, sun streaming in through high windows and splaying dusty shafts of gold across the room. They fell on a massive elk head with an imposing rack, his black sightless eyes catching the glint of the sun.

"This is beautiful," Shelby said, taking in the vast room, her builder-mind marveling at the twenty foot ceilings with perfect round log trusses. A river rock fireplace dominated the room, its stately mantel a single half-log. Two leather sofas flanked the fireplace with two Indian print chairs completing the group. A giant Navajo rug hung on the wall next to the fireplace. "Jack, this house could be in *Architectural Digest*!"

She peeked in rooms marveling at the craftsmanship. "I've seen pictures of log houses in building magazines, Jack, but nothing that equals this." She examined the staircase, the banister and rails made from like-sized barked logs. "Did these come from the ranch?" As soon as Jack answered one question, she had two or three more. She walked over and studied the dusty elk's head. "Did you bag him?" Jack nodded.

When she finished looking in most of the rooms, she walked through the breakfast nook into the kitchen. "Whoa, what happened here?"

Jack laughed. "Not much, is it?"

"Wow, you got that right," she said in dismay.

The appliances looked old and abandoned. The windowsill of the dirty window over the sink facing the Rockies was lined with dead potted plants. "Somehow it looks worse than I remember. I was going to remodel it, but the café came up for sale and Ellie wanted out of here so I never bothered. Pretty sad, huh?"

"The house is magnificent, the kitchen needs help." She glanced around. "Lots of help."

Jack led the way back to the entry way. "Funny how we take things for granted like the view of the mountains. I had forgotten how beautiful they are. You being a builder and saying this house is special means a lot."

She touched Jack's arm. "This house is an absolute treasure, Jack. Thank you for showing it to me and the ranch. And for letting me ride Solitaire. I loved every minute of it."

Jack locked the door. "Me, too. You've made me see things a lot more clearly."

"That's nice to hear. Thank you for telling me about Ellen. What a wonderful woman. I have to tell you, the picture of you two on the dresser in our room almost made me cry. You looked so happy, Ellen too—pure joy. The picture is beautiful." She glanced at him, hoping she hadn't said too much, but he was smiling. "You're remembering that moment."

Jack nodded. "Ellen called it the fifth season. She was always coming up stuff like that."

"I don't understand, what did she mean?"

"There are four seasons up here, some Ellie enjoyed and some she didn't. That summer was absolutely perfect, the weather, her health was good, we were good—happy and in love," Jack said, obviously remembering. "When I asked what she meant by a fifth season, she said it was when we have it all, a sense of wellbeing, when life right this moment is precious, and tomorrow no longer holds our hopes and dreams. She told me she wanted me to recognize and appreciate that our summer was exactly that, the fifth season." Jack's eyes had filled with tears.

Shelby reached for his hand and held it. "That is beautiful, Jack. You are so fortunate to have experienced that with Ellen." They sat in comfortable silence for a time, then Shelby turned to face him. "I'm still curious," she said, smiling at him now.

"I'm flattered. I'm not interesting enough to warrant your curiosity but ask away."

"You haven't mentioned kids. Do you have children?"

He shook his head. "We assumed we would, but it just never happened. We didn't do that fertility stuff. I was worried about Ellie's health and I figured it was me anyway. I'm fifty years old, too old now but I admit it would be nice to have a son or daughter. How about you?"

"No kids either, Bobby's choice, not mine. I'm forty so I know exactly how you feel."

Shelby and Jack were still sitting on the porch deep in conversation when Bobby roared into the driveway, sending up a cloud of dust that enveloped them.

Chapter Nine

"Thanks, Jack. That was a cool development—first class." Bobby rested his hand on Shelby's leg. "Your pants are damp."

"I waded into a creek. It was fun," she said quickly.

Bobby rambled on during the ride about the impressive electric gates mounted into basalt rock pillars, the swanky clubhouse, the tennis courts and lush golf course. Jack asked a few questions. Shelby listened only enough to catch the general drift; Bobby didn't seem to notice.

Reliving the ride, she could visualize the amazing scenery and house, how Jack opened up to her, and their water fight. Aware of his thigh touching hers, it felt like an electric current passing between them. Shelby breathed a sigh of relief when they reached the café.

Jack suggested they get cleaned up while he went to work in the café. Shelby took a quick shower, then asked for a towel. Shaver in one hand, Bobby held up two fingers of his other hand, then made the sign of the cross. That meant two more days in Troutsprings and he was thanking heaven for it. Shelby dried off behind the shower door and said nothing to Bobby.

Today her emotions had run the gamut: compassion, sympathy, astonishment, joy, and attraction, all wrapped up in one man and one place. She could not forget that moment at the creek on their fly-fishing trip, then Jack's unmistakable look today at the river. *He's*

*been widowed three years, so probably hormones, but what does it say
about me having those feelings?*

As soon as they dressed, Shelby and Bobby went downstairs to the
café. She offered to help and was surprised when Bobby offered too.
Jack had said this Saturday night would be the busiest, August 26th
was the start of the annual Pine Ridge-Troutsprings Fishing Tournament. In addition to Ellie's regular customers, a lot of out-of-state
tournament entrants would show up for dinner and drinks, and Jack
was right. Customers stood two and three deep at the bar waiting for a
table. Bobby was helping Jack as chef, smiling and joking with
customers. It struck her as odd how he appeared to have no animosity
when the two of them worked side by side; it surfaced only when the
three of them were together.

Cooking as fast as they could, Jack and Bobby hardly kept up with
the orders. And this was one night when even Adele could not have
done the job by herself; the two of them served patrons on a dead run.
Ronnie brought a friend to help, and the two washed dishes and
restocked glasses and plates as fast as they could.

Fish stories wafted around the café, the laughter loud and the
smoke so thick it made Shelby's eyes burn. By midnight, the rowdy
standup crowd had thinned but the bar and tables were still packed.
Shelby and Adele continued to deliver trays of beers to the crowd,
mostly men now; there were fewer women this evening. Tournament
entrants had on official baseball caps and those that hadn't worn a hat
had red faces and arms from hours in the hot August sun. The
fishermen had an air of conformity, their clothes, their hats, their
manner of speaking. They were all in a festive mood except for two
men, late arrivals who did not fit.

Shelby noticed them right away when they came in around eleven;
they didn't look like fishermen. They looked more like the guys that

hung around California's Venice Beach as they stood at the bar drinking beer until two stools became available. One guy had blond spiky hair and wore cut-off jeans and a jeans jacket. The other man had cotton pull-on pants and a T-shirt that showed his muscular build. He wore a baseball cap, his black ponytail protruding from the back. Both he and his friend looked like bodybuilders.

Shelby kept glancing at them as she helped Adele deliver customers' beer orders. The two seemed unhurried, drinking slowly and talking only with each other. Announcing he had to be up before dawn to be in the tournament, Virgil left at midnight and Jack took over bar tending.

By one a.m. the barstools were vacant except for the two body-builders, a table of four fishermen still drinking and talking, and two couples at the poker and twenty-one machines drinking and pushing buttons. The fishermen rose, bade good night to Jack, and called thanks to Adele who walked them to the door, then went behind the bar to help Jack.

"I'm going to take a break," Bobby called out to her. Shelby acknowledged him with a brief wave and continued working. As soon as she and Adele wiped the tables and put the chairs back in place, Adele went behind the bar and shooed Jack away, saying she would finish up.

Jack came around the bar and sat down on a stool. Shelby acknow-ledged his smile, his steady gaze making her forget the uncomfortable feeling over the two men. The gamblers called out their promise to leave when Jack did. "Whenever, it's your money," he chided them.

The two bodybuilders finally rose and moved to the end of the bar. Fear out of nowhere made Shelby tense, her eyes on the blond guy. He asked Adele how much they owed and held out a bill in his right hand. She rang up their tab and took the bill from his outstretched hand. As the cash drawer slid open, the blond produced a gun from his left jacket pocket and leveled it at Adele. "Okay, just keep your cool and no one will get hurt," he said.

Shelby held her breath as the ponytail thief produced a long hunting knife. He positioned himself with his back to the doors. Nervous, he kept shifting his weight from one foot to the other while waving the knife from side to side. The gamblers directly in back of Shelby had evidently stopped playing because the machines went silent and she heard a stool scrape the floor. The accomplice at the door jerked his head in their direction and raised the knife up and back, poised to throw. Shelby felt his eyes lock on hers. She froze, the cleaning cloth hanging from her hand. Her eyes moved to the gunman who retrieved a crumpled paper sack from his right jacket pocket and thrust it at Adele, his eyes on Jack. "Put all the bills in the bag. Don't bother with the change."

Jack, who had been looking directly at her, swiveled his stool slowly toward the gunman. Shelby recognized his expression, the same steely look he had when he confronted Bobby. "You're nothing but a dirty punk," he said in a low, even voice.

The man leveled the gun straight at Jack. "I'm not afraid to blow you away, old man, so don't try anything stupid. Hurry up, Red," he said to Adele. Her hand shook as she pulled a large wad of bills from the register and stuffed them in the bag. The thief, his eyes still on Jack, made a grab for the bag from her outstretched hand but barely caught the edge of the paper. It ripped and the thief was left holding a small piece of the sack as the bills fell to the floor. Instinctively Adele bent to pick them up.

Eyes wide, Shelby watched the scene unfold in slow motion. For a split-second the gunman took his eyes off Jack and tried to see what happened to the money. Just as Adele bent over, Jack lunged toward the gunman. The robber's eyes flew wide open in disbelief, the 9mm Kurz discharging. "You stupid!" the gunman screamed.

Jack catapulted backwards off the stool, landing with a loud crash, his mouth open and the front of his shirt covered with blood. Shelby tried to scream but no sound came out. The wound in the middle of his stomach instantly began pumping blood over his shirt onto the floor.

The knifeholder lurched forward. "Jesus, you killed him!"

"Shut up!" the gunman roared. "Let's get outta here." They backed out the door with a warning to everyone to stay put. The money lay forgotten on the floor. The minute the door closed, Adele was calling 911 as Shelby ran to Jack's still form. On her knees, she pressed the cleaning cloth firmly against the spreading stain. Leaning closer, she could detect shallow movements of his chest. "He's alive!"

The gamblers knelt on the floor beside Shelby. One man lifted Jack's head and his wife slid her sweater under it. "Where is your husband, Shelby?" the woman said, her voice quaking.

* * *

Sitting on the wooden steps enjoying the cool night air and his second Marlboro, Bobby began to feel good for a change. The trip was almost over, for which he was beyond grateful. A vacation from hell for sure, but he'd stuck it out to make Shelby happy. Hoping he was getting points for his sacrifice, he breathed in the cool pine-scented air and listened to the wind through the trees. Noisy pickups and cars rattled past and in between vehicles, Bobby heard snatches of music and laughter through the vehicles' open windows. The amount of traffic at this late hour was surprising. The moon had passed its zenith and disappeared behind the café.

Bobby stood up and walked to the middle of the parking lot, gazing up at what looked like a zillion stars. He heard a muffled bang, surprising because he saw no cars at the moment. Finished with his cigarette and curious at the sound, he started toward the café.

Just as he reached the bottom step, two men burst through the doors straight at him, backsides first. "What the hell?" Bobby yelled.

The gunman spun around toward him; Bobby heard the explosion and felt searing pain at the same time. He screamed and toppled backwards, his head smacking the hard dirt with a sickening thud. The stars were swirling. He couldn't seem to draw a breath, and his left leg felt like it was on fire. Flat on his back, strangely the only sound he heard were boots hitting hard dirt close by, then a vehicle motor roar, tires spinning, and then eerie quiet.

He couldn't move or sit up so he laid prone, the stars continuing to swirl as a strange searing pain emanating from his leg seemed to be overtaking him. And then nothing.

Chapter Ten

Past the dark silhouette of the pilot, Shelby spotted a distant massive blanket of light reflecting up into the dark sky. *That has to be Missoula.* The crew's exit from the Bell copter could not have been faster or more efficient. Shelby had to race to keep up with the gurneys, almost to the entrance of the trauma center. Inside she took hold of Bobby's hand as she watched Jack's gurney being rushed down the hall. The flight nurse was running along beside it, holding onto the IV. The other copter nurse was already talking to an ER physician a few feet away.

She felt Bobby squeeze her hand, wanting her to lean down. "Try not to talk, Bobby. Save your strength," she said.

"I was shot in the leg. My mouth is fine." He pulled Shelby closer. "So much for your fucking health spa on wheels vacation idea. Thanks a shitload!"

Too stunned to reply, she let go of his hand. Jill grabbed hold of his gurney and she and the physician raced alongside it down the hall where Jack was taken.

The next few hours were hectic and stressful, as Shelby had to complete the paperwork for Bobby and Jack. She chose a private room for Bobby; Ms. Foster from Admitting advising that, "After Mr. Ketchum is out of surgery, he will go to Intensive Care on the third floor." Ms. Foster glanced at her watch. "Six a.m. I'm sure you're exhausted. I suggest you wait in the surgery waiting room. It's quiet and comfortable and I'll make sure you are kept informed."

Shelby found the surgery waiting room on the main floor, thankfully empty and quiet. She collapsed onto the sofa, her mind ricocheting between the shooting, Jack, the trip and Bobby's ugly words—her marriage was coming apart. She dozed off, for how long she didn't know, until her cell phone rang. It was Adele. Shelby glanced at her watch: 9:45 a.m.

"I'm still waiting, Adele. I haven't heard anything about Bobby or Jack. I'm assuming Jack is alive or they would have notified me. I wish that made me feel better."

Adele responded with an "Amen to that."

Still the only one in the surgery waiting room at 11:00 a.m. Sunday, Shelby was so deep in thought she was unaware of the doctor's presence until he spoke. "Mrs. Stamford?"

Startled, she jumped up. "Yes, I'm Mrs. Stamford."

"I'm Dr. Adams. I dealt with your husband's wound and I'm happy to report he is doing fine, resting comfortably in recovery. I don't believe there will be any permanent damage. The bullet missed the bone and, thankfully, didn't tear the tissue as much as I initially feared. As for Mr. Ketchum, his condition is critical at this point.

"Oh, thank God he's alive," Shelby whispered.

The doctor motioned for her to have a seat, then sat down beside her. "About Mr. Ketchum, his vitals are stable and, considering the nature of his wound, he is obviously a tough guy. And lucky because the bullet just missed his aorta. He lost a lot of blood from the initial wound and internal bleeding. The next twenty-four hours are critical." Shelby asked if she could see Jack. The doctor shook his head.

"No, I'm sorry. He is heavily sedated and on the respirator. Besides, he wouldn't even know that you were there."

"Oh, he would know," Shelby said firmly. "I am certain of it. I just want to let him know that he's not alone. Please, two minutes, no more."

Dr. Adams gave her a tired smile. "I've learned never to question a woman's intuition. Two minutes only, promise?"

"I promise, thank you." She followed him to the intensive care unit where he spoke to a nurse who then led Shelby to Jack's room. She tiptoed in and paused. In a bed with its guardrails up and Jack's upper body slightly elevated, Jack looked dead! She fought to hold back tears. *No, he cannot be dead!* She concentrated on Jack's chest, finally detecting it was moving up and down slightly, but with a steady rhythm. There was a plastic tube down his throat and a smaller one piggy-backed to it, plus a tube in each nostril. Connected to a heart and intravenous monitor and two or three other machines she could not identify, Jack was surrounded by cords and wires and monitors beeping and flashing signals. A respirator issued a steady swooshing sound.

Shelby bent close and touched his forehead gently. "Jack, it's Shelby," she whispered. "They won't let me stay long. I know you can hear me, Jack. Know that you are not alone. I'm right here. You've got to fight, okay?" A tear trickled down her cheek and landed on Jack's hand. "Don't you give up, Jack Ketchum. Please fight. Adele is coming over and both of us will be right here fighting with you."

Shelby slipped her forefinger under Jack's still hand—that strong, tanned, weathered hand she'd seen gently stroke a horse, build a camp-fire, and expertly cast a line into the river. Now it was punctured with needles, her teardrop glistening in the dim light. Shelby raised her finger under his hand and closed her eyes, as if touch could transmit her message. She felt Jack's fingers curl around her forefinger—ever so lightly but unmistakably!

Shelby let go the tears she had been trying to hold back; they fell onto the sheet beside Jack's arm. *He will fight; he is fighting.*

Shelby thanked the nurse then took the stairs to the second floor and slipped into Bobby's room. A nurse making notations in his chart nodded at Shelby, then quietly exited. Groggy and obviously in pain, he opened one eye when Shelby whispered, "How do you feel?"

"Like crap." His voice was thick from the drugs. "Did Jack—?"

"He's alive and the doctor says the next twenty-four hours are critical."

Shelby wanted to tell Bobby how much his ugly words hurt but he looked helpless and in pain. He wouldn't have heard anyway, he was already drifting back to sleep. Shelby heard her name paged over the intercom. *"Shelby Stamford, please pick up a white courtesy phone."* She went to the nurses' station and answered the call. It was Adele, her voice sounding artificially light. There was a long pause. "Well, did the old geezer survive?"

"He's alive, Adele."

Shelby heard a muffled sob. "Oh, thank the Lord." She could hear her crying. Adele cleared her throat. "How about Bobby?"

"He came through okay. In pain but fine. Are you coming over?"

"That's why I'm calling. What do you need me to bring?"

* * *

Two o'clock Sunday afternoon Shelby found Adele in the hospital coffee shop. They ordered lunch and as soon as the waitress walked away, Shelby said, "My God, Adele, how could this happen? In L.A. maybe, but not Montana! Jack cannot die. He is too good a person."

Adele seemed more like the old Adele. She patted Shelby's hand. "Damn straight he's a good person, and tough. He will fight with everything he's got."

"What about the two men, have they caught them?"

"Not yet but the sheriff from Pine Ridge got good descriptions from everybody."

"That's right. There were witnesses that saw the whole thing."

"Anyway, the sheriff would like to ask Bobby if he saw their vehicle. But even if Bobby didn't, the sheriff thinks they'll catch them. With the tournament going on, somebody will surely have seen their car or truck."

"I don't know what Bobby saw. I've only seen him for a total of maybe five minutes."

"Tough ending to your vacation. I never heard how you ended up in Troutsprings."

"Long story. Long and sad and I'm not sure you'd want to hear it."

"I'm not going anywhere."

"The short version—it was for the two of us to get away together. I was hoping it—"

"Would put Humpty Dumpty back together again? Honey, I'd like you to think I'm wise beyond my modest years, but the truth is Jack mentioned you two were having a battle royale when you rolled in. And you don't have to be a psychologist to see Bobby doesn't like Montana and you do. You two are so different. Does he have someone else?"

Shelby nodded. "He doesn't know I know but if he did, he'd say she doesn't mean anything and give me a line I've heard before."

"So what now?"

"Not sure, but I know I don't want to go back to life the way it was. I need some time away from Bobby, away from L.A. Maybe—"

"Montana is away from L.A.," Adele said.

Adele's quick comeback made Shelby smile. "Yes, it is, but right now I'm worried about Jack." Shelby glanced at her watch. "We'd better go check on him." They went to the intensive care unit and inquired about Jack Ketchum. "Are you family?" the nurse asked in a hushed tone.

Adele spoke up. "Honey, we're all he's got."

"Mr. Ketchum's blood pressure dropped. He's been taken back into surgery on the main floor. You can wait in the surgery waiting room and I'll tell Dr. Adams where you are."

Shelby and Adele exchanged stricken looks, then made their way to the surgery waiting room. Three hours later, Dr. Adams entered, looking more haggard than before. He was still in green scrubs. He nodded to Shelby and she introduced Adele.

"Mr. Ketchum started bleeding internally. We had to go back in and repair the rupture. He's still alive, which is a tribute to his strength. He must have a terrific will to live."

"What do you think his chances are, doctor? Please, just tell us," Adele said.

"At this point it is strictly up to him. Leave a cell number with Janet at the desk. I'll call if anything happens. I'm going to catch a nap in the doctors' lounge but I'll be close by. Get some rest and we'll see how he's doing in the morning." He gave them a weary wave.

"He's right. Let's find a hotel and get some sleep," Shelby said. "But first I'd like to check on Bobby again. Can you wait a few minutes?"

"Take your time, hon. I'm going to sit here and pray."

Shelby took the stairs to the second floor and entered Bobby's room. He was asleep. She stood gazing at him, her thoughts jumbled. *Is this the end of the road for us? What if you had died in that parking lot? All the fame and money you've chased wouldn't have made a difference. I've made a decision. My life is no longer going to revolve around Bobby Stamford. It's up to me now.* Shelby took a deep breath and touched his arm. "Bobby?"

He opened his eyes and took a few seconds to focus. "Shel, where the hell am... Oh yeah, the Missoula Ritz. What time is it?"

"A little after six. Would you like me to ring for a pain pill or some dinner?"

"Great idea. A Percodan with a side of fries, please."

"Would you stop it? I've had it with your sarcasm. And I don't want to hear anything more about this being my fault. You got that?" Shelby's words were clipped and crisp.

Bobby reacted with surprised indignation. "Well, sorryeee. I was about to ask how Jack is. What put the damn burr under your saddle?"

Shelby stared at him, no trace of emotion. "Jack is fighting for his life. They took him back to surgery because of internal bleeding. And you're it. You're the damn burr."

"Shel, come on. I just got my ass shot off. What do you expect me to do, sing you love songs? I'm sorry for what I said." He grasped her hand. "C'mon, baby, don't be mad."

Shelby felt the torrent of emotions that began on the helicopter and heightened during the endless hours of waiting all of a sudden evaporate like vapor from a tea kettle. *I'm not ready to let go of my anger, but right now I'm too tired to hang onto it.* "We'll talk in the morning. I'm beyond exhausted." She turned on her heel and left.

Shelby found Adele on the phone with Cavanaugh's Inn; they had a room. Both gave their cell numbers to Janet in ICU who reported Jack's condition remained unchanged. "Dr. Adams is asleep in the doctors' lounge, but he's instantly available," she said.

They went directly to the hotel dining room and each ordered wine. "Your mind is racing at warp speed," Adele said.

"Since four this morning," Shelby said. "I can't turn it off. It's like in a free-fall. I'm at level ten on the anger scale and all these thoughts are crashing down one on top of another."

"Hopefully the wine will help—two would probably be better, followed by a hot bubble bath soon as we get to the room. Do you have to call anybody about Bobby?"

Shelby shook her head. "Trust me, there's nothing wrong with Bobby's mouth. If he wants to call someone, he can do it himself. But how about Jack? Any brothers or sisters?"

"He had one sister, quite a bit older. She passed away a few years ago. Ellie's folks were from the east, a card-at-Christmas kind of family. I'm the closest thing to a family Jack's got."

"It's pretty obvious he is still hurting over Ellie's death."

"He was devastated. So was I. Ellie loved being around people. She felt isolated at the ranch so Jack bought the café for her. He's a cowboy, loves the outdoors, horses and ranching. I find it kinda weird that a cowboy would love to read, but Jack does. World history, Native American history, geology, biographies, poetry, different subjects— you saw his library. But as opposite as they were, Jack and Ellen had a great marriage. Unfortunately no kids, though."

"Speaking of marriage and family, you've never told me anything about 'Adele,' like marriage, kids and all that. I feel like we're family so is it okay if I ask why? Have you been married?" Noticing tears welling, Shelby immediately reached for Adele's hand.

"You want the drawn-out, sad version or the NBC nightly news wrap-up report?"

"I want whatever version you want to share with me, Adele."

"Okay, short version." She took a deep breath. "Married late. Paul Carson. A wonderful, handsome, athletic guy. A super son, Timmy. Paul and I celebrated our twentieth anniversary of a great marriage eight years ago. He was football coach at Missoula High when he and

Tim went on their annual snowmobile ride with a group they had belonged to for years. Short version, the group got caught in an avalanche. Half survived. Paul & Tim were in the half that didn't."

"Oh my God, Adele, I'm so sorry! That is horrible. No wonder you didn't mention it."

"I meant to but we've been so worried about Jack, whether he was going to pull through or not, there never seemed to be the right time to talk about it."

Shelby could not suppress instant tears, the shocking news taking her breath away. Spying their empty wine glasses, she silently held up one in each hand. The waiter filled both.

After they each regained composure, they sat sipping wine as Adele talked softly about the difficult years that followed. It suddenly dawned on Shelby that Adele's sense of humor and ready laughter were how she had coped and perhaps was still coping with a life-altering tragedy. At the end of their third glass of wine, Adele patted Shelby's hand. "You're right, Shelby, we are family, and I'm here to tell you I'm damned grateful for it."

"Me too. I was an only child and now I've got a sister? Lucky, lucky me!"

Later, a hot bubble bath helped ease Shelby's sorrowful thoughts for Adele, followed by gratitude for her friendship. *No matter what I do or where I live, Adele and I will always be family.* Shelby climbed in the twin bed closest to the open window, a gentle breeze touching her face as she closed her eyes and said a prayer for Adele and Jack and "Bobby too."

Adele had said earlier that she intended a "one- or two-night trip back home" tomorrow to talk to Virgil about Ellie's Café and "bring some of Jack's and my clothes and whatever you want me to bring of yours." *What a thoughtful person. She really is Jack's family and now mine.*

She could hear the shower; Adele was getting ready for bed. From out of nowhere, Shelby thought of her dad, tall, handsome David Longren with his Indiana Jones hat and aviator sunglasses, the father with the ready smile. *Where in Peru is he?* She couldn't remember the postmark on the envelope. *Does he ever think about me? What is his life like?* Next came thoughts of her mother, at the moment in Paris. *She's probably paying more attention to the gardens at the Louvre than the art.* She said a prayer for them too, then turned off her lamp and welcomed sleep.

Chapter Eleven

Bobby retrieved a mirror from the bedside drawer, checked his reflection, then downed the last of his breakfast coffee. *One more day of this swill and I will die voluntarily.* Instinct told him to deal carefully with Shelby this morning. She seemed in a strange mood last night, something else definitely going on. *Could be fatigue, but crap, 9:30 and still no Shelby?* He had been ready for over an hour, an hour of silence. He hated silence as much as being alone. Bobby retrieved his cell phone and called hers. She answered on the seventh ring. "Where are you?"

"I was in ICU with Adele, checking on Jack. He looks alert and Dr. Adams said his vital signs have improved. Isn't that great news?"

Bobby gazed at himself, checking his hair this time. "I couldn't be happier, truly I am."

"I hope you mean that, Bobby."

"Of course. Hey, it's nine-thirty. When are you going to get here?"

"Soon as we get a quick bite in the coffee shop. Not long."

"Okay," Bobby said. He rang the nurse and asked for a *Wall Street Journal* and *L.A. Times*. A candy striper arrived within minutes with both papers; he gave her a ten. "Keep the change, sweetheart." For the next hour, Bobby glanced over both newspapers. Finished, he rechecked his reflection and was combing his hair when Shelby came through the door.

Caught off guard at the sight of her, he forgot the mirror still in his hand. Dressed in a thigh-high, tight skirt and sleeveless blouse, her long blond hair softly framing her face, Shelby looked tanned and gorgeous, much like she did when he first saw her ten years ago on his way to New York. Flight attendant Shelby Longren was a knockout in a short black skirt, white military-style blouse, and a jaunty scarf around her neck.

The same beautiful legs, big brown eyes, a dynamite smile that he couldn't resist, and a diamond on her ring finger that Bobby remembered only made the challenge more interesting. Confident and friendly, she had treated him with the same poise she showed everyone, even the little old lady in the seat next to his in first class. Shelby Longren liked to laugh and he made her laugh a lot in those days. But she didn't seem to laugh much anymore.

Surprised that she didn't kiss him, she instead asked, "How are you feeling?"

"A lot better, thanks. You look great. Did you sleep okay?"

"Surprisingly well, considering how worried I was about Jack." Shelby sat down in the bedside chair and looked up at him as though waiting. It made him uncomfortable.

Bobby exhaled a deep breath. *Here I go.* "You know, Shel, Dr. Adams said I can do my physical therapy anywhere, and I need to get back to work. I need to get back to L.A. While I was waiting for you I read the *Journal* and the *Times*." He grinned. "Did you know that L.A. has twenty-thousand bistros? How cool is that! People here don't even know what *bistro* means. How about we go home and celebrate over dinner at *Trois Mec* in Hollywood. According to the *Times*, scoring a table there is tricky, but you know me. I'll get us one or we can go wherever you want. You liked our drive down the coast highway. You thought that was fun, right?"

He waited, expecting Shelby to say something but she merely

continued looking at him, which was unnerving. "Okay, if that doesn't sound good, how about I call Santa Monica Rental, have them pick up the Eagle and get it back to L.A.—however. I can't drive and it's such a long trip I don't want you doing it. Let's book a flight home. One more day in Montana and I'll—"

Shelby leaned forward. "We need to talk. Bobby."

"That sounds ominous. Can't it wait 'til we get home? Aren't you anxious to see your—"

"I'm not leaving." She remained perfectly still, her expression unreadable.

The words landed like a blow. "What the hell do you mean you're not leaving?"

"Just that, Bobby. You are free to go back to L.A. whenever and however you wish. I'm going to stay here. For a while anyway."

"You gotta be kidding! I wouldn't have gotten shot if you hadn't dragged me on this trip. Now you're bailing on me when I need you the most? What kind of wife are you?"

Her brown eyes flashed anger. Shelby stood up and looked him in the eye. "You're the one who bailed, Bobby, a long time ago."

He'd already had enough of her gushing about Montana and ragging on him. The inequity galled him. "I drove your Eagle RV-Palace a thousand miles. I helped in the café and did all the other dumb things you wanted me to do. So what do you mean I bailed a long time ago?"

Shelby's expression did not change. Not the reaction he expected. "Listen, Bobby, I am not going back to California right now because I'm not sure I want to be married to you. I need time and a place away from L.A. to think things over and I figure Montana is as good a place as any. I agree that you should go back to L.A. but I'm going to stay and help take care of Jack."

"Jack? Why and what do you mean help take care of him?"

"He has no family, Bobby. No one," Shelby said. "I'm going to help Adele take care of him until he gets back on his feet. That will give me time to decide what I want to do."

"That's crazy, baby! Listen, I know you're upset, but we can talk this out back home. C'mon, I need you, Shel. And what about Skyline? How can you abandon your business?"

He watched her rise, walk to the end of the bed and turn to face him, her hands on the foot rail. "My business will be fine. I've talked to Enrique. Darryl agreed to take over foreman duties and our two custom homes are in the final stage. Enrique will do a good job with those."

What the hell is happening? Bobby's mouth went dry; he felt like throwing up.

Shelby kept staring at him as if letting what she said sink in. "Bobby, I can't count the times I've heard you say to your clients 'put your cards on the table, baby.' Well, that's what I'm saying to you. Put your cards on the table, Bobby. You either want me and want to be married or you want to play your game. You can't have it both ways. But if you do want me in your life, the rules of this game have changed."

"Rules of the game, what the fuck are you talking about?"

Shelby's hands went on her hips. "Do you know what room you're in?"

"What do you mean?"

"The number of this room, what is it?"

"Hell, I don't know—or care. What are you talking about?"

"It's Room 226. The Spindrift Motel. Ring a bell?"

Bobby's heartbeat revved to rocket speed. Speechless, he could only stare at her, calm a minute ago but now with contempt in her eyes. It felt difficult to take a breath.

"I've spent a lot of hours in a waiting room here, a great opportunity to think about our marriage. When the admitting clerk said you'd be on the second floor, I asked if Room 226 was available. Prophetic, don't you think? Sorry, but secretaries are not included with this one."

She smiled, but he saw tears welling. "I know all about Terri Armstrong." There was dead silence. "You're not nearly as clever as you think."

"Why haven't you said something? Why…"

"I'm going to rent a place here until Jack can go home. Adele is going to keep Ellie's open and come and go from Troutsprings to help when she can. When the doctor says it's okay, Adele and I will take Jack home and I intend to stay until I know he's all right."

"Why, Shel? You don't know him that well. Or Adele. Is this to punish me?"

"This is not about you, Bobby. This is about me, and I know them well enough."

"Wow, when you say put your cards on the table… Don't do this, Shel, please. I really wish we could talk this over at home. Maybe we could go to a counselor…"

"You need to understand, Bobby, I stopped the divorce after Brenda because I thought you were a good guy who made a mistake. But the mistake I made was thinking that behavior was the exception. I didn't want to throw in the towel like my parents. Divorce is giving up."

"Shel, don't. Please."

"Hear me out. What I realized is that it really is just a game to you. You love the chase and the conquest but when you win the woman, the deal, or whatever constitutes the game, it no longer has value, so you start the chase all over again—that's Bobby Stamford. The exception would be your being satisfied and sincere. You are sincere just enough to keep me from leaving. What a revelation. I thought it was my fault." There was no hint of anger in her voice.

Too shocked to speak or react, he watched Shelby quietly exit, his heart still thudding, the mirror forgotten in his hand. Silence invaded; he hated silence. When his heartbeat finally slowed, Bobby became aware of the mirror. He put it away, then lay back against his pillow. *She's just blowing off steam. She'll be back within the hour. Shel would not do this to me.*

At nine p.m., with the hospital eerily quiet and sleep begging for his attention, Bobby laid the newspapers aside and closed his eyes. Shel had not returned. "Well, I'll be damned."

* * *

The following morning Shelby went directly to Intensive Care on the second floor. The nurse said Jack was being monitored and suggested she come back in an hour so she could see him and catch Dr. Adams at the same time. Shelby glanced at her watch, then took the stairs to the second floor. She knocked briefly, then entered. Dressed in slacks and sweater, Bobby was stretched out on the bed, a newspaper in his hands. She noted two crutches propped against the bed and a wheelchair parked under the window. He glanced up at her but said nothing.

"Hi, Bobby. How are you this morning?"

"If I were any better, it would be a sin. How the hell do you think I'm doing?"

"I'm not here to fight," she said. "I came to see how you're doing and let you know the insurance I took out on the Eagle is taking care of getting it back to L.A.—no cost to us. If you need a ride to the airport, I would be happy to take you." She stood at the foot of the bed.

"I'm sorry. It's just hard for me to leave without you. I can't believe it."

"I know, but I've explained why I'm staying."

Bobby's expression turned quizzical. "Yeah, you did, but are you sure what you're doing? Staying to take care of some old guy? Though I admit he is a nice old guy."

"Jack's fifty, only five years older than you. You can drop the insults, they're childish. And yes, I have thought this through. I am doing this for me, but there is no way I could make you understand. I haven't been able to so far."

Bobby smiled. "That's okay. I've pretty much had it with your 'Up with Montana, down with L.A.' speech anyway. Why don't I just have my people call your people?" Bobby smiled.

Button one pushed. "I wasn't going to bash L.A. I was going to say that I hope we can talk after you get home and settled. You call me or tell me when I can call you."

"I'm going to be swamped when I get home. The Covington Project is closing at warp speed, the biggest project of my career. I was counting on my wife being there to support me, not playing footsy with some old fart who considers Inglenook Chenin Blanc actually fit to drink."

Button two pushed. "So you're saying you won't or can't make any time at all to talk to me? If that's the case, then I take it you're not interested in working things out."

"If you really wanted to work things out, you'd come home with me. Remember, I said that, as busy as I'm going to be, I'd be willing to go to a counselor. I have no idea how much time I'll have or when, but with you in Podunk, Montana, it isn't like trying to get hold of you in—"

"Santa Monica? At the Spindrift?" she said.

"Very funny, Shel."

"Interesting. Bobby Stamford doesn't like sarcasm."

"What I'd like is for my wife to come home where she belongs. Instead, it sounds to me like you're going to sit up here and play judge and jury, deciding the fate of our marriage. And if I want to have any input, it'll be by phone. Does that sound fair to you? It sure doesn't to me."

"I shouldn't be surprised you'd put a negative slant on what I'm trying to do. I have tried to talk to you about this—in person, in L.A. But you weren't interested so now I'm going to try another way and I'm asking you to please give me some time."

Bobby tossed the newspaper aside. "Well, baby, that's just the chance you'll have to take. I'm not chopped liver, you know. I can't guarantee that after you do all this soul-searching, I will take you back. I may be the one to change my mind."

Button three—that's a launch. Hands gripping the bedframe, Shelby leaned forward and stared hard at him. "You arrogant sonofabitch. Take me back? Bobby Stamford, the guy who never let his marriage stand in the way of a good time? The screw 'em until he gets caught, then Mr. Contrite who wants to buy his wife a trinket at the Ritz Carlton to calm her down?" Heart pounding and suddenly feeling dizzy, Shelby began to laugh, near-hysterical laughter that made her realize she was losing control. She couldn't stop. Bobby's smile faded and he looked scared. Holding tight to the bedframe, she tried deep breathing but it didn't help. She was sobbing one moment and laughing the next. Unable to gain control, she held onto the bed for dear life. *There were so many things I wanted to say, Bobby, so much I wanted to hear from you.*

Desperate to get away from him, she let go of the bedframe and started for the door.

"Wait, Shel. Wait, please. I'm sorry, I didn't mean it. I—"

"D...don't...talk... you... you... sa...said it all" was all she could manage before bolting from the room. Hands covering her face, Shelby stood outside the door, a half-step from hyperventilating. *I can't see Jack now.* Shaking and gasping for air, she remained stock-still for what seemed an interminable time until her breathing slowed, then she instinctively headed for the surgery waiting room startling a passerby as she ran by. Thankfully, the room was empty.

Two hours later, Dr. Adams came through the door. "I thought I might find you here. Don't get up," he said cordially and plopped down on the couch across from her. His smile immediately vanished. "You don't look well. Are you all right? You're almost as pale as Jack."

"What I am is exhausted. I was going to come back up but... How is Jack?"

"The nurse said you stopped by. After three weeks, good news. We turned off the respirator last night. We left it in place but turned it off to see if he could breathe on his own. Jack did fine so we removed it this morning and have been monitoring him closely all day. He's breathing on his own and glad to have all those tubes out." He gestured to his throat. "Jack's been off assisted breathing for twelve hours now. His blood gases are good and his vitals are strong. I'll have him transferred to a regular room in the morning. Now we can introduce some food."

"That is wonderful news. Thank you so much for all you've done," she said.

The doctor's smile returned, broad and genuine. "Jack Ketchum is one case I will give thanks for when I say *my* prayers tonight."

* * *

The following morning, Shelby went to Jack's room and peeked in. Sound asleep and with all of the tubes gone, the sight of him helped to erase the ugly scene with Bobby. Jack sleeping peacefully did more than that; it brought back the idea she arrived at during her two hours trying to pull herself together in the surgery waiting room. Waiting outside Jack's door and filled with resolve, she squared her shoulders. *No reason to wait any longer.*

She and Jack and Adele needed a place to stay until his release, and then for an unknown period afterward for Jack's "physical therapy and rehabilitation," as Dr. Adams called it.

Decision made, she remembered Jack's nurse telling her about the complex where he and several hospital employees lived. The three-block walk invigorated her and, after a tour of the ground floor, two-bedroom apartment at the Mountain Shadows Apartments, Shelby wrote a check for the deposit and one month's rent. Walking distance from St. Patrick's Hospital, the apartment complex had ten fully equipped units available for shorter periods for visitors and university or hospital personnel.

Tiny compared to her house or Jack's, but it seemed perfect for a short stay for the three of them and it was close to the hospital. When Martin, the complex manager, handed her a key, she told him she had arranged for a hospital bed for Jack. "The front bedroom, please, and could you have the regular bed put in storage? I'll give you a heads up the day before Jack is released."

Shelby walked back to the hospital and directly to Jack's room. Shaved and combed, his *I'm-happy-to-see-you* look was so obvious she couldn't help but respond and kissed his cheek.

"I have never seen a more beautiful sight than you comin' through that door."

"You're looking pretty good yourself, mister."

"That's nice to hear. I had eggs and toast and coffee! Do you have any idea how much I missed coffee? They don't have an IV for that." Jack chuckled then winced from the pain.

"Was the food awful?" Shelby said, remembering Bobby's contemptuous remark.

"Slightly better than the IV, but it beats tubes down the throat. How is Bobby doing?"

Oh boy, how do I handle this? "He's fine, Jack, but I do need to talk to you about him."

"Fire away. Geez, Ketchum, that was a poor choice of words," he said and placed his hand over hers. He listened, and when Shelby told him Bobby had returned to L.A., Jack looked shocked and alarmed. "I might as well tell you the rest." She told him about renting the apartment and her plans to return to Troutsprings to help with his therapy until he got back his strength. "And I'm going to help Adele run the café until you are fully recovered."

Shelby noticed he blinked a couple of times but said nothing. "I realize what I did was presumptuous, Jack, but everything just seemed to fall into place. I simply could not go back with Bobby, I just couldn't." Saying it outloud made her aware how impertinent her actions must seem. He was looking at her with those intense blue eyes. "I wish you'd say something, Jack."

Red splotches appeared on his gaunt face. "Dammit!"

"Are you mad at me?" she said, trying to remain calm.

"Not at you, at Bobby. I should have decked him that day. Maybe it would have knocked some sense into him. What an idiot. I hope you—"

Shelby could see him becoming agitated. "Jack. It's okay. He's gone. Don't get upset, it's not good for you. Please?"

He put his head back against the pillow and closed his eyes. "Sorry," he whispered.

Shelby looked down at his hand covering hers, the same hand that grasped her forefinger when they weren't sure he'd make it. "Upsetting you is the last thing I want to do. I stayed to help you, not kill you off with my problems," she said. "So the plans are all right with you?"

Jack opened one eye and grinned at her. "Never let it be said that Jack Ketchum was dumb enough to turn down an offer like that. Of course it's all right with me."

"Okay then, first things first. You are now a non-smoker. Dr. Adams forbade it so let's get that straight, right off. You got a problem with that?" Shelby stared hard at him.

"Oh Lord, I know when I'm beat and that's the second time." He gave a tired smile.

* * *

Shelby visited Jack every day, arriving after his breakfast and staying until he napped. Adele drove over twice each week. Their visits were spent playing poker and dominoes with Jack. Shelby could see Adele's presence proved to be good medicine for him. Dr. Adams started Jack's therapy the day after he was moved out of Intensive Care, slowly at first, getting him to walk the hallways, then progressing to breathing and strengthening exercises in the hospital's therapy labs. It visibly sapped Jack's strength and he took a long nap each afternoon.

Shelby spent that time bicycling around Missoula. Jack's nurse, Ken, loaned her his bike. He wanted to lend her his truck but she refused, preferring to tour the university and town on bicycle. Her favorite ride was around the University of Montana campus with its stately old brick buildings, the magnificent bronze Grizzly mascot, and a forest of beautiful pines intermixed with sycamores, maples, birch and hawthorns sporting every color of fall.

During quiet times Shelby thought about what to do about her marriage but all that came to mind were hurtful things so she postponed those answers until tomorrow. Counting back, it surprised her that it had only been eight weeks since the shooting, but so many life changes.

Back at the hospital later that afternoon, she was with Jack when Dr. Adams said he would be releasing him in "a couple of days." Jack grinned at the news and was on the phone to Adele as soon as Dr. Adams left the room. He pressed the speaker button so Shelby could hear.

"Great news! I'll get Virgil to run the café and I'll be there soon as I can!"

* * *

Shelby finished up at the apartment and was at the hospital at 11:00 a.m. when Jack was officially released. The nurse told her Dr. Adams was due any minute but she could go in. The door was partially open and she could hear laughter. "Come in," Ken said. "He's bragging about the Troutsprings fishing." Jack was dressed, shaved, and ready to go but definitely thinner.

"You look spiffy, cowboy. How are you feeling?" Shelby kissed him on the cheek.

"Better now that you're here." Ken gathered up the tray of shaving material. "Soon as I finish with a couple more patients, I'll be back to take Mr. Gorgeous here to the apartment. I'm in 215 right across the courtyard, Shelby, so I can come over any time he gives you trouble."

Dr. Adams arrived and asked Shelby to step outside so he could check Jack over. When he called her back in, Adams explained the medications Jack needed and what to look for when changing the dressing on his wound. "Well, Jack, you've been a great patient. Ready to go?"

"You bet, Doc, and I thank you for everything you did. You saved my life."

"You are welcome, cowboy, but you took a bullet in the upper abdomen that just missed the aorta. I want you to take it easy and no smoking okay?" He wished Jack good luck.

Shelby nodded at Jack with a raise of her eyebrows. "You heard the man," she said.

"I did, I did. Now can we blow this joint?"

Chapter Twelve

The flight to LA was long and tiring. Bobby had a hard time managing the crutches; his leg throbbed, he had a headache, and he was exhausted. Despite his father picking him up at LAX, Bobby missed Shelby not being there to smooth the way and make things easier.

"What the hell happened?" Adam asked Bobby, barely settled in the Escalade. "You go on vacation and end up getting shot? And why isn't Shelby with you? Why is she still up there?"

"Dad, lighten up, okay? I feel like hell and I don't want to go into this right now. I need to lie down and get a pain pill."

"Of course, Bobby. Sorry, it's just that this whole situation is such a shock."

"I know, Dad, I know." They rode the long distance in silence, Bobby's head back on the head rest, his eyes closed. Adam called the house on the car phone as they turned off the Coast Highway and when he pulled up in the driveway, Oscar and Esther were standing outside.

Bobby noted Esther's shocked expression when Oscar rushed forward to help him out of the car and position the crutches under his arms so he could straighten up. She came forward and looked up at Bobby with soulful eyes. *"Oh, Señor, es muy malo por accidente y Señora Stamford no es aqui."* Shelby had told him that when Esther was nervous or upset, she reverted to solely Spanish. Seeing tears in her eyes, Bobby had to look away, a sudden catch in his throat. "Thank you both very much" was all he could manage to say.

Navigating the long walk to the house, Bobby waited for Oscar to open the front door then asked, "Did Mrs. Stamford call?"

Esther answered him, "*Si, Señor,* Señora called this morning to say you would be arriving today and we should have everything ready for you." Esther brushed a tear from her cheek.

Adam deposited Bobby's bags in the entry and immediately headed to the family room bar. Bobby paused in the entryway and looked around as though seeing it for the first time. The grand half-oval entry with its parquet-hardwood floor, the wide stairway following the curved wall up to the second floor; after Ellie's Café it seemed palatial. Bobby blinked at the sight; he could almost hear Shelby's hammer and see her, in jeans and baseball cap, creating it.

He hobbled into the great room and gingerly lowered himself down into his chair, Oscar without a word helping lift his leg onto the ottoman. "This place is beautiful, Bobby. What can I get you?" Adam said from the bar.

"Scotch—a big one," Bobby said. "Guess I never noticed just how beautiful it really is."

Oscar closed the front door. "*Señor,* may I help you up to your bedroom?"

"Thank you, Oscar, but I won't be able to get up and down those stairs. Can you fix up the guest room for me and bring down some of my clothes and bathroom stuff?"

"*Si, señor,*" Oscar said and disappeared up the stairs.

Adam brought Bobby his scotch. "Can you drink with a pain pill?"

"I'll wait to take the pill until I eat, otherwise it would do me in."

"Tell me, what happened, son."

"You talking getting shot or Shelby?"

"First, how you got shot."

"A robbery. I happened to be in the wrong place at the wrong time. I was lucky it was just my leg. The owner got it in the gut."

"Did he live?"

"Yeah, he made it, but barely."

"Why didn't Shelby come home with you? I thought everything was good with you two. She seemed happy the night of her birthday party."

"Yeah, everything seemed fine," Bobby said, hoping to end the discussion.

"So the trip went badly, but there must be more to her decision than that."

Realizing his father wasn't going to let go of this, Bobby downed half of his drink. "Shelby is not sure she wants to be married to me so she's staying up there to think things over. The trip was officially for my health, but evidently she was counting on it to work out some issues she's unhappy about. The biggee was she found out I had a little get-together with Terri. How, I'll never know, but that almost did it. There's also the issue of kids. She said she's waited long enough and that I don't care what *she* wants. Does this look like I don't care what she wants?" He gestured at the house with his glass.

"Shelby wanting children doesn't strike me as unreasonable."

"I don't need to hear that now, Dad," Bobby said, not bothering to mask his irritation.

Adam drained his glass and rose to refill it. When he returned he chose Shelby's chair and turned it to face Bobby. "I've never pried into your affairs." Their eyes locked briefly over that word. "Aside from being grateful to have Shelby in the family, a divorce would not be good right now. This sounds crass but with Covington Square being launched fairly soon and our firm working to promote Stamford Development as an environmentally friendly, pro-community company, having the Stamford name involved in a divorce would undo a lot of that effort. Not to mention the financial impact could be disastrous."

"I know, Dad, I know. I tried like hell to talk her into coming back with me. I even offered to go to counseling! One thing I found out, Shelby's never in doubt. Right or wrong, when she decides something, that's it. I don't think the Pope could have changed her mind."

"Maybe I shouldn't ask, but do you love Shelby?"

"Jesus, Dad, what kind of a question is that? We've been married ten years."

"That's no answer. Don't try to con a con man."

Bobby held up his empty glass. Adam refilled it and returned to the same chair, obviously waiting for an answer. "Do you love Mom? You've played around plenty."

"Yes, I love your mother. And yes, I am guilty of some indiscretions, more than I'd like to remember. Call it maturity, Bobby, or finally figuring out the big picture, but having a history with one woman who truly cares about you beats the hell out of a high you get playing around."

"Is this the exalted Adam Stamford talking, the guy who charmed every secretary he had out of her pantyhose? Who are you trying to convince with that speech, me or yourself?"

"You, son, and I hope you take this to heart." His father's whole demeanor changed; he looked and sounded emotional. "Remember when your mother was diagnosed with breast cancer? It scared the hell out of her and me even more. When it hit me that she might not make it, I realized how much I loved her and I stopped playing around. That was twenty years ago when a lot of my buddies were also playing around. A lot of those guys got divorced, Bobby. They married women half their age and had two or three kids they wish they'd never had.

Today every one of those guys is wondering how long they'll be able to satisfy a younger wife. Even now I know guys my age, still married and still boinkin' chicks with tight asses and breast implants and fretting themselves into a coronary unit."

Bobby flashed to the Spindrift Motel, the sweating, the chills and nausea. "You had this revelation twenty years ago and didn't say shit? What kind of father are you? If you thought I was making a mistake, why didn't you say so? All we ever talk about is business."

His father's face flushed at the criticism. "Would you have listened? Would it have made you say no to Brenda or to Terri? I don't think so. You would have thought I was a hypocrite like you're doing right now. This revelation or whatever you want to call it came from watching what happened to those friends and business associates. Good guys who, I guess, never stopped to think what they had. Even more important my revelation came from here," he said touching his chest. "I have a question for you and I want you to think about it before you answer."

"If you want to know if I'm depressed, the answer is yes. Otherwise—what?"

His father's stare was unnerving. "Have you ever stopped to think beyond Covington, beyond developing? About your future, what you want from life and who you want to be with when you're my age?"

Stung, Bobby could hardly breathe, his eyes locked on the father he had emulated, the man who taught him everything he knew about business but had a life-changing revelation and chose not to share it with his only son. "No, I haven't," Bobby whispered, trying to ignore the mental image of Terri spoon-feeding a wizened Bobby Stamford. "Jesus, Dad, I didn't think this day could get much worse but bingo! You did it!"

"It's not totally my fault we haven't talked like this. Once you landed the Covington property, it was like you were possessed. I admit it was a coup, Bobby, but I have to confess that's when I felt like I lost my son. I wasn't part of it. Covington was all you wanted to talk about and every minute of your time was devoted to it."

"What do you mean 'lost your son'? I did it for Stamford Development, the business you spent your life building, where all your time and effort went, more time than you ever spent with Karen or me when we were kids. I guess you never had a revelation about *your* children."

His father's eyes narrowed, his jaw clenched. "You say you did Covington for Stamford Development? Well, there wouldn't be a Stamford Development if I hadn't worked my ass off ten- and eleven-hour days and weekends when you and Karen were kids. You don't think I regret that? I'm grateful that Stanford Development is the huge success it is, but your mother sharing those tough years, keeping the family together when I wasn't there? If she weren't here now to share the good times, none of it would mean a goddam thing."

"So you're telling me this revelation caused you to go back on everything you've done and been. And I emulated you? I can't believe you quit the game!" Bobby said in total disbelief.

His father physically recoiled, eyes wide. "Quit the game? What game?"

"The game—the fucking game that I've watched you play ever since I was old enough to remember. The one all the rich guys play." The more he thought about it, the madder Bobby became. "You know, spreading the bucks, kissing the right ass, shaking the right hand, being president of the country club, having pictures on your wall with the governor and every USC coach! Wasn't all that to have power, call your own shots, have whatever woman you wanted—be the fucking winner! If it wasn't for that, then what the hell was it all for?"

"Calm down, Bobby, you're talking crazy. There is no game. I worked hard, yes, and I did some things I'm ashamed of, but my goal was to make Stamford a success, to give all of us a good life. Nothing more! What did you think it was for?"

Bobby spoke through gritted teeth. "I just told you what I thought it was for."

He dropped his gaze to his empty glass. Silent moments passed, the scotch softening his anger. Bobby looked at his father. "Then you tell me, Dad, you've been around longer than me, screwed around more than me, and put the business first over everything. So how is it you're still married and my wife is in Podunk, Montana, happier to be with people she hardly knows than with me?"

His father's intense stare disappeared, a tired or a sad look taking its place. "Maybe I was more discreet or maybe I wasn't as much of a player as you thought," he said quietly. "What I do know is I made sure your mother knew I cared about what made her happy. Can you say that? Have you ever asked Shelby if she is happy?"

"Fuck, I don't know," Bobby said. "Probably not. Maybe I thought all of this," he gestured at the darkening room, "showed how I felt. Right this minute I'm not sure what the hell love is or whether I could feel it if I did know."

Overcome by a hollow, weary feeling, he dropped his chin to his chest. "I thought I made Shel happy, but I'm finding out everything I thought I knew, everything I've been busting my hump doing, counts for nothing. It's all smoke. You always said, 'you have to pay your dues.' Well, I watched you and did what I saw you do. And the Covington project? I was riding a wave—the biggest goddam wave of my life. Now I don't know what to think."

Bobby moved his leg off the ottoman. "What I *think* right now is I'm going to take a big honkin' pain pill and go to sleep."

Chapter Thirteen

Bright sun greeted Jack as Shelby escorted him out of the hospital. He glanced back at the huge complex as the cab drove away, the place and the people in it that saved his life. He said a silent prayer of thanks. Shelby made him lie down as soon as they got to the apartment and the next thing he knew it was evening.

The open window next to his bed ushered in a cool breeze. How good it felt. He could see a courtyard with lots of trees and grass, a beautiful sight after hospital rooms. Anything green, anything not made of steel or plastic seemed gorgeous. And there was something else—a wonderful aroma drifting through the partially open door.

Jack spotted a new robe neatly folded at the foot of his bed and a new pair of leather moccasins on the floor directly below. He slipped them on and had to smile at the image of Shelby sneaking them in to surprise him. Jack made his way to the dining area where he could see Shelby through the cut-out opening. She was humming softly with the radio and slicing tomatoes into a salad. "Is that pot roast I smell?"

He sat down at the pass-through and watched as she moved around the tiny kitchen. "I thought you said you couldn't cook? You certainly can't tell by how good it smells in here."

She smiled. "Pot roast it is and I agree it does smell good. I said I can't cook gourmet stuff, but I figured you would like something basic for your first meal out of the hospital."

"You figured right and I'm starving. I think this is the first time I've actually felt hungry since I got shot. How long until dinner?"

"About fifteen minutes. I just have to mash the potatoes and stir the gravy."

"Whoa! I must have died and this is heaven. An angel in the kitchen and mashed potatoes and gravy? Yup, this is definitely heaven."

Shelby chuckled. "I'm no angel and I suggest you reserve your judgment. The potatoes may be lumpy. I set the table, but would you rather I bring a tray to your room?"

"Absolutely not. I don't want to eat another meal in bed. Sitting with you at a regular table is a real treat. By the way, this robe and the moccasins feel really nice. Thank you."

"A little getting-out-of-the-hospital present from Adele and me. It looks good on you."

"It feels good." He rubbed the soft sleeve. "I'll give Adele a call after dinner and thank her too. Seems like you two are getting to be good friends."

"We joke that we are family. I feel like I've known her forever. We've crammed a lot of life into a short time. I wish she were here with us. Okay, gravy's almost ready. You've got ten minutes, better move it, fella."

Jack used the ten minutes to comb his hair and freshen up then returned to the table. Shelby placed two plates of food on the small table and two glasses of red wine. Jack held her chair for her. "Thanks but I'm supposed to be taking care of you, remember?"

"Hey, I'm shot-up, not dead. Is this?" He lifted the wine glass.

"Yes, for a special occasion." She handed him the bottle. "I think it is appropriate."

"A wine with horses on the label!' He couldn't help smiling. "*14 Hands Vineyards, Columbia Valley 2010, Hot to Trot Red Blend?* Are you trying to seduce me?" he said, watching her blush. "Just teasing, this wine and your cooking is really thoughtful, thank you."

Shelby insisted on opening the bottle then poured wine in both glasses. "Here's to Jack Ketchum, you are one tough guy."

Smiling, Jack raised his glass. "Here's to you and Adele. I feel like we're family too." Jack discovered just how hungry he was. The dinner was delicious, the hospital seemed far away; the apartment was cozy and Shelby looked relaxed. The strained expression on her face when Bobby was around was gone. "How are you doing, Shelby, you feeling okay?"

"You mean about Bobby?"

He nodded. "A lot has happened since you came to Montana. You okay with it?"

"Actually I am, surprisingly so." She tipped her glass in a mock salute.

Jack treasured the dinner she fixed and this quiet time with her. They talked about their fishing trips, about Adele and the café, lingering over the food, enjoying a home-cooked meal.

"You know, when I first met you I figured you for a city gal. Then I find out you have not one, but three horses, you ride like the wind, and you're a Class A builder. What do you do for a hobby, brain surgery?"

She grinned. "Only when I run short of money. The building thing started as a hobby then morphed into a business. I've always loved horses, ridden since I was a kid. My Mom preferred that I liked horses better than boys." Shelby paused. "Speaking of horses, I wonder how Lolli and Solitaire are doing?"

Jack's fork paused in mid-air. "That's terrible! I haven't given a thought to the ranch, the horses, or the Café. I forgot everything!"

"The ability to shut everything out is probably what helped you pull through this. Dr. Adams said you survived only because you wanted to live, no other reason. So don't lament."

He listened as she talked about Jenkins and his sons taking care of the ranch, and Adele keeping the café open. The café reopening had gone fine. Business was good, customers asking about him and sending him prayers and good wishes. Humility flooded over him like a shower, Shelby staying to help care for him, Adele and Virgil taking care of the café and ranch. "I don't know the right words to thank you, and Adele and Virgil and everybody else," Jack said.

Shelby just nodded. "How about asking for seconds? That's one way. In fact you'll hurt my feelings if you don't have seconds on something."

"A little bit of everything then. That was delicious."

"Want a cup of coffee with it?"

"Can we wait and have that in the living room?"

"Certainly. You are feeling better and I am encouraged." Shelby brought him more food and sat down, elbows on the table, chin resting in her hands. "Tell me what makes cowboy Jack happy besides a gourmet meal like this?" She nodded at his plate with a mischievous look.

Jack took his time answering, giving serious consideration to her question. Finishing the last few bites, he answered, "Well, a frosty morning with the sun shining makes me happy. The promise of a whole day ahead. That first cup of coffee. Putting my line in the water and feeling the tug of a big trout. Riding around my place and seeing that things are like they're supposed to be. You know, hay stacked neat in the pole barn, fat cattle, dogs and cats running around. It doesn't take a whole lot."

"You have all those things, except a dog. Actually I am surprised you don't have one as much as you love animals."

"I did have. His name was Smoky, a gift from Ellie. That was a long time ago, he was just a pup. He died of old age about a year after she passed. I don't know why I never got another one. I should have. Smoky was like my shadow, he went everywhere I did."

"You must miss him. What kind of dog?"

"Golden Lab, and yes, I miss him."

"Life dishes out hurt, doesn't it?" Shelby said thoughtfully. "But you are fortunate, Jack. Your life is simple, a good life. You have your beautiful ranch, good friends, and Adele."

"My life isn't complicated. I like that. I read the newspaper and see on TV all the bad things going on. I never thought it would happen in Troutsprings, but I'm glad I live there anyway. What about you? What makes Shelby happy?"

She smiled and shook her head. "A couple of months ago I could have told you exactly what made me happy. Right now I'm not sure, but I'm beginning to think my life is one of those complicated ones you see on TV, and just as messed up. Come to think of it, I'm happy to be right here, right now. I can't explain it, I don't understand it myself."

Jack pushed his empty plate away. "Maybe you needed a rest from trying to please somebody else all the time. Perhaps tending to your feelings for a change is what feels good."

"Jack Ketchum! You didn't fall off a turnip truck." Shelby rose and offered to bring their coffee to the living room. "Would you like to watch television or play cards?"

Jack stretched out in the big chair, his feet on the ottoman. "No TV or cards. I'd love to just sit here and talk with you. I don't often get the chance to have a classy lady all to myself." He closed his eyes. "A cigarette would sure go great with this coffee."

"Forget it, mister," Shelby said and stretched out on the couch.

"Can't blame a guy for trying."

"Talk away, Jack Ketchum. I love to hear your stories about Montana and the ranch."

"No way, tell me about Shelby. I want to know how you got to be a builder. Bobby told me about the remodel you did and the houses you've built. I'm impressed."

Jack studied Shelby as she talked about her life, noticing when her smile disappeared, replaced by a somber expression. Her father was a mining engineer. He loved to build things and when she was little she followed him around. While her friends were playing with Barbies, Shelby was learning to use a square and a level, her first project a dog house when she was nine. Her father cut the lumber but she built it, roof and all.

Shelby's countenance seemed to deteriorate when she said shortly after her tenth birthday her parents divorced. "I was devastated. After that I only saw my father during the summers because his work took him to Mexico, South America, Canada, wherever mining jobs took him. To make spending money I built dog houses and sold them. My first business—that was fun!"

Shelby smiled again. "My mom and stepdad got me a horse for my thirteenth birthday. We didn't have a corral, no place to keep her, so I built one." That produced a second smile.

"So how did you get from dog houses and corrals to houses?"

"Dad bought a cabin not too far from where I grew up near Montrose, Colorado. After the divorce, because of it, I suppose, he took the summers off and, from the time I was thirteen until I went away to college, I spent the summers with him at the cabin and visited my mom a couple of evenings a week. The cabin hadn't been lived in a long time. It needed help so Dad and I started working on that place."

A slight smile told him she was remembering. "We started with a deck, then a new kitchen and bath, and over those five summers we literally rebuilt the place, even furniture for the deck. I loved those times." Shelby straightened up, a faraway expression on her face.

"Where is your dad now?"

Her voice dropped to a whisper. "Peru. He's in Peru."

"How long has it been since you've seen him?"

"Five years, just before he left for South America. As far as I know, he hasn't been back to the States since he took that job."

"And no visit to Peru?"

"Jack, you're relentless!" Shelby gave him a stern look.

"People on turnip trucks have to be that way. That's how we come up with profound insights." He was relieved to see a smile. "You haven't answered my question."

"No visit to Peru. I know you're going to ask why, so I'll save you the trouble. He's never invited me. I figure he's so wrapped up in his work he has no time for me."

"Do you hear from him?"

"Yes, on my birthday and Christmas. He'll call or send a card and usually sends me something. He wrote a card a couple of months ago."

"Will I get shot again for asking if you wrote him back?"

"No, but I might poison your cereal in the morning."

"Did you?" he pressed.

"No, and don't ask why. I just haven't gotten around to it." Jack started to say something but Shelby interrupted him. "Okay, I will. Are you satisfied?"

"Absolutely." He put his head back on the chair and patted his stomach. "I'm as good as an old guy can get."

"I don't like the word *old*, Jack. You're not or you wouldn't have survived that bullet. But it's odd you say that. Bobby loved slamming you by calling you 'that old man.' We got into it pretty good a couple of times over that."

"Really! What was his reason or is that just Bobby?"

"That's Bobby for sure, but maybe he was jealous. I have no idea what his problem was."

"Jealous? I'm flattered."

"Well, why not?" A smile replaced her somber expression. "A good-looking young cowboy? He should be jealous."

"Is this part of my therapy?" Jack chuckled softly.

"Absolutely not and I'm offended you think I don't mean it. You are not old and I don't want you saying it. Got it?"

"Yes, ma'am. I think I'll call Adele and Virgil. Then this young, studly gentleman will say good night." Jack left Shelby puttering in the kitchen to make his calls. As he hung up, it dawned on him: the apartment, the phone, and all the groceries. *Who paid for all of this?* He nearly had to wrestle the information out of Shelby. She paid for everything and Jack had to threaten to leave, to walk out of the apartment in his brand-new robe all the way to Troutsprings if she didn't let him reimburse her. "You are tough!" he admonished her.

Her eyebrows shot up. "Me! I was about to say the same about you."

Shelby put the last of the dishes in the dishwasher and rinsed her hands. "How did it go tonight at the café?"

"Adele said it went great. She also said she misses you. And the big news is, the sheriff notified her they caught the guy with the knife. They figure it's just a matter of time until he rats on his partner."

"That is great news. Did she say where?"

"No, but I'm sure we'll get the whole story when she gets here tomorrow."

She handed him his pills and a glass of water. "You know you're spoiling me," he said.

"Is my patient complaining? Already?"

"No, I'm loving this. The excellent dinner, the nice conversation and good care. We never got around to talking about your mother, so don't forget where we left off."

"Okay." Shelby sighed an exaggerated sigh.

"Thank you, fair lady." He put out his hand. Shelby extended hers and Jack pressed it to his lips and then bowed slightly.

"Jack Ketchum, you are a constant surprise. I figured you for a rural Montana cowboy, but that's a very cosmopolitan gesture." To his delight, Shelby's demeanor had totally changed. She was smiling and joking; she looked and sounded happy.

"You'd be surprised what you can learn from those old Cary Grant movies," he said over his shoulder as he walked toward his room. Glancing back as he entered the hallway, Shelby was still standing there looking down at her hand and smiling.

He got ready and then slowly lowered himself onto the bed. The rails had been removed and the head was slightly elevated. It felt good and sleep beckoned quickly. As he fell asleep he saw an image of Shelby sitting atop a prancing horse, a wild beautiful look on her face, the image blurring and swirling with images of Ellie asking him what made him happy, Ellie turning blue then saying nothing at all.

Jack woke with a start and opened his eyes to rid himself of the nightmarish thoughts. He pulled back the curtain and looked out at the courtyard trees silhouetted against a bright harvest moon. *I miss you Ellie. If we could have had a son or a daughter, a part of you would still be with me and it wouldn't be so hard to let go.*

Memories of Ellie engulfed him. Petite, pretty and blond, Ellen Sorensen always the life of the party, their first meeting right here at the university his freshman year. Both dorms had thrown a party. Ellie, smiling mischievously picked Jack Ketchum. She could have had any guy there, but she approached him and asked if he would dance with her. It wasn't as much that he asked her to be his girlfriend as it was that Ellen Sorensen from Danbury, Connecticut, slipped her hand into his that night and lead him into the relationship—willingly.

Ellie, I'm feeling something that I thought died with you. And it's for a woman that belongs to someone else.

The last image as sleep claimed him was of Shelby standing knee-deep in the river holding a string of fish and telling him Ellen was in God's hands, not his.

Chapter Fourteen

After sleeping a good part of Sunday, Bobby arrived at the office Monday morning, greeted by fifteen staff members welcoming him back and expressing sympathy over the shooting. Adam greeted him as though their conversation had never taken place.

Terri followed Bobby into his office with a mug of coffee. "Wow, did I miss you," she said. "You didn't have to go away and get shot to make me realize how much I want you."

Her eagerness brought a rush of good feelings: successful and in-charge, and horny enough that he forgot his throbbing leg.

"How about dinner tonight?" Terri suggested. "I could come to your place."

"Not my place, let's go out. I need to work until seven. Is that okay with you?"

"You sure we can't go to your place?"

She must know about Shel. How the hell did she find out? Surely Dad wouldn't tell her.

"No, Oscar and Esther are there. They adore Shel, and besides I need to see and be seen."

Bobby eased himself into his chair. "Later, baby, okay? Thanks for the coffee. Now would you ask my father to come in so I can catch up on everything?"

She gave him a pouty look on the way out. Bobby took a sip of coffee and gazed at his top-notch office. The coffee was perfect.

Jamaican Blue Mountain blend, fresh ground with a touch of cinnamon. Now that's coffee. Man, it's good to be back to civilization! Glancing at his desk, he noticed that the picture of Shelby was no longer there. Bobby opened the drawer and there it was in the back corner, face down. *Strange, did Terri do that?* Taken on their forty-foot Hunter, sailing back into Marina del Rey, it showed a smiling, tanned Shelby in shorts, tee shirt, and wearing a jaunty sailor's hat. *I remember that day, glorious weather, sailing along the shore line.* He started to put it back on his desk then changed his mind. *I don't need a reminder.*

He immediately began to feel better; this was his world. Stamford Development's suite occupied the ground floor of a seven-story building on Wilshire Boulevard. Two heavy glass doors trimmed in brass and etched with *Stamford Development, Inc., Established 1975* opening into it. The other floors, leased to attorneys and stockbrokers, helped fill the parking lot with Beamers, Jaguars, Mercedes, and Lexus.

Stamford's offices had been decorated by none other than Matalyn Jeffries & Associates, L.A.'s most prestigious interior designer. An "only-only in L A" feature was a floor-to-ceiling glass wall showcasing an exterior lush garden with a waterfall. "This will guarantee no doubt in your clients' minds that they are dealing with the best, most successful development firm in the L.A. basin," Jeffries said. And she turned out to be right; they were the top firm.

Adam tapped on the door then entered. "How are you feeling? You look more rested."

"Better, thanks. I slept a lot yesterday. By any chance did you tell Terri about Shelby staying in Montana?"

"No, of course not, but she happened to be in my office when you called the morning you left. Maybe she put it together from my end of the conversation. Why do you ask?"

"Oh, just curious."

"Hey, if you need a lift anywhere, a lunch or an appointment, I'll be happy to drive you."

"Thanks but I can handle it." *Chrissake, he doesn't have a clue how that talk yesterday hit me.* Bobby had spent the rest of Saturday depressed, unable to fathom that he'd devoted his career to a game his father said did not exist. *You may not think so, Dad, but you can bet your sweet ass this is a game. I didn't land Covington and get this far to change now. I'm playing.*

Anxious to get the conversation back to business, Bobby asked what had transpired during his absence. He made notes as they talked about pending deals and new clients. Discussion concluded, Adam rose. "As far as Covington is concerned, I've talked every day with Stuart, so I suggest you call him. By the way, any word from Shelby?"

"Nope, nothing."

"That's too bad. I was hoping she would call."

"Why is that? I always had the impression you and Mom didn't totally approve of Shel, the fact she's not from an old L.A. family."

Adam shot him a disapproving look. "That's about as crazy as that game you were talking about. Martha sometimes comes across as uppity, but she admires Shelby and so do I."

Damn, why did I say that? Bobby spent the morning returning calls and making appointments. He intended to clear his desk and get working on the Covington project, Stamford Development's boldest undertaking: an environmentally friendly, up-scale shopping center on the most exclusive, most expensive real estate in southern California— the Coast Highway between Oceanside and Del Mar.

And it was his baby. He had courted Charles Covington's favor before he passed away, then become like a son to Alice Covington since her husband's death. He capitalized on his mother's long-standing friendship with her and his own USC background. He phoned Alice two or three times a week, marking it on his calendar so he wouldn't forget. He visited monthly, taking a gift or flowers and staying long enough to drink tea with her. He hated tea. He made sure Alice's birthday was special, with a gift and lunch at whatever posh restaurant she chose. Assuring her she was family, he included her in the Stamford Christmas. And it finally paid off.

The minute the ink was dry on the sales agreement, Bobby found her the perfect condo in a gated complex close to his mother. And that done, Stamford Development Inc. became owner of the sweetest piece of real estate north of the Mexican border, eighty oak-studded acres that sloped down to a broad expanse of Highway One frontage overlooking the Pacific. Bobby fairly salivated every time he thought about it. His last pitch to Alice, the one that sealed the deal, was naming the shopping center Covington Square.

"Oh my, Charles would be so proud," she had said when he made the proposal.

Bobby had a vision, a revolutionary concept of a center designed and engineered from day one as environmentally perfect as a shopping center could be. The substantial additional cost could be recouped with higher-than-average rents and he had the market study to prove it. Instead of a commercial eyesore, Covington would be an asset to the community and a model for shopping centers of the future. Endorsement by CAPE, the powerful California Alliance for the Protection of the Environment, and its president, Frederick Houghton, was the key and his ticket to the big time. National fame. He had it on good authority that if he pulled this off, every major magazine, newspaper, and network would be breaking down his door.

Environmentalists and developers; oil and water; good versus evil, natural enemies working side by side? Unheard of, impossible? Bobby intended to make it happen. There had been opposition, strong opposition from rich and influential residents of the area, all wanting to keep it in its natural state, perhaps a park. *Yeah, right, a zillion-dollar park. This is my ticket to the top and if I have to bend a couple rules, so be it. You want a park? I'll give you one, with a few hundred exclusive shops thrown in—Bobby Stamford's kind of park.*

Desk cleared, Bobby called Stuart Flaherty, Stamford's corporate attorney and his best friend. His secretary put the call right through. "How you doing, Stuart, free for lunch? I want to get caught up on Covington. How about meeting me at the Bistro?"

"Good to hear from you. I don't book lunch on Mondays so I am free. See you at one?"

Bobby and Stuart had met at USC, Stuart on a tennis scholarship. Defeating Bobby in a tournament, he offered to coach him so he could also be on the USC tennis team. Stuart coached but Bobby never made the team; instead they became fast friends. What made Stuart unique in Bobby's mind was he did not play the money game. He was a dedicated lawyer because he loved the law and, coincidentally, Stuart Flaherty was a card-carrying, tree-loving, pro-Sierra Club environmentalist.

His advice on every project, "Don't fight 'em, just do it right. It will cost a little more but in the long run it'll pay off. Time is money, right?" It was this policy, incorporated into their planning from the onset, that garnered Stamford their sterling reputation with civic and municipal bodies charged with the responsibility of overseeing development.

"Bobby, it's great to see you. Adam told me you got shot. What the heck happened?" He motioned to the crutches. While they ate Bobby told him about driving the Eagle, trying to quit smoking, the crappy healthy food and ended his story with the shooting. Stuart didn't interrupt, totally absorbed in Bobby's story. "You're lucky there's no permanent damage."

"Yeah, but it was the vacation from hell. Pretty country though, right up your alley. Rivers, lakes, forest everywhere, not many people —environmental utopia. Drove me nuts."

Stuart laughed heartily. "I remember at USC when you found out I belonged to Sierra Club, you thought I was a member of some UFO spotting group. I wasn't sure we would ever be friends, tennis or not. I figured you for a real hard-ass."

"And I figured you for a blazing liberal, an environmental whacko. Now here you are representing a development company. What's that saying about strange bedfellows?"

"It worked out better than okay, didn't it?" Stuart said, obviously amused at the anomaly.

"You're a good attorney and friend. If I haven't said thanks lately, I do so now."

Bobby listened as Stuart brought him up to date on the Covington project. After having told him years ago that he didn't need to hear "irrelevant details that only the attorney needs to understand," thankfully Stuart skipped over the glut of regulations Bobby knew existed. He went straight to the part Bobby wanted to hear. "The final step, a public hearing on the architectural elevations, is set for October 5th, a little over a month away. I plan on using the next few weeks to meet with members from the San Diego County planning staff to iron out any wrinkles."

"That sounds terrific. What do you need me to do?" Bobby said.

"Well, now that you're back, I'd like to set up another meeting with Houghton at CAPE. I've been keeping him apprised of this. He's coming around and I work with his right-hand man, which is a woman, by the way. Kathryn Alexander, a sharp gal. Here's her card. I'd like you to be there, have them hear the commitment from you. They're leery but intrigued by the project."

"What's this gal like? How old is she?" Bobby wanted to know.

"Okay, no need to use your charms on her. Kathy is legit and second in command because she's earned it. She's not your type any-way, doesn't wear makeup, loves the outdoors."

"Okay, okay, counselor, but I would still like to know how old she is."

"Hard to tell, maybe around our age. Got a little gray in her hair, but pretty. No pranks, okay? This project is getting done on merit. That's the only way I work."

"No pranks planned. I just want to be prepared, help our merit in whatever way I can." Bobby signaled for the check. "Things are coming along even better than I'd hoped."

"I hear your words but they don't match your face. For a guy who survived getting shot and is about to launch a history-making endeavor, you don't look happy."

"That's why you're a good lawyer, you don't miss a trick."

"What's up?"

"Shel didn't come back with me. She's in Montana thinking things over. She found out about Terri."

"Uh-oh, not good. I'm sorry to hear that. The two of you couldn't work it out?"

"No, and I really tried. Except for the first few days, we fought the whole trip. Soon as we got there, she was in love with the people and Montana! All of a sudden she's one of them, bashing the hell out of L.A. and everybody in LA, including me. Then the robbery happened and the whole thing blew. She's taking care of the old guy that got shot."

"How old?"

"Fifty. Why?"

"You said she loved the people. Think she might be attracted to him?"

"Are you kidding? He's a cowboy hick. Impossible."

"Nothing is impossible. Depends on the circumstances and where she's at." Stuart tapped his temple. "After Brenda and now Terri, you can't be totally surprised. Are you sure you want to be married? Maybe you'd be happier single."

"Not sure. I came back thinking to hell with Shel and marriage. Terri was right there, *is* right there ready and willing."

"Then you ought to be happy."

"I know I should."

"But?"

"I'm not, which drives me nuts and I can't figure out why. Ironic, isn't it? Terri was hired to help with the PR campaign and she's the straw that could bring down my house of cards."

Bobby took note of Stuart's thoughtful gaze. "Bobby, as your lawyer and best friend, may I offer some advice? Give Shelby the time she needs but keep the lines of communication open. It sounds cliché, but it's true. I'm sticking my neck out here but be careful with this Terri. Don't let her call the shots. You don't know if she has a hidden agenda. It would be counter-productive to let her monopolize all your time so you don't have an opportunity to think."

"You know what? I can see that being a potential problem," Bobby said.

Stuart rose. "I'll line up a meeting with Houghton and call as soon as I get a time. Maybe we can have dinner after."

"Okay, buddy, thanks," Bobby said.

They made their way out of the restaurant, Bobby hobbling along, pausing to greet clients and shake hands with acquaintances and a few secretaries.

"How ya doing, Bobby? What happened, Bobby? Let's get together, Bobby."

"Sure, sure, let's do it. Call me," Bobby replied, accompanied by a smile.

The smile was genuine. Meeting on a multi-million-dollar deal, a gourmet lunch at a posh restaurant, with expensively clad colleagues and acquaintances vying for his attention? Bobby Stamford was back and it felt damn good.

Stuart helped Bobby get into the Porsche, then peered down at him. "If you need to talk, call me, okay? And I mean that."

"Thanks, I know you do. Say hi to Vickie and the kids." *Damn, I forgot to ask about them.* For the second time on his first day back, Bobby Stamford felt a twinge of remorse.

He drove directly to Dr. Caldwell's office, dreading to face him. The nurse first checked his blood pressure, then Doc came in. "Your blood pressure is okay, 140/90. Still taking Altace?"

"Yes, and I need a refill. Could it be called in and have it delivered to the office?"

"No problem. Let's have a look at your leg, then I'll have Shirley set up some physical therapy sessions. How well you play tennis and golf and get around in general is going to depend on how serious you are about the therapy. Now let's check your weight."

Bobby drove back to the office, the visit with Caldwell turning out better than expected. The miserable food on the trip accomplished one good thing; he was four pounds lighter than when Caldwell hit the roof. The follow-up EKG was all right too, an improvement.

Only a few Stamford employee cars were in the parking lot when Bobby arrived at the office. Terri's silver Lexus was gone and his father's parking place was empty. Bobby navigated on crutches to Terri's desk and scratched a memo. *Find out what you can, ASAP, personal, business, and education on Kathryn Alexander—CAPE.*

In his office wading through the papers from Stuart, he looked up to see Terri enter promptly at seven, smelling of expensive perfume. She closed the door and clicked the lock in place. Terri had changed from her chic business suit into a pale yellow dress, tight and short.

Bobby watched her walk slowly toward him to the center of the room and then stop. "Do you like?" she said, twirling on tiptoe slowly around.

He took a long, hungry appraisal, his eyes traveling the length of her body from head to foot, out her slender, outstretched arms to graceful fingertips. She continued to turn. His glance rested on Terri's perfect round breasts, then moved down over her flat belly. The dress stopped midthigh and there were no stockings on those smooth, golden legs. She came forward to his desk, a slight smile on her lips, her eyes like a magnet pulling him in, eyes with the promise of heaven.

"Jesus, you got me going," he said.

"Good, I like getting you going." She made her way around the desk and stopped in back of him, her hands on his shoulders. "Put your arms on the desk, straight out in front of you."

"What are you going to do?" Bobby said, closing his eyes.

"You'll find out."

She started to rub his shoulders and neck, pushing his chin down to his chest. Magic fingers took away the tension and sent a shiver through his body. She rubbed slowly and firmly, bending forward with her cheek alongside his, massaging his shoulders, then out along his arms until her fingers reached his. Her hands retraced their route back up his arms. She kissed his cheek as she rubbed, kissed his neck, then the other cheek, small kisses, traveling kisses, making him hold his breath in anticipation.

Enveloped by her fragrance, he felt her smooth silky arms against his cheek as her hands massaged him. She straightened up and pulled him gently back against her; he could feel her breasts with the back of his head. He turned his head and rubbed his cheek against them, his heart beating faster. Terri turned Bobby's chair ever so slowly until he was facing her. Her eyes held his. She knelt in front of him.

"Are you in a hurry to go?" She asked, her voice a husky whisper.

Bobby couldn't speak, conscious only of her eyes and his own breathing.

Terri loosened his tie and began to unbutton his shirt, taking her time on each button. He closed his eyes again and put his head back, feeling her hands rub his chest lightly and then tangle her fingers in his chest hair. She dug her nails into his chest, little digs, making him press against her hands, wanting more. It hurt. It felt wonderful.

Terri helped Bobby out of his chair, careful of his leg, down onto the cushy green carpet in back of his desk. He lay with his shirt open, the rest of his clothes on the chair and then he watched as she slowly pulled her dress off. There was nothing underneath.

Terri climbed on top of him and he was ready for her. She rocked gently at first, then harder, her eyes closed and her head back. Bobby put his hands on her waist, eagerly swept along in her passion. "Baby, you feel so good," she whispered, then said nothing, demanding with her body that he join her.

Terri rode him, moving harder and faster until little beads of perspiration formed on her forehead. She kept moving, a look of rapture on her face. Bobby's passion could not wait. He arched his back and drove himself deeper into her. Terri had brought him with her and she was ready. They came together, a crescendo of thrusts and shudders and sounds, then silence.

Terri remained completely motionless, silent with her head down, hands resting on his bare chest. "Okay," she whispered, then slowly rolled off and onto the floor beside him. They lay side by side, staring up at the ceiling, listening to the sound of their own breathing.

Finally, Terri turned onto her side, her face close to his. He felt her warm breath on his cheek, her kiss. "Welcome back, baby. Welcome back to L.A."

Chapter Fifteen

Shelby soon learned that October in Montana meant cool mornings with a layer of sparkling dew. And, delightfully, a grand show of fall with yellow and gold leaves skittering across the landscape. For a Californian it was an exciting harbinger of change.

Jack had finished his four weeks of therapy with stoic resolve, anxious to get home and concerned about work needing to be done on the ranch before winter fully arrived. Dr. Adams said the results of Jack's therapy were nothing short of a phenomenon, how quickly his appetite returned and his steady weight gain of the pounds he'd lost. On their last visit, Dr. Adams congratulated Jack for making him look good and elicited a pledge that he would continue a "some sort of" therapy program in Troutsprings. Jack assured him that the cattle work waiting for him would be therapy "aplenty." After saying their thank-yous and goodbyes with Dr. Adams, the staff and Ken, Shelby could see it was closure for Jack. He was ready to go home.

Jack, Shelby, and Adele departed Missoula on October tenth, Adele driving north along the eastern shore of Flathead Lake. Astounded at the change in the trees, Shelby couldn't take her gaze off the patches of green pines and leafed trees ablaze in fall colors. Jack agreed to stop for lunch in Big Fork on the northeast shore of the lake, but encouraged Adele and Shelby to "get with it, no need to linger over our coffee." Adele and Shelby took his impatience in stride.

But Shelby was unprepared for the rush of memories upon arriving at Ellie's Café. She cringed thinking of her fight with Bobby the day they arrived, and then more pleasant thoughts of the evening crowds and helping Adele and visiting with the customers.

The recollection was short-lived as Jack was out of the back seat of Adele's car almost before it came to a halt. "I would so like to get down and kiss the dirt, but you two would have to help me up," he said. Jack stood in the parking lot, hands on his hips, staring at the old café with a happy smile. Adele was the first through the doors and once inside, Shelby was surprised at how good the place made her feel.

The Saturday night dinner crowd, on seeing Jack at a table, turned the evening into a celebration. Shelby tried to help Adele waitressing but she would have none of it, so Shelby had dinner with Jack and watched a display of affection like none she'd ever witnessed. Jack's neighbors and friends took turns approaching the table to pat his shoulder and others to shake his hand. She witnessed smiles and tears, toasts and laughter and promises "to get together."

The last to approach was Jim Jenkins. He looked a lot older than Jack. Bent forward in a straight line from the hip, with a slight hitch in his walk, Jenkins had lively blue eyes and a wild shock of silver hair. Jack rose to greet his life-long friend. It was obvious the two men had never hugged. Shelby watched Jim gather Jack in his arms, shaking his head as though unable to find the right words, hugging for a brief moment then slapping his shoulder with gnarled hands. Jim pulled out a handkerchief and wiped his eyes. Jack did the same with a napkin from the holder. Shelby was determined to stay close to Jack. They stayed until the last customer disappeared.

Adele approached. "You look better already, Jack. How does it feel to be home?"

Jack rose. "This was one of the best moments in this old geezer's life." He escorted her to the door. "Thank you, Adele—for everything." She offered her hand but Jack pulled her to him in a warm embrace. "I'm just glad you're okay and back home." She blew Shelby a kiss.

Jack turned off the lights and they made their way upstairs. Shelby stood before her door then turned to Jack. "Your friends are really something. You should feel very special."

He looked down at the floor. "What I feel is humble. Between you and them it was almost worth getting shot." He gave her a tired smile. Shelby stood on tiptoe to give Jack a kiss on the cheek as he instinctively turned his face to hers. Their lips met briefly, lightly, but Jack did not pull away. Instead he gathered her close in his arms and pressed his lips against her temple. Shelby lifted her face to his, Jack's lips touching hers, a sweet lingering kiss.

He pulled away. "Shelby, I…"

Shelby put her forefinger to his lips. "Good night, Jack. I am so glad you're home," she said and entered her room, the room she had shared with angry Bobby. The porcelain bird on the dresser still sat beside the picture of Jack and Ellen. The room looked exactly the same but things were no longer the same. Shelby suddenly felt overcome by uncertainty. *My God, I'm supposed to be thinking about my marriage, but I wanted him to kiss me. And more.*

Shelby donned her pajamas and got in bed, staring unseeing at a book. Jack's kiss, as innocent as it was, ignited a strong desire, difficult to ignore. There was a quiet knock on the door. Shelby cleared her throat. "Come in."

Jack had on his robe, blue pajama legs showing. "Mind if I come in for a minute?"

"Of course not, come in." She patted the blanket.

He sat down on the edge of the bed. "There's a lot going on in that pretty head of yours."

Shelby avoided his eyes and propped the book up straight. "What makes you say that?"

Well, for one thing, you've got the book upside down." Jack reached over and turned the book upright, then replaced it in her hands.

"Oh, for goodness sakes. I don't know what's wrong with me."

"Would you like to talk about it?"

Shelby closed the book and laid it aside. "I'm not sure I know what you mean."

"I'm trying to figure out if that was your doing or mine. If I did something wrong, I didn't want to go to bed with you in here mad at me."

"No, Jack, I'm not mad. That was a goodnight kiss, nothing more." Eyebrows raised, his look signaled he was wondering if she had something else to say. Shelby remained silent.

Jack exhaled, his shoulders relaxed. "Okay, I just didn't want to upset you. You were kind of quiet at dinner anyway. Are you all right? I wish you would talk to me."

Shelby clasped her hands together and shrugged her shoulders. "All of a sudden I'm not sure…about anything, Jack. This is your home, you belong here and you're well now. Maybe it's time for me to go. I don't know what to do. I feel all mixed up."

Jack moved closer. He took her in his arms and stroked her back. "This is your home as long as you want it to be. You haven't given yourself a chance to figure things out since you've been here. You were fighting with Bobby when you got here. You tried like hell to keep him happy your whole stay and since the shooting you've been fussing over me. Now it's time for Shelby to start thinking about what *you* want to do. Big things take time, Shelby. Hard answers don't come easy. Give yourself a chance, okay?"

"You're doing fine now, Jack. You don't need me anymore."

He pulled away and stared at her. "Is that a fact? I've got a place that's falling apart and a certified California builder on the premises. What do you mean, I don't need you?"

Taken aback, Shelby wasn't sure how to respond. "Really, you would like some help? Are you talking about here or the ranch?"

"Take your pick, but I was thinking here. Talk about being needed, good Lord, Shelby, you've come to the right place. I have so much work to do winterizing everything. What if some Californian puts his foot through the porch downstairs? I'll get my butt sued off."

"I could fix that," she said automatically, remembering the loose and broken boards on the porch. "If you want me to, I could replace the whole porch and fix the railing while I'm at it." She leaned back and pulled the covers up to her chin. "I would like to do that," she said.

"All right! That's what I want to hear, a lady with a mission."

"Okay, I'll take your word. Adele told me the same thing—give myself some time."

Jack's hand rested on Shelby's blanket-covered shin. "Having your help these two months is why I got well so fast. It wasn't the medicine or the physical therapy. It was having you around. Our walks, our talks and all the care you showed me. Do you have any idea how much your being here means to me?"

She felt like Jack must have read her mind. "I... no. I guess I didn't realize it."

"Well then, I am sorry." Jack reached his hand forward, inviting Shelby to grasp it. He put his other hand over hers. "I'm kinda walking a fine line here, so stop me any time. You popped into my life one day out of the blue and, somehow now you're here." Jack touched his heart. He looked at her earnestly. "Adele too, she told me the same thing. I'm sorry things are messed up between you and Bobby. I'm sorry you're unhappy. I'd do anything to bring back your smile and that sparkle in your eyes when you rode Solitaire." Jack looked down, "And you would leave a big hole in our lives if you left now. I know you are trying to work things out and I respect that, but I want you to consider this your home. Not just this building," he looked around the room, "but here with me and Adele. We don't want you to go."

Shelby exhaled a deep breath, instantly feeling better. "Thank you, Mr. Jack Ketchum."

He smiled at the thank you. "A bit of unsolicited advice?"

"What's that?"

"Maybe if you were to deal with some of the unfinished business, you'd feel like you're making progress. What do you think?"

"Like Bobby? I'm not sure what you mean."

"Like your dad. I know that bothers you, I saw it on your face. I think you ought to write him and let him know you're here and invite him for a visit. And if you want to call Bobby and talk or scream and holler—whatever, just do it. This is your home. If you want to invite your mom, do it. That's dealing with the things that make you feel uncertain. You don't have to decide anything right away. Take your time."

Jack stood up, smoothed his robe, a serious look on his face. "Dr. Ketchum, psychiatric help, five cents." His serious look gave way to a grin and then he kissed her on the top of the head. "Good night, Shelby, sleep well. We'll talk again in the morning."

Shelby turned off the lamp. *He's right. I haven't heard from Bobby, haven't called him either. If I want to take control of my life, I need to get started.* Shelby felt her body relax, the hollow uncertain feeling beginning to subside, replaced by the prospect of fixing the café's porch. *I can work at the same time I try to figure things out—I'd much rather do that than just sit around. I'll be helping Jack and myself. That was a great idea he had!*

Shelby awoke Monday filled with a new resolve. She had an early breakfast with Jack, and together they took a look at the porch. Determining what she needed, Shelby phoned her list of the lumber and supplies to Builders Supply in Columbia Falls and said she would be in later in the day to pick it up. She drove Jack to the ranch, but before she would leave him she extracted his promise to wait for Ronnie and Chuck before doing any lifting.

Back at the café, Shelby took action on the first of her issues; she wrote to her father.

Monday, October 3rd

Dear Dad,

Don't faint—a letter from me and it isn't Christmas or your birthday. I wanted to say thank you for my birthday gift and let you know that I am living in Montana—for now. Without going into the details, Bobby and I have separated and I'm not sure whether it will be temporary or permanent. If that sounds a bit uncertain, it's because I am.

I am staying with a gentleman, Jack Ketchum, at his café-home. That reads a lot different than the situation, he is strictly a friend. A couple months ago he was shot in a robbery in his café and I helped take care of him. So when I needed a place to stay while I think things over, Jack said I could stay here. What's that saying about truth being stranger than fiction?

I've thought a lot about the argument we had when you left for Peru. There hasn't been a day go by since then that I haven't regretted it. Mom is busy with her own life and sadly the same is true of my husband, neither seem to need me in theirs. I believe that was the essence of our misunderstanding, wanting to be a part of someone's life that you love and care about.

I hope this letter finds you well. I am so hoping to hear from you soon! Please write to me in care of Jack Ketchum, P.O. Box 17, Troutsprings, MT. 59905-0017.

Much love,
Shelby

When Shelby discovered she didn't have her father's address, she placed a call to Esther.

"Esther, hello! How are you and Oscar and...everybody?"

"*Señora, hola tambien!* We miss you very much is how we are. Nothing is the same without you." Her voice resonated with sadness. "Are you coming home soon?"

"Not for a while, but I miss you and Oscar too. How is Bobby doing?"

"I think Señor Stamford misses you. We sometimes see him sitting in the living room in the dark. May I ask if he has called you?"

"No, I haven't talked with him since he left."

"*Madre de Dios*, I do not understand these things."

Esther put Oscar on the phone, and a few minutes later, Enrique. He sounded excited, telling her that all her hard work teaching him had paid off. "I just received notice that I passed the exam. I am now a licensed contractor, thanks to you!" She could hear the pride in his voice. Cherokee was doing fine, the other horses too. "Skyline is humming right along, boss, but it's not the same without you," Enrique said quietly. "But hey, whatever you need to do to take care of yourself, know that I am handling things just like you taught me, okay?"

Esther came on the phone again with the address, then bade Shelby goodbye. *"Adios, mi hija."* Shelby could hear her crying. *My daughter, she called me her daughter.* Teary-eyed, Shelby pictured Esther with her salt-and-pepper hair, white apron over her plain black dress, and her ever-present Nike shoes. Shelby brushed away tears, then took a deep breath and dialed Bobby's number at the office. *Item number two on my to-do list.* A cool female voice answered.

"May I speak to Bobby? This is Shelby."

"Just a moment, please. I'll see if he's in."

Her heart pounding, she wondered what to expect. Bobby answered immediately. "Shel... hi! How are you?" He sounded cheerful.

She breathed a sigh of relief. "Fine, Bobby. I just wanted to say hello and find out how your leg is and how you're doing."

"I'm great, Shel, really great! The leg is coming along, but because I sit more than I should, it hurts at the end of the day, otherwise it's good."

"I'm glad to hear that." Suddenly not sure what to say, she hesitated. "Well, I know you're really busy, so I—"

"Wait, Shel, please. Don't hang up." His forced cheerfulness disappeared. "I'm really glad you called. Tell me how are you doing? Are you feeling okay?"

Her throat felt bone-dry and constricted. "I'm doing... okay, I guess, but I just talked to Esther and she started to cry. So am I now. That hurts."

"I know. They're both sad. They sort of move around the house quietly without saying much. They did ask if they could have Enrique and his wife and daughter over for dinner to celebrate his passing his test. I said sure."

"That was nice of you, Bobby. Thank you." There was another long pause.

"Shel?"

"What?"

"I'm afraid to say much. I seem good at sticking my foot in my mouth. But I have to ask, have you given any thought to coming home… do you miss me?" His voice broke.

A wave of uncertainty engulfed Shelby. "I have, but it seems that the more I think about coming home, the more uncertain I get."

"You didn't answer the rest of my question. Do you miss me?"

"I miss how it could be, Bobby. I'm the one who is calling, if that counts for anything." A tear rolled down her cheek. *Damn. I don't want to cry.*

"I'm afraid to call, Shel. I want to give you the space you need and I don't know what to say. I usually make matters worse. But I miss you, Shel. I wish you would come home and things get back to normal."

Shelby tried, but could not hold back her tears; she had no doubt Bobby could hear. "I think that may be the problem, Bobby. Normal is good for you but it isn't for me."

Shelby heard a muffled "Tell him I'll be right with him," then Bobby said, "Shel, dammit I've got a meeting right now on Covington. Can I call you back? How about I call tonight from home? That way we can really talk. I want to. Want me to call you on your cell?"

"It's on the fritz and I haven't had a chance to get it fixed. Let me give you the café landline." Shelby gave him the café number, then thoughtfully hung up, her mind filled with his sad tone, his saying how he missed her and wanted to talk. *Is there any hope for us or am I being a fool again for even considering it?*

Shelby dropped off the mail on the way to Columbia Falls and, after picking up the building materials, she arrived at the ranch in time to pick up Jack.

That evening they dined on Bobby's Santa Fe sandwich addition to the café's menu. Jack's face had a drawn look. He was clearly exhausted and sat willingly while Shelby cleared away the dishes. She urged him to retire early, saying she was going to watch television. He offered no resistance, thanked her for fixing dinner and slowly climbed the stairs.

With her cell phone on the fritz and no phone in her room to receive Bobby's call, Shelby turned on the television over the bar. She turned off the overhead wagonwheel chandeliers, the television providing sufficient light. Bobby had said he was going to call from home and there was a one-hour time difference. She wondered if he remembered that.

Shelby waited, minimally involved in the television program, sitting for a while and then getting up to stretch and check her watch. *He agreed we need to talk and said he wanted to talk.* Shelby tried to dismiss it but hope did emerge, hope that Bobby would tell her he wanted to work things out, that he valued their marriage and wanted to make her happy. The phone remained silent. Shelby picked up the receiver to make sure it was working.

It was. The café was cold. She couldn't go upstairs to get a sweater, she might miss the call. Shelby paced to keep warm, a desperate feeling taking hold. *I don't get it, he said he would call. Even Bobby is not that callous. Hopefully he's okay.* Minutes dragged on; she picked up the receiver again and heard the flat hum of a dial tone. Standing up, leaning against the wall, the realization hit.

It took her breath away. *He's not going to call. He never intended to call.*

Chapter Sixteen

The following morning the sun had barely risen when Shelby attacked the rickety porch with a vengeance. Driven by silent fury, she started ripping away the old wood with a heavy-duty nail bar. Anyone observing her could easily have identified her rage: the clenched jaw, the force and abandon with which she worked. How long she kept it up she didn't keep track, but all of a sudden she realized she had better stop. The muscles in her arms felt on fire. Glancing at the sun midway to its zenith told her she'd been going at it for over three hours!

Shelby sat down on the steps and tried pouring coffee from her thermos into the cup. Hands trembling, she held onto it with both hands as she drank, her eyes taking in the destruction she accomplished. *Good therapy! I can finish removing the porch today.* Resting as she sipped her coffee, she noticed a lot of pick-ups rumble by in both directions loaded with firewood. Some horns sounded and arms and hands appeared, waving at her as they sped by. She determinedly willed away thoughts of last night's telephone vigil and waved at the passersby in return.

Coffee finished, she walked around to the back of the café to survey the growing pile of debris—half the old wood with another half to go. Frantic movement close by in the trees caught her eye. It was chipmunks darting up and down their vertical freeways in the poplars and aspens carrying winter food. She spotted two gray squirrels with big, bushy tails doing the same thing. They kept a wary eye on her, fussing when she moved.

Shelby slowed the speed of her work the rest of the day. Mid-afternoon it turned cold and blustery, gusts creating dust devils in the dirt parking lot, swirling leaves in a circular motion. She wore her customary baseball cap and worn jeans she'd brought from home, and borrowed one of Jack's heavy flannel work shirts. The thick shirt felt good and so did the familiar work. Jack arrived from the ranch around 4:30 p.m. just as Shelby was cordoning off the porch with yellow tape to keep traffic from falling through exposed studs. That night Shelby's fatigue matched Jack's.

The next few days flew by, Shelby refusing to think about Bobby but making her daily call to Enrique to discuss Skyline business. She focused her concentration on the porch project and began work from the time Jack left early in the morning and quit when he arrived at the café. On Thursday Shelby had enough new wood installed that customers could enter the café through the front doors. During that week she received four remodeling job offers.

The project took two weeks to remove the rotted wood and replace it with pressure-treated outdoor board. Wide, sturdy steps now ran the width of the building along with a new railing. Shelby had spotted a heavy snow grate when she picked up her lumber from Builders Supply. Wanting to surprise Jack and Adele, she bought two of them and inlaid both of them side-by-side in the porch in front of the double doors. She finished the job by staining the new lumber to assure it would hold up against the rain and snow.

Her first day after finishing, Shelby noticed Jack. He looked exhausted with no color in his face. They had settled into a routine, breakfasting together, sharing the news of the day, then each went to work. Sunday and Monday nights when the café was closed, Shelby prepared dinner for the two of them. She and Jack both thanked Virgil and Adele for continuing to operate the café. Right now Jack's re-entry into ranch work left him totally exhausted at the end of the day.

The first Sunday after she finished the porch, Shelby declared, "Time out," insisting Jack take the day off and asked if they could "go out to dinner," and if so, "Where?" To her surprise, he agreed and chose a charming Italian restaurant in Pine Ridge. They enjoyed their dinner with wine and then headed back to Troutsprings, both admitting they were exhausted.

As Jack drove his truck south along the ridge, Shelby glanced at the lights of homes scattered atop the foothills. A cold blustery wind whipped the giant pine trees with full force. Clouds scurried across the darkened sky, intermittently blotting out the moon. Jack said it was another front from the north. Shelby could smell the rain in the air and feel the chill. "Nice evening, huh?" she ventured as Jack swerved to miss a pot hole.

"Uh-huh. Nice," he said absent-mindedly.

Shelby looked over at him and waited. He seemed deep in thought. Finally, he turned to meet her gaze. "Where were you?" She smiled at him.

"I was just thinking that we're both working so hard, we're too tired at night to talk. How are you? Feeling less mixed up?"

"Better than when we first got back from Missoula. I don't feel as much an outsider now. When I was working on the porch, it seemed everyone who drove by honked and waved at me."

Jack turned on the truck's heater. "That surprises you?" he said.

"It did, at the time. Why? Is that funny?" she said, feeling a bit defensive.

"Well, it occurs to me you can take the gal out of L.A. but you can't take L.A. out of the gal. That's a city attitude."

"Jack Ketchum, you are an anti-urban snob," Shelby exclaimed.

"Guilty for sure. I've only been to L.A. once on vacation with Ellie. We did the tourist thing, Disneyland and some other places, but I didn't take to it. Not many people down there I'd care to take up with, which I guess is why you were such a shock."

Shelby glanced over at him. He looked serious. "Bobby and I've discussed this, but it usually ended up in an argument. Now I see why. It isn't fun being on the receiving end."

"But I said you were different. You don't fit the typical L.A.—"

"You're digging yourself in a hole, Jack Ketchum. I'm different now, but ten years ago I might not have appreciated Montana or the people because I was part of that world."

"Nope, you were never like that. That's the world that produced Bobby Stamford," Jack argued. "C'mon, I bet you know a lot of guys just like him, the ones that think money is power. And if they didn't have it to buy or do what they want, they'd be complaining all over the place. Bobby belongs in that world. He couldn't last a winter in this one. You're not like that."

"He has some good qualities," Shelby said. "You make him sound like he can't do anything and he buys people."

"You going to tell me that's not true?"

"No, dammit, I can't, but for some reason I don't like hearing you say it."

"Then you must still be in love with the jerk."

Shelby glanced at Jack, his hands tightly gripping the wheel. Stung by his condemnation, she said nothing, both of them remaining silent for the rest of the ride.

* * *

Jack lay in his bed, hands behind his head, staring into the darkness. He'd just trod on forbidden ground criticizing Bobby, a revealing mistake. Shelby reacting the way she did told him she still loved Bobby, the realization hurting a lot more than he thought it would. Before their discussion in the car, Jack experienced the same rush of desire for her, the same way he felt on their ride around the ranch and when she kissed him the night they returned from Missoula.

Admitting he had that feeling most of the time now, a mixture of desire, respect, need, and protectiveness, it dawned that he had fallen in love with Shelby Stamford. *Too bad, Ketchum, you're in for a world of hurt.* Jack thought back to Ellie, how much he loved her and now three years later, out of the blue a woman from L.A. happens to show up in his life and awakens a need in him. *How ironic is that. Three years living in a cocoon, then I fall in love with another man's wife.* Seeing no answer, he forced his thoughts to what immediately lay ahead—the ranch.

He awoke the next morning welcoming fall chores; they would leave no time for hurt feelings and disappointment. Standard chores meant bringing in the herd from the open range to the winter pasture closer to the barn. Next came branding and vaccinating the stock, culling the yearlings and weaning them from the cows, and determining which cows and bulls he would offer for sale in December, and bulk them up. It also meant repairing broken fences and fixing equipment.

He and his neighbor Jim Jenkins had used the buddy system for as long as Jack could remember, sharing chores, major pieces of equipment, and repairs that inevitably went with them. Jack had grown up with Ed, Clay, and Darryl Jenkins, all of whom inherited their father's work ethic and values. Their fall chores already completed, they were ready to help Jack.

Jack felt stronger but far from fully recovered from the shooting, the major lingering effect exhaustion at the end of the day. Dr. Adams had said it could take as little as six months and a maximum of a year to return to normal. Unfortunately Jack needed to be back now, ready to face long days of strenuous work. High schoolers Ronnie and Chuck, both well-muscled from farm work, helped afternoons when they weren't busy after school, both boys eager to add to their car-money fund. With the round-up scheduled to begin the following morning, Jack spent the day getting things ready. It would take two full days to get all the cattle in. The Jenkins sons would be over at dawn. Old Jim said he'd help until late afternoon like he always did, riding his favorite bay stallion.

Satisfied he was fairly organized, at four o'clock Jack quit and headed back to the café. Not long after he arrived, he started pouring himself a beer when Shelby entered. She and Adele had spent the day shopping in Missoula. "Wow, what'd you do, buy out every store?" Shelby must have had a dozen bags in her arms.

"I tried, but this was all I could carry. Oh, Jack, Adele and I had so much fun! I am really looking forward to tomorrow," she said, setting the packages on a table. She approached the bar. Relieved and grateful she no longer looked or sounded angry, he asked if she'd like a beer.

"You bet, then dinner please. I'm starving, then straight to bed because I'm exhausted."

"Well, I've got the perfect meal for you, chicken grilled to perfection and sweet potatoes." Jack picked up on her mood, over dinner listening to her talk about her day, then after dinner recognizing a tired, happy Shelby, they both climbed the stairs.

* * *

Up at dawn the next morning, he was downstairs at the stove, coffee ready, eggs and sausages sizzling on the griddle when he heard Shelby on the stairs. He turned around and what he saw took his breath away. Shelby, her slender shapely frame clad in tight jeans, a denim shirt and jacket, a red farmer's handkerchief around her neck, and feet thrust into new cowboy boots. On her head, a straw cowboy hat encircled by a leather band was pulled low on her forehead.

And to his enormous relief, she was smiling at him. *Maybe I misread her reaction last night. I certainly hope so.* He whistled. "You look like Ms. Montana, not a cowpoke." She turned around, hand on her hip, the sight of her sending electric current through him.

"What'd'ya think of your new cowhand, Montana?" she drawled.

"I think Montana might as well throw in the towel right now. He doesn't have a chance." With that, Jack tossed up a spatula full of sausage links with one hand and caught them with the plate in his other hand.

"Don't you drop my breakfast!" She was laughing. "I don't work well when I'm hungry."

"I'm going to have trouble working at all," Jack said with grateful seriousness.

He was amazed at how quickly she caught on to what needed to be done. They split into three teams of two, old Jim and Clay were one, Darryl and Ed the other. He teamed with Shelby to round up the herd from the range across Stagecoach Road from the ranch. Jack watched her riding Lolli, amazed at her ease maneuvering stubborn cows and their young in the right direction. She instinctively guided the mare to the left or right, or let Lollie react and either press or hold back. And he could tell she loved it, waving her hat and hollering an excited *yahoo* when she outfoxed a stubborn cow. The Jenkins soon forgot

Shelby was female and even forgave her for being from "*Califor-niahhh.*" She earned their respect with horse savvy and hard work.

Jack wondered what her outlook would be the following morning. Shelby groaned when she rose from her chair at breakfast but there was a smile on her face. It took two full days to gather up the herd scattered over the large summer ranges. They drove the slow, bawling, obstinate creatures around rock outcroppings and trees, through double gates that led to the winter pasture on the south side of Stagecoach Road. At times, dust billowed up and around them so thick they could hardly see.

It took until five o'clock for the herd to be secured, the air frosty from a cold wind blowing straight from Canada. The Jenkins crew said their goodbyes as soon as the last steer went through the gate, dispersed into either one of the smaller winter enclosures or the barbed-wire pastures to keep steers separated until vaccinations and branding could be completed. The final chore: the cattle needed to be fed.

Jack transferred large round hay bales from the pole barn into the back of his pickup, where he remained. Shelby's job was to drive into the pasture. She used the running board to get up and into the driver's seat of Jack's Ford Super Duty Dually Diesel "monster truck" as she called it, then drove into the pasture. Together they rolled the bales out of the truck bed and broke out the hay on the ground into a long line.

After the last bale was dumped, Jack looked up at Shelby, standing in the truck bed. Standing tall, she was taking in the scene, the cattle, the setting sun and mountains, seemingly oblivious to the cold and dust. Strands of hay clung to her clothes and hair, her ponytail had loosened and tendrils of hair curled about her face.

"Now you look like a cowpoke." Jack smiled up at her, his hand resting on the tailgate.

"I feel like one!" Grabbing the truck bed's side wall, she vaulted over it landing on the ground with both feet, startling a few cows. "Ta-dah!!" she said and came up laughing.

"You're showing off again, lady. I couldn't even do that!" He laughed, remembering the way she jumped off Solitaire.

It was dark by the time they took care of Lolli and Solitaire. "Please say you're super tired too or I'm going to feel like the Ancient Mariner." He glanced over at her. Her hat was off, a faint smile on her lips. Above her eyebrows Shelby's skin was white, the rest of her face a light sienna shade of Montana dirt.

"I'm pooped," she said. "A hot bath is what I need."

"Good, then it's not just me." Though round-up was muscle-straining, dirty work, Jack was encouraged. It was getting done, Shelby was at his side, and he needed nothing more.

The next three weeks were a flurry of the same long dusty days filled with bawling cattle. They worked from dawn until dusk. Jack and Shelby establishing a morning ritual of kibitzing who could groan the best; he won more than half the time. It took two of those three weeks and all the help the veterinarian, the Jenkins clan, and Shelby could give, to get the herd vaccinated. The following week they spent branding and administering pregnancy tests. She rode, branded, and lunched with the Jenkins, plying them with questions about past round-ups. Shelby watched one steer get castrated, then refused to watch another.

For Jack, the chores were a joy, Shelby beside him helping, joking and making him feel alive. He often caught himself admiring the way she rode and moved. Sometimes when she became aware of him staring at her, she would touch the brim of her hat with her gloved hand and give him a smile that made his knees weak. To his delight, she seemed happier than he had ever seen her. Problems, Bobby, or

talk of L.A. never arose, causing Jack to picture Shelby sharing the
ranch with him, riding on their property, spending snowy winters by
the fire. The more he gave into this fantasy, the more he felt an
underlying panic of her suddenly announcing she was returning to
L.A. and Bobby.

When that happened, Jack had to force himself to think only about
the present.

Work was halted an entire day by an unexpected trip to Kalispell
when Jack was called by the district attorney to testify against the
thieves at the Flathead County Courthouse. It forced him to re-live the
shooting, remember the fear, the pain and struggle to regain his
strength. He tried concentrating on being grateful that he survived, and
did fine until the bailiff marched the two men into the courtroom, both
dressed in jailhouse orange. They looked Jack in the eye, a smirk on
both faces and contempt in their eyes. Jack was half over the railing
separating them when the bailiff grabbed him. Only Shelby's and
Adele's forceful warnings calmed him down.

Because of the shooting, the start of fall chores had been delayed
an entire month, finishing in late November instead of mid-October.
Ordinarily that would have frustrated him, but not now. The cattle
were taken care of and the rest would just have to wait until spring.

Back at the ranch the following day, Saturday, Jack thanked Jim
Jenkins, paid his sons, and handed Ronnie and Chuck their final ranch
checks just as the sun set. Frosty cold with the wind blowing and light
fading, Jack and Shelby headed back to the café, looking forward to
celebrating completion of fall chores over dinner at the café.

The dinner crowd was rowdy. Adele blamed it on the full moon.
As they ate, Jack and Shelby talked about cattle and ranching and
made plans to drive back to the ranch the following day. She wanted to
see it again now that the work was all done.

"Well, you've completed your first round-up," Jack said, toasting her with a glass of beer. "You came through like a veteran. What do you think?"

Shelby raised her glass. "I think I'll never look at a steak the same way again."

Chapter Seventeen

Shelby was pleased when she came down Sunday morning; Jack had brunch all prepared and he looked rested. He greeted her with a light kiss on the lips then Shelby even surprised herself, kissing him back and not so lightly either. "Hey, I liked that!" he told her. They lingered over coffee, the Kalispell and Missoula newspapers, then Shelby asked if they could drive to the ranch.

They arrived around noon, Shelby drinking in the sight of the bright sun overhead, the impressive log house silhouetted against the dark forest and mountains. All around her a strong wind ripped the last of the leaves from the trees, skipping them along the ground like tiny colorful acrobats. The sight made Shelby smile as did Jack. He looked as happy as she'd ever seen him, a peaceful kind of joy. The thought occurred that never in their ten years of marriage had she ever seen an expression like that on Bobby's face. *Don't think about him now.*

She glanced at the smokeless river-rock chimney rising above the ranch house and wished she could be inside with Jack, a fire in the giant fireplace and good smells coming from the kitchen. After their frenzied month, the ranch felt serene and quiet, the polar opposite of everything L.A., which at the moment seemed a world away.

Another thought occurred to her that if this were indeed her home, she would cherish its beauty, the golden acres of hay, the trees and river that formed its border, the stunning house and the life it represented.

Dangerous thoughts, Shelby, what about your life in L.A., what about Bobby? The thought of Bobby not calling her back wiped out any positive thoughts of him and L.A. She took Jack's hand, wanting to walk the grounds. They paused to watch stock graze on dwindling piles of hay and she commented on the clouds skittering across the sky. She walked up to a pen of yearlings and watched the frisky calves chasing each other. "This place is fantastic, Jack. I loved every day working with you. Do you remember when you asked me what made me happy and I had no answer? Ask me now."

"I do remember. Okay, beautiful Shelby, what makes you happy?"

"This moment, the vista," she said gesturing at the mountains. "These little guys, happy as can be. Everything as it should be."

Jack nodded. "I know what you mean. It's a sense of peace, a feeling of things being in order. I'm glad we came out, Shelby." He climbed up on the corral fence and hooked his heels on the second rung. "I love it here, it does something," he touched his heart. "It's hard work but ranching has been a good life for me. I find it surprising that a gal from L.A. could feel the same way." His gaze and smile spoke volumes and made her heart race.

Shelby looked up at him framed against the blue-purple mountains in the background, a thoughtful expression on his tanned handsome face. Everything about Jack Ketchum seemed to radiate peace, everything except when she caught him looking at her—like right now. His blue eyes staring down at her signaled he wanted her.

Shelby stood motionless as he climbed down from the fence and gathered her in his arms. He had hugged her before in a friendly embrace; this time it was different. She could smell his aftershave, feel his warmth and his strength as his hands pulled her tighter against him.

"You are a special man, Jack. I've never met anyone like you—ever." Shelby said, her lips seeking his. Jack responded with a kiss, a lingering kiss where she could feel his heart beating fast under her hand. Shelby broke Jack's hold and without either of them speaking a word, she led him toward the barn. Once inside, she waited as he pulled the heavy door shut then slid the bar into place, red lights beginning to flash in her mind. *If you do this, Shelby Stamford, you can't take it back.* Now it was her heart beating fast.

Jack turned back to her and took her hands in his, warm hands, strong hands. "Are you sure about this?" he asked in a husky whisper. Jack Ketchum, ever the gentleman, was offering her the opportunity to change her mind though his voice and touch said he wanted her. The flashing red lights vanished as quickly as they appeared.

"Absolutely," she said. She wanted him every bit as much as he wanted her.

Jack led her up to the loft, removed his jacket and asked for hers then spread both on the soft bed of new hay. Shafts of sunlight streamed down through the skylights, bathing the loft in a golden glow. Shelby first removed her jeans and boots then Jack did the same, the still angry surgery scar on his chest a glaring reminder how close she had come to losing him. She sat down on the jackets, unaware of the cold, her heart racing.

Jack knelt down beside her and helped her out of her sweater. Eyes never leaving his, she lay back as he rolled up the sweater and put it under her head. His eyes traveled over her. "You are so beautiful, Shelby." She waited as he rubbed his hands together to warm them, then gently cupped her breasts, kissing her face, her throat, her breasts, her stomach. Soft kisses, sweet kisses, kisses tinged with passion, until she called his name.

"Jack, please. Make love to me. I want you."

She gazed up at him as Jack entered her, recognizing need and desire and longing on his handsome face, the same feelings she was experiencing! *Is this real or am I dreaming?* No, it was real. Jack was here, strong and warm, whispering her name, moving gently at first then harder. Wanting nothing to do with gentleness she moved with him, coaxing, demanding, rocking with such fierceness that it brought them both to a climax, sending Shelby soaring, circling, and tumbling, then floating back to earth.

She heard him moan and whisper her name. Withdrawing, he supported himself on his elbows and looked into her eyes. "My God, Shelby, was that real?"

Her answer was to kiss him again, a lingering kiss which, to her amazement, rekindled her desire and evidently his too. As he returned her kiss, she rolled them over, mounted him and began moving again, enticing him slowly this time. They made love again, taking their time, enjoying each other's body slowly building to a climax that lasted longer than the first, exploding through her body and the deep recesses of her mind where hurt and betrayal lay hidden.

Shelby rolled off onto her side, her head resting on his shoulder. "Now I'm cold," she murmured. "But gloriously happy." Jack kissed her forehead, pulled a jacket around her, and held her tight against him, his warmth, his strength and closeness eliciting the same feeling she experienced standing in the river, wonder and joy! *I've never felt this with Bobby.* As wonderful as the feeling was, its revelation came as a shock.

The café was dark and quiet when they returned from the ranch. Jack told her he needed food. Clad in pajamas and robes, they hurried downstairs to the café kitchen. "Wow, Jack, listen to that wind. Is this a regular Montana storm or is it working up to something major?" She waited, but Jack was peering in the refrigerator. "Hey, cowboy! Are you ignoring me?" she said.

Jack smiled and shook his head. "Regular storm. Nothing special.

Not ignoring you. I just don't have a care in the world. I am alive, totally in the present, and sad memories laid to rest. All because of you. How's that for an answer?" She had to laugh; he looked joyously happy.

Shelby made pasta with left-over vegetables and fresh tomatoes, then Jack added some cut-up cooked chicken from the frig. After she served it up on two plates, Jack carried their dinners upstairs on a large tray ahead of her as she followed with a bottle of Chardonnay and wine glasses. She sat in the middle of Jack's king-size bed as he settled the tray in between them. He poured their wine and raised his glass. "To the most beautiful woman in Montana."

"To the most handsome Montana cowboy and soft, sweet-smelling hay." They clinked glasses and then Jack shook his head and laughed.

"Exactly what are you laughing about, Jack Ketchum?"

"Everything! You drive me wild with desire. You're so beautiful I can't believe you're here with me. And just know that if I am in the middle of a fantasy, I never want to wake up."

"It's no dream, Jack." Shelby leaned close and kissed him. "It's very real." She marveled at him, his expressive blue eyes and happy smile, only for her. And for the first time in ten years she fell asleep wrapped in a loving man's arms.

Bright sun greeted her Monday morning. It streamed through the window of Jack's room onto her face, rousing her from sleep, bright rays stretching across the bed enveloping Jack, asleep beside her. *Making love with you was a different experience.* Admitting she had pondered that revelation, but she was still unsure exactly what made it so.

She recalled making love with Bobby but then was distracted by Jack rolling onto his side, his face towards her, his hair mussed, hands clasped together under his chin. Yesterday in the loft he had been demanding, patient, passionate and sweet at the same time, but thoughtful too, clearly caught up in her passion, complementing it, enjoying it and making it his own. It dawned that Jack gave her not only his body but his heart. *You and I made love, Bobby and I had sex, you give heart and soul—what a difference.*

Shelby grinned, guiding a thick strand her hair lightly over Jack's forehead. He rubbed his forehead and burrowed deeper into the pillows. She did it again, this time dragging her hair over his nose; he swatted it in his sleep. Chuckling, this time she did it across Jack's lips. His eyes flew open and the instant recognition registered, Jack grabbed her with the quickness of a cat, wrestling her onto her back, kissing her neck and blowing on it, sending Shelby into fits of laughter. She tried to get away but he held her down, kissing and tickling until she gave up.

"Okay, okay," she managed to say. "Stop or I'm going to develop a permanent stutter."

After they showered and dressed they went downstairs, Jack wanting to know what she wanted for breakfast. About to answer, Shelby heard a knock on the door. Jack opened it and greeted Julie, Troutsprings' postmistress, who handed Shelby an envelope. "A registered letter from Peru!" she said, clearly impressed. "I've never had a letter from Peru and it being registered I thought I would bring it over."

"Ohmigosh, it's from Dad!" Shelby thanked Julie profusely and heard Jack thank her too. She had the letter opened before the door closed.

5 November

Dearest Shelby,
What a wonderful surprise to get your letter. The news about

you and Bobby surprised me, as did Mr. Ketchum getting shot and you being right there when it happened. I hope this letter finds you well and Mr. Ketchum fully recovered. Thank you, Shelby, for bringing our situation out in the open. It was way overdue and I am so sorry. I should have understood how you felt about my leaving. The argument at LAX was the symptom, not the disease and I regret my part in it and that it has kept us apart for so long. I miss you, Shelby. I could really use a hug from my favorite daughter.

I have more stored-up vacation days than I can use in my lifetime and I need a break from the dirt and heat, not to mention work. I've always wanted to see Montana. Are there hotels nearby? If it is okay with you and, depending of course on Mr. Ketchum's condition, I will see if I can't arrange some time off. Please let me know.

Love, Dad

Through teary eyes, she watched Jack pour coffee into two mugs and hand one to her. Shelby handed him the letter. "I can't believe that's all it took—a short note. Why didn't I write before, why didn't he? If you hadn't hounded me, Jack, I may never have written."

He read it then handed it back to her. "But you did and he responded by return mail. That should tell you something."

"Are you sure it's okay with you if he comes for a visit?"

Jack lifted his coffee mug in a toast. "Are you serious? More than okay. I'm looking forward to meeting him. The question is how do you feel about seeing him?"

Shelby paused. "Excited. A little nervous, a tiny bit angry. If I hadn't written, would he? Or would things have stayed the way they were, forever?"

"Who knows, Shelby, but my gut says don't dwell on the why, just appreciate the what is. Life is too short to question good news, take my word for it."

Shelby giggled. "Another turnip-truck insight. Do you ever tire of being right?"

"Tough job but somebody's gotta do it, and I seem to be the only one on that turnip truck." Jack started whistling as he started their breakfast.

Shelby re-read her father's letter, wondering what he would think of Montana, of Jack Ketchum, and a daughter he hadn't seen in five years. So much had changed since she last saw him; the move to the Santa Monica house and Skyline Construction. But there were also things that hadn't changed. Bobby was still…Bobby, no children to make her father a proud grandpa. *He's finally coming to see me and I'm in Montana trying to figure out what to do with my life with more questions than answers.* She looked up from the letter and watched Jack, still whistling as he cooked. When he noticed her eyes on him, he leaned across the counter and kissed her full on the lips.

It is wonderfully obvious that I make Jack Ketchum happy! Shelby's concern vanished.

After breakfast Jack said he had ranch business to take care of and told her, if she wanted to write her father, that he would mail it on his way to Kalispell. Shelby wrote a quick note, apologizing for it being short, but confirming she absolutely wanted him to come to Montana.

As soon as she finished, Jack left and Shelby put in her daily call to Enrique. Things were still going well and he told her again to stay as long as needed or wanted. "Good experience for me, boss." He sounded confident and happy. Shelby hung up, insecurity creeping into her thoughts. Bobby hadn't called in over a month and Enrique, without actually saying it, with his tone and words let her know he didn't need her at all. *Enrique spent the whole call assuring me and not one question.* Her confusion returned, full force. It occurred that Bobby may have been right after all that the decision about her life and their marriage was already made, but by Bobby Stamford and that's why he hadn't called.

Admitting she needed to find out, she called his office and was informed he was on his way to a meeting. Shelby hung up and dialed his cell phone. After a slight delay she heard it ring. "Hello," a female voice.

"Is this Bobby Stamford's number?"

"Yes, it is. May I say whose calling?"

"His wife!" Shelby said, not masking her annoyance. A pause with muffled voices in the background followed then Bobby answered. "Hey, Shel! You okay? Is there an emergency?"

"I thought maybe you had one. You said you'd call me back from home, remember?"

"Shel? I really can't talk now. I'm on the freeway going to a plan-ning commission meeting in San Diego on Covington. I'm dictating notes to uh…my secretary for the meeting. That was stupid of me not to call. I got home too late and figured you'd already be in bed. You wouldn't believe how fast things are happening here, meetings every day, working late every night. But I will call soon, I promise. Shel? Are you there?"

"Do you actually give a damn?" Shelby slammed down the receiv-er, mad at herself for allowing negative feelings to intrude after the wonderful afternoon and night with Jack. She felt angry but didn't know why. Shelby refilled her mug and sat at the counter, trying to pinpoint why she was upset. The female voice? *No… well, maybe a little.* The charade Bobby put on? Bingo! He was like a chameleon, his persona dependent on the situation; elaborate explanations, always a promise amidst a flurry of activity. What did the real Bobby think? *Is there a real Bobby?*

Her call with Enrique no longer disturbed Shelby; she knew him. He merely wanted to show her he was responsible. *Enrique has nothing to do with my anger. It's Bobby. And dammit, my mother who is so self-involved she couldn't quit talking about Paris long enough to let me tell her something important.* And her father! *Accepting five years of exile from his daughter without a fight, only to fold over of a one-page note.*

A knock on the café door rousted Shelby from her negative thoughts. She peeked out the front window of the café; Adele's Jeep Cherokee was parked in front. Dressed in jeans, boots, and a parka, she strode in, her energy crackling like the cold November air. "First big snow is on its way, I can feel it," she announced and then poured herself a cup of coffee. "You look great, Shelby. What did you do to yourself?" She was staring with open curiosity.

"Finally rested, I guess. I've been worn out fixing the porch then working at the ranch." Shelby hoped that satisfied her curiosity.

"Well whatever, it did the job. Catch me up, how are things. Any news from Bobby?"

"Nothing relevant but I did just call him. He talked about the Covington project but all of a sudden I feel like I should go home. I don't get it, Adele. If I were to do that, it wouldn't be because I want to, but because I'm afraid of what will happen if I don't. Does that sound crazy?"

"Yes, and I've been down that road. Remember the saying: a familiar bad situation is better than fear of the unknown? It has kept a lot of women in bad relationships. My advice? Feel whatever the hell way you want, just don't act on it immediately. Agreed?"

"Agreed, especially today. I am so excited. My Dad is coming from Peru for a visit. I haven't seen him in five years so I certainly wouldn't want to leave now."

"Tell me about this daddy of yours, how old is he and does he have a girlfriend?"

"Adele! You're incorrigible."

"Tell me something I don't already know." She laughed. "I still want answers."

"He'll be sixty-three in January and I assume still handsome. He's an engineer."

"You said a mining engineer. What's his name and when did you last see him?"

"David Longren. I admit it still hurts when I think of the last time I saw him, though it's stamped in my memory like it was yesterday. I watched him disappear into a tunnel at LAX. He was angry at me and didn't look back because I didn't want him to go. He told me he had to go, that he had too many years with El Dorado Mining to quit." Shelby remembered that moment all too well, how much his terse reply hurt, the overwhelming feeling of being alone as she stood in the parking lot watching his airborne plane become a speck on the horizon.

"Did he ever marry again?" Adele asked, ending Shelby's sad thought.

"I have no idea. Maybe he got married in Peru and just didn't want to tell me." Shelby couldn't help notice a look of disappointment flit across Adele's face.

"Well, I'm looking forward to meeting this David Longren. I've got this hunch that he is going to arrive in Montana, handsome as ever, unmarried, and crazy as hell about redheads."

Chapter Eighteen

Bobby's intercom buzzed, interrupting his concentration on a planning and zoning request for vertical down-drains to insure maintenance of the natural slope of the Covington property. "This better be important," he grumbled. Terri was in San Diego at Stuart's request and Miss Telford was filling in for the day; Terri would have known better than to put a call through.

"I asked not to be disturbed, Miss Telford," he said.

"It's some lady from the local NBC affiliate. I thought it might be important! Do you—"

"Got it." He cut her off and punched the blinking light on his phone. "Bobby Stamford."

"Mr. Stamford, this is Leigh Anne Kinney with KXLA. How are you this afternoon?"

Four magic letters, KXLA, prevented him from dismissing her as he scribbled her name on the November 15 page of his calendar. "I'm fine, thank you, what can I do for you?"

"Well, it seems you and your project, Covington Square—I believe it's called—have come to the attention of the powers that be here at the station. We understand that it is a revolutionary concept: developer working side-by-side with environmentalists. And CAPE at that."

Bobby pictured her: thick glasses, plump, no makeup and, though he thought he detected a hint of sarcasm in her voice, he kept his impatience in check. "Those are all true, Ms. Kinney, and I am working on it even as we speak. Is there something particular you wanted to discuss?"

"Yes, of course. KXLA is interested in doing an introductory piece on your project, a preliminary of sorts, anticipating, of course that you and CAPE eventually make it to the altar."

"I see, and this would involve...?"

"An interview with you, which I would like to do at your office. Then some footage at the site with you explaining the concept. We would like to close with a statement from CAPE. It shouldn't take more than half-an-hour at your office and about the same at the project site."

Her casual tone and demeanor bothered him, "a half-an-hour here, half-an-hour there," and especially her remark, "anticipating of course that you and CAPE make it to the altar." *That sounds flippant. Is she trying to make light of the project? Or worse yet, an exposé and she's trying to dig up a scam? Jesus, I'm either getting paranoid or extremely careful.*

"I would be happy to explain the project to you. However I'm sure you understand that an undertaking of this financial and political magnitude, I...we would want assurance that it is covered with the consideration it deserves."

"Meaning what, Mr. Stamford?"

"I approve the finished piece before it's aired," Bobby said all at once on an exhale, furiously doodling on the calendar in front of him.

"Ordinarily that is not our policy so I would have to get back to you on that."

"I understand. Why don't you check it out and get back to my secretary." He replaced the receiver and went over the conversation in his mind, hoping he'd sounded properly cordial yet professional, even as his insides churned.

It didn't take Miss Telford long to spread the story. Adam Stamford came striding into his office without knocking just as Bobby hung up the phone. "Well?" Adam said.

Bobby gave his father a mock salute. "It's just possible that Stamford Development may have moved into the big time. I'm talking national big-time."

Everything went right the rest of the day. The architect was pleased with the prospective down drains and wanted the specs faxed to him so he could look them over before sending it to his construction liaison in San Diego. And Terri would be in San Diego until very late, for which he breathed a sigh of relief. She was occupying all of his off-time, the very thing he promised Stuart he would not allow. Terri couldn't seem to get enough of him, which made him wonder if he was the aphrodisiac or was it the sex itself. She had incredible energy; he was sure she was responsible for at least five of the pounds he'd lost.

After their Spindrift Motel get-together he viewed Terri Armstrong as a gold-medal athlete in sex. And now, thankfully, he was fit enough to go two hours with her and not end up in emergency. But she was becoming possessive, flaunting their relationship at the office: sexy looks, innuendoes, kissing him with his office door open. *Not Bobby Stamford style.*

Wanting to share his good feelings with someone, preferably gorgeous and appropriately impressed, he regretted Shelby's absence, but decided he'd try Paige Williamson, a divorcee from Bel Air; he'd seen her at the club. Great figure and a dynamite tennis player, he met her when he'd wandered over to see what the crowd at the club was watching, and ended up staying for the last of her match. Captivated by her good looks and competitive spirit, he ended up buying her a lemonade at the court-side bar, at which Paige gave him her card and a look that signaled a go-ahead to call. There was no answer at her home, so on a whim he called the club.

"Would you page Paige?" he quipped to the operator.

She answered on the sixth ring, out of breath. "Paige Williamson."

"Paige! Bobby Stamford. Did I get you off the court?"

"Yes, you did and I was winning."

"Sorry 'bout that. I should make it up to you, how about dinner tonight?"

"Is that implying a consolation? You don't think I can win now?"

Bobby leaned back in his chair. "Bobby Stamford has never been a consolation prize in his life. Winners only."

He heard her chuckle. "Then I'll have to kick some serious butt. Pick me up at seven?"

"Seven it is." *I should run for president. I can't do anything wrong today.* He confirmed her address and directions as his intercom buzzed again.

This time it was Terri. "Hi, baby, miss me?" she whispered into the phone.

"This is not your cell number, where are you calling from?"

"The PC office."

"The planning commission! Then take it easy, will you? Keep it professional."

"You didn't answer me," she cooed.

"Dammit, Terri, what if someone hears you, you sound like a hooker in heat."

There was a long silence, then her petulant voice. "Mr. Stamford, this is Ms. Armstrong, Covington public relations. I'm calling to set up a meeting this evening, nineish for dinner. I feel it's imperative we go over what I've accomplished today." Her voice dropped to a husky whisper. "And besides, I want to fuck your brains out." He heard her throaty laughter. "Give me credit for some brains, Bobby. I didn't get where I am by being stupid."

Her statement sent a chill down his spine; where was it she thought she had gotten, PR for Covington, into his bed, in line to replace his wife? It was a disturbing thought. "Can't make it tonight, Terr, I've got a meeting."

"Terr? This isn't Shel you're talking to, Bobby. And don't give me that shit about a meeting. I'm your secretary, remember?"

He assumed a professional tone. "This just came up, Terri. I will see you at the office in the morning. I'm anxious to hear what you accomplished. Gotta go, have another call—"

Bobby hung up before she had a chance to reply. *She's getting to be a pain in the ass. I'm going to have to deal with her.* He didn't want to destroy his good mood thinking about a hostile Terri. And since everything had gone so well, he decided to call Shel. Each time she had called she made a big deal out of the fact that she was the only one calling. Virgil answered the phone at the café. Shelby was upstairs and he offered to 'run right up and get her.' Bobby heard voices in the background; he forgot it was six o'clock there.

Moments later a breathless Shelby picked up the phone. "Bobby, what a nice surprise." It registered in her voice and it made him feel a twinge of guilt for not calling more often.

"Yeah, hi yourself! I forgot it's six o'clock there, can you talk? How are you?"

"I'm fine, sure I can talk. What's up?"

"I had an exciting thing happen today and wanted to share it with you. KXLA is interested in doing a story on Covington and me. They think the concept is newsworthy, environmentalists in bed with developers." Bobby instantly regretted his choice of words. "You remember, I told you about CAPE?" he added quickly.

"How exciting, tell me all about it."

Bobby went over his conversation and the fact that KXLA seemed enthused about it. Shelby sounded genuinely happy for him. He made a polite inquiry about her day and immediately regretted it; he didn't have a lot of time. Shelby excitedly told him Jack was throwing a party "in a little while to celebrate finishing fall chores." She went on about the fun she had on the cattle drive, the cute little yearlings, branding the cows, and the sky being *sooo* blue. Shel not mentioning their problems, he decided not to ask her when she was coming home. After listening for a few minutes, he hung up feeling a bit deflated; she sounded excited about his news but just as excited over some cowpoke party.

He left for the country club where he could shower and change; he kept a sport coat and tie in his locker for just such an occasion rather than driving to Santa Monica and back. Thinking about Shelby on his drive to the club, the fact she hadn't filed for divorce was a good sign. She hated even the mention of divorce and said several times that she would not want to throw away ten years of "history together." *I just need to be patient, but in the meantime there's no reason I can't enjoy my momentary freedom.*

Except now Terri Armstrong was infringing on that.

Paige Williamson was a dead ringer for Gwyneth Paltrow. He figured she was in her mid-to-late thirties, and she had money. Her house was modest by Bel Air standards, but it was immaculately kept, by a gardener no doubt. A uniformed woman, Mexican or Guatemalan, answered the door. Paige gave him a tour of the house, which turned out to be grander than it looked from the street. In the garage she showed him her brand-new Mercedes CLA 250. "I just love it, 208 horsepower. Zero to 60 mph in 6.9 seconds."

Bobby had to laugh; she knew more about cars that he did. Over dinner at *Chez Michele* he also learned that Paige's life was her friends, tennis, and the club, pretty much in that order. She seemed genuinely excited about his potential entry into national news, but when the dialogue turned to relationships she asked point-blank if Shelby had filed for divorce.

"I want to be honest with you, Bobby. I am interested in you enough to suggest you call, but I have a lot of friends and my life is full. I would not want to be party to your divorce or anyone else's. This town is big in population, but small with regard to character. I don't date married men or go out with my friends' ex-husbands. That's why my reputation survived my divorce and I want to keep it that way, nothing personal." Her demeanor was sincere and friendly but Bobby felt as though he'd been summarily dismissed.

"I understand, Paige." He covered his embarrassment. "This dinner wasn't intended for anything more than to get to know each other. Nothing personal taken."

After a pleasant dinner Bobby drove Paige back to her house, refusing her offer of a nightcap on the pretense he had an early breakfast meeting. Paige kissed him on the cheek when he escorted her to her door, and graciously accepted his explanation. "I wish you luck with your project, Bobby. I'll be watching for you on the news. And I wish you well with your personal life. Keep my card, just in case," she said with a smile. Classy and aboveboard, Paige was the antithesis of the Terri Armstrong he was getting to know.

Bobby's Porsche joined the evening traffic and, needing time to think he switched to the slow lane. Some significant things had happened today that he did not want to skate over. Paige had openly brought up an issue that he knew existed in their social strata, her forthrightness in glaring contrast to Terri's duplicity. Paige's situation also brought something else disturbing to think about; some poor sucker had worked his butt off to buy that house and now she was living in it, complete with maid and gardener, no doubt with enough spousal support to spend her days playing tennis at the country club. *Shit, that could easily happen to me.*

Equally disturbing was Shelby being as excited over a cattle drive as she was about her husband's hard-won recognition. Bobby pulled down the mirror. "What's that saying about when the going gets tough?" he said to his reflection then flipped the mirror back up. "The tough get going."

It took four days for Leigh Ann Kinney to get back to him. The powers that be, she told him, were willing to gamble on his approval. Bobby suggested they do the project site footage first so she could get a feel for the scope of Covington Square. Bobby was able to delay the taping for one week; he had a lot to do to prepare for it.

The following morning Terri breezed into his office, iPad in hand, an impassive expression on her pretty face. "It's a go for the KXLA piece. Here's what I want you to do—"

"Yes, sir," she interrupted.

Bobby ignored her. "We'll need a second sign, future site of yadda, yadda, yadda, something prestigious but not the final one. We'll need a special sign for the ground breaking ceremony. The interview is Monday so put it up Friday, I want a flagpole next to—"

"Yes, sir. Absolutely, sir."

"Terri, please. See if Banners can get the logo flag finished. I want it hanging up there along with the U.S. and California flags. And see if you can get a dozen or so brochures. I know we told them we wouldn't need them for another six weeks, but push, okay?"

"Right away, sir. Is there anything else, sir?" Terri stood up and turned to leave.

Bobby looked up from his desk. "Sit down."

She continued toward the door. "I said sit down!"

Terri came back and sat in a chair facing the desk. Her eyes were frosty pools.

"What's the problem, Terri?"

"What makes you think there's a problem?"

"Cut the shit, okay? This is a big deal. I don't need to worry about your PMS or whatever the hell it is. This is business and you were hired to handle PR for Covington. I need someone who wants this to succeed as much as I do and I'm getting the impression that's not your agenda."

Her eyes widened, the frostiness replaced by a flicker of uncertainty.

"It is my agenda, it's just that I…I thought…"

Bobby softened his tone. "Look, Terri, I don't know what you thought, but I need to make one thing perfectly clear. Covington Square is the most important project of my career. First and foremost, we are a team—a professional team. I depend on you, trust your professional integrity and confidentiality. Covington is the highest of stakes. I will not allow whatever personal relationship that you *may* think we have to threaten it. Anything that screws this up is out. It's as simple as that. Do you understand?"

He watched her face as he spoke. A hint of anger, alarm, doubt? She said nothing.

"And while we're on the subject of personal relationships, there's something I'm unhappy about." Her face paled. Bobby realized he had her on the ropes. "I may be separated but I am still married. You knew that from the beginning. I don't appreciate the sexual innuendoes in front of the staff, or kissing with the door open. That's unprofessional, it's blatant, and I don't like it." There was a long silence. "Terri, say something."

He saw tears welling. "I'm sorry, Bobby, I didn't mean to compromise the project or embarrass you. I realize how important confidentiality is." She rose and brushed away a tear that had spilled onto her cheek. "I'd better get on this. We only have a week."

"Good girl." He nodded. *Score one for Bobby Stamford. You just have to be firm.*

* * *

Terri returned to her desk just outside Bobby's office. She glanced around to see if anyone was watching her. Noting Miss Telford's curious stare, she sat down and began Googling phone numbers to get Bobby's orders underway. She could feel the heat emanating from her face and neck. *Did I hear you right—good girl? I may have underestimated you, Bobby Stamford. But you sure as hell have underestimated me.*

She called Banners, Inc. and Stadium Supplies, and fairly hissed when they questioned the short time she gave them to complete her demands. Each firm readily relented when she said she had someone else who would handle her perfectly reasonable, unscheduled request because of *some goddamn unforeseen circumstances!*

After she hung up, she sat fuming until she decided on a shift in tactics. There had never been an objective that she set her sights on that she hadn't gotten: a man, a job, an acceptable car. The Lexus had been a gift from generous Lyle, married owner of the dealership; the furniture in her apartment a gift from sweet Bernie, newly divorced. And her lifetime membership at The Westood Fitness Club bestowed upon her by Larry Larsen, co-owner of the club, all gifts legal and enforceable before the unfortunate dissolution of each relationship. Clothes, trinkets, and money were small-time stuff.

But she did acknowledge never having the biggest developer in southern California in her sights before. His wife was a problem, but not insurmountable. His health was of concern at first, but that seemed to be improving. Admitting her mistake of figuring Bobby Stamford to be merely a rich spoiled playboy had almost proven fatal to her plans, as was underestimating the importance of the Covington project to his career. *It's not too late, I can fix all that.*

Terri Armstrong's fiery good looks and driving desire were gifts inherited from her Mexican mother for whom she was named. Theresa Maldonado Armstrong had also passed down the art of gentle and, if necessary, not-so-gentle persuasion. The wife of Howie, insurance salesman, wannabe rich and successful businessman, but-never-quite-made-it, Armstrong. Terri's father's greatest achievement, she remembered, was at age eleven, when she and her mother attended the opening of H.T. Armstrong's Fireman's Fund insurance office. But even sharper in her memory was how embarrassed she was by his office being located between the Pico Gallo Chicken Take-Out and Dr. Thompson's Podiatry Clinic in the Lincoln Avenue shopping center in Anaheim, California.

She had grown up aware of and close enough to the Beverly Hills, Rodeo Drive lifestyle to want it, but light-years from having it. But mature for her young age and lying about it with assistance from her mother, she began a job at Disneyland at age fourteen, working every day after school, every summer and holiday, saving every dime she made. A two-year stint at Anaheim Junior College opened the door to a series of secretarial jobs in high-end offices, a professional wardrobe second to none, a relentless burning desire and a few broken hearts along the way. Now here she was with a killer apartment in Westwood and a plum job with infinite possibilities for advancement.

Terri dug into her work with the fervor that landed her the job at Stamford, Inc.

* * *

Bobby and Adam Stamford checked the Covington site on Sunday, November 19th, the day before the scheduled taping. The sign was perfect: taupe background, distinctive white with black lettering, and bearing the Covington logo, a giant oak tree with a seagull super-imposed.

Future Site Covington Square
600,000 square feet • Exclusive Shops and Restaurants
Environmentally Designed and Engineered
Phase One Opening Fall, 2016
Stamford Development, Inc.

Atop the flag pole, a U.S. flag, a California flag, and strategically placed beneath both of them, a Covington Square flag, the Pacific breeze ruffling all three perfectly for a television shot. Bobby asked Adam to stand near the sign, then took a picture with his Smart phone; he wanted to gauge the impact the scene would have on a small screen. He studied the picture; the sign was framed by two giant oak trees, the flags, and a few billowy clouds for ambiance. Bobby had to smile. *Now if I could only hire a seagull to fly over.*

He told his father to pray to the big developer in the sky for no rain and go easy on the smog. Evidently HE heard Adam, for Monday dawned clear, sunny and smog free; and Ms. Kinney turned out to be photogenic with an excess of television savvy. She said to Bobby she was new with KXLA, recently recruited from the NBC affiliate in Atlanta. Very professional, she seemed genuinely enthused about the story. Bobby applauded her effort to rid herself of her southern accent which slipped in occasionally when her concentration lapsed; she acknowledged his compliment.

"Thank you, it was difficult. I assure you, Mr. Stamford I haven't gotten where I am by not doing my homework." Ms. Kinney positioned Bobby where Adam had stood.

What is it with women? Always assuring me how they got where they are?

She went over the details with her cameraman and reviewed her notes, then informed Bobby they had already taken an aerial shot using the station's traffic chopper. "I will ask a couple of general questions about construction and the environmental aspect as we walk around. Then I'll follow up on the points we discussed in our phone conversation. Part of both shots will be included on the evening news. The completed half-hour piece will air as a community interest piece that I host." Bobby clutched the set of rolled up plans and nodded he was ready.

The minute the camera light went on Ms. Kinney's southern accent disappeared; she spoke distinctly, not too fast, not too slow. When the breeze ruffled her hair, she deftly swept it aside with a graceful hand, never missing a beat. She held the microphone with her other hand up to Bobby with her first question. "Mr. Stamford, the idea of engaging environmental approval from the very beginning is a unique concept. Could you give us your thoughts where the idea came from and what you hope to accomplish?"

Bobby was on fire with enthusiasm. She hadn't told him what her questions would be because she wanted his answers to be spontaneous but they hadn't been difficult to anticipate and he had practiced different answers in front of the mirror. Ms. Kinney was the consummate professional, interjecting questions or comments at the right moment, making him feel at ease. When he flubbed an answer, she said 'no problem,' and they re-did it. He could have kissed her.

The final piece was magnificent and, according to Stuart, the equivalent of a half-million dollars in advertising. It gave Bobby a rush as he watched it in his office with Leigh Anne; she was dazzling, the morning sun dancing off her shiny hair. And he couldn't have looked any better if he'd hired her as his agent. Leigh Anne assured him that despite CAPE's CEO Frederick Houghton not issuing glowing comments on the project, his reserved dignified acceptance of the Covington concept was more effective than an effusive endorsement. "I trust you are pleased, Mr. Stamford?" she said, handing him the disc.

"Please, call me Bobby. I am more than pleased. You did an excellent job and I would love to buy you dinner to celebrate the finish of a great collaborative effort, though I prefer beginnings to finishes?" Bobby said, noting her trim ankles, pretty legs, and the absence of a wedding ring as he escorted Leigh to her car, a Beamer that still had Georgia plates.

First thing the following morning Bobby called the florist and ordered two dozen Georgia peach-colored roses to be delivered to Ms. Kinney at KXLA with his handwritten card: Thank you from one pro to another. Superb job!

That done, her home phone and address went into Bobby's personal address book.

Chapter Nineteen

The twisted dirt road from the La Orroya mine snaked its way down the western slope of the Andes into bustling Lima, the capital of Peru. David Longren had made the trip a hundred times during the last five years, the road testing his patience, the Volkswagen Bug's tires, engine and durability. He passed groups of natives leading llamas and alpacas loaded with baskets of potatoes. The women, wearing traditional Bolo hats, were dressed in layers of bright colors and leather *huaraches* with soles made from tires. Carrying their babies in colorful slings on their backs, they seemed undaunted by sparse oxygen in the 8,000-foot cool Andean air.

He began the drive at dawn to allow time for flats, engine trouble, road delays or accidents, but leaving early was all for naught when he became engulfed in Lima's chaotic traffic. His Varig flight, scheduled to depart at noon, hopefully allowed him time to go by one of the exclusive boutiques in the Zona Rosa to buy a gift for Shelby, perhaps an alpaca poncho or hand carved artifact from Brazil wood. He also wanted to buy a bottle or two of Piso at the airport duty-free shop. That fiery drink would help tame any cold Montana night.

He had intended to arrive yesterday, a full day before his flight. But after he had cleared the mine before yesterday's scheduled blast and then pressed the electronic switch, there was no explosion. He had to call La Orroya's explosives expert at another site, who showed up quickly. After retracing the circuits he found the short which allowed work to resume but too late to attempt the hazardous drive. Disappointed, David had looked forward to a rare treat, spending the night at his apartment in San Ysidro, having a late dinner at Paulo's and then wandering the busy streets of the Zona Rosa with its European atmosphere. However, after five years living and working in and around a deep hole in the earth amongst Indians who spoke Quechua instead of Spanish, he had acquired infinite adaptability.

Adapting to life in Peru, David remembered the plethora of surprising challenges to an engineer from Colorado. Most immediate was surviving the traffic in Peru's capitol of Lima where he had an apartment. His first surprise: that ten million Limaños considered traffic lights merely to be suggestions rather than electronic signals representing law and order. Another surprise: five-car wide streets with no lines, narrowing into a two lane street without warning resulting in chaos. But perhaps the most evident: the majority of Lima's streets had no ninety degree angles, instead arcing off into great circles, in the center of which stood a magnificent statue, the figure staring benevolently down on grid-locked captives. Lima drivers were known to stop because of an accident only if there was blood and sometimes not even then.

How could he possibly explain living five years in this city of ten million people to Shelby? Admitting he couldn't, David settled on a hand-carved statue of a prancing horse for her, the dense dark wood bringing the animal to life with its flowing grain and shiny depth. He bought a set of bookends carved from the same wood, and a set of silver demitasse spoons hand crafted from pure Peruvian silver. He was certain Shelby would like the horse, and felt sure he could find homes for the other gifts. He made it to the international section of Lima's airport with not a lot of time to spare and, as expected, encountered long lines and unruly crowds. Accepting that they were awesome factors over which he had no control, David quashed his impatience. Three thousand four hundred miles, and seven and a half hours later, the Boeing 767 landed on the Ft. Worth-Dallas runway at 10:30 p.m. Dallas time. Retrieving his bags, David went through customs and then caught a Hampton shuttle to the hotel.

During the long flight, he looked forward to a hot shower, an American dinner, and a good night's rest before his flight the following morning. The first thing he checked out upon arriving at his room was the spacious bathroom with a hair dryer and a telephone! Next he put a luxurious thick towel to his face; what luxury! David showered off the last remnants of Andean dust then called for room service. Sitting in his tenth floor room and facing a window that gave him a view of the city, he ate a ten-ounce filet mignon with all the trimmings, savoring it down to the perfect round mushroom perched on top.

Afterward, he stretched out in the huge tub with more water than he would use in a week in La Orroya, an opportunity to soothe sore muscles and because it was such an indulgence. The water felt amazing, his head resting on the rim, his eyes closed. *Why didn't I write Shelby a long time ago? Tell her the truth that I was worried that if we didn't put it back together soon, our relationship would be gone forever. Guess now I'll be doing it face to face.*

David Longren acknowledged that the lure of adventure and his thirst for knowledge of other cultures had cost him his marriage. His mining engineer degree from the Colorado School of Mines prepared him for his chosen profession, but history classes on the pre-Columbian civilizations of the western hemisphere were what fueled his desire to seek work in Mexico, Chile, Bolivia and Peru.

Laura Olsen, his girlfriend from nearby University of Colorado, had also professed a love of travel and an equal interest in ancient Indian cultures—that is, until her first trip as his wife to Peru on his first job. The grinding poverty, the primitive conditions and scarcity of Americans quickly dashed her purported interest. Their new life together changed overnight from one of shared adventure to separation and differing directions. When his beautiful daughter was born, David kept a standing two-month reservation with the airlines, taking maximum time off between jobs and lulls in exploration. Not wanting to give up his career or family, he stayed in a loveless marriage, finally admitting when Shelby was ten that it was a mistake.

He prized his photo album of their summers at the cabin in Colorado, in his mind the yellowed pictures and frayed pages testimony to his commitment to be a part of his daughter's life. Now surrendering his resistance to thinking about his far-away daughter and the fact they had lost their closeness, hurt somewhere so deep inside that it stung his eyes with unshed tears.

Guilt, anticipation, fear, a sense of time lost, crowded into his thoughts on his first night in five years in North America.

* * *

Troutspring's first official big snowstorm arrived on November 23rd. Shelby awoke, instinctively knowing something was different even before she looked out the window. "Jack, wake up, come here! It looks like a Christmas card. Even the parking lot is beautiful. There isn't a track or footprint on it!"

Jack rolled out of bed, pulled on his jeans and sweat shirt and joined her at the window. "I was about to say wait until February, you might not think it's so beautiful, but I don't dare."

Shelby grabbed her sweater and jeans, rushing around trying to pull on both all at once.

"What are you doing?" He moved out of her way.

Shelby located her boots. "Going outside, I can't wait." She grunted with effort, her foot refusing to slip into the boot. Feeling akin to being on a pogo stick, she hopped around the room trying to get her boot on without sitting down. "This damned thing!" She glanced at Jack who was running a comb through his hair, observing her in the mirror. He turned around and leaned against the dresser, arms folded across his chest, and a grin on his face.

Shelby lost her balance and dived for the bed. Both hands grasping her boot, she looked at him and broke into a laugh. "Boots one, Shelby zero, thanks a lot, Montana. You could help you know." She motioned to her boot. Jack obliged with a push against the boot with his thigh.

Shelby pulled on gloves, a knit cap and jacket then dashed down the stairs and out the front doors. She ran to the middle of the parking lot then turned and looked up at the bedroom window. Jack was holding the curtain open. "Come on down." She yelled, motioning to him. Shelby whirled around and around, arms straight out, looking up at the leaden sky inviting the snow to cover her face. Whisper quiet, it looked like a pure white, all-encompassing cloud burst. The café was crowned in white, snow obscured the mountains; and the pines surrounding the café were already drooping from the night's snowfall.

The café doors closed and Shelby saw Jack exit and stand on the porch. He had a camera and was snapping photos. She raised both arms in a victory sign; she lay down and made a snow angel, then got up and moved to a patch of un-trampled snow. Swinging her arms and leaping with scissor-like strides, she completed a figure eight. Jack moved off the porch, his hair and shoulders quickly covered with snow. Shelby pointed at the design she'd made.

Jack looked up from the camera. "A big bow, well done!" He was laughing.

"It's a figure eight, not a bow! Can't you tell?" Shelby hefted a snowball straight at him.

Jack ducked and the snowball hit the café. "Hey, missy, remember who won the last fight? I wouldn't egg on the big guy if I were you."

"Oh yeah, big guy?" Shelby picked up two handfuls of snow, shaped them into a ball then eyeing him with a devilish look, drew her arm back to throw just as he snapped a picture. Jack whirled around and started for the porch, her snowball splatting in the middle of his back, apparently sliding down his collar for he hollered and scrunched up his shoulders. "Okay, okay, it's a figure eight." He laughed. "Come on in and have some coffee with me, slugger."

Jack brushed the snow off Shelby's back and they both scraped their boots on the new snow grates. "Good job on the grates," he said.

He poured their coffee and switched on the television. The Today Show was on NBC, Anchor Lester Holt interviewing a politician. They both heard a car and Shelby peeked out the window. A uniformed man got out of a truck and walked toward the café. Jack opened the door for him. "Telegram for Shelby Stamford," he announced.

"I'm Shelby." She accepted the telegram. Jack tipped him; the young man thanked him and quickly exited.

"Who's it from?" Jack said.

"I don't know yet. I hate telegrams, you read it, okay?"

"I thought you were an optimist," he said and slit the envelope with his pocket knife. Jack glanced over the paper. "Your dad is David Longren, right?"

Shelby's heart did a flip-flop. "Yes. Has something happened to him?"

"Well," he said quietly, "he must be okay. He's arriving at the Glacier International Airport on the twenty-eighth. That's Thanksgiving Day." Jack handed her the telegram across the counter. She read it over then read it again. "I can't believe he's really coming! It's summer in Peru, did you know that? What am I going to say to him?"

"What about Happy Thanksgiving? Or welcome to Montana might be ni—"

Shelby began pacing around the tables. "Do you think he's coming because he's sick and that's why it only took that one little note?"

"Would you hold on? Stop pacing and listen to yourself. Come here." Jack held out his arms. Shelby came around the counter and slipped into his embrace. "Don't invent worries. Just think, you're going to spend Thanksgiving with your dad in all this beauty you're so excited about. If he's tired of heat and dust, David Longren is going to love it here. This is what you call good news, right?"

"You're right, you're absolutely right. I'm being paranoid. What a day, first the snow and now this. It's making me crazy. And starved. Feed me, Montana Jack."

Jack served them French toast at a table by the window. "I've been thinking about something, wondering when to bring it up."

"Uh-oh, you look serious. Is it something bad?"

"No it's not bad but I don't know if it's good either. You tell me. Ever since I showed you the ranch and the house, I've been thinking. You are right about that place. I belong there, not here." He gestured around the café.

"Jack, really? Move back to the ranch? But what about the café, would you still try to run it? How would that work?"

"Hear me out before you think up a bunch of problems." He put his hand over hers. "Adele actually runs this place and has ever since Ellie died. She tells me what to do and then does it herself. She does all the ordering and knows more about it than I do. I bet she would jump at the chance to own the café. Adele has more energy than she knows what to do with. Even if she doesn't, Shelby, I want to go home. What do you think?"

"I think you are the wisest, most handsome, the sexiest man I

know, Jack Ketchum. That is a brilliant idea! Adele would love to own
the café, I just know it." She paused, hesitating whether she should
reveal to Jack what Adele told her, then after pondering briefly, she
decided it would be okay. "Jack, Adele told me about her husband and
son, how horrible that was for her. And I think if she owned the café, it
would be the perfect thing for her. She loves this place. And you out at
the ranch, that is so exciting!"

Shelby sat back sipping her coffee when a worrisome thought
popped into her mind causing her to pause her coffee cup in mid-air.
*Jack said HE belonged there. Maybe that's his gentlemanly way of
saying he's ready to get on with his life. I certainly wouldn't blame
him.*

"Earth to Shelby, earth to Shelby." Jack's eyes were peering at her
over her cup. "Where were you? A minute ago I was the wisest,
sexiest, all that stuff kind of guy. What happened?"

"You said *you* belong there. I couldn't agree more, but I don't want
to intrude. I'm—"

"Shelby Stamford." Jack removed the cup, set it down and took her
hand in both of his. "I want you to come to the ranch with me. You
and your dad." He squeezed her hand. "I wish you... I wish things
were diff... Oh never mind, you're making me a worry-wart just like
you!"

She exhaled a sigh. "Thank you, Jack. I would love to come. A
visit with my dad in Montana instead of L.A. would be the chance of a
lifetime—especially at the ranch."

"Okay then," he said. "We have a lot to do to whip that place into
shape. We've only got five days counting today. I think I'll call
Ronnie and Chuck, hopefully they're out of school this week and if so,
the job will be easier. If not, we'll do the best we can. What do you
say?"

"Why don't you call Adele first, I'm anxious to hear her reaction."

Shelby remained at the table while Jack called Adele. She was evidently home for Jack leaned against the café wall, a smile on his face, talking, gesturing with his hand, listening and shaking his head in agreement. Ten minutes of conversation and Jack returned to the table.

"That was quick, what did she say?"

"You might have known we'd get in an argument."

"You didn't look like you were arguing."

Jack broke into a grin. "That's because I won. Well, sort of, the best you can ever win against that woman. She would love to buy it, but she started rattling on about getting a loan on her house. I told her to forget it and that's what we were arguing about. Ellie's Café is paid for so no need to involve a bank. She can pay me. I told her it was an offer she couldn't refuse. I'm surprised you didn't hear her holler over here. I told her we'd get to the paper work later. She's excited, know what she asked me?"

"What?"

"She wanted to know if it would hurt my feelings if she changed the name. I said Jack's Place would make a fine name. You should have heard her holler over that, but I told her to change it to whatever she wants. Adele said she's thankful and really proud of me but I'm still an old geezer." Jack was chuckling and shaking his head.

Shelby couldn't believe a ten minute conversation and the café sold, two people settling something as important as the sale of a business that quick and easy, Bobby would laugh at them.

"I'm proud of you, too, you studly gentleman."

"I like that better than old geezer. Now let's get this Thanksgiving show on the road."

Shelby pictured the ranch house, her thoughts racing as she waited for Jack to call Ronnie on the upstairs phone. Five days was scant time to rid a house of years of dust and cobwebs, to get telephone and electrical service reestablished and operational. Shelby rose and found a notepad and pencil on the counter, for a moment suddenly feeling dizzy. *Guess I got up too quick or it's all this excitement. Dad coming, Jack moving back where he belongs, Adele buying this place. This is all too much.*

The café phone rang. "Ellie's Cafe," Shelby answered.

"Not for long," Adele sang out.

"Congratulations, Ms. Entrepreneur. I take it you are happy about owning Adele's Cafe. It does have a nice ring to it."

"I just had to call back, Shelby. The more I think about it, the more excited I get. Since I don't have to put a mortgage on my place and pay big loan fees, I can put a little money into Adele's. I want to change things, make it my place. You're so good at that, will you help me?"

"Are you kidding? I would be honored. Do you have any idea how much fun we can have turning this place into Adele's?"

"Thanks, Shelby. By the way, Jack told me your dad sent a telegram and is on his way. I'm inviting myself for Thanksgiving. I thought I'd better let you know."

"You're one sentence ahead of me. Thanksgiving wouldn't be Thanksgiving without you. Jack's upstairs trying to get hold of Ronnie and Chuck right now to help us clean up the ranch house—"

"That's also why I called," she interrupted. "I was going to close the café this week anyway because of the holiday. I'm hoping we can meet at the ranch, just tell me when. We'll whip that place into shape in nothing flat. I want that daddy of yours to be nice and comfy."

"Adele Carson, whatever vitamins you're on, sister, I want some."

Chapter Twenty

For the next five days, Shelby joined Jack, Adele, Ronnie, and Chuck, attacking the ranch house like an industrial cleaning crew, from early morning well into each night. The boys were on their Thanksgiving holiday and couldn't believe their good fortune at earning car-money in the dead of winter. Equipped with vacuum cleaners, dust mops, ladders, brooms, buckets, rubber gloves and sponges, the five cleaned and polished, passing each other on a run. The kitchen was the final room, which somehow the already-exhausted house-warriors still managed to turn from an out-of-date, unkempt disaster into a shiny, clean center ready to cook a Thanksgiving feast.

At the end of five ten-hour days not only was the house clean, it was also operational, thanks also to a steady host of repairmen and installers hooking up appliances and repairing equipment. Wednesday, the day before Thanksgiving, was equally busy, Jack and the boys bringing loads of clothes from both closets and all of the books from his bedroom library—a huge load by itself.

"It's possible these books may have to stay in those boxes for a while," Jack told Shelby as he was about to leave on his "make sure we got everything" load. He also promised to bring fixings from the café to make dinner, rustler's stew for all of them.

Shelby and Adele promptly left for Kalispell for what Shelby called the finishing touches, plus the groceries for their Thanksgiving meal. They split the extensive list of accessories, each breezing through stores in determined fashion. Following that was an equally hurried visit to ShopMart, which resulted in three carts of groceries that they had difficulty finding room for in a Jeep already crammed full of purchases. Adele could hardly see out the windows.

"We belong in the Shoppers Hall of Fame," Shelby said as they pulled up in front of the ranch house. She and Adele left the grocery unloading and putting away to the guys. With the cleaning now done, Shelby was anxious to put the finishing touches in place.

"I'll start with the living room. What room would you like to do?" she asked Adele.

"The kitchen now that I don't mind going in there. Okay, let's rock and roll."

Shelby liked tackling the living room, finding just the right places for a handsome duck decoy, Indian clay pots, a huge mountain-scene painting, dozens of varied sizes of scented candles, several ending up on the six-foot half-log mantle, others along with magazines, baskets of pine cones, and dishes of nuts and candies on the room's tables. After finishing with new towels and rugs in the bathrooms, fatigue dawned with such force that Shelby felt giddy and nauseated at the same time, a reminder that they hadn't eaten since breakfast.

As she descended the stairs, she sniffed wonderful smells coming from the kitchen, Jack's stew, warm, fresh French-bread, and coffee. She paused on the last step and gazed around the living room. *It looks beautiful!* The flickering firelight danced across shiny floors, bathing the room and furniture in its warmth. Everything looked fresh, clean, and inviting and Jack was calling for everyone to hurry up.

When she entered the kitchen Shelby stopped in her tracks; there was no resemblance to the forgotten room she had first seen. The old stove shined, the windows sparkled and the floor was spit-spot clean. A wine-colored cloth covered the large round table, and in the center a huge pot of rustler's stew. Jack stood with his hands on the back of a chair. "Dinner is served!" His smile said it all; the transformation was complete. "Come and get it!" Jack dished up five bowls of stew and said there was "plenty more where this came from." They all ate their first bowls without talking, but on refills between spoonfuls each one shared his or her thoughts on their "amazing accomplishments" in the last five days. Shelby ate just as heartily as Jack.

Nine o'clock and dinner over Jack paid the boys, and then Adele, admitting even she was tired, offered to drive them home. Jack closed the door and turned to Shelby. "Three hours to Thanksgiving. I'd say that qualifies as a photo-finish."

"Amazing but it's the three of them that made it possible." Shelby said. "I'm exhausted."

"Me, too," Jack said. "But I'd like to pour us a couple of brandies and sit by the fire to enjoy what we've done." Jack and Shelby stretched out on separate couches near the fireplace. "This place has never looked like this. Not ever." Jack spoke quietly.

"Really? I imagined Ellen doing a great job, her loving beautiful antiques and all."

"Ellie loved furniture and pretty things but she didn't seem interested beyond that. You have a knack for decorating. I watched you earlier putting all this together. You were really enjoying yourself. I would love to see your home in L.A. I bet it's beautiful."

"It is really nice," Shelby answered. "No prettier than this, just different. But this place is an absolute treasure." She studied Jack; he was silent for a long time.

"A $1.79 for your thoughts," she said quietly, staring at the fire.

Jack smiled. "A whole $1.79?"

"Yes, you're so quiet you must be thinking deep thoughts."

"Oh, just pondering life, how things can change. Like how you just

happened to break down where you did and now here we are." Jack
rose and held out his hand. "Come to bed with me, beautiful lady. You
are exhausted and so am I. I just want to hold you. This is going to be
our last night together unless your dad sleeps awfully sound."

* * *

Shelby awoke late the following morning; she had slept so hard she
had a headache. Only when she opened her eyes and looked around,
did she remember where she was. Jack wasn't beside her, but bright
shafts of sunlight flooded the room. *It's Thanksgiving and Dad is on
his way*! The thought of five years to catch up on made her shiver with
anticipation, but there were also hurt feelings to be ironed out and
misunderstandings to explain. How different this visit would be if it
were taking place in L.A. She opened the drapes; the sun was dazzling.

Yesterday's unexpected storm had departed. Jack was right; if her
father was tired of heat and dust, he would love the Montana she saw
from the window. Sunlight shining through icicles hanging in front of
the window and flashing diamond daggers of color in all directions.
White fields stretched outward before her eyes, their undulating
surface creating a subtle pattern of shade and light. In the distance,
majestic mountains rose into a cloudless sky, with snow clinging to the
dark crevices that lead up to their white crowns.

This is so beautiful, it's almost surreal.

Figuring that Jack was feeding the stock, she showered and dressed
then hurried downstairs. The fireplace had been recently filled with
logs; the house looked beautiful, sunlight streaming in the windows.
Shelby headed for the kitchen and her date with a huge turkey. She had
promised Adele she would get the big bird in the oven before leaving
for the airport. And Adele said she would then drive over while they

were gone to make the dressing and finish getting things ready for dinner.

Looking around the kitchen Shelby suddenly remembered her Mayan family, Bobby, the Stamfords, and her horses! She hadn't given them a thought or her mother and Dennis in the last five days! Shelby prepared the turkey and put it in the oven then sat down and made her phone calls. Everyone seemed appreciative of her call and wished her well, except for Bobby. When she wished him "Happy Thanksgiving," his reply was "Same to you." Vowing to let nothing ruin this day, an excited Shelby, steadied by Jack, left for the airport to greet her father from Peru.

* * *

Inside Glacier Park International Airport, Shelby and Jack waited in a spot where they could see her father exit the Delta flight 207 tunnel. She could not stand still; pacing back and forth, sitting down and then rising to pace again. She glanced at Jack seated with his legs stretched full out, boots crossed, a thoughtful expression on his face as he observed people.

Shelby was about to sit down when she heard the announcement that the flight from Dallas via Salt Lake City to Kalispell had landed at Gate Nine; passengers would be deplaning through the tunnel. Shelby looked at Jack, seeking support or assurance, she wasn't sure. He rose and came to her side. "It's going to be okay," he said and gave her a comforting squeeze.

Hands clinched as she peered over and around people, Shelby spotted David Longren exit the chute. The passengers in front and around him dispersed and there he was. He stood still, looking around; tall, lean, silver sideburns, Indiana Jones hat, tanned face and aviator glasses.

Shelby's mouth suddenly went dry and her heart raced. He removed his glasses, then dropped his suitcase where he stood and looked straight at her. Shelby, tears flowing down her cheeks, covered the last two feet with a leap. Her father had tears too as they collided in a wordless fierce embrace. She could feel his body shake with silent sobs. Or was it hers?

"Shelby, Shelby," he said, rocking both of them from side to side. He pressed his lips against her wet cheek. "I don't know what to say," he whispered.

"Dad, I can't believe you're actually here. This is the best Thanksgiving ever!"

"Thanksgiving? I've been away so long I forgot." His voice sounded just like she remembered, his words now tinged with a slight Latin accent. "Thanksgiving, what an appropriate day to arrive. I hope you are as thankful to see me as much as I am to see you." He took out a handkerchief and wiped his eyes and face.

"You'll never know how much," she said and steered David to Jack's side.

"Dad, this is Jack Ketchum, the man I wrote you about. Jack, this is my—"

"I know," Jack interrupted. "This is your favorite father. Good to meet you, David, welcome to Montana." Jack smiled and shook his hand warmly.

"Good to meet you, too, Jack," David Longren replied. "From what Shelby wrote, I'm glad to see you have recovered. She obviously took good care of you."

"I want to set the record straight right now. Shelby... only set me back two or three weeks," Jack said with a straight face.

David's somber demeanor vanished, immediately acknowledging Jack's humor.

"Good grief," Shelby sighed. "I'm in for a time with the two of you to contend with."

To Shelby's delight Jack and her father gained an instant rapport, chatting easily through the wait for the luggage. She clutched her father's carry-on bag and walked between them, holding tight to his hand. Jack and David each carried a large suitcase.

On their drive to the ranch she watched her father, his gaze marveling at the mountains and trees. When Jack turned into the driveway off Stagecoach Road, Shelby touched his leg. "Stop for a minute, Jack, please." They stopped under the arch. The sun, a low red ball, was ready to drop below the horizon, silhouetting the huge pines surrounding the house, smoke pouring from the chimney and lights glowing from the windows. "Is that not a beautiful sight? It looks like a greeting card, doesn't it?" she said to her father.

"May I?" David got out of the truck, hands on his hips as he took in the scene. "Indeed it does and this air is wonderful!" He got back in the truck. "Broken Arrow, great name, Jack."

"Thank you. The first time my dad put in some of these fields, he found lots of arrows, all broken, so that's what he named it." Jack parked next to Adele's car, nosed into the fence near the front walk. They barely reached the porch when she swung wide the huge front door.

"Hello! Happy Thanksgiving," Adele said, a huge smile greeting them. Shelby took note how chic she looked in forest green slacks and matching sweater, her hair swept back.

"Adele Carson, this is David Longren. Dad, Adele is a good friend of Jack's and mine."

"Well now," Adele stepped forward and extended her hand. "Good looks run in the family. I could tell just by looking that you're Shelby's father."

David didn't miss a beat. He took her hand, bowed and then pressed her hand to his lips. *"Si, señora hermosa,* I am the guilty one. What can I say?"

Adele, for all her bravado for a moment looked flustered. "Shelby, you said he was good-looking, you didn't mention he was charming, too. That was Spanish for what?"

"I think he called you beautiful lady," Shelby said with a smile.

The fireplace was glowing and the house smelled of turkey and dressing, and the spicy fragrance of pumpkin and apple pie. After a few moments of pleasantries, Jack accompanied the new guest up to his room, deposited his luggage and advised that champagne would be served as soon as David was ready to come down.

"You look like your dad," Adele said in a quiet voice as she buzzed around the kitchen.

Shelby began setting the table for dinner. "I'll take that as a compliment."

"It was meant as one. He's gorgeous."

Jack was opening a bottle of champagne and listening to their exchange. "Hey, you two, I'm beginning to feel like an old ugly dog," he groused.

Adele put the finishing touches on a sweet potato casserole. "Honey, chopped liver you're not. You're just too much like my brother to think of you as gorgeous. Although," she looked up, appraising him, "you're one damn fine specimen."

"I'll second that." Shelby laughed. "Damn fine." The three were engaged in lively conversation when David came down from upstairs.

"Sounds like I'm missing out," David said. He placed a tissue-covered package in front of Shelby, another in front of Adele, and one in front of Jack.

"What's this?" the three asked almost in unison.

"Little mementos of Peru," David answered.

Shelby opened hers first; it was a hand-carved horse. "Ohmigosh, it is beautiful!" she exclaimed, turning it over and over, extending it for Jack and Adele to see.

Jack received bookends, Adele the set of sterling silver spoons, both of them thanking David profusely. Next they shared a holiday toast. All four stood at the kitchen counter sipping champagne, Shelby, Jack and Adele taking turns plying David with questions about Peru when the telephone rang. Jack reached for the wall phone. Shelby watched his happy smile disappear and he glanced her way.

"Just a moment." He turned to Shelby. "It's Bobby. Want to take it in the living room?"

She nodded and then sprawled in one of the chairs facing the fireplace. "Hi, Bobby."

"Hi, Shel. I was kind of short with you earlier, sorry. Happy Thanksgiving—again." His voice seemed like a stranger's.

"And the same to you." Shelby looked around the room, at a loss for something appropriate to say. Bobby asked about the weather. She told him thirty degrees and last night's storm had left twelve inches of new snow. Beverly Hills, he informed her, was seventy-three degrees at half past five and the Stamford clan had been served their hors d'ocuvres and cocktails on the patio when he arrived at four. It clicked in Shelby's awareness that Esther said he'd left the house around nine. Six unaccounted hours. *Same old Bobby, same old song.*

"Let me grab the portable phone," Bobby said. She could hear voices in the background. "There, that's better." Bobby's voice took on an intimate tone. "Baby, it's good to hear your voice. It sounded like people were there, did I reach the café? Is buddy-boy Jack open today?"

"No, that was Adele and my father you heard."

There was a long pause on the other end of the line.

"Your dad is there?"

"Yes, he just arrived a few hours ago."

"How very cozy."

"Why the sudden sarcasm, Bobby?"

"As I recall there are only two bedrooms at the Troutsprings Hilton. I know you're not going to sleep with your father."

"We are at Jack's ranch house. There are four bedrooms here," she said coolly.

"Oh." There was another long silence. "Sorry."

Shelby knew exactly what Bobby would do next. *Here comes persuasion.*

"Shel, do you miss me?"

"Do you miss me?"

Bobby chuckled. "You do realize that you are developing an irritating habit of answering a question with a question? Yes, I miss you and we need to talk. Can you fly down?"

"My dad just arrived, Bobby. I can't leave now."

"Can I come up then? How about I fly up? I could be there tomorrow."

"I don't think that would be a good idea, Bobby…not right now." *Here comes the anger.*

"Well, why the hell not? You're still my wife. How long am I supposed to sit around and wait for you to make up your mind?"

Bingo. "Bobby, my father literally got here less than an hour ago. You need to understand I haven't seen him in five years. I don't know how long he's planning to stay but I'll let you know as soon as I find out. How is the Covington project coming along? Are you ready to break ground yet?"

"It's great, just great." Control returned to his voice. "If all goes well we'll break ground the end of January or for sure in February. This is big, Shel. The KXLA piece showed Sunday and the papers got hold of it. The phone hasn't stopped ringing. They're calling it a showcase project. I'm being lauded as the developer of the future. I wish you were here to share it with me. It just doesn't have the same meaning without you."

"I'm happy for you, Bobby. You've worked on Covington for five years. You deserve it. I will talk to Dad and get back to you so we can make some plans, okay?"

"Yeah, okay. You take care, Shel."

"I will. You, too, and be sure to give the kids a hug from me."

The phone clicked without a goodbye. Shelby sat picturing the Stamfords. Adam presiding over the mammoth table, the family gathered around, dinner being served by stout Margaret, who had been with them before Shelby joined the family. She hung up and stared into the fire. Bobby sounded hurt, sad, and then angry. Shelby's rational mind reminded her he could turn it on and off like a faucet. Her emotional side tugged at her heart.

"Mind if I come in?" Jack's voice sounded behind her.

"Of course not, I was just coming back."

Jack came around and sat in the couch facing her. "Are you okay? You look sad."

"He knows how to push my buttons."

"I've witnessed that firsthand. He could be an accordion player," Jack said with utmost seriousness. The mental picture of Bobby playing an accordion made Shelby smile.

"You're absolutely right and I'd make a good monkey at the end of the leash. I'm not going to let anything spoil this day. Thanks for reminding me."

They stood up and she reached for Jack's hand. "Okay," Jack said.

"Adele says dinner is ready and we had better get in there or she'll have their wedding date set."

Dinner was leisurely, pleasant, and convivial, the food so good that all four diners had refills, Jack and David a third time. Everyone lingered over the meal long after the men had pushed their plates away. Shelby rose. "Adele made a pumpkin pie and an apple pie, Dad, that I swear are the best I've ever had, so don't think of giving up yet." She heard groans, then added. "Okay, let's put the turkey away and have dessert in a little while in the living room?"

David sat on the couch and motioned for Shelby to sit next to him. She experienced a familiar feeling from long ago, snuggled against him with his arm slung casually over her shoulder. Jack was happy for her; she could see it in his eyes; Adele's too. The evening ended with everyone eating a slice of both pies. "I'll never eat again," Shelby moaned.

"I need to walk to Kalispell," Jack lamented.

"I'll jog behind you," David groaned.

Adele looked at them with calculated superiority. "Wusses, all. I feel like a million bucks." She donned her heavy jacket. "Thank you, Jack, and you, Shelby. This was a wonderful Thanksgiving. And David, it is so good to meet you. We love your daughter and I'm glad you're going to be with us for a while."

Jack had slipped out and started the Jeep while Adele and Shelby removed the dessert dishes. The motor purred quietly as the three escorted Adele to her car, snow crunching beneath their shoes. Shelby glanced up at the sky and gasped at the sight, millions of stars, the sky awash with them. The full moon's brilliance danced off the snow. David opened the door of the Jeep and stood, staring up at the sky. "I've never seen anything so beautiful," he said.

Shelby was about to agree when Adele spoke up. "Well, thank you, sugar. You're gorgeous too." She laughed at her own joke and hopped into the car. "Bye, everybody!"

David was still chuckling when Adele's car disappeared from sight. "I don't think I've ever met anyone quite like that lady."

Chapter Twenty One

Exhausted from Thanksgiving and the week of preparations, Shelby slept late Friday morning. She brushed her teeth, staring at her reflection, wondering since the round-up, why she felt as though she had run a marathon at the end of each day. *I guess I'm not as tough as I thought.*

She went downstairs and, not finding Jack or her father, she threw on a jacket, cap, and gloves and went in search of them. Instantly revived by the cold air, she marveled at how much bluer the sky seemed here than it did in Santa Monica. Was it no smog, actually brighter, or was it her imagination? One thing for sure, the sun glistening on the snow made the snow sparkle.

Taking her time, she walked down the driveway toward Stagecoach Road, then paused to look back. *I love this view, smoke pouring from the chimney, a foot of snow on the roof, melting into icicles.* They hung from the eaves like ornaments, catching the sun's rays and flashing a dazzling kaleidoscope of colors. Shelby inhaled, letting her eyes feast on the setting. *This is another world and it's beginning to feel like home. Uh-oh, that's an unsettling thought! Abandoning my home, my marriage, my business and the life I've built over the last ten years—what kind of person does that?*

Thankfully, spotting Jack's truck in the winter pasture stopped her self-contemplation. Jack and her father were rolling a hay bale off the back. Though a football field away, she could see her father standing in the pickup bed, looking around and gesturing at the mountains. Her father's Indiana Jones hat identified him as did Jack's Stetson. After observing them for a few minutes, she decided their hats weren't the only thing that set them apart. Still amazed at Jack's seemingly rapid recovery, his effortless motions moving the hay bales gave the appearance of a man far younger than his fifty years. Her father spotted her and waved. Shelby climbed over the fence and tramped through snow across the open field; she was breathing hard when she arrived.

"So, Dad, Jack is teaching you ranching already?"

"He is," David replied. "And this is infinitely better than mining gold."

Shelby stayed with them until they distributed all of the hay then she and David rode on the pickup tailgate back to the house. Jack served pancakes in the sunny breakfast nook. "I thought you liked my pancakes?" he asked, eyeing her barely eaten food.

"I think I ate too much yesterday, my tummy is advising me to beware of food this morning. Don't worry about me starving to death."

Jack nodded. "Tell me, David, has your daughter always had such a healthy appetite?"

"Indeed she did. The summers we spent at the cabin I was never sure who ate more, she or her horse." David chuckled, his eyes were twinkling.

"Okay, guys, be nice. Do you want leftovers for dinner or to eat at the café?"

"Great idea," Jack said. "How does a T-bone steak sound for dinner, David?"

"Trust me, Jack, any steak sounds good to me. Actually Adele suggested it last evening. She told me she was buying the café from you and she seemed pretty excited about it."

"Adele's run the place for a long time anyway. It's time for me to get back to ranching."

After breakfast, Jack begged off, saying he had to call Adele about the sale so Shelby asked her father if he'd like to go for a walk. They took the same path that she and Jack followed on horseback, a tramped-down cattle trail. At first, both hiked in silence taking in the beauty then Shelby stopped and held up her hand. "Listen, isn't the quiet wonderful?"

"You have no idea how I appreciate it. Blasting and mine work is noisy business."

"It's so different here from L.A., Dad, almost another world. You seem to like it here but I was surprised that you took me up so quickly on my invitation," Shelby said tentatively.

"Our getting together was long overdue, Shelby. It's my fault and I feel terrible. You shouldn't have had to do it. Most of all, I'm sorry for letting five years slip away." He opened his arms and Shelby stepped into his welcoming hug.

"I'm sorry too that I got mad. I knew deep down you couldn't end your career right then and I shouldn't have asked. You were right about the argument in the airport. It was the symptom, not the disease." They resumed their walk.

"Life can get so screwed up," he said, the fierceness in his voice surprising Shelby.

She brushed away a tear. "Are you talking about us?"

"No, just life in general. 'Us' is no longer screwed up, at least I hope not."

"No, we are not and we're going to keep it that way. How long can you stay, Dad?"

"Would I be overstaying my welcome if I hang around through Christmas?"

"Not at all, that would be fabulous!" Shelby fumbled for a tissue and dabbed her eyes.

Not breaking their gait, David glanced at her. "Why the tears, pumpkin?"

"Five weeks! That's longer than we've been together since our days at the cabin. That's over twenty years. I feel like our lives are whizzing by, you spending yours in one hemisphere and me in another. I hate that. I always have, especially now."

Now it was David's turn to dab his eyes. "Tell me, what happened with Bobby?"

Shelby slowed, struggling to sum up the last ten years into a succinct, understandable explanation. She spoke haltingly at first, telling him about Bobby finally achieving his dream, Covington Square and all that it meant to his career. She explained Bobby encouraging her to start Skyline Construction and then, between Covington and her business, how their lives seemed to drift apart. Her father's eyes grew wide when she told him about her hunch to follow Bobby, then still in her Snoopy nightshirt, she saw him get into a Lexus and eventually turn into a motel.

"Good Lord, what a waste of ingenuity."

"Ingenuity he definitely has, but that made it pretty clear he doesn't value our marriage."

When she explained her reasons for their vacation in the Eagle and it breaking down in Ellie's parking lot, David let out a low whistle. "Wow, isn't that interesting."

"Why, what are you thinking? Fate? Karma?"

"You have to admit it's pretty amazing about how many events had to happen to land you in that parking lot at that moment and Jack be right there to help you. Then he gets shot and there you are when he needed help—sounds like fate to me. I don't know Jack, but he strikes me as genuine, a man of integrity, something that obviously doesn't apply to Bobby." David squeezed Shelby's hand. "That's not a blanket condemnation, but it does seem odd that Bobby has integrity in business but not in his personal life. What do you plan to do, or do you know?"

"I'm not sure and that's the trouble. Bobby called yesterday, and I hate to admit it but most of my time on the phone I spent predicting what tactic he was going to use next. And the sad part, I was dead on. It made me realize that's been his pattern of behavior from the start."

When they reached the creek, Shelby paused at how different it looked: bare trees and the boulders covered with snow. David brushed off two of them. "Pull up a rock," he said.

"Don't mind if I do."

"So where is all this introspection leading?"

"Hopefully for some clarity and Bobby to value our marriage. I wanted so very much for ours to work and not end up like you and Mom, promise to love one another forever then kiss it off and break everyone's heart." Shelby noticed a flicker of pain cross his face. "I'm sorry, Dad."

"Is that what you think I did? Kiss it off?"

"I admit I did at first but later, much later, I realized you and Mom are so different you were doomed from the start. Now I'm thinking that may be the case with Bobby and me. I want children but he doesn't. I've come to realize I can't love him the way he is and I don't believe he can change. I'm not even sure it would be fair to ask him to change."

"Pretty insightful, sounds like you've already made up your mind," he said quietly. "Where does Jack fit into this picture?"

"What makes you think Jack's in this picture at all?"

"The fate aspect, the look in his eyes when he sees you and the way you look at him."

"It makes no sense, Dad. I'm on a trip that I hoped would save my marriage and the next thing I know I'm on Jack's doorstep, literally, and my whole world goes off its axis."

"I remember a saying I heard years ago that explains a lot of things. 'The heart has reasons that reason cannot know.'" Shelby listened, her eyes on her father's face. "Think about it, Shelby. That explains the unexplainable, those times when your heart doesn't follow logic or reason—it doesn't have to because you know it in here." David touched his chest. From the look on his face, Shelby could tell that saying had been important to him at some point in his life.

"That's a thought-provoker," she said. "Shakespeare?"

"No, Blaise Pascal, a seventeenth-century religious philosopher. I like it because it is as true today as it was then. Universal truths hold up through time, so listen to your heart. Does Jack have feelings for you?"

"He's never told me he loves me if that's what you mean. I know he really loved his wife. I'm not sure he's over her, although selling the café may be a sign he is letting go."

"Sometimes, pumpkin, men don't say how they feel as much as they show it. Jack strikes me as a man to whom talk is cheap." At that Shelby sighed. Her father pulled her to her feet and took hold of both hands. "Okay, what's with the big sigh?"

"Conflicting feelings, but talking about it with my dad helps." She managed a smile.

"So you feel a little better?"

"You're here. Of course I feel better."

"Then I'm happy. The trip has already accomplished one good thing."

* * *

Jack left the ranch hoping to find Adele at the café; he needed to talk. He breathed a sigh of relief at the sight of her Jeep in the parking lot. She was humming along with the radio when Jack let himself in. She greeted him with a smile. "Hey, Jack. How you doing?"

"I'm not sure." He sat down at the bar. "I gave Shelby and her dad a chance to talk."

"How are those two, anyway?"

"You mean how is David Longren."

"Okay, so I think he's cute. No law against that."

"No law," he said. Jack could feel his heart racing, wondering where and how to start.

Adele turned to face him. "Something's wrong. Tell me, what is it?" Jack could only shake his head, feeling like a fool. Adele came around the bar and sat on the stool next to him. "Jack Ketchum, we've been friends since Moses. You tell me right now what's wrong."

"Okay, but you have to give me your word you won't repeat anything we talk about."

"You sound crazy. Repeat what?"

"If you don't promise, I'm not saying another word."

"Okay, okay. I give you my word. What's this all about?"

"I'm in love, Adele, in love with another man's wife. I can't help how I feel and, dammit, it's driving me nuts."

Adele nodded, seeming to digest his words. "I'm not surprised you're in love with her. She's a beautiful, amazing woman. I see your wedding ring is gone. Have you told Shelby?"

"Of course not!"

"Why not?"

"She's married. How can I say anything? I'm pretty sure she's still in love with Bobby, or thinks she is." Jack remembered his argument with Shelby on the ride home from Adele's.

"Do you think she has feelings for you?"

"Yes, I do but I know for a fact she's mixed-up about her whole situation. I don't want to put more pressure on her. She hasn't been feeling well, like all this worrying is wearing her out."

"Has she said anything about going back to Bobby?"

"No, but when he called last night she looked sad, like maybe she misses him."

"Well, I know her father wants to stay through Christmas. I asked David last night and that's what he said, so she can't be planning on leaving for another month."

"Really? David said through Christmas?"

"Yes, and a lot of things can happen in a month." He caught her mischievous look.

"You talking about me or you two?" He managed a grin.

Adele put her hand on his arm, her expression serious. "Don't drive yourself crazy, Jack. Shelby loves you. I can see it when she looks at you. She may not realize it yet, and you're right that she's mixed up. She wants to do the right thing. Just give her some time and have faith."

"Faith! She's married, for God's sake, and she wants kids. I can't give her children." He shook his head in disbelief. "I must be out of my mind."

"Jack, you were there for me when I lost Paul and Tim. Faith was all I did have then."

"I'm sorry, Adele. I remember very well." He nodded. "Then you don't think I'm a fool?"

"Honey, if you're a fool, I'm the village idiot. I believe in love and, call me nuts, but I still believe there's some wonderful guy out there that's gonna love me as much as I love him. No, Jack Ketchum, keep the faith. You are not a fool."

Chapter Twenty Two

Beverly Hills, the heart and soul of L.A.'s upper crust populace, was where Bobby preferred to shop and get his Christmas spirit. In the three blocks that comprised the Rodeo Walk of Style, one could shop in over a hundred world-famous stores and boutiques: Versace, Ferragamo, Louis Vuitton, Chanel, Hermes, Cartier, Harry Winston, plus Bijan, which operated on an appointment-only basis. And Bobby's favorite, Armani. He loved to walk the three blocks on Rodeo between Santa Monica and Wilshire and let the full impact of the wealth and power it represented inspire him. Rolls and Ferraris were not an uncommon sight, neither were casually-clad celebrities.

One never took notice. It simply wasn't done.

Bobby waited at his favorite table on the second floor overlooking the indoor patio at The Courtyard on Rodeo Drive, a noontime favorite. A cocktail waitress, wearing a short Santa suit, black fishnet stockings, and high black boots, took his order. "Double scotch, please," he said and settled back, watching her shapely derriere disappear and the Christmas spirit invade.

He could certainly use some holiday cheer after Shelby ruined his Thanksgiving by staying in Montana. Notifying his mother that Shelby would also not be attending the Stamford Christmas dinner, Martha Stamford requested that he come "sans date, darling." When he relayed that to Terri, it initiated a week-long snit, ending only when Bobby surprised her with a modest emerald drop necklace.

Bobby found it difficult to figure out his mother. Blue-blood Martha Weston Stamford had opposed his marriage to a flight attendant. They never became close, but now that Shelby was gone, Martha constantly inquired if he had heard from her and wanted to know if she was remaining in Montana because she was ill. Martha suddenly sounded as though she cared a great deal about Shelby. Bobby often wondered how he turned out to be such a cool guy with his mother doing the raising.

Stuart showed up with a full briefcase for their last meeting on Covington until after the holidays. The latest hitch was a request from the Planning Commission that required several arterial street design alterations. The request, now attached to the Tentative Tract Map, would be part of the conditions for approval. "You look tired, Stuart. Am I working you too hard?"

"I'm fine, Bobby, just trying to finish up coordinating the street improvements with the city engineers. Nothing that can't be dealt with but I don't want to leave anything hanging. Vicki and I are taking the kids to Colorado on a family ski holiday. We leave the day after they get out of school. Zach and Lindsay are really excited. They insisted we rent a unit that has a fireplace, and both of them wrote Santa and told him our condo number."

Bobby summoned the cocktail waitress. "Good for you and glad you're getting away."

"Sorry the meeting with CAPE was delayed. Houghton and Kathryn Alexander were both in Washington, D.C. Maybe I should send Vickie and the kids on ahead and follow later."

"Not on your life. You go as planned. I have a luncheon date with the infamous Ms. Alexander next week and I will take care of every—"

"We're awfully close on this, Bobby," Stuart interjected. "You sure I can trust you with her? And what about Houghton?" Stuart was smiling but Bobby could see he was serious.

"Ms. Alexander said he is still in Washington. Don't worry, I'll behave. Besides that, it would wreck your family trip for Vickie and the kids if Dad isn't there to ski with them."

"Thanks, Bobby. With all that's been accomplished, let's assume everything will go smoothly. Just be cool with Kathryn. We've gotten their approval every step of the way. She just needs assurance that we're sticking to our commitment clear through phase three."

"Not to worry." *Give me some credit, counselor. I can handle Kathryn Alexander.*

Stuart presented Bobby with the pending papers, a list of names and telephone numbers of key people, answers to possible questions, and his notes. He wrote down the telephone number of the Snowflake Condominium office and handed it to Bobby.

Bobby wished Stuart a good trip, and as soon as he returned to the office, he instructed Terri to buy ski sweaters and hats for the Flaherty children and have them Christmas-wrapped. He wanted to deliver them himself. She wanted to know their sizes. "I don't know," Bobby said. The boy is eight, the girl five, you figure it out." He waved her off, anxious to make a call.

There was no answer at Jack's ranch house. *Damn, the middle of December in Montana, for chrissake. You should be in the house once in a while. Where the hell are you?* Bobby had given a lot of thought to Shelby and their marriage in the last two weeks. He wanted her back; life was better with her. Beautiful and classy, yet she took care of everything—exactly what he needed in his position. The biggest contention, children, shouldn't be an issue much longer. Her biological clock was quickly running out. *Kids are cute when they're somebody else's.*

His biggest fear was basic economics. After seeing Paige William-son's setup, Bobby mentally calculated then confirmed with Stuart that if Shelby divorced him, it would cost him four, maybe five million, depending on her attorney. Not to mention a hefty amount of spousal support. *No way do I want to cough up that kind of money.*

Bobby tried the ranch house again, cradling the phone on his shoulder as he wrote *Shelby* at the top of a yellow pad, then scribbled a list of things to discuss with her. The phone rang a dozen times. *Still no answer.* Satisfied he had enough ammunition for his call, Bobby left the list near the phone to remind himself to try again.

He didn't even try to count the party invitations he'd received; it looked to be one every night for the rest of December and he needed to make an appearance at all of them. All the title companies threw parties, as did the major suppliers, contractors, legal offices and, of course, Stamford competitors. He especially liked to attend those, wearing one of his Armani suits, graciously talking a little business, complimenting this or that project, then glancing at his Rolex and moving on to the next party.

Stamford Development's Christmas party was the affair by which all others were judged. No office of any importance planned a party on December 23; that date belonged to Stamford. Founded by his grandfather, John Weston, then bought by Adam Stamford, theirs was the oldest development firm in L.A., with a client base that read like *Who's Who in California.*

Bobby tried Shelby one last time before he left, but still no answer. In his car, he called the Flahertys on his cell to make sure they were home, then called Dominique's Vintage Wines in Westwood and asked them to ice a bottle of Mumm's Cordon Rouge. He picked it up a few minutes later.

Vickie answered the door of their Spanish-style home in the older section of Brentwood. "Bobby! Nice to see you, come on in." She kissed his cheek and ushered Bobby into the large foyer. "Stuart, Bobby's here," she called up the stairs.

Stuart came bounding down, dressed in navy blue sweats. "This is an unexpected treat. Come on in the family room." Bobby handed him the bottle of champagne.

"I happen to know this is your favorite. Merry Christmas."

"How thoughtful," Vickie said. "And ice cold. How about I get some glasses." She disappeared toward the kitchen. Stuart led Bobby through a rounded archway into the spacious family room. Flames from the gas fireplace flickered evenly as colorful lights glowed on the Christmas tree, and there was a wonderful aroma coming from the adjacent kitchen.

"Don't you say a word, an environmentalist with a gas fireplace," Stuart said with mock sternness. "I would have gotten rid of it years ago but the kids love it. Sometimes it's necessary to compromise one's beliefs in the interest of family harmony."

Vickie returned with the champagne and three tall flutes on a tray. Bobby was surprised when he was re-introduced to Zachary and Lindsay. Zachary gave him a firm handshake and Lindsay was equally polite, then both played a board game on the floor in front of the fire.

"Zachary looks like a miniature version of you, Stuart," Bobby said, watching Zachary.

"I know. I keep telling him he's going to grow up to be as ugly as I am. You ought to see him play tennis."

"How did the tennis tournament go?"

"We won. Father and son champions, right, Zach?" Zach flashed his dad a smile.

"Lindsay is starting tennis in the spring," Vickie said.

"You two are making me feel old," sighed Bobby.

"Can you stay and have a bite with us?" Stuart asked. Vickie nodded her approval. Bobby had intended to stop for a quick glass of champagne, give the children their gifts, then go to the Colonial American party. But something about the closeness of the family made him accept. The wonderful aroma turned out to be chicken marsala, quinoa, and a spinach salad. Both children helped their mother serve dinner. Bobby was impressed with their table manners and social skills. After dinner, they cleared away the empty plates.

"Why don't you both thank Mr. Stamford for joining us, then scoot off to bed? It's your bedtime," Stuart said.

"Before you go I have a little gift for you." Bobby retrieved the shopping bag from the entryway where he left it.

"That's really nice of you, Bobby," Vickie said. "What do you say, kids?" Both said thank you as he put the packages in their arms. They tore through the beautiful wrapping. Lindsay held the sweater up to her chin, her grin with two missing front teeth, indicating her approval. "Totally cool," Zachary said and pulled the sweater on over his clothes. Brother and sister thanked Bobby again and disappeared up the stairs with their mother.

"Great kids, Stuart. Have a wonderful holiday. Forget L.A., forget Covington. I'll only call if we have an earthquake and the Covington property ends up in the Pacific."

Bobby bade his friend good-bye and headed for Wilshire Boulevard; he still had time to make an appearance at the party. The noise and excitement of a party no longer appealed to him; a light rain was falling and home sounded good but he had promised his father he would represent Stamford. Bobby turned on the windshield wipers, their rhythmic beat inviting contemplation. *What the hell, those kids weren't so bad. A pint-sized Bobby Stamford would be okay. I can at least offer to have kids. That ought to help get Shelby back home.*

Bobby pulled up at the curb and a uniformed attendant handed him a claim check and took his car. Music pulsed forth; the party was still going strong. Matching boxwood topiaries on either side of the colonial facade were festooned with twinkling white lights. A huge designer-decorated Christmas tree filled the foyer. Once inside, he felt revived as he looked around the elite crowd.

Bobby spotted George Wrenstead, Colonial's President, and they made eye contact. George immediately extricated himself from his guest, shaking hands and greeting partygoers as he made his way across the large room toward Bobby. A cocktail waitress appeared, took Bobby's order, and returned with a scotch just as he reached George's side. As they chatted, Bobby's eyes roamed over the crowd.

He spotted her immediately, her back to him, a glittering red dress clinging to her every curve. Terri Armstrong was looking up into the face of a young, tanned, good-looking guy, touching his arm in an intimate way. Bobby stayed his obligatory time with Wrenstead, until he was able to free himself when someone else approached. Bobby moved in Terri's direction.

"I love sailing," he heard her say.

"Great! I could arrange a sail on my boat. I'm out almost every weekend," the man said.

"Terri!" Bobby tapped her scquined shoulder.

She spun around. "Bobby, how wonderful to see you!" The emerald drop necklace rested against bronzed skin that was visible right down to her inviting décolletage.

"Why don't you introduce me to your friend?" Bobby said.

"Of course. Steven Lange, this is Robert Stamford. Steven is a commercial real estate broker, Bobby. He specializes in retail leases in Beverly Hills." Terri flashed Bobby a dazzling smile. Bobby judged

Lange to be in his early to mid-thirties. He gave Bobby a firm hand-shake.

"Nice to meet you, sir."

Sir? Who are you calling sir, you little prick? "A commercial broker and you sail? What kind of a rig do you have?"

"A thirty-foot Ericson, Bruce King design." He sounded proud. "Do you sail?"

"I do." He shot Terri a glance. "A forty-foot Hunter. I moor it at Marina del Rey."

The fellow looked properly impressed.

Guess I trumped him. Why am I jealous of this little shit anyway?

"See you at the office, Terri. Good to meet you, Lange. Maybe we'll meet in the Marina bar." He gave them his practiced smile and touched his eyebrow in mock salute.

"Yes, sir, good to meet you, too—"

Bobby moved off mid-sentence. He had intended to leave after talking with George Wrenstead but instead decided to stay and work the room. He conversed with other Colonial officers and a few wannabe developers who seemed flustered at being zeroed in on by the now TV-recognizable Bobby Stamford. He knew exactly where the red dress was at all times; wherever it went, Mr. Good-Looking Tan Face was never far away.

Bobby spotted a blonde. Beautiful, tastefully dressed in a chic black suit, her long hair falling softly onto her shoulders. He instinc-tively moved toward her. *Perfect. Red Dress and Mr. Cheap Boat are close by.* "Excuse me, we have met. You are the friend of Leigh Anne's that she works out with all the time?"

The blonde returned an amused smile. "Leigh Anne?"

"Leigh Anne Kinney, KXLA, the news lady?"

"Very innovative. Has that ever actually worked for you?"

Bobby chuckled. "You would have to ask. I figured I was safe because you'd surely seen her on TV. Was it that bad?" He moved closer and inhaled. She wore a fragrance he recognized, and whatever it was, Brenda Langley had worn it. "Okay, I admit that was pretty lame."

She eyed him over her drink. "Tell me, would you have been embarrassed if I had said yes and put you on the spot to remember my name?"

"Not to worry, I'd have found a way." He held out his hand. "Bobby Stamford, Stamford Development. A very Merry Christmas to you and what is that amazing perfume? I want to remember it." They touched glasses. Terri glanced his way, her eyebrows arched in surprise.

"Rita Forrester, Attorney. Merry Christmas to you as well. It's Gucci Guilty."

Bobby had to chuckle at her backatcha reply. He loved three-play, the step before foreplay: seeing if the chemistry lasted past the intro-duction, finding out the occupation and marital status. They exchanged cards. Rita Forrester was in private practice, specializing in real estate law. Thirty-eight, graduate of Hastings law school in San Francisco, divorced, and not involved with anyone. That took five minutes.

"I look forward to giving you a call," he said as she moved away.

She nodded and smiled. "I look forward to it as well."

Satisfied that Red Dress saw their exchange, he turned toward Terri and raised his empty glass in a silent, smile-less toast.

Chapter Twenty Three

With Stuart gone Bobby's next few days were dizzying. He met with engineers, architects, planning and zoning; he took calls from several well-known contractors who wanted to know when the job bids would be awarded. His days seemed consumed by Covington, but Bobby decided Stuart's absence was a good thing. Necessity forced him to become familiar with the maze that constituted the permit process: a tangle of regulations on design, landscape, parking, pollution, noise, engineering, public safety, even maintenance. All cumbersome, tedious and expensive, and everything he learned came in handy when he met CAPE's second in command.

Bobby's lunch with Kathryn Alexander went smoothly. Afterward he knew he should call Stuart to reassure him but didn't, not wanting to intrude on their vacation. Stuart was right, Kathryn wasn't his type. The biographical file compiled by Terri was invaluable. He knew what clubs Kathryn belonged to, her political affiliation and graduate school. And he had subtly used them all. She was wary but friendly, stating point-blank: "You being aware of the tremendous additional costs to build totally green, I'm curious why you would undertake this concept?"

He knew better than to try and con her so his answer was: "Fame of a sort. I admit it was a personal goal to seek national status as the developer of a radically important concept." That made her smile but she bought it and they agreed to meet again when Houghton returned.

Bobby had reached Shelby three times in the past couple of weeks; she sounded happy. She was enjoying her father's visit and thankfully did not mention Jack Ketchum one time. *I knew that hick didn't figure into this.* Still, he was annoyed that Shelby didn't come home as soon as Thanksgiving was over. Her answer: she was sorry but her father wanted to stay in Montana through Christmas and there was nothing she could do about it. In their last conversation she promised when the holidays were over, she would come to L.A. Bobby held up offering to have children until her visit. He wanted to do that in person, over a romantic dinner.

His mother called, saying that one holiday dinner was quite enough for her to be responsible for, so the Stamford family Christmas dinner would take place at the Bel Air Country Club. Bobby was relieved; it would be glitzy and festive and the country club was the place to see and be seen. Past Presidents and Supreme Court Justices were not an uncommon sight. The family planned to convene afterward at Rick and Karen's house to open gifts with the children.

Bobby implored his mother to find out from Karen what the children wanted, then buy it, have it gift-wrapped and labeled from Uncle Bobby. His gift to Shelby, already wrapped and mailed, was a set of custom-made tools—the best money could buy. They were the building-trade equivalent of Nike golf clubs complete with the finest leather engraved toolbelt. In his quest to get Shelby back, he swore to leave nothing to chance.

He ignored Terri after the Colonial party and she treated him with cool indifference. Their business dealings were brief and professional and Bobby was actually relieved. She was now some other guy's problem. He had Rita Forrester and Leigh Anne Kinney's numbers and invitations from both to call. They might not be gold medalists in bed, but they would be a lot easier to control. Actually, things were going along swimmingly in all departments.

Bobby put everything on his desk away and locked his files. All work stopped as of five o'clock, December 22nd. Stamford Development's Christmas party began at six o'clock the following day, December 23rd, and he had some last-minute shopping to do. Matalyn Jeffries, Stamford's decorator, had sent four of her staff members over. Bobby could see them through his open door, directing the junior Stamford staff in unloading their vans. Matalyn herself would be popping in during the day and tomorrow to make sure everything met her exacting standards and to marvel at her own creativeness. Martha Stamford had selected the menu and wines with the caterer, none other than Wolfgang Puck of Spago. Bobby made it a point to be gone during the day; he preferred to arrive at five o'clock dressed and ready to meet L.A.'s elite.

December 23rd Bobby arrived at the party exactly at five and had to admit Matalyn had outdone herself this year; the decorations were magnificent. An unspoken rivalry existed among local interior designers and Matalyn Jeffries had guaranteed both Bobby and Adam that this year's tree would "blow away the competition." The deep green carpets and forest green granite counters were the perfect palette on which to create a Christmas wonderland. The employees' tree, put up at the beginning of December, was replaced by the much-anticipated pièce de resistance of the party: the eighteen-foot flocked tree that occupied the foyer.

Covered in twinkling colored lights, it was decked out with tiny ceramic replicas of famous southern California landmarks: a lighted miniature duplicate of the Hollywood Sign, a perfect Norton Simon Museum, the USC library, Dodger Stadium, the Rose Bowl, the Franciscan Mission, the Matterhorn at Disneyland, authentic-looking ceramic street signs blinking Hollywood and Vine, and a detailed Coliseum. Hung exactly right, each one was handmade, perfectly detailed and exquisitely painted, a showy tribute to this money-driven political sphere of influence, and a tribute to the foresight of the development industry that created them.

Bobby did a double-take as he toured the office. The twenty-foot conference table, centered with an ice sculpture of a Christmas tree, was laden with giant shells filled with fresh oysters, cracked crab, a variety of pasta salads with fresh seafood, the sculpture surrounded by crystal bowls with jumbo prawns hooked over the edge, platters of rare roast beef and lamb, all delectably prepared and artfully displayed. Two chefs, each with two assistants, served the elegantly-clad guests.

Bobby acknowledged that the old and new money of L.A. showed up, the fat cats who owned Boardwalk and Park Place, the hotels and railroads. Bobby took note of his mother fussing over the President of USC while Adam made sure to greet several former USC football players retired from the NFL. Bobby greeted judges, senators, congressmen, and several top people in L.A. County and City government. If there happened to be a municipal, educational or judicial emergency, the corresponding representative would come to the Stamford party knowing his or her boss would be there. The Chief of LAPD never missed the party.

The guests went wild over the Christmas tree. A photographer from the *L.A. Times* showed up early and took pictures of it, the reporter interviewing Matalyn Jeffries. Both reporter and photographer stayed to get candid shots of the guests and a story for the society page.

The party netted a dozen confirmed new clients and four potentials. Between Bobby, Adam and Martha, every guest was personally greeted and wished a Merry Christmas by a Stamford. That was a standing order from Adam and endorsed by Bobby, a matter of good breeding and good business. Bobby had sent personal invitations to Rita Forrester and Leigh Anne Kinney. Leigh Anne phoned her regrets that she would be in Atlanta for Christmas but would be available on New Year's Eve if he was free.

Rita came to the party looking smashing in a shimmering sequined dress. "You look dynamite, counselor. I'm sorry we haven't had a chance to talk since the Colonial get-together. If you could stay after the party, we could have a nightcap."

"That would be nice. This is some party, Bobby. Thank you for the personal invitation."

"My pleasure," Bobby said, taking note of Terri watching him, which he noticed she did throughout the evening. He gave Rita a kiss on the cheek and hurried off to mingle. The last guests left around midnight.

Bobby stood at the door along with Adam and wished the departing guests a happy holiday, his father and mother leaving shortly after. With the office quiet, the lights dimmed, and the food removed, Bobby joined Rita in his private office. The chef had prepared two plates. Bobby hadn't eaten a morsel for he had greeted more than his share of guests. They sat across from each other on matching couches, separated by a table with a bottle of Domaine Chandon sparkling wine chilling in a bucket. Bobby filled their champagne flutes.

"I had heard about Stamford's Christmas bash," Rita said, "but it exceeded all the buzz. I don't think I've ever seen so many important people in one place. You're to be congratulated."

"I admit we go all out." He raised his glass to Rita, then took a long sip. "It's a way to thank our long-time clients, get some new ones, and provide the powers that be in this city with the opportunity to socialize."

"I now realize you were joking with that lame come-on. You are really quite charming, Bobby, and I recognize this is your element." Rita raised her glass in return and then drank.

Bobby heard a noise from the darkened outer office. "Hang on to that thought. I'll be right back." He put down his glass and walked into the central suite, the Christmas tree lights the only illumination. Terri was sitting with her shoes off, her feet propped up on a desk, swigging champagne directly from the bottle. "Yo! Bobby. How goes the conquest of the counselor?"

"Terri? You're drunk!"

"No shit!"

"What the hell are you still doing here? Where is Mr. Thirty-foot Ericson?"

"Now, now, just because I was a little friendly to a nice guy doesn't mean you should be trying to lay a friggin' lawyer—an old one at that." Terri's head fell back as she laughed.

"I'm calling you a cab. You need to go home and sober up. Drunk is not your best side."

Terri took another drink from the bottle and hurled it at Bobby. "Fuck you."

Bobby ducked, the bottle flying by just as Rita Forrester came out of Bobby's office.

"Bobby? Is everything all right?"

"No problem, Rita. Unfortunately just an employee who's had too much to drink."

Terri stood up, swaying uncertainly. "Just an employee? Had too much to drink? I have not had too much to drink! I am sotally tober," she slurred.

"Terri, that's enough. I'm sorry about this, Rita. Perhaps I'd better see to it Ms. Armstrong gets home. She is hallucinating."

"I understand, Bobby. These things happen. Give me a call when you can."

Bobby left Terri standing, holding onto the desk. "Stay here." He walked Rita to her car and waited until she drove out of the parking lot, then let himself back in the office. The room smelled of champagne and wet wool. Terri was nowhere to be seen. Bobby walked toward his private office, following a trail of shoes, Terri's black suit jacket, next a skirt, panties, and finally near the couch, a black lace bra. Terri was stretched out on the couch, naked except for the champagne bottle balanced precariously on her stomach.

"Bet you can't balance one of these." She laughed and the bottle started to fall. Bobby reached over and grabbed it before it spilled.

He sat down across from her. "You are out of line. Get dressed, I'm taking you home."

"C'mon, baby, let's have a little fun first." She swung her arm inviting him closer, but hit the small Christmas tree on the coffee table. Bobby caught it mid-air.

He jumped up. "I want your ass out of here in the next five minutes. You got that?"

Terri blinked as if trying to focus. She struggled to sit up, bare feet on the floor, chin resting on her hand. Bobby sat back down, deliberately keeping his eyes on her face.

"Or what?" she said blankly.

"What the hell do you mean, or what?"

"What's the big Bobby Stamford gonna do? Spank me? That'd be fun." She giggled. "Or maybe you're planning on firin' me." She shook her head. "Not a good idea, legal stuff can get sooo messy. CAPE might not endorse your little project if they knew everything about you that I know. And Adam wouldn't like it either, his son fucking the PR assistant."

"Stop it, Terri, you're making a fool of yourself. Get your clothes on."

Terry sat up straight and her smile disappeared. "I've told you before, Bobby, do not underestimate me. But you are doing it again. That's not very wise." She stared at him coolly with no trace of a slur in her voice. *She wasn't drunk at all, she was pretending!*

Her threat and total clarity hit like an electric shock. "What do you want, money?"

"No, sweetie, money I can get anytime. I want Bobby Stamford all to myself, no old lawyers or TV babes. C'mon, honey, let's have some fun." She lay back, one leg on the couch, the other leg dangling over the edge. She closed her eyes and began rubbing her breasts.

"Do your job, Bobby. You want to keep little Terri happy, don't you?"

Chapter Twenty Four

Shelby and her father strolled along Kalispell's Main Street arm in arm as gusty winds swirled snow around them and the other Christmas shoppers. David patted her gloved hand. "This has been wonderful, getting to spend time with you and meeting Jack and Adele. I'm glad Christmas is two whole weeks away."

"I know and I don't want to even think of you leaving. Let's not talk about it." Their first errand of the day had been to ship boxes of gifts, one huge one for the Stamford clan directly to Karen and Rick's house via UPS, a second one to Esther, Oscar, and Enrique, and a third box to Laura and Dennis Baxter in Montrose, Colorado. Shelby told her father about Bobby's gift. "He considers himself a pretty good chef so I checked out cookbooks online. I liked the description of Gordon Ramsay's *Three Star Chef* so I bought the set of three books. It isn't often a chef with thirteen Michelin Stars gives away his top secrets but Ramsay does. I think Bobby will like that."

David told her when he found a gift for Adele, his shopping was done. Shelby soon found out he wasn't easily pleased. They browsed in shop after shop, glancing at possible gifts, until finally he stopped before the window of a jewelry store. "I see what I want." He chose an initial pin, a fancy gold A, with a single small diamond. Shelby recognized her father's thoughtfulness. He was making a statement, just what the statement was, she wasn't exactly sure.

"That's perfect, Dad, elegant and personal. She will love it, now how about some food?"

"You bet." David slapped his gloved hands together. "I'm starving!"

"Okay, Tavern on Green Street, here we come," she said and laughed as he made the sign of the cross. Shelby noted it was snowing harder, coating the branches of maples in the sidewalk planters, the bare branches festooned with miniature white lights. Shelby glanced back, locking into her memory bank the Christmas picture of Main Street in Kalispell. *In case I don't come back.*

Finding Tavern on Green Street, they were swept through the double doors aided by the wind, the warmth inside briefly stinging their faces. They both stopped and inhaled. "Good smells and fresh coffee!" her father said. He ordered steak sandwiches for both of them.

"This is so much fun, Dad. I don't want this day to end."

"You're having fun and it shows. Is it possible your being away from Bobby's shenanigans is the reason? Or maybe it's being around Jack?"

"Possibly both," she said. "You look better than when you arrived too. How much is attributable to Adele and how much is my doing?"

"Touché." He grinned and toasted her with his coffee cup.

Shelby paused as the waitress served their food. "I have to go back to L.A. after the holidays. I promised Bobby we'd talk."

"Do you know when you're leaving?"

"No, but I need to set a date. What are your plans or do you have any?"

David paused eating, obviously thinking over her question. "I don't know. I haven't even called the office. I guess I'm not anxious to go back, either."

They left the subject up in the air, Shelby instinctively feeling their mention of leaving had put a damper on the day. David, behind the wheel of Adele's Jeep, waited outside a shop while Shelby ran in and picked up the gift she'd ordered for Jack.

Though her father's three weeks had flown by way too fast, she felt they'd both made a concentrated effort to savor every moment. Up early, their days began over coffee, her listening to him talk about his job, filling her in on Peru, Inca history and its architecture. It pleased her that he wanted to know about Skyline and asked if she had any pictures. "Yes, I do. They're on my iPad at the ranch. Remind me when we get back, okay?"

Lunch finished, they headed back to Troutsprings, neither one mentioning Bobby on the drive, and her father artfully avoiding any mention of her mother. He let her know how much he enjoyed helping Jack with the cattle and, despite the cold, how he loved the three of them taking wintry rides. "Patches is a great horse."

Her tummy full and the Jeep nice and warm, Shelby put her head back, hesitant to bring up Adele though she was curious how he felt about her. It seemed they were attracted to each other but then, she reasoned, who wouldn't like her dad or Adele. Shelby loved the four of them socializing over dinner at Adele's and the ranch, then playing dominoes or cards. *Like a real family. But the evening ten days ago when all four of us decorated the tree is when I saw the spark between Dad and Adele. That was a nice evening.* Shelby remembered with four people it didn't take long to finish the tree. Finished and the tree lights on, David opened the champagne that Adele brought and they toasted "the most beautiful tree in Montana!" Afterward, Adele wouldn't let them relax; she wanted to dance and insisted Jack find his CD's.

Music playing, both men hesitated until a slow song came on and Adele summoned David to dance with her. Shelby watched as her father closed his eyes, his cheek next to Adele's as they danced; he looked so happy! She and Jack joined them, first dancing to slow songs, then faster ones, and finally all four rockin' and rollin' until they collapsed on the couches laughing at each other. At evening's end, she saw her father kiss Adele, a romantic kiss on the lips.

She finally broke their amiable silence as they neared Troutsprings. "You and Adele are getting along great. She is unique but there's a lot more to her than her huge zest for life."

David remained silent for a few minutes then glanced over at her. "More often than not, zest like that comes from having survived great personal tragedy."

"Wow, is that an autobiographical comment from my father?"

David Longren's thoughtful expression instantly disappeared. "It's Christmas. I'm with my daughter. Let's not be serious."

"Okay, but you have to promise we'll talk about this before you go back to Peru? Otherwise you're not leaving Montana."

"I promise. I should learn to keep my mouth shut," he said.

* * *

Shelby decided that if she had ever imagined Christmas in Montana, she would not have done justice to the real thing. A fast-moving storm on Christmas Eve day snarled traffic for travelers but for those fortunate to be spending the holiday in one spot, it was glorious. Adele closed the café and put a sign *Closed for Remodeling-Watch for Reopening* on the door. She asked if they could celebrate Christmas Eve at her house and it was agreed they would open gifts on Christmas Day at the ranch.

Adele served a special dinner in the dining room of her cozy Pine Ridge home, the table elegantly decked with gold candles, miniature poinsettias, and her best crystal and china.

"Oh, Adele, how beautiful," Shelby exclaimed, eyeing the table.

They took turns taking selfies with their phones but Jack wanted a real photo so he set his Nikon on a ledge, put it on automatic and then dived into place for a photo of all four of them with glasses raised. A tape of Christmas music was playing in the background.

Jack, Adele and David were talking and laughing. Sitting opposite them Shelby couldn't help but visualize the black-tie dinner the Stamfords were no doubt having about now at the country club. She had talked earlier with Bobby, Karen and the children. *Different worlds.* Glancing around the table, Shelby couldn't suppress a smile at getting to spend Christmas with her father, their relationship restored and wrapped in the warmth of Adele and Jack. Taking it all in, it pushed the uncertainty of her future to the farthest reaches of her mind.

Adele and David topped each other's funny stories and Jack joined in with tales of past Christmases at the ranch. Her father seemed at ease, even making the coffee. Adele called him "Hon," but then Adele called everyone "Hon."

Finally, Jack stood up and looked at Shelby. "Are you as sleepy and tired as I am?"

"Did I nod off again?" Shelby asked. "Yes, I am exhausted. Besides, we need to get home so Santa can come. Are you ready, Dad?"

"I'm going to stay here tonight, Shelby, and help clean up this lovely mess that Adele has made. We'll drive over in the morning."

He said it so casually and with no awkwardness that it sounded as natural as if he were offering to take out the garbage.

Jack shook David's hand. "We'll see you tomorrow, whenever you get there. There's a pro game on, the Lions playing the Cowboys. Think Adele and Shelby will let us watch it?"

"You must be kidding!" Adele said, hands on her hips. "If there's a game on, you'll have to fight me for a seat in front of the TV."

Jack kissed her cheek. "Thank you, Adele, for a wonderful dinner, beautifully done."

Shelby announced. "We'll be eating on the coffee table in front of the TV because I'm not missing the game either," she said. She hugged and kissed her father and Adele, then she and Jack rode home in amiable silence. When they arrived at the ranch, he loaded wood in the fireplace, plugged in the Christmas tree lights, and put on another CD. "I thought you were tired," Shelby said.

"Not that tired. It's been years since I spent a Christmas Eve here. Let's not rush through it. Can we sit and just soak it up for a while?" He patted the spot next to him on the couch, his arm stretched along the back.

Shelby removed her shoes and joined him. He looked around the room, his gaze coming to rest on the tree. "That tree is magnificent, perfect for this house. If someone had told me last Christmas that tonight I would be here in front of a fire at my ranch with the most beautiful woman in Montana, I would have figured they'd had too much homebrew."

Shelby smiled. "What are the chances of that happen—"

"A million to one," he whispered and kissed her parted lips.

Shelby turned, her upper body facing Jack and her legs stretched out on the couch. Jack cradled her against him and kissed her again, a long, lingering kiss. He kissed her lips, her eyes, her face, his breath quickening, his heart beating faster under her hand. One boot rested on his other knee. He gently pressed her back so she rested against the triangle formed by his leg. Jack began to unbutton her silk blouse with his right hand, his eyes never leaving hers.

"I'm just helping you get ready for bed," he said in a husky whisper.

Shelby felt his desire as much as she saw it in his eyes. Her blouse fell open and she raised enough for him to unhook and remove her bra. He pressed his hand gently in the valley between her breasts, palm side down, turned his hand over, then palm side down again. "Do you have any idea how beautiful you are?" he whispered.

Shelby said nothing as she ran her forefinger slowly around his mouth. His hand still rested between her breasts. "I think we should both stretch out. What do you say?" she said.

Shelby got up then Jack took the long flat cushions off both couches and placed them together on the floor in front of the fireplace. "Don't go away," he said and disappeared up the stairs. In an instant he was back with pillows and a blanket. Jack had the ability to take Shelby where she had never been with Bobby. Perhaps it was his patience, his touch, or his eyes looking at her with enough desire to ignite her own. Whatever it was, the effect was electric and it swept her along in a tide of passion in concert with his. Shelby wanted him, wanted to give herself to him; they made love tenderly at first, building in intensity until both bodies glistened, oblivious of all except the two of them. Their passion was all-encompassing, driving mind and body to its final destination. Shelby fell asleep in the total peace of Jack's embrace.

The following morning, she was awakened by a kiss on her forehead. "Wake up. Merry Christmas!" She peered at Jack through one eye. He seemed bright and much too alert.

"Are you always this cheerful this early in the morning?" her voice cracked.

"I am when I have a night like last night. I'll make us coffee. We need to put these cushions back. We sorta trashed the couch."

Shelby stretched and yawned. "I remember you. I picked you up at that dinner party last night. What'd you say your name was?"

Jack lopped her with his pillow. "Let me put it to you this way.

The longer you lie there, the greater the chance I'm gonna want to do it again. If you want a Christmas with presents and food and the football game, you'd best hustle your little behind up to the shower. Otherwise, you're fair game." He was grinning at her.

"Okay, okay, I'm out of here." Shelby grabbed the two pillows and blanket and made her way up the stairs. "But you're a lech!" she shouted from the top stair. Shelby heard him holler "thank you!" as she opened the bedroom door.

They were cleaning the kitchen after breakfast when Jack paused, dish towel in hand. "I notice you haven't mentioned your dad not coming home last night."

"I know, isn't that neat? I hope he spent the night with her, not just at her house."

"Really? You never cease to amaze me. A lot of daughters in your situation might be jealous of his attention to another woman."

"There you go on that turnip truck. I love Adele. If my dad and she were to get together, he'd be one lucky man. Adele, too. My dad is a little gun-shy at marriage, but he's great."

"Great runs in your family." Jack flashed a grin and snapped a dish towel in her direction.

Adele and David showed up at half-past eleven, laden with arms full of brightly wrapped gifts. David added them to the pile already under the tree. Adele was right behind him, checking packages with her name, shaking, sniffing, and listening as though they were ticking.

"You are terrible. Cut that out," Shelby admonished. All four sat on the floor in a half-circle around the tree. They prompted Shelby to open a box marked from Bobby, an elaborate set of tools. "Wow, look at these, Dad." She glanced at him. "Of course, they're from Bobby."

Jack handed Shelby a rather large box, which looked to be professionally wrapped. She shook it gently. "Not heavy? I can't imagine."

Placing the box on the coffee table Shelby tore the paper away and brought out a cowboy hat. "It's gorgeous." She put it on, then turned to Jack. "A cowboy hat. I love it and it's a perfect fit! How did you—"

"There's something else in there," Jack said.

"Really?" She reached in and brought out a leather vest the exact same color as the hat. "Wow, I have never had a *real* cowboy hat or vest. I love them!" She promptly put on the vest, then donned the hat. "How do they look?"

Jack was staring at her, a big smile on his face. "Like you're the best-looking cowgirl in Montana! I'm glad you like them."

Her father and Adele opened their gifts and by one o'clock, almost time for the impending kickoff, the great room was trashed, awash in Christmas paper, boxes and ribbons. Everyone stood, said their thank yous, and wished each other a Merry Christmas. Jack, David and Adele began picking up paper.

One gift for Jack remained, far back under the tree. Shelby scooted it out and watched with anticipation as he opened it. Adele and David leaned forward to peer in the box. Jack folded back the tissue and the smell of new leather greeted them. He whistled as he pulled out a pair of hand-tooled, custom-made cowboy boots. "I…I don't know what to say. I've never seen such good-lookin' boots. Shelby, how did you ever?" He rubbed them, then put them to his nose. "They even smell good. I won't be wearing these out with the stock." The tan boots were embossed with an intricate design splayed across the pointed toe of each boot, and on the outside at the top of each boot were the initials JJK embossed in the leather.

"There's another present, Jack. Wait a sec, I'll get it," Shelby said and left the room.

Jack glanced at Adele and David. "Do you know what she's up to?"

"I hear nothing, see nothing, and know diddly," Adele said. David shrugged his shoulders and put a purposely blank expression on his face.

Shelby returned and put down a fairly large Christmas-wrapped box on the floor at Jack's feet, then knelt on the floor beside it. David and Adele stood right behind her for a good view.

The lid was wrapped separately and there were holes in the box... and movement. Jack glanced up at Shelby with a puzzled look, then removed the lid and peered in the box. Two sleepy brown eyes, surrounded by soft golden fur, stared up at them.

"Well, I'll be damned. Look at you!" Jack reached in and lifted a chubby Golden Lab puppy from the box, its tail wagging furiously and all four legs trying to walk in mid-air. When Jack hugged the squirming puppy to him, the pup became a bundle of furry, licking, yelping canine. Jack laughed and buried his face against its tummy. "He smells good, a new puppy smell, almost as good as new boots." The puppy licked Jack's face and wriggled, wanting to get loose. "Shelby, he's," he held the squirming pup up for a look, "yes, it's a he. He is beautiful!" Jack's eyes danced with delight. "What a great gift, thank you." Jack put him on the floor and stood to give Shelby a kiss. The puppy took off running, sliding on the shiny wood floor, charging through boxes and Christmas paper. "He's the cutest little guy I've ever seen," Jack said, watching as the puppy surfaced from under a pile of paper.

"What are you going to name him?" David asked.

Jack looked at Shelby. "What about Shadow?"

Shelby nodded. "Shadow is a perfect name."

* * *

There were few days in her life that Shelby remembered being perfect. This Christmas Day was one, no fraught nerves, no disappointments, no feelings of being judged or not fitting in. There was laughter, love, companionship, and little Shadow who followed them everywhere. He was Jack's dog, of that there was no doubt. When Jack sat, Shadow curled up at his feet, his chin resting on top of Jack's boot. If Jack went in the kitchen, Shadow followed, tail wagging, running to keep up. Finally, Shadow fell asleep in his basket, a gift from Adele and David, on his back, his round belly gently rising and falling in sleepy bliss.

It was late when her father left with Adele. The house was quiet except for the sound of the crackling fire. Jack patted the couch, an invitation for Shelby to sit beside him.

"Okay, but just a second, okay? I'll be right back," She hurried upstairs to the bedroom and began taking her clothes off. A few minutes later, she stared at her reflection, stark naked except for her cowboy hat and vest. "I can't believe I'm doing this, oh what the heck, why not!"

Jack was on the couch facing the fireplace with his back to her when she descended the stairs. "Jack, I have a question. Do you think that the hat and vest look good on me?"

He rose and turned around, the look on his face changing from mouth-open shock to a big smile. "Well, that's the first time I've seen them worn that way, but YES, you look Fabulous!"

"Well, thank you. I do have one last gift for you, cowboy," she said. "Biblical sex, are you ready?"

"Biblical sex, what is that? His eyes and his expression signaled just what she hoped his reaction would be.

Shelby smiled. "It's sex so good that you think you've died and gone to heaven."

He laughed out loud and opened his arms. "Oh! My! God! You bet I'm Ready!"

Chapter Twenty Five

S helby knew something was up the moment Adele and her father showed up for breakfast on New Year's Day. They entered the kitchen, both looking like the cat that swallowed the canary. Adele had a large rolled-up paper in her hand and David looked about to burst, hiding a secret.

"Hi, you two," Shelby said from her chair at the kitchen table, a sleepy puppy in her lap. "That looks suspiciously like a drawing, Adele. Is it?"

"You guessed right, Shelby, and I have your daddy to thank for it." Adele unrolled the paper on the table and anchored it with a coffee mug on each corner. "As professional as if it were done by an architect. David put on paper the changes I want to make to the café." Jack entered the kitchen and stood next to Adele and David, the three of them peering at the drawing over Shelby's shoulder. She spotted the changes immediately. The present porch was enclosed which added significant table space; new windows were added on the front wall, plus there were four or five tall "bar height tables" in the large empty space in front of the gambling machines.

"Wow," Shelby exclaimed. "This is a better use of the space. What do you think, Jack?"

"That you did a great job on the drawing, David. A larger dining area and adding bar tables is what Shelby said, a better use of space. You will bring in more money this way, Adele."

"Hot damn," Adele said, clapping her hands together.

David sat down next to Shelby. "What do you say, Skyline Construction? Do you think we could pull this off? We have almost a month."

"Are you serious? Could you stay that long?" Shelby felt excitement flush her face.

"Shelby, remember our summers at the cabin? I may be an old fool but those times were magic for me. We can have that time again! What do you say?"

"I don't have to think about it, Dad. Adele, you got yourself a couple of builders so, first thing tomorrow, Dad, we'll go to the café, take all our measurements and figure out our supply list. It'll be another photo finish, but I think we can do it."

"I told you Shelby couldn't pass this up." David and Adele exchanged a high-five.

"One last thing, gang," Adele said looking and sounding serious. "Twenty-seven days from today is the scheduled grand re-opening, but I want to have a preview party the night before." Adele glanced down at Shelby. "Pretty important date, January twenty-sixth?" She enunciated the date again and raised her eyebrows.

Shelby thought for a moment as she stroked Shadow. *January twenty-sixth, why does that date sound familiar?* "Dad's birthday! I can't believe he agreed to a party."

David's expression said it all. "Adele tricked me. She asked my astrological sign and I told her I had no idea. So she says in order to find out, she needs to know the month and day. Is that sneaky or what! So I find out I'm an Aquarius, but the next thing I know she's planning a party and threatened to put a hammerlock on me if I say no!" Shelby burst out laughing, which woke up Shadow so she gently put him on the floor.

"Now you know the real Adele." Jack was laughing too, then a minute later, he said "Uh oh," and looked at Shelby. "I know you're good, but that isn't much time. Can you get it done?"

Shelby exchanged glances with her father, then nodded. "We can do it. But, Dad, that means you and I both have phone calls to make. I don't look forward to calling Bobby."

"Same here," David said, admitting that he didn't relish telling his self-made millionaire CEO John McGinnis it would be another month before his return. John McGinnis took the news better than Bobby Stamford.

Shelby threatened to hang up if Bobby didn't quit yelling. She finally got him to admit he would be busy for the next thirty days anyway with the final preparations for the Covington ground-breaking. He told her he would let her know the exact date of the ceremony.

"And I damned well expect you to be here. Oh I almost forgot, your father is invited if he wants to swing through L.A. on his way back to Peru." That part, Shelby thought, was a good idea.

She recognized two things from this building project. Adele meant a lot to her father; he was risking his position with El Dorado to accomplish something important to her. The second was that her father wanted to give the two of them the opportunity to relive a very special time in their lives. As for herself, she wanted to be near him for as long as she possibly could.

One thing she would need but didn't seem to have at the moment was stamina. The only thing she could blame it on was the porch project which turned out to be a significantly physical challenge. Then on the heels of that came the fall chores at the ranch—even more taxing. Looking back, she had to admit she'd been busy working on one project or another from the moment she arrived in Montana. *That can't be it. I was always working at home too.* Shelby decided the real culprit was the stress of not knowing what her future held, and no way would she turn down this opportunity to work with her father again—and help Adele.

Adele made no effort to hide her excitement about the party. In between cleaning and changing the interior look of her café, she drove to Kalispell for building materials, which allowed Shelby and David to keep working every hour of daylight. Like they did years ago, they cut lumber and hammered and nailed side by side; they discussed problems they ran into, her father visibly enjoying every minute and Shelby feeling their bond grow stronger each day. Another positive of the project was seeing Adele and her father's relationship blossom. He spent more nights at her house than he did at the ranch.

Shelby tried to ignore the recurring thought of her father going back to Peru and her promise to return to L.A. Instead, she savored working side by side with him, having Adele and Jack close by, and she even refused to view the temperature as a problem. Though arriving first thing on several mornings, she did take note of the thermometer on the outside of the café showing zero. Anticipating the weather before they began the project, she and her dad tacked heavy plastic over the front of the café and Adele rented a large space heater that kept them "warm enough." More importantly, Shelby ignored the temp and sore muscles because they were on schedule and because of something Adele had said. "I have to tell you, Shelby, if this remodel job accomplished nothing else, it has allowed me to witness the rekindling of a wonderful memory in the minds of two people I dearly love."

* * *

January twenty-sixth dawned cold and blustery. The snowstorm abated in time for the highway department to plow the roads. The neon

Adele's Cafe sign glowed iridescent colors into the chilly night, but inside Adele's Cafe sparkled for its grand preview. Giant red bows adorned the top of every window. A twelve-foot sign, *Happy Birthday David,* hand-lettered on butcher paper by Ronnie and Chuck, hung above the bar. Helium-filled balloons with long streamers filled the ceiling and each table was adorned with a flower arrangement. A huge cake occupied the center of the buffet table.

Shelby and her father stood visiting with party guests when at 8:00 p.m. Adele clapped her hands to quiet the room. "Okay, everybody, keep hold of your cocktail glass or beer mug because we've got a couple great things to toast!" Shelby was surprised how many people she recognized from waitressing when she first arrived. And all of them were in a party mood.

"The least important thing first... thanks to Shelby and David here, tonight is the official opening of Adele's Café which I'm here to tell you is all spiffied up and raring to go!"

Shelby had to laugh at the crowd's reponse: glasses and beer mugs raised along with cheering and whistles and yahooing and laughter. "Thank you, thank you all," Adele said, her smile saying it all as she bowed then raised her glass. "Okay, enough about me," she said.

"Now for the second reason of this shindig." Adele turned toward Shelby and David and waited for everyone to sit down then she held up her wine glass. "I want to propose a toast to David, our guest from Peru, on this his sixty-third birthday. David, here's to you, to your health, to love, and to the banquet life has to offer. We wish them all for you, today and always."

Everyone toasted David, then Adele again, then the construction crew, the remodel job, the Montana Grizzlies, Peru, God and the U.S.A. Hank, a football fan from Missoula, stood up. "Hear, hear." He raised his glass. "Here's to those who wish us well, all the rest can go to…" Whistles, cat-calls, and laughter followed. Virgil proposed they eat before dinner got cold.

The beer and wine flowed freely, the conversations and laughter loud and rowdy. After dinner Shelby watched her father open one gift after another. He beckoned Adele to his side and told the crowd how much he had enjoyed his stay in Montana and thanked everyone for welcoming him so warmly. Shelby felt Jack squeeze her hand; she glanced at him and he had the same frightened look on his face as Adele, standing next to David with her hand on his shoulder.

Shelby held tight onto Jack's hand. The moment she dreaded had finally arrived. Her father was leaving tomorrow and after a brief stop in L.A., he would be flying twelve thousand miles away. It was summer in Peru; they spoke a different language there. He would be on a different continent, in a different time zone, another world.

Shelby glanced at Adele, the same lost feelings registered on her face. Adele's smile was gone. Tears brimming, she nodded at Shelby. Her look brought back something David had said on their first walk. He said he lamented "living alone longer than most people have been alive."

Fighting to retain control, Shelby was thankfully distracted by Virgil lighting the candles on the cake. "David, be sure to make a wish before you blow them out," he said.

Her father looked up at her, then at Adele, and finally at Jack. "I know my wish, but how about helping me, everybody?" The guests circled the cake. "Okay, on the count of three."

Shelby kept her eyes on Adele still standing by David's side; her expression was a mirror of her own feelings, frightened and suddenly feeling lost.

* * *

Sunday arrived much too quickly for Shelby. The Delta 737 lifted above the snowy terrain and she looked down on the tiny buildings of the Glacier airport. Every nerve sent conflicting signals to her brain. *Stay. No, you have to go. You said you would. Don't go!*

Shelby looked over at her father, obviously lost in his own thoughts. When she hugged Shadow goodbye earlier, soaking his soft fur with her tears, her emotional roller coaster felt like it had careened off its track. At the airport she and Adele hugged, each unable to hold back tears.

Jack had pulled her to him and they held each other. "We never really talked about us, Jack," she whispered. We should have, why didn't we?" she said. He looked as pale as he had in the hospital. Eyes downcast, she turned and bolted toward the gate without looking back.

The last thing she saw of Jack Ketchum was the pair of hand-tooled cowboy boots she'd given him for Christmas.

On the plane, Shelby felt her father take hold of her hand. She grasped it with a death-like grip. He was trying to comfort her, she realized, but he didn't look much better than she felt.

At the moment he appeared to be struggling with feelings of his own. Thankfully, half an hour into the flight the flight attendant delivered coffee. Shelby closed her eyes and put her head back against the seat as her father put down her tray table. "Shelby, you are ghostly white. Are you okay?" he whispered, extricating his hand from her tight grip.

"I'm not feeling well," she whispered without opening her eyes.

"Talk to me. You're scaring me."

She opened her eyes and blinked, trying to focus, but dropped her chin to her chest. "I feel really bad," she whispered.

"How, pumpkin? Feel bad how?"

"I don't know what I'm doing, Dad. I'm not in control anymore.

Everything I do hurts somebody, and I'm hurting!" He took her hand once more, but she stiffened. "Could you let me out? I need to get to the bathroom."

He grabbed the coffees as she scrambled over him. Shelby made her way unsteadily down the aisle, holding onto seat tops with each step, and barely making it into the bathroom before vomiting in the toilet. She rinsed her face in cold water with one hand while holding onto the edge of the sink with the other. She felt clammy and her ashen reflection in the mirror scared her. Shelby exited the restroom and leaned against the door, trying to breathe evenly, not sure she wasn't about to throw up again. She stood there for several minutes until she felt in control, then made her way back to her seat. David had moved over, leaving the aisle seat open.

He opened her air vent and took her hand. "Breathe deep. Again. That's better." His voice was a soothing, reassuring whisper. "This is the right thing to do, Shelby. You had to go back sometime. Hard as it is, you need to confront Bobby and figure out what you want to do. Remember what I always told you when you were little and something made you sad or upset?"

"This too in time shall pass?"

"Right." He smiled. "And it will, Shelby, it always does."

Shelby put her head back and closed her eyes. Weariness brought sleep that ended only when the Boeing jet touched down on the LAX runway. Bobby had a sleek black limousine with a uniformed driver waiting for them.

* * *

Jack took Adele's arm as they made their way back across the snowy parking lot of Glacier International Airport. "You drive, okay?" Adele said when they reached the Jeep. Jack shaded his eyes and watched as

Shelby and David's jet grew smaller in the distance. A terrible feeling gripped him; it felt like a part of him had just been ripped away.

He started the car and tried to click the seatbelt into the receptacle but couldn't, his eyes were brimming with tears. He looked over at Adele. She had blotted her eyes and was applying make-up to her cheeks. "They're gone, Adele. I can't believe they're gone. On a scale of ten I'm not even registering. How about you?"

Adele applied bright red lipstick and then flipped up the mirror. "Like my heart just got stomped on. How the hell did we ever let this happen to us anyway?"

"Beats me. All I know is, I don't want to be by myself in that big house today. How about coming over and we'll have our own Super Bowl party?"

"I don't want to be alone either. But let's not cry in our beer, okay? I'll cook something great. We'll holler our heads off and get roarin' drunk. Stop by the café and I'll grab some groceries." Adele switched on the radio just in time to hear the weather; there was a storm headed toward Flathead County with sub-zero temperatures and a wind chill factor of twenty degrees below zero. "Do we need to stop by your house and turn the heater up, make sure the pipes don't freeze, and get your PJs and toothbrush? You can have Shelby's room. If we get roaring drunk, you don't need to be on the highway."

"Well, I plan on doin' just that, Hon, so you'd better swing by there, too."

* * *

For Shelby, the sad goodbyes with Adele and Jack were in stark contrast to the joyous reaction from Esther, Oscar, and Enrique. Esther wept openly, hugged her and refused to let go. Shelby introduced David to her Mayan family. Enrique and Oscar shook his hand and carried on a conversation in Spanish. Esther released Shelby only long enough to offer her hand to David with a polite greeting, then put her arm back around Shelby's waist and walked with her into the house. Enrique helped the driver unload the luggage from the limousine.

A bright sun shone above, the day balmy compared to the snowy landscape they left. Shelby stood in the entry and gazed at the house and landscape beyond the huge windows. *This is so different, flowers, green everywhere instead of white. Like another world.* In control now, she turned to her father. "I'll give you a tour later. I am anxious to see my horses. Want to go with me?" She led the way, the four of them following.

The stables looked small and new compared to Jack's mammoth old barn. Three of the four half-doors were open and three curious mares peeked out when they heard her voice. Shelby approached the stalls; the horses nickered and shook their heads. "Oh gosh, I should have brought carrots."

"I'll get some," Enrique said and sprinted off toward the house.

Shelby stroked Cheyenne and Dakota and rubbed her face against each one's neck in her version of a hug. Their ears flicked back and forth in response. She hugged Cherokee, then peered into the pregnant mare's stall. "Cherokee, you're huge!" she exclaimed. "Look, Dad."

David stepped forward, held his hand out to Cherokee and looked into the stall. "A foal. When is she expecting?"

"Late March, early April." Shelby pressed her cheek against Cherokee's forehead. "You look wonderful, girl. Enrique and Oscar took good care of you, didn't they."

Enrique returned with the carrots and Shelby gave one to each mare. David stepped back and watched alongside the Flores family. Esther whispered something to Oscar, then clasped her hands together, a smile on her face.

When they returned to the house Oscar started to haul Shelby's luggage up the stairs. She was suddenly confronted with something to which she had given little thought. "Oscar, wait. I would like my luggage put in the downstairs guest room for now. And Dad's in the other one."

Shelby and Enrique went over Skyline matters at the kitchen table, then he bade them goodbye. David stood at the edge of the foyer, surveying the great room, then walked through the main floor, looking up at the high ceilings, rubbing his hand over the Palos Verde stones in the fireplace, finally stopping at the massive windows.

He gazed out at the grounds. "This is truly magnificent, Shelby. So different from..." David cleared his throat. "Just beautiful." He walked back to the television and turned it on. The second quarter of the football game was just beginning. "Oh, I'm a happy guy." He went to the bar and poured himself a drink. "You know where I'll be for the next couple of hours," he said, stretching out in Bobby's chair.

Shelby placed a call to the ranch. Adele answered; she sounded tipsy. "Happy Super Bowl, Hon." She giggled. "We're havin' a party, eatin' chips and dip and drinkin'." Adele's voice became distant. "Here, Jack, tell her what we're drinkin'."

Jack came on the phone. "Shelby, I'm so glad you called." He sounded sober. "What you said at the airport about us not talking, I am so sorry! I didn't know... you being married, I was afraid to press you. I....I wish..." She heard him stifle a sob. "I miss you already," he said, definitely not sounding tipsy. He sounded sad and upset and it made her heart ache anew. She heard a long sigh, then he asked about their flight.

"I've had better. Are you watching the game?"

"Yeah, we're watching. Adele has Shadow in her lap. Are you watching?"

"Sort of. Dad just turned it on. Jack, I…this is so hard, I don't know what to say."

"It's okay, Shelby, you did what you had to do. I…understand," he said, his voice faltering. "I hope you will call me once in a while. You'll probably want to know about Shadow." Jack cleared his throat. "Oh, I almost forgot, when does David leave for Peru?"

Shelby was taken aback at the change of subject. "He…uh, he's going to hang around here for a few days to see Bobby."

"Sure, of course. Well, tell him goodbye for me. Does he want to speak to Adele?" She interpreted that as Jack was anxious to get off the phone.

"I'm sure he does, I'll get him. I promise I will call, Jack. Take care of yourself."

"You too, Shelby."

Shelby handed the phone to her father and bolted from the room. She rushed to the bathroom and stood inside, her back against the closed door. *He said he misses me, that he's sorry we didn't talk. We didn't because I'm married and he was afraid to press me? He said everything except I love you.*

Not sure what to think, Shelby resolutely rejoined her father and watched the Super Bowl in silence.

Chapter Twenty Six

Over the last five years Shelby had become accustomed to Bobby working late and on weekends, but not on Super Bowl Sunday. On that day, the house was usually filled with clients and guests, important people who expected to be elegantly entertained Stamford-style, with gourmet food and wine. Not this year, the Covington project took precedence over the Super Bowl.

In the family room watching the game with her father, she heard the back door close and Bobby call out "Shel?" then enter the family the room. "Oh, there you are. And, David, I'm glad you took me up on my invitation. Great to have you aboard."

David rose and shook Bobby's hand. "Good to see you too."

Shelby rose from the big chair, not sure what to expect. "Hello, Bobby."

"Don't you just hello me." He gave her a long hug and a quick kiss. "God, it's good to see you. Let me look at you." He gave her a quick glance-over. "You look fantastic."

"It's good to see you, too," she said. Bobby had definitely lost weight.

He promptly poured himself a drink and sat on the huge arm of Shelby's chair, their attention returning to the game. In between plays and comments on the game, Bobby inquired about their flight and wanted to know if their limo was on time and the driver courteous. Bobby rose and to went to the bar. "How about a refill, David?"

"Yes, thank you." Her father handed him his empty glass.

As soon as the game ended, Esther appeared to announce that the salad was ready, the table set, and the barbecue hot, "as Senor Stamford instructed."

Bobby excused himself, to change clothes he said, then came back down and began grilling salmon steaks that Shelby had to admit were perfect. She and her father both said so at the same time, causing all three to chuckle, easing Shelby's tension for the rest of the meal.

Bobby did not ask about Jack or Adele, nor did he make a comment about Montana or the two holidays Shelby spent there. Conversations after dinner were bits of Stamford family news, inquiries about David's job and living in Peru, and nothing about the office or Covington.

Esther served coffee and dishes of frozen yogurt. "You changed me forever, Shel. I can't believe I'm eating yogurt and thinking it's good," Bobby said. "*Gracias*, Esther, *muy bueno*."

Shelby covered her smile with her napkin, seeing Esther's surprise at Bobby's Spanish. After they finished their coffee, David rose. "That was a fabulous dinner, Bobby. It has been a very long day and that bed looked awfully inviting."

Bobby rose too. "Of course, Dave. If there's anything you need, just let Oscar know."

David leaned over and kissed his daughter on the cheek. "Good night, pumpkin. You look exhausted so don't stay up too late, okay?"

"I won't, Dad. Good night."

Bobby came up to Shelby and took her hands as she rose from her chair. He placed her arms on the top of his shoulders and settled his hands around her waist. "You look wonderful, Shel, but tired. Are you all right?" He looked and sounded concerned.

"On the flight I thought I might be coming down with a cold or something but whatever it was went away. I am tired though, actually more like exhausted." she said.

"Then let's go to bed. A good night's sleep in your own bed is just what you need."

Shelby looked at him, aware that he was waiting for a sign from her, but she could give him none. What she felt was anxious and uneasy. "Bobby," she said as gently as she could, "I had Oscar put my things in the guest room next to Dad's."

Bobby instantly pulled her to him, cradling her head against his shoulder. "Shel, please, don't do this," he whispered against her face. "Please, give me a chance."

"Bobby, I'm not ready... It's too..."

"That's okay, baby. Just sleep in our bed next to me and let me hold you. Please?"

Shelby took a deep breath and pulled away. "I'm sorry, Bobby." She removed his arms and backed up, still facing him. "What time are you going to work tomorrow?"

Shoulders slumped, he looked crestfallen. "Early, unless you want me to go in later."

"I thought I'd take Dad on a tour tomorrow, but we could have coffee before you leave?"

Bobby nodded. "Or, if you bring him by the office around one o'clock tomorrow, I'll take you both to lunch. How about that?"

"That would be really nice." Shelby gave him a tired smile. "Lunch tomorrow, then. We'll be at your office at one. Good night, Bobby."

"Good night, Shel." She left her husband standing in the dining room looking after her with eyes as soulful as Shadow's.

Her father was on his phone when Shelby came into the kitchen the following morning. "I understand, John, but this couldn't be helped.

My daughter isn't feeling well and I won't leave her until we check it out. I'll be back to work next Monday."

She poured herself a mug of coffee and sat down at the island. "Trouble?"

"They want me back, whether I still have vacation time or not. We're drilling new test sites on the adjacent property El Dorado just bought."

"Who was that you were talking to?"

"The CEO, John McGinnis. He said they really need me."

"I need you too."

"I know, pumpkin, that's what I told him." He came over and gave her a kiss on the cheek. "But a dad's gotta do what a dad's gotta do. How are you feeling this morning?"

"Better than on the plane. I would have sworn I was coming down with something."

"Do me a favor, will you?" David said as he refilled his mug. "Even though you feel better, make a doctor appointment. You scared me yesterday."

Shelby kept her promise and called Caldwell's office. Thursday morning at nine was the first available appointment, the same day as the ground-breaking ceremony. The Covington event was set for three o'clock Thursday afternoon.

After breakfast, Shelby and her father checked on her three mares and gave them their accustomed treat. He walked around the stables, looking closely at the construction. "I meant it, Shelby, when I said you are good."

"Thanks, I learned a lot about building from you."

"That was a such a fun time, wasn't it? Happiness in a sea of sadness."

"What do you mean, a sea of sadness?" She looked at her father. He was leaning against a post looking out over the hills.

"Remember in Kalispell when you asked about my autobiographical comment? I didn't want to talk about it then, but I told you I would before I leave. I will, if you'd still like to hear."

"Of course I want to hear." She motioned for them to sit down on a bale of hay.

"Thirty years ago, I was where you are right now. I'd been married ten years to someone I thought I knew. We had such dreams, so many plans. Laura said she wanted to travel with me, but she didn't. She told me she was interested in Indian cultures, but she wasn't. What you said about hearing what you wanted to hear, seeing what you wanted to see, that was my situation. I don't know if your mother deceived me, but eventually there came a time when I had to admit I didn't know the real Laura and I couldn't keep up the facade any longer. So I left."

"You said a sea of sadness. What did you mean?" Shelby said softly.

"That's what I see when I look back over my personal life. The marriage, the years apart, the loneliness, it was like a sea of sadness except for our summers. Now here you are in the same predicament. I feel like I'm watching you live my life over again. To admit you no longer love someone you promised to spend the rest of your life with…is the hardest thing I've ever done." His voice cracked.

He changed mid-sentence from talking about me to talking about himself. They both rose and Shelby put her arms around her father. He hugged her tightly, rocking them from side to side. "I was so angry with you, Dad. Angry that you could leave us, leave me. I see now how unfair I was. Why didn't you ever let me come visit you?"

"Shelby, I begged Laura. She was adamant that you not leave the

country. She said if I pressed it, she'd take me to court. That's why I
bought the cabin. I quit any job that wouldn't give me three months off
in the summer. I made a lot of people mad at me in those days."

Shelby leaned against the post. "I am so sorry. I never knew any of
this. I don't understand why Mom would do that. I told her lots of
times I wanted to visit you. She always came up with some reason, a
trip or something. I thought you didn't care so I gave up asking."

"I am so grateful you did write. If you hadn't, we wouldn't be here
right now."

"You know why I wrote that note?"

"Why?"

"Jack kept hounding me. He brought it up every day. I did it to
keep him quiet." Shelby shook her head at the irony.

David nodded. "I knew I liked that guy. Now I know why."

They strolled back to the house, arm in arm. "Would you mind if
we go by the two houses Skyline is building?" Shelby asked. "They're
close to completion and I would like to look them over. Then we'll
drive in and have lunch with Bobby."

They arrived at Stamford Development at one o'clock. Bobby
graciously gave David a tour of the offices, introducing him to the
staff as they went. Adam was equally gracious and Terri Armstrong
was nowhere to be seen. Bobby took Shelby and David to The Courtyard for lunch. He was the Bobby she knew ten years ago: friendly,
attentive, and totally engaging.

After lunch they drove south along the Coast Highway to the
Covington site. The Pacific formed a small bay across the highway
from the property. Crews and machines were finishing a large area for
the ceremony, leveling and then filling in with gravel. Bobby showed
where the tent and new sign would be, then stood on the leveled-off
spot and pointed toward the bay.

"When phase one is complete, you will be able to sit on this spot in a beautiful open-air patio, eat your lunch, and listen to the sound of the surf. Is that view not spectacular?"

Shelby and David wholeheartedly agreed. Bobby drove back up the coast highway to San Clemente. They walked along the beach, then had dinner at the restaurant on the pier. Outdoor heaters allowed them to sit outside and witness the sun drop below the horizon. The broiled red snapper was tasty and the beer ice cold. Bobby held Shelby's hand. He made her laugh and asked questions of her and David. Bobby was in his element, exactly where he wanted to be, and it showed. He flashed a dazzling smile, his handsome face mirrored serious thought and humor next, then a look at Shelby that said volumes if she read it correctly. For a few hours, he was the Bobby she fell in love with ten years ago but, unable to forget their ugly fight in the Missoula hospital, Shelby did not let her guard down.

They arrived back at the house after dark and David went directly to bed. Esther and Oscar had retired to their quarters and the house was quiet. Bobby led Shelby to the living room and set a match to a prepared fire. It crackled into flames, lending a soft glow to the darkened room. He opened a bottle of wine, poured two glasses and handed one to Shelby.

"What a great day, Shel. Your dad looks good and it's nice to have him here. And you look wonderful. It is so good to have you back." Bobby walked over and touched the rim of his glass to hers, crystal echoing in the quiet room. He returned to his seat and sipped his wine.

She touched the glass to her lips; the wine tasted bitter. "Thank you for a wonderful day. Dad enjoyed visiting with Adam and getting to see Covington. And the dinner was lovely."

Bobby put his feet up on the coffee table and his head back against the soft cushions. "You promised we'd talk," he said quietly. "Here we are by ourselves. Talk to me, Shel. Tell me how you feel, what you've decided to do." His voice relayed tenderness and caring.

"I don't even know where to start."

"Why don't you start with right now. Tell me how you feel about coming home, about being here with me."

"Honestly? Confused, wondering why you didn't call me back that night. Sad that you went back on your promise and, frankly, not sure I can ever trust you."

"I understand your disappointment...and your sadness. You have every right to feel both," Bobby said. "I am truly sorry, Shel."

You say all the right things. Do you mean them? Is this the real Bobby?

He leaned forward. "I learned something with you being gone. It's not as good at the top if you're up there by yourself. I hope you'll give us another ch—"

"I don't want to hurt you, Bobby. I simply can't give you an answer now. I've been back a little over twenty-four hours and this is the first chance we've had to spend any time together."

Bobby's stare looked earnest. "I was hoping your coming back meant you had already made up your mind. I hate living in limbo."

"I don't like it any more than you do, but this involves the rest of our lives. It's important to take the time and for us to talk like this," she said.

"Maybe there's still hope then?"

"There is always hope, Bobby. It just depends on...a lot of things."

"Shel, does Jack Ketchum have anything to do with your decision?"

"Why would you ask that?"

"Stuart thought he might. Did you sleep with him?"

"Did you sleep with Terri?"

"There you go, answering a question with a question." His voice took on a harsher tone. "You know I've admitted I did wrong. If that hick is somehow involved in this, I think I have a right to know. If he isn't, then what's the hold-up? Why am I having to wait for an answer?"

"Our problems are longstanding, Bobby. Jack isn't part of that."

"I feel what I'm asking is pretty reasonable. Do you love me or not? Do you want to stay married to me or not?"

Shelby leaned forward. "I've told you it's not that simple. I want things to be diff—"

He threw up his hands. "What do you want from me, Shel? You want to be starry-eyed and dewy-lipped, like things were ten years ago? Isn't that a bit unreasonable?"

The mellow mood disappeared. Poof and it was gone. "Starry-eyed and dewy-lipped? Is that what you think I've been talking about all this time?"

"What I think is, when we got married I made a commitment and so did you. I'm keeping mine and I don't think it's fair for you to unilaterally decide the fate of our marriage."

"Unilaterally?" Shelby felt anger uncoil somewhere deep inside. "This is not about being starry-eyed. It's about caring and respect. Or rather the lack of it. Brenda and Terri wouldn't have happened if those two things were present. That is what has gotten us to this point."

Bobby's expression flashed hostility. "You always turn things around to be my fault. I'm not the one who walked out, Shel. I didn't give up on us, you did."

Shelby sighed. "Your saying that tells me you just don't get it. You don't listen."

"I'm listening to you. I'm the one asking for another chance."

"On whose terms?"

"I'm even willing to give you a baby."

It took a full minute for his statement to sink in. When it did, it hit like a slap in the face. Shelby's reply came out like gunfire with a silencer. "You are what?"

"I've thought about it and if that's what it takes, I'm willing to…"

Shelby jumped up, no longer able to contain her anger. "If that's what it takes? You are willing to give me a baby—if that's what it takes!" Shelby could feel and hear the rage in her voice, her heart pounding. Bobby evidently heard it, too. His face went pale.

He stood up. "Dammit, Shel, you're taking it wrong. That's not how I meant it. I meant it in a good way. I was trying to—why are you getting so mad?"

"What was all that at the restaurant, a performance? Now we're back to the real Bobby!" Her words were delivered clipped and crisp. "Children are not bargaining chips! I will not keep going over and over the same issues. Rather than say something I may regret, I suggest we continue this discussion when I cool off—which may be a while! Is that perfectly clear to you, Robert Stamford?"

Bobby rose, his voice barely an audible whisper. "Absolutely clear."

"Then goodnight." Shelby whirled and walked from the room without a backward glance.

Chapter Twenty Seven

"I'm sorry we were roped into this ground-breaking thing," Shelby lamented to her father as they encountered bumper-to-bumper traffic on the way to Bobby's office. "This being your last day, I was hoping we could picnic at the beach and soak up some sun."

"It's okay, I had coffee with Bobby this morning and he was as nervous as a cat in a room full of rocking chairs. He said they're expecting two hundred invited guests plus it's open to the public. I take it that CAPE endorsement is a big honor. He asked if I had a suit to wear."

"I'm not surprised." Shelby's anger matched her disappointment in Bobby and made her question whether they had anything left to talk about. But, unwilling to ruin the last hours of her father's visit, she forced those feelings aside. "You look great. You've been in the States five weeks and this is the first time you've worn it. Montana dress is definitely more casual."

"I love Montana: the weather, the scenery and the people," her father said.

"Does that apply to Adele, too?" Shelby had to keep her eyes on the traffic, cars changing lanes and slowing abruptly.

David patted her shoulder. "For someone who claims she's confused, you sure want straight answers from your dad."

"Well…does it apply to Adele? And if so, why are you leaving?"

"I have to return to Peru, Shelby. I've stayed longer than I intended. Adele is a fabulous woman but I have a job. Besides, it will give me an opportunity to think things over."

Shelby took a quick side-glance. Her father had a thoughtful look on his face. "That doesn't sound very positive," she said, the similarity of their situations hitting home.

"No, but perhaps safer. I've made enough mistakes in my life."

Shelby dropped David off in the Stamford parking lot at eight thirty and promised to call as soon as she could and then drove the six blocks to the medical complex. Dr. Caldwell's lab technician drew blood for a complete blood count and asked for a urine sample. Linda, the nurse, recorded her blood pressure, pulse, temperature and weighed Shelby. She was up eight pounds.

"Holidays in the company of excellent cooks," Shelby commented.

Linda entered her findings on an iPad plus the reason for her visit: fatigue, nausea, and emotional highs and lows. She gave Shelby a gown for her exam, including a pelvic. Shelby glanced at magazines and wondered what Jack and Adele were doing. Dr. Caldwell kept her waiting half an hour and, as always, apologized for his tardiness.

Forty-five minutes later, again dressed in the pale blue suit she chose for the ceremonies, Shelby waited in his office. The doctor entered with her chart in his hand and half-glasses perched on his nose. "Your blood results are all within normal parameters, hemoglobin is fine; glucose, too. Everything looks good. You said your last periods have been irregular?"

"Yes, and I only spotted."

"Have you been under any stress?"

"A ton of stress would be more accurate. Bobby and I are kind of at a crossroad and I'm not sure about anything. Sunday I felt like my emotions were totally out of control. That's never happened before, but you know Bobby." Tears welled, and Caldwell handed her a tissue.

"Well., I am extremely sorry to hear you and Bobby are having problems. I find him difficult at times too, and I don't have to live with him." He glanced at her over his glasses. "But stress is not the reason for your symptoms, Shelby."

"Uh oh, that sounds ominous."

"Shelby, I assure you it's not ominous." The doctor came around the desk and sat in the chair facing hers. "I hope that despite your present issues with Bobby, you will consider this good news. You don't have a medical problem, Shelby. You are pregnant."

Shelby saw his lips move but the doctor's words did not register. She had known him for ten years; his expression was serious. "Excuse me, what did you say?"

He smiled. "I'm obviously not connecting with you. You are pregnant, Shelby, two and a half months, perhaps three, judging from how things feel. Are you all right with this?" His look was sympathetic.

"I'm…it's not really sinking in. Maybe I'm in shock. Are you sure, or could it be a mistake?" She spoke in a tremulous whisper.

"Yes, I'm sure, Shelby, no mistake. We can schedule an ultrasound for you or you can select a gynecologist and he or she can order it, the choice is yours." Dr. Caldwell rose and moved to the door, his hand on the knob. Shelby stared into space. "Ultrasound?" She remained in the chair, her posture and expression unchanged.

"I've broken this news to literally hundreds of patients and I can never predict how they will react. Tell you what, Shelby, we'll schedule the ultrasound. That will give you time to digest the news and pick out an obstetrician. I'm going to put you on prenatal vitamins to make sure the baby and you are getting calcium and so forth. Linda will be right in. And then if you have any questions, I'll come back in before you leave. Okay?"

Shelby could only nod when Caldwell closed the door. She heard music and voices in the other rooms and saw the doctor's framed credentials on the wall, but everything seemed far away, distant. *Two and a half months, maybe three—that would be mid-November. Oh my God, that time in the barn. I'm pregnant with Jack's baby! But... he said he couldn't have children!*

The truth registered with hurricane force; it took her breath away. A lifetime of hope in those three words, words she had dreamed of hearing with Bobby as happy as she. But Bobby wasn't here and the baby wasn't his. *How could I have not put it together? I was doing so much physical work I assumed it had to be that. Never, never in a million years.*

Half an hour later Shelby left the office, still dazed, an ultrasound appointment card in her hand. She got in her car and flipped down the visor mirror, wanting to see if she looked any different. Her face was flushed, her eyes sparkled, and her mouth was turned up at the corners.

I cannot believe it. Yes, I can... I am pregnant!!!!

It was eleven o'clock. She had two options. She could drive back to Bobby's office and get involved in the madness of the Covington preparations. Or she could drive to the beach. *I need time to think.* Shelby drove south and pulled off the freeway in San Clemente. She walked out on the pier, small whitecaps lapping against the pylons. Waves stroked the shoreline on her left and right and she took the same outside table where the three of them had dined a few nights before. The slate blue Pacific stretched out before her for as far as she could see.

Warm for the last days of January, the sun felt good on her face and the breeze ruffled her hair. She watched with new delight as huge pelicans dived from great heights straight into the water and seagulls swooped and swirled in front of her in a graceful airborne ballet.

Shelby hugged herself and furtively glanced around to see if anyone was watching. All of a sudden she remembered she hadn't eaten anything today and she was starved. The waiter asked for her drink order. *No wonder wine hasn't tasted good.* Shelby ordered milk with her lunch.

Fully absorbing the truth during the two hours she sat staring at the sea, she drove back to the site and sat in her parked car for a few minutes. Reliving the doctor's words, she couldn't stop smiling, images appearing of a little Chloe or a little Jack, riding horses, playing hide-and-seek, blowing a kiss bye-bye. Then something nagged in the back of her mind, something Jack said about children when they talked on the porch of his ranch house, the day of the water fight. *We thought we'd have children but it never happened and now I'm too old.* Shelby's happy bubble clouded over, negative thoughts intruding into hers. *He said he's too old, which is nonsense. Still, if he doesn't take this as good news, I could be raising this baby by myself.*

Shelby's emotions once again bounced from joy to uncertainty. She desperately wanted to talk with her father, but first she needed to get in touch with Jack. *I will not allow any negative thoughts about this baby.* She shook off those feelings and mentally pulled herself together, then headed toward the crowd, a solid line of cars and news vans along the curb. A stage had been set up: a podium banked by microphones and two rows of chairs behind the speaker's lectern. Giant matching terra-cotta pots overflowing with petunias flanked the wide entrance to the tent, already filled with people. Flags with the project's logo fluttered in the breeze.

The leveled-off spot in front of the platform held hundreds of folding chairs. The crowd had begun to gather as cameramen and reporters were setting up, dragging cords and shifting camera positions. It dawned why Bobby had been so preoccupied; this was a full-blown media event. She squared her shoulders and entered the tent. Stuart Flaherty, Bobby, Adam and Martha Stamford and her father were standing before a table admiring an elaborate scale model of Covington Square. All three phases were depicted, complete with tiny plastic people, oak trees, bushes, cars, and tables on the patio where she and her father had stood earlier. Shelby walked along the table, eyeing brochures of the various shops, restaurants, boutiques and bookstores. All chic, all first-rate, along with literature and applications to join CAPE as well as brochures from Marcel's, New York's leading fashion chain and the anchor store in the center.

David was the first to spot her. "Shelby, we were getting worried about you." He kissed her on the cheek and led her to the group. Martha Stamford looked her up and down, Shelby elevating her chin, readying herself for another jibe. "Shelby darling, you look positively radiant. Not at all like your father described. David had us a bit worried."

"Leave it to your child to make a liar out of you," David interrupted. "Shelby, you do look a lot better. Is everything okay?"

"Fine, Dad, everything is fine."

Adam and Stuart greeted her warmly. Memories of Bobby and last night's argument had been swept aside by her fantastic news.

The tent filled quickly with significant arrivals. Shelby spotted Terri, a clipboard in her hand, directing people, pointing to the scale model and giving out brochures. City and county officials and important guests crowded into the tent.

Bobby grabbed Shelby's elbow and steered her around, introducing her to one person after another. His excitement bubbled over, affecting everyone with whom he spoke. At 2:45 P.M. Terri escorted the luminaries to their respective chairs on the platform. Shelby whispered to Bobby that she and her father would sit in the audience but he would not hear of it. There were two seats reserved for them next to his on the platform. He held Shelby's hand as they made their way to their seats. The special guests were seated in the first rows facing the stage.

The biggest luminary, literally and figuratively, was Frederick Houghton, President of CAPE, California Alliance for the Protection of the Environment. He stood six feet, five inches, distinguished and graying, wider around the middle than at the shoulders, impeccably dressed, and exuding power and authority. Seated immediately to Bobby's left, Houghton looked like a J.P. Morgan or a Rockefeller. Next to him was Kathryn Alexander, also from CAPE. Mr. Houghton was scheduled to follow Bobby on the program.

By three o'clock the milling crowd had found seats, quieted down and was waiting expectantly. Television cameras switched on, reporters making their opening statements with microphones in hand. Then Terri cued Bobby. He rose and walked to the bank of microphones.

"Good afternoon, distinguished guests and ladies and gentlemen. Covington Square was born as all projects are, as a dream, a spark, an idea. And today we are here to break ground and begin the realization of that dream. We seek not simply to develop this property, but rather to introduce a new concept to development. Our goal from the beginning was, and remains, using the highest standard of environmental research and design and combine those goals with the best elements in development. Covington Square has been called a model for development in this twenty-first century, a model I assure you Stamford Development holds in the highest regard."

Bobby presented facts about the project: the three phases, the projected completion dates, and an invitation to return for the grand opening. The crowd applauded enthusiastically. Bobby introduced Frederick Houghton and returned to his seat beside Shelby.

Houghton's speech was a coup for Bobby and Adam. Houghton acknowledged that the concept of "going green" on such a large-scale project was a first. "I have to admit that we were surprised and pleased when Stamford Development first approached us and sought CAPE's cooperation and guidance, not merely focusing on the bottom line. And from that day on, our advice and input was sought on every step of the way to find the best environmental approach in each phase of design. It is CAPE's opinion that Covington Square will be the leader in shaping the future of new developments!" After the lengthy applause, Houghton challenged other developers to show the same wisdom and vision.

There were four more short speeches, one a moving tribute to Bobby and Adam Stamford delivered by Alice Covington. Her faltering voice and remembrance of her husband and how proud he would be of the Covington project drew the biggest applause of all. Bobby assisted her to her chair, Shelby and David sharing a look. *That was a brilliant bit of strategy. Bobby's got them eating out of his hand.*

Next was the Photo Op, the principals turning the earth with shovels sprayed metallic gold. Alice Covington was to have participated but she told Bobby she felt faint and remained in her chair. Martha Stamford sat next to her and asked someone to bring water. Alice's gold shovel was thrust in Shelby's hand and she was directed to stand in between Bobby and Adam.

A slew of newspaper photographers and television cameras recorded the occasion.

Karen, Rick, and Chloe attended; the boys were in school. After the photo op Chloe held tightly to Shelby's hand as they circulated among the crowd. Shelby had noticed Terri Armstrong during the ceremony. She and Bobby avoided eye contact and hardly gave each other more than a glance or nod. She took care of everything while avoiding being within twenty feet of Shelby.

Bobby had his back to them across the span of standing guests. Shelby estimated if she wanted to speak to Terri, she had about three minutes before he would spot them. *Should I acknowledge her? Probably not. Oh, what the heck, let's see how Bobby reacts.* Approaching, Shelby tapped Terri's shoulder. She spun around, shock registering on her face.

"Terri, I wanted to congratulate you on the job you've done on this project. I happen to know Bobby has properly rewarded you, and you deserve everything. You've done an excellent job. It's nice finally getting to meet you." Shelby glanced over her shoulder.

Bingo! Bobby sees us, uh-oh, panic on three faces—both of his and Terri's.

Arms flailing, Bobby appeared to be swimming as he tried to get through the crowd, a set smile on his face. Irving Ross, the Marcel representative, intercepted him two feet away, gesturing and gushing over the project and Marcel's place in it. Bobby's panic-stricken eyes were staring straight at them but he dare not be rude to the rep of his biggest tenant. Just as Bobby extricated himself with a laugh and pat on Irving's back, Shelby and Chloe moved away.

"Who was that lady, Aunt Shelby?" asked Chloe.

"Nobody, sweetheart, no one important," she answered, experiencing a sense of closure.

Shelby next happened across Alice Covington, a tiny woman in height and stature, who greeted Shelby warmly and cooed over little Chloe. Shelby and Alice were visiting when Bobby finally reached Terri's side. She had a good view of them over Alice's head. Bobby looked angry. They whispered to each other excitedly, then Terri whirled around and left him standing.

The official ceremonies concluded, Shelby and her father were among the fifty special guests invited to a post ground-breaking party at André's, a neighborhood restaurant. Frederick Houghton and Kathryn Alexander were invited but politely declined. Stuart told Bobby not to expect their attendance, that CAPE walked a fine line between acceptance and fraternization.

Monsieur André Bourges greeted them at the door of his restaurant. Bobby had told Shelby and David that though André had been the driving force behind the opposition, for some unknown reason he had reconsidered. Shelby did note how very solicitous the Frenchman was to Bobby. The party was convivial; there were toasts, backs slapped, hands shaken and kudos given to Stamford Development Inc., particularly to Bobby. He graciously acknowledged Stuart Flaherty.

"Wave at Uncle Bobby, Chloe," Shelby said, and then spotted her father talking to Karen, Rick, and the elder Stamfords, Martha Stamford resplendent in a pale gold Ungaro suit. Shelby approached the group and her heart skipped a beat when she looked at her father, a handsome, charming gentleman. *How is it he is still single after all these years? Will he forget Adele? When he finds out I'm pregnant, will he change his mind and want to be a grandfather?*

Shelby visited briefly with her in-laws and then handed Chloe back to Rick. Chloe blew Shelby a kiss from her father's arms. As soon as dinner was over, Shelby and David begged off, informing family and inquiring guests that he was leaving the following morning for Peru.

Later that evening, Shelby sat on David's bed as he packed the suitcase he had used for the L.A. part of his trip. "I don't want you to go, Dad."

"You're not making this easy."

"I know but I'm afraid I won't see you again in this century."

"Why don't you come to Peru for a visit? We'll take the train to Machu Picchu, sit on the hotel porch and look out over the Cordillera. It is spectacular. I'll show you Cuzco and—"

"I can't right now, Dad. You see how messed up my life is. I don't know what I'm going to do. And Enrique's been handling Skyline. I need to take care of that too." *And the baby.*

"Of course, pumpkin, I understand. But whenever you can, you must come. We don't want five years to pass until we see each other again. Promise me."

Chapter Twenty Eight

Jack tried to keep busy after he and Adele spent Super Bowl Sunday supposedly watching the game. They had royally tied one on, both lamenting Shelby and David's departure with Jack Daniel's Tennessee sour mash whiskey. They laughed and cried and drank straight shots. They chased down bowls of chili with cold beers, then groused about their ill-fortune with more straight shots.

Only occasionally did they pay close attention to the game, and after it ended Adele fell asleep on the couch with Shadow curled up against her. Jack threw a blanket over them, stoked the fire and went to bed. Since then, Adele had been busy at the café, snowmobilers and skiers, Troutsprings and Pine Ridge residents alike trying out the new dishes she introduced. She also advertised in the Pine Ridge and Troutsprings papers, hiring Ronnie and Chuck to distribute leaflets announcing the new ownership and that Adele's Café was now open for lunch as well as dinner. It had paid off; she had a good steady crowd.

Shelby hadn't been gone a week, but it seemed like a year. He had the pictures he'd taken of her propped on his desk. Jack wrote Shelby three letters, laboring over each word, trying to explain how he felt. He told her he loved her and shared his fantasy about her living at the ranch. He asked if she could love him back or if she had found out she still loved Bobby. He folded each one neatly and put it in a book he kept on the coffee table.

Jack had the daily feeding and the stock needing veterinary care to take his mind off Shelby. It didn't help. There was machinery to repair and fences to fix, plenty of chores to keep him busy. A fellow rancher stopped by the previous day and asked to buy four good-producing cows from Jack to introduce new blood into his stock. Jack sold them, then went about his work. Shadow followed him around and Jack was grateful for it.

On Thursday, February first, the weatherman predicted eight more weeks of winter. A depressing thought. Adele stopped on her way to work to ask if he would look at the freezer at the café; the compressor was going on and off constantly. She promised him a Chicken Cordon Bleu dinner, a new concoction. Adele wanted to see if he liked it.

They hadn't spoken of David or Shelby; they hadn't talked at all. Jack figured the real reason for her visit was to see how he was holding up. She seemed fine. That was depressing too.

Jack arrived at Adele's Cafe at five o'clock. "How you doing, Adele?"

"Hey, partner, doing great! How about you?"

"Absolutely, positively dandy!" he replied in an equally loud voice.

"Atta boy, you say it enough times you'll start to believe it."

Jack checked the freezer. There were enough dust balls under it to stuff a mattress, evidently one place Adele hadn't cleaned. He vacuumed underneath it and the motor sounded better already. The place looked different, clean and fresh, with valances over the windows and colorful silk flowers in clear vases on each table. New bright cocktail napkins with *Adele's Café* imprinted on them were stacked on the bar and on the new tall round bar tables Shelby and David had built. Virgil put down a bowl of popcorn with Jack's beer.

"Makes customers thirstier n' hell, Jack," he said and went back to tending bar.

Jack ate alone at a table and enjoyed the new addition to the menu. A few customers came up to visit, lamenting the cold and snow and telling him they liked what Adele had done to the place. Adele stopped by the table and tried a bite. "It's good, isn't it?" Jack agreed and finished his meal, then moved back to the bar. Virgil drew him another tap. Lester Holt was on NBC with the evening news.

"Same ol', same ol'," Adele said as she paused a moment to watch. "Murder, war and politicians saying they didn't do anything wrong." She went back to work. Jack was finishing his beer as Lester Holt signed off. "And now for news beyond the day's headlines. In a state that in recent years has suffered riots, earthquakes, devastating fires and floods, some good news. Stamford Development, one of southern California's largest developers, and Frederick Houghton, head of California's powerful environmental group, CAPE, today showed the rest of the country what can happen when opposing forces work together. Let's go to Leigh Anne Kinney at KXLA, our NBC affiliate in Los Angeles, for a report."

Adele stopped dead in her tracks and Jack's hand froze in mid-air, the mug half-way to his lips. A pretty young woman stood in front of a crowd. In the background a tall distinguished man could be seen speaking from a podium, though it was the reporter's voice they heard. Adele walked up and stood beside Jack, her eyes fixed on the reporter. "Stamford Development, a major developer in southern California, today broke ground with the blessing of The California Alliance for the Protection of the Environment, CAPE, on Covington Square, which they hope will be a model for future environmentally engineered and designed shopping centers."

The camera panned the stage. Jack and Adele zeroed in on Shelby, flanked by David on one side and Bobby on the other. Shelby, David and the others on the platform stood up as Bobby and the speaker shook hands, then waved at the crowd. Bobby had a triumphant smile on his face as he held Shelby's hand high with his own.

Jack and Adele looked at each other in unspoken shock.

The reporter continued. "According to Robert Stamford, the developer, the additional cost to the project is justified. Development should reflect the true cost to the environment."

A pan showed the tall man, Shelby, Bobby, and three others smiling with shovels in their hands. Lester Holt appeared again and spoke in his resonant voice. "Thank you, Leigh Anne. This story just proves, folks, you can mix oil and water. Good night from NBC Nightly News."

Jack stared blankly at the screen. He didn't see it or even the television set. What he saw was the image of Bobby Stamford, smiling and confident, holding Shelby's hand high in his hand, his own fantasy disappearing like a puff of smoke. Jack's chest hurt where he'd been shot, or was it his heart breaking? Jack Ketchum felt old and tired and he wanted to be alone.

Adele was talking to him. "Jack, there could be a hundred explanations for that scene. Don't go jumping to conclusions."

"I already jumped. I don't need explanations." Jack left without a further word. As soon as he got home, he phoned Ronnie and Chuck and hired them to do the chores. Then he called the Jenkins and asked if they would watch over The Broken Arrow Ranch. He had to get away.

Jack didn't want to talk to Adele; he wasn't in the mood for another pep talk about keeping the faith and love conquering all. He couldn't bear hearing Shelby tell him she decided to stay with Bobby.

He didn't need to hear it; he saw it in the triumphant look on Bobby's face.

Jack closed the house, hooked the horse trailer up to his Ford 350 diesel dually pickup, then put his camping gear and little Shadow in the truck cab and took off. He told himself it was time to replace the cattle he'd sold and introduce new blood into his stock.

Once on the road, he tossed his cell phone in the glove compartment and headed south.

* * *

The following day Shelby drove her father to LAX and waited in the terminal until she saw the Varig 747 take its place in the line of departing planes on the runway. She called the ranch on her cell phone. *No answer. Jack, where are you?* She had made her decision and there was no point in putting off telling Bobby. He'd said he was tired of waiting. She hoped he was in his office. With the festivities over, maybe they would finally have the time to talk. She glanced at her watch, almost noon as she pulled into the parking lot. Shelby entered the foyer of Stamford Development, an excited Miss Telford greeting her and wanting to know if she had seen Bobby and herself on television.

Miss Telford didn't wait for an answer. "Bobby and Mr. Houghton from CAPE made the national news last night! You were on there too, sitting next to Bobby. Two whole minutes, I timed it! It was at the end of Lester Holt's broadcast on NBC." She rolled her eyes and clasped her hands together. "We are sooo proud of Bobby."

"Absolutely, Miss Telford, that is exciting."

Miss Telford blushed as though she had just been selected Miss America. "I'm going on and on and you're here to see Bobby, I'll buzz him."

Bobby immediately came out of his office, a broad smile on his face, and strode toward Shelby. "Well, what a wonderful surprise." Everyone stopped to watch. Shelby saw it coming but could not ward off Bobby's hug or kiss. The staff broke into applause, all but Terri. Bobby laughed and then bowed slightly, spurred on by the employees' reactions.

He ushered Shelby into his office with a "hold my calls," said in Terri's general direction. Bobby had either forgotten their heated discussion or chose to ignore it. He closed the door and walked to his desk. "Champagne?"

"No champagne, thanks. I just saw Dad off. I thought maybe we could—"

"Have lunch on this glorious day? Of course, because it isn't every day you get to take out a national newsmaker. Nice of you to think of it. Would you mind if I ask Dad to join us?"

Dammit, what was I thinking? I can't tell him today, the biggest day of his career. "No, of course not, Bobby, ask him along."

The three had lunch on the vine-covered outdoor patio of The Bistro in midtown Beverly Hills, Bobby and Adam bombarded with congratulations as they walked to their table.

"Wow, you two," she said to Bobby and Adam, "it seems you know most everyone."

"Thankfully, that's true," Bobby said, he and Adam both acknowledging congratulations by shaking hands and patting backs. Shelby could see Adam was as pleased as his son.

At the table as they waited for their food, Adam was cordial, talking about the importance of family and how much he and Martha had missed her during the holidays. Their lunch arrived, Adam asked about Montana, the weather and the building projects Bobby said she had done. Over coffee, her father-in-law assured Shelby they would love to see her at upcoming family gatherings. Bobby listened as he ate, nodding his head especially about the family part. *That was the reason he wanted Adam to come..*

Shelby dropped Bobby and Adam off at the office, then phoned Enrique from her car. It was Friday, payday for the Skyline employees. Enrique met her at the house and they did the payroll together for the first time since she returned. Shelby enjoyed seeing her crew again.

"You've done a wonderful job, Enrique. You got your license and the remodel job finished. Both houses are looking great, you should be proud of yourself."

"It was nice you being as close as the phone. Sorry about all the long-distance calls, but knowing I had you to turn to, made it easier to make decisions."

"No big deal about the phone calls. That's the least of my problems."

"I'm worried about you, boss. Would I be out of line if I asked what the problem is?"

"Of course not, you're like my brother. It's complicated and it may affect you."

He looked puzzled. "That's not an answer."

"I know. I'll explain as soon as I can. In the meantime would you like a few days off?"

"Thanks, but not until the houses are finished. We're so close I would like to see them through to the end if that's okay with you."

"Of course. Hopefully I'll know more about my situation and we can make some plans."

Enrique gave her a curious look. "Whatever you say, boss."

"You can't call me that anymore. We're partners."

"Okay, partner, see you on Monday."

Bobby had the weekend packed with parties and guests. He was the happiest Shelby had seen him since Covington began. There was no reference to their talk. He acted as though it never happened, asking both evenings if she would come upstairs to sleep in their room. When she declined, his reply was something akin to "no problem.'" Saturday night he insisted they have dinner with the family at the country club. Shelby acquiesced.

On Sunday, Bobby invited the Flahertys and two key Stamford executives and their wives out for dinner. He said it was to thank them for a job above and beyond the call of duty. Again, Bobby gave her no opportunity to speak to him.

Shelby lost track of how many times she tried to reach Jack over the weekend. A vague uneasiness elevated with each unanswered call. *If I don't get hold of him soon, I will fly to Montana and ask him straight out if he loves me. I need to know. Then I'll tell him about the baby.*

Cell phone in hand and determined to talk with Bobby before he left for the office, Shelby stood sipping coffee at the kitchen island when he came down Monday morning.

"Gotta run, Shel, I'm late for an appointment," he said in a cheerful voice.

"You're avoiding me, Bobby. Please sit down. Whoever it is will just have to wait."

Bobby set his briefcase on the floor by the door and sat on a stool, facing her across the island. She put her cell phone on the island, then poured his coffee and set the cup in front of him. "I have come to a decision, Bobby."

He cleared his throat. "You have?"

"Yes, I have and I'm sorry, Bobby, I—"

"Shel, no! Don't say it. Don't say divorce." His voice was little more than a whisper.

"You have your life, Bobby. I'm not part of it and I haven't been for a long time."

"You're not being fair, Shel. I will make you part of my life if you give me a chance."

"I don't think I could make you understand if we talked a million years. You know how much I hate divorce, Bobby, but if I stayed married to you I would be living a lie. I don't want to hurt you or your family, but I don't want to hurt anymore either."

"I know I screwed up with—I didn't realize what I had, Shel. I do now and all I can say is I am so sorry I hurt you. And I give you my word, it won't ever happen again." His tears matched the despair in his voice. He ran both hands through his hair.

Tears welled in Shelby's eyes too. "It's too late, Bobby, too late for us. I loved you so much and I waited. I wanted you to love me back, but you didn't—you couldn't. So I buried myself with my building." Shelby motioned toward the stables. "I want more out of life now."

He looked the picture of abject misery. "Want more? You live in a ten-million-dollar home. You can build whatever you want, buy whatever you want. I'm telling you I can change and I want our marriage to succeed. Can't we try again?" He looked panicked, as though running out of ideas. They eyed each other across the granite island, visible and rock-solid like the chasm that separated them. His pain showed in his posture, on his face and in his voice. Bobby wiped his eyes with a handkerchief. "Tell me, does Jack Ketchum have anything to do with this?"

Shelby straightened up, girding for what she knew was coming. "Yes, Bobby, he does." She made sure to look straight at him with an unwavering gaze.

Bobby's eyebrows arched. "Are you in love with him?" His words were whisper-quiet.

Shelby drew a deep breath. "Yes, very much. And I don't know how else to tell you…"

"Tell me what?"

"I am pregnant. With Jack's baby."

Bobby's transformation was instant. The veins in his temple bulged and his pupils dilated. He stared at her in disbelief. His face at first pale, Shelby watched a flush start at his collar and spread upward, splotching his cheeks. "You are What!" He spit out each word.

Shelby's voice remained quiet and firm. "I am pregnant."

Bobby rose, and without taking his eyes off her, swept the coffee mugs and her cell phone off the island in one swift, powerful motion. Shelby did not flinch when all three hit the wall, the cups shattering coffee and ceramic fragments all over the kitchen, her cell ending up on the floor near his briefcase. Bobby stared at her, loathing contorting his face. He walked to the kitchen door, picked up his briefcase and looked down at her phone. He glared at her, then stomped on it, sending metal shards over the kitchen floor.

"Are you crazy!" Shelby yelled.

He smiled. "That's a Stamford Development phone," he said over his shoulder as he opened the door to the garage. "I want you out of my house and out of my life!"

Chapter Twenty Nine

Stunned, Shelby sat staring at the shards of her destroyed cell phone and the sea of broken pottery. *I should have seen that coming.* She rose to begin cleaning up the mess when Esther came through the door, hands instantly flying to her cheeks. "*Madre de Dios!*" Shelby just looked at her and said, "Bobby."

Esther rushed to Shelby and held her, rocking the two of them gently side to side. When she let her go, she shook her head. "*Este es muy malo.*" She shushed Shelby away. "I fix, I fix."

The house remained quiet for the rest of Monday. Shelby tried to reach Jack on and off the remainder of the day, no answer at the house or on his cell. Bobby did not come home after work which came as no surprise. *I'm sure Terri is giving him the sympathy he needs.*

The next day Shelby tried again to reach Jack all day and late into the evening, still with no answer. Scary dreams awakened her in a panic Wednesday morning at 4:00 A.M. Dawn still hours away, she tried both numbers with the same results so she hung up and called Adele at her house in Pine Ridge. A sleepy voice answered. "Hello?"

"Adele, it's Shelby. I'm sorry for waking you up."

"It's okay" came a muffled reply.

"I've been trying day and night to reach Jack since last Friday. There's no answer at the house or on his cell and I'm scared. Do you have any idea where he is and if he's all right?"

There was a long silence. "No, Hon, I haven't seen or heard from him since he left. Come to think of it, he didn't say anything about why or where he was going, which isn't like Jack."

"What is it, Adele? I can tell by your voice that something's wrong. Tell me what it is."

"I don't know where he is, Shelby, but I think I may know why." The whispered tremor in her voice took Shelby's breath away.

"Adele, I called to tell Jack that I came to a decision and told Bobby I want a divorce." She waited expectantly for a response but heard only silence. Shelby gripped the phone, each second of silence elevating her panic level, revving her heart rate and constricting her breathing. Adele not answering confirmed Shelby's worst fears. *Something has happened to Jack and she can't or won't tell me!* Uncertainty and fear triumphing over nerves and now fighting for air, she hung up the phone without saying goodbye.

* * *

Adele replaced the bedside phone in its cradle, Shelby's panic still echoing in her ear. Wide awake over her news about Jack, Adele suddenly realized that she hadn't kept track of just how long he had been gone. She counted back to last Friday on her fingers. "That's five days!" she murmured. "Jack's not that irresponsible, maybe something really has happened to him."

Her concern now full blown, Adele mentally considered calling Shelby back but having to tell her she had no answers. Or better, she could try to get some answers first. Acknowledging being caught off guard at that hour and not sure which of Shelby's concerns to respond to first, then Shelby hung up before she could respond! *She sounded like she was hyperventilating. I don't want to make her worse.* That thought made up her mind; she called Jim Jenkins.

Reluctantly she woke him up and the minute he said hello, she said, "Adele here, Jim. This is an emergency. Jack hasn't answered his cell phone since he left and I'm scared maybe he's hurt and needs help. Did he tell you where he was going?"

"No, not where he was going." Jim sounded more alert than she expected. "All he told me was he was headin' south to buy cattle and didn't know when he'd be back. I didn't think to ask him. Come to think of it though, he sounded kinda serious and quiet."

"Uh-oh. When he stopped by your house was he in his truck with the horse trailer? And did he happen to mention a town?" She heard his breathing. Jim was thinking.

"Yes, ma'am, on the truck and horse trailer, but he didn't mention a town. All I can say about that is when we used to go cattle buyin' together, our first stop was always Jackson, Wyoming. We'd stay there one night, then move on. How many days has Jack been gone?"

"Five, I think," Adele said, trying to remember what Shelby said.

She heard Jim counting. "Five days? Then I'd bet money he's in Dodge City, Kansas. That's where we always ended up. We'd drink beer and eat steak. We had ourselves a—"

"Sorry, Jim, but I need to find Jack right now! Any idea where he might stay?

"Well, there was only one place we ever stayed. The Dodge House Hotel. I'd try that."

"Thanks, Jim, I owe you a dinner!" Before she could hang up, Jim said to hold on.

"Adele? That ain't like Jack and I'd appreciate you callin' me back if you don't find him. 'Cause if you don't, me and my boys will go lookin' for him."

* * *

After her call to Adele, Shelby stopped trying to reach Jack. Him leaving like he did and not answering her calls when he could see who was calling, said it all. *He must have thought it over and changed his mind. I don't get it. Was I just a good lay?* Her gut told her otherwise, but she could think of no other reasonable explanation. Rationally, if he had been in an accident Adele would have been notified by now.

Shocked and feeling betrayed at Jack's behavior plus having to deal with Bobby, Shelby had to admit she was mentally and physically exhausted. *This is my house too. Bobby cannot arbitrarily kick me out and I'm not leaving until I feel better and know where I'm going. I need time to find an apartment so, tantrum be damned, he's not getting his way this time.* She wrote Bobby a note advising she wasn't going to leave until she was ready, then propped it up in plain sight on the island in the kitchen so he'd be sure to see it.

She occasionally heard his voice but he didn't come near her room. Even hearing his voice made her angry. She halfway wished he'd knock on her door so she could tell him how childish and stupid his tantrum was and that she wasn't leaving until she was damn-well ready. And after learning why she was never allowed to visit her father in Peru all those years, her mother was now on her shit list too. Thinking about Jack, if he wasn't hurt or dead, it royally pissed her off that that he didn't have the guts to level with her. *The only family I'm not mad at, besides Oscar and Esther, is Dad! I should probably call him, but what would I say?*

Shelby took a nap when she felt tired, she ate what Esther cooked, and she soaked up the afternoon sun sitting on the patio, sometimes reading apartment ads in the paper, other times remembering scenes from her life: her mother's wedding to Dennis and how alone she felt, the excitement of getting her first horse and the disappointment her father wasn't there to share it.

Shelby vividly remembered her return to California, and eleven days ago learning that she was pregnant. She remembered that moment, how her hopes soared and then were dashed by the man with whom she conceived this child. *Conceived in love, I thought!* She hadn't spoken to anyone except Esther for a week and that was just fine and dandy.

Friday morning, Shelby was reading the paper on the patio when Esther approached, the portable house phone in her hand. "*Señora, es muy importante, por favor.*" Esther nodded, encouraging her to take the call. It was the Imaging Center reminding her of her ultrasound appointment Tuesday. The clerk asked a couple of questions: was this a routine appointment or was she having problems? And did she want to be informed of the sex of her baby? Did she want to know if it was a boy or a girl?

Thoughts of her baby filtered down into the depths of Shelby's psyche, the image touching her, chipping away at the numbing, hurtful feelings that had brought her to her knees. Picturing her baby, she cast off her anger and disappointment, and then quite without reason, Shelby's heart made the resolution to be healed, a decision her rational mind had been incapable of making. *I wanted a child. I dreamed of having a child and now I am. I may not get the whole dream, but I have love enough. I can do this.*

Shelby woke up Saturday feeling anxious "to do something!" Esther was delighted when Shelby asked if she would like to go shopping with her. They first went to an electronics store and an hour later Shelby walked out with a new cell phone, briefly lamenting that she had no one she wanted to call. Next they looked at cribs and strollers. They held up baby outfits of every kind, oohing and aahing but not buying until she learned whether the baby was a boy or girl.

They enjoyed a wonderful lunch, Esther beaming like a proud, happy grandmother-to-be who told Shelby she felt "*muy felicidad*" to have her back.

Tuesday, 9:00 A.M. sharp, Shelby arrived at the Imaging Center. The female radiologist kept glancing at the screen but saying nothing as she guided the instrument over Shelby's belly. Shelby asked if everything looked okay and was assured it did, also that the images would be sent electronically to Dr. Caldwell "within the hour and should be available at his office by the time she could get there." Excitement mounting, Shelby called Dr. Caldwell's office on her new cell phone and asked if she could come over and wait. "Sure," Linda told her. "I'm sure he will work you in as soon as we can after we receive the images online."

Shelby checked her watch. 10:00 A.M. *I want doughnuts—lots of doughnuts.* She went by the bakery and picked out a variety for Dr. Caldwell and his staff. Still warm, they smelled of yeast and cinna-mon. She had doughnut crumbs around her mouth when she walked into the office and handed the box to the receptionist. "A dozen minus three," she said.

"Good, huh?" the receptionist said.

"Delicious," Shelby replied.

A few minutes later, Linda invited Shelby to wait in Dr. Caldwell's office. Another thirty minutes went by, then Caldwell opened the door, a donut in one hand. "Thanks for the treats, Shelby! Let's go in the lab. The big screen computer is in there." Shelby followed him. Linda was already working at the computer.

"How are you feeling?" Caldwell said, brushing crumbs off his face.

"Much better, and excited. Does everything look all right? Is the baby okay?"

"Absolutely fine," Caldwell answered, he and Linda exchanging quizzical smiles. He invited Shelby to sit on a stool in front of the computer and he stood beside her. "Remember when I told you about your pregnancy and you went into such a state of shock? There was something I suspected but I didn't mention because it seemed you'd had about all the good news you could handle at one sitting. Now you can see for yourself."

Shelby stared at the huge screen. "I'm not sure what I am looking at."

The doctor pointed with a pencil. "Here is one fetus. And see this?" He pointed to a different area. "Here is another fetus. You can just see the head." Caldwell tapped a key and another screen appeared. The picture was clear; there were two tiny negative profiles.

Shelby's hands flew to her cheeks. "Am I seeing what I think I'm seeing?"

Linda hugged her first and Dr. Caldwell started to shake her hand but then hugged her too. "Yes, you are, Shelby. You've got twins in there and both are fine. How about that!"

"Twins, really? I can't believe it! That's the most wonderful news I've heard in my entire life," she said to Caldwell, detecting a bit of moisture in his eyes.

He cleared his throat and returned his gaze to the screen. "I can't tell the sex of either fetus yet," he said huskily. "But they look well-formed. They're small but that's okay at this stage. Are you eating well?"

"I'll do better," Shelby said, staring at the screen.

The doctor put his hand on her shoulder. "I hope and pray that I will never get over the thrill of seeing life." He printed both images. "Babies' first photographs. You've made my day."

"And you've certainly made mine," Shelby replied, clasping the papers to her chest.

She drove back to the Canyon Hills Drive house in a state of euphoria. Oscar and Esther's old clunker car was gone; they were probably buying groceries. Shelby went through the kitchen, grabbed three carrots and went straight out to the corral. She approached the fence and gave treats to two horses, then called Cherokee, who walked up and put her head over the top rail. Shelby put her arms around the mare's neck, burying her face against it, feeling Cherokee's warmth, inhaling her smell. Like Shadow, she had a wonderful smell all her own.

Shelby could feel the horse's pulse with her cheek. "Remember last July when we found out you were going to have a foal and I was so envious? Now look at me." Shelby stepped back to show Cherokee. The mare's head moved up, then down, which Shelby chose to interpret that she understood her mistress's excitement.

"I'm going to have two! Bless you, Grandma Longren, for being a twin!" she called out to the sky. *I have so much to be thankful for.*

Chapter Thirty

David Longren had been back in Peru for ten days, hard at work for nine. Coming back felt akin to jumping onto a moving train from an overpass—"Jump fast and hang on!" El Dorado was behind schedule drilling test sites on its new acquisition and John McGinnis was not a man who liked to be behind at anything.

David began working twelve-hour days his second day back, re-establishing his routine: rise before dawn, work until dark, then return to his apartment which was nothing more than two rooms in a dormitory on the La Orroya clearing. After showering and cooking his meal, he fell into bed, only to repeat the same routine the following day. For years the hefty salary he earned had made up for the loneliness and adversities, but it seemed pointless and empty now.

It had been a grueling Monday, mapping the terrain of the new acquisition by helicopter, choosing test sites, looking for the easiest and cheapest way to get equipment in. John McGinnis had been on David's heels all day, with him in the helicopter, asking questions, pressing for answers and instant decisions. Hundreds of thousands of dollars of equipment stood poised and ready. At dusk, McGinnis left in the helicopter for Lima and the comfort of his apartment and family. He asked David if he wanted to catch a ride to his own apartment in Lima, but David declined. He was exhausted and another big day awaited him. McGinnis, satisfied with their decisions, said he would remain in the city.

David stood for a moment watching the copter disappear, then walked to his office and glanced through today's reports and memos on his desk. A bright yellow envelope had been tossed on top of his pending box. If it hadn't been so bright he would not have spotted it. Envelope in hand he walked toward his apartment, the clearing light not bright enough to make out the return address but bright enough to see a tire track across it.

Thankful that his apartment was warm after a long day in the cold Andean air, he first located his glasses. The letter was from Adele! Recognizing her handwriting he felt a catch in his chest. David propped the envelope against the salt shaker on the tiny table and headed to the shower. Wanting to savor the letter, he chose to enjoy it after dinner. There was no telling as to its contents; Adele Carson could be charmingly unpredictable.

He took his usual quick shower; there was not an abundance of water at this elevation. Dinner was also hasty, for sustenance, not pleasure. David ate, eyeing the propped-up envelope, picturing her cozy home, remembering the warmth of the fire and Adele. He missed her, the fun, their laughter and the closeness. He missed Jack too. He turned out to be a good friend.

And he desperately missed his daughter. It had been easier when he and Shelby only exchanged cards, when he never heard her voice or felt a hug. But memories of her remained fresh, her laughter, their talks, their Christmas shopping, then the wonderful time they had remodeling the café. The way she'd held his hand on the plane when she was frightened.

His trip had accomplished what he'd hoped it would do, rekindle a strong love between father and daughter. But it also spawned a gnawing need to nurture that relationship. His trip also created an unexpected void in his life, caused by the absence of one pie-baking, live-life-to-the-limit, lovable redhead.

Dinner finished, David stretched out on his bed and switched on his reading lamp. He instinctively sniffed the envelope, hoping to detect a familiar fragrance. It may have left Montana smelling of the wonderful perfume Adele wore; now it smelled of an earthy mixture of Peruvian hands with a dash of rubber tire thrown in.

Wednesday, February 7th

Hey You Handsome Fellow!

I suppose you think I'm missing you just because I'm writing all the way to South America. Well, forget it. I'm doing just fine. I think I'm the only one who is, but I'll get to that later. I just thought I'd say hello and tell you I baked an apple pie today. Got the crunch topping all ready to put on top and I'd send it, but it might lose something in the translation. (ha-ha)

Adele's Cafe is doing great and it's the season when it should be slow. I've done some advertising so I am busier than a one-armed paper hanger on a hot day. I'm not sure what I'll do when summer comes and it really gets busy. Oh, the problems being a business tycoon!

I don't know if you have talked with Shelby since you got back. She woke me up this morning at 4:00 A.M. wondering about Jack. Seems he's disappeared and is not answering any of her calls on either of his phones. Anyway she said she told Bobby she's filing for divorce. But since she thinks Jack has abandoned her, she plans to stay in L.A. Her exact words were: Jack won't take my calls and I don't know where he is, so it looks like this is where I'm going to stay. She sounded terrible, David, and she hung up without even saying goodbye. I am really worried about her.

I haven't talked to Jack for over a week myself. He's been miserable since you two left. He won't talk about it so there's not much I can do. I tell you it's hard to be positive, but I am. I don't believe in moping. It causes wrinkles.

I have made a decision and I figured I'd better let you know. You realize, of course, I could have any number of handsome, rich men. But I decided you are the one. I'm picking you over all the others who have applied. The truth of it is, I love you, David Longren. Do you have any idea how lucky you are? I always knew there would be a good, decent (gorgeous!) man out there who would love me as much as I love him. I know you went back to Peru because you had to for your work, but also because you needed to think us over.

You've probably decided the same thing about me by now, anyway, but I'm not much for waiting around for somebody else to make the first move. It's time for you to retire. Sixty-three is the exact right age and Montana is the best place to do it because that's where I am.

Let me know the date and time of your arrival. I'll pick you up at the Glacier Airport.

All my love,
Adele

P.S. I'm sending some snapshots Jack took so you won't forget us.

Encased in three sheets of stationery, the pictures had escaped ruin by the tire. There was a picture of Adele behind the bar, a close-up with a soft light on her pretty face and a slight smile on her lips. She was wearing a green sweater, the pin he'd bought her clearly visible. On the back she had written "Montana business tycoon." There were three pictures of Shelby taken in the snow, one making a victory sign, one cavorting in front of the camera, and one about to let a snowball fly at the cameraman. The handwriting on the back was Jack's, a date only: November 18th. The last picture was of the four of them on Christmas Eve.

David sat up on the edge of the bed and held the bright yellow sheets directly under the lamp. He re-read the letter and re-read it again, then examined the pictures, drinking in every detail. Laughter began low in his gut, traveled up through his chest to his throat and engulfed him, shaking his body, then turning into tears without him realizing it. David pressed the letter to his lips and let the tears fall.

You wonderful, refreshing woman. Here I am, wondering whether I should give up a lifetime of being single and lonely—that's crazy! You've picked me? I'm the luckiest bastard on two continents. How incredibly right you are. It is time for me to give all this up. David looked around the room, recognizing the irony. *Benedictine monks who've taken a vow of poverty live better than this. I'm spending my life making some rich guy richer when I could be with a beautiful woman, in a warm home, with love and warm apple pie—with crunch topping! What the hell was I thinking?*

The part about Shelby scared him. Certain that his cell phone would not work, David donned his jacket and walked back to the offices in the center of the clearing. He let himself in and dialed Shelby's number on the company's secure line. The phone rang a dozen times. David reluctantly replaced the receiver and then had to talk to himself to quell his growing fear. He was away from a phone all the next day, but as soon as he arrived at camp from the field on Tuesday, David went directly to his office and called Shelby's number again. She answered this time, sounding out of breath. "Shelby, it's Dad. I was worried about you. Are you okay?"

"I'm better now."

"Have you come to a decision yet?"

"Yes, and I'll be staying in L.A. I told Bobby I'm filing for divorce and you know him, he didn't take it well. I'm still at the house though. I'll let you know soon as I have a new address. I miss you so much, Dad, and wish you were here. How are you?"

"Missing you terribly. It is just so lonely here, Shelby."

"Dad?"

"What, pumpkin?"

"You're going to be a grandpa. Twice."

"A grandpa? Oh my gosh! Really? Who? When? Wow, I am speechless!"

"Dad, did you hear me say twice?"

"I did but I have no idea what that means. A grandpa twice?"

"It means that I'm pregnant with twins."

David let her words sink in, the full impact computing in his brain, the word "twins" conjuring up the mental picture of his mother and her twin sister. "I'll be damned, Shelby, that twin gene theory of skipping a generation is really true!"

"It must be, Dad. I was as shocked as you are."

"It's wonderful, but how'd Bobby take learning about the baby and you divorcing him?"

"Bobby isn't the father, Dad. Jack is," Shelby said.

"Really? Jack's the father, you're divorcing Bobby but staying in

L.A.? I don't get it. I got a letter from Adele saying you sounded terrible on the phone. I take it this is the reason."

"Partly, Dad." He heard her sigh. "It's too complicated to explain over the phone. We can talk about it when you come for a visit. I am better now than when I talked to Adele."

"Okay, but is everything is all right with the babies?"

"Yes, mother and babies are in good health."

"Excellent! Well, I may be confused but I have some good news, too. I've also had time to think and you were right. Adele is a remark-able woman. I'd be a fool to let her get away."

"Oh, Dad, now you're going to make me cry. That is fabulous! Have you talked to her?"

"Not yet, but I'm in my office so I'm going to email her right after we hang up."

"Don't tell her about the babies, okay? I'd like to tell her myself. By the way, are you aware that tomorrow is Valentine's Day?"

"No, I wasn't, so thanks for reminding me! I will let you give Adele your wonderful news. What a Valentine's gift you've given me, Shelby. I feel badly about your confusing situation. I wish I could give you a hug."

"I wish you could, too. Come to L.A. as soon as you can, Dad. Maybe we can get Adele to come down when the babies arrive."

"Give me time to settle my affairs, and I'll be there as soon as I can. But where exactly?"

"Esther and Oscar will know where I am. They will pick you up. I love you, Dad."

"I love you too, Shelby. Take care of yourself and the babies. See you soon."

David sat holding the receiver long after he hung up. He could see his reflection in the window. *The babies are okay, so is Shelby. What I don't get is what's going about the babies and Bobby and Jack? I need to get there soon. Grandpa, that sounds wonderful! Oh my Lord, Adele a grandmother to twins? Is the world ready for that?*

He emailed John McGinnis requesting an immediate appointment in La Orroya or Lima. He had a replacement in mind if McGinnis would agree, but this grandfather-to-be was going home regardless. He wanted to be with his daughter and the babies and he would find a way to be with Adele too. He had no doubt he would be able to do both.

David sent a second email, this one to Adele Carson: *Dearest Adele. Happy Valentine's Day, my love! I cannot turn down your offer of warm apple pie with crunch topping, so please stop taking applications immediately! I accept. Will email you as soon as I know my date and time of arrival. I can hardly wait to see you. I love you too, Adele! Lucky David.*

* * *

Bobby gazed down at the main floor of The Courtyard from his second-floor table and sipped his scotch as he waited for his guests. This meeting was after-the-fact, but today was another landmark day. Frederick Houghton, Kathryn Alexander and Stuart Flaherty were expected momentarily. This luncheon with CAPE was to discuss the future of development in southern California, a planning session for the twenty-first century no less, with Robert Stamford as the recognized spokesman for the industry.

He'd taken as much care dressing this morning as he had done for the KXLA piece. Bobby was anxious to announce to CAPE that, indeed, Covington had affected the thinking of developers on a larger scale. A national story in *Fortune Magazine*, "*California Developer with a Dream*," would appear in an issue due out in the next few weeks. *Go ahead and admit it, you finally made it. You're number one. You won the game, the one your father spent a lifetime teaching you and then said didn't exist.*

Bobby had reluctantly resigned himself to the divorce. He'd done everything in his power to make Shelby happy—he'd given her everything. Her thanks? Getting herself pregnant with another man's baby. And after Terri's threat and her prank pretending to be drunk, he'd called the detective and given him names and leads. Terri was about to get her ass in more hot water than she could handle. Unhappy former lovers were a wealth of information and, as an added precaution, the detective was checking into Howie Armstrong. Any man with a daughter as cunning as Terri couldn't be totally clean. Bobby intended to free himself of double-dealing women with an agenda and play the field. No legal entanglements.

Arriving early, he checked with Chef Rudy to make sure the arrangements were perfect. They were. Bobby made a trip down to the men's room on the main floor. He checked his hair and straightened his tie. Waldo, the men's room attendant, brushed the shoulders of his cashmere jacket. Bobby tipped him a five-spot and exited.

He walked back toward the stairs, pausing at the base to survey the crowd. That's when he spotted them, Terri Armstrong and Leigh Anne Kinney being seated at a table near the fountain in the center of The Courtyard. He then glanced at the entrance doors. Right on schedule Stuart was escorting Houghton and Alexander in from Rodeo Drive.

"Jesus, what timing." Bobby paused at Terri and Leigh Anne's table, forcing a smile as Stuart, Houghton, and Alexander walked toward him. Terri jumped up and greeted Houghton. He smiled. "Yes, I remember you, Ms. Armstrong. You did an excellent job on the ceremony." Stuart and Bobby exchanged furtive glances and then Stuart directed Houghton and Alexander toward the stairway, telling them "our usual table upstairs is ready."

As soon as they were out of earshot, Bobby turned to Leigh Anne and Terri. "What a surprise. What are you ladies up to?"

"I thought it would be nice to show Leigh Anne around L.A. She's new here, you know." Gazing into Terri's gold-flecked, hazel eyes, Bobby wondered, for the first time in his forty-some years, if he had finally met his match. "Nice idea. You two enjoy your lunch." He turned on his heel and fought the urge to kill.

As soon as the CAPE lunch was over, Bobby returned to his office, his all-important meeting a blur. He hoped he hadn't made a fool of himself with Houghton and Alexander. On top of that, as they were leaving, Stuart took him aside and said to call him ASAP. He looked worried. Back at his office, Bobby first called the detective he had hired to check out Terri and left a message. "Find something on her and fast! If you get anything, call me!"

He called Stuart next, dreading to hear there was another problem. Stuart sounded grave, and as Bobby listened to "the issue at hand," as Stuart called it, he broke out in a sweat. "Fidelity International just informed me via registered letter they're putting on hold all financing on Covington—not a dime until the ownership of Stamford is determined."

Bobby exploded. "What the hell does that mean? I own it with Dad and Mom."

"You forgot about Shelby. I didn't realize she had filed, but Fidelity received notification of the divorce. Remember, according to California's Community Property law, your wife holds a twenty-five percent vested interest. Fidelity's Board held an emergency meeting and the consensus was they do not want to be involved in your divorce. Their position is, until clear ownership of the corporation is proven, Covington Square is on hold, dead in the water."

Bobby stared in disbelief at the phone, his life's dream, the crowning achievement of his career and his ticket to the top was dissolving. *The Fortune Magazine story, CAPE!* The phone still in his hand, he heard Stuart talking. "Meet with Shelby. See if you can talk to her and perhaps come to some agreement. Needless to say, Bobby, we need you to do that ASAP."

"You want me to deal directly with Shelby?" Bobby closed his eyes, visualizing the coffee mugs crashing against the wall and then stomping on her cell phone. "I'm screwed."

"If some agreement can't be reached, Bobby, Covington won't be launched on time and if that happens, Stamford stands to lose a million in sunk costs." Stuart sounded desperate.

"What can I possibly say to her, Stuart?" Bobby said, his mind spinning out of control. Stuart kept talking to him, calmly coaching him to think rationally until finally Bobby regained a measure of control. It took an entire hour, but Bobby called Stuart back and asked him to draw up an Indemnity Agreement. "Soon as you do, I'll try to convince Shel to sign it."

"Try, Bobby. If Shelby signs an agreement that holds Fidelity harmless regarding any corporate ownership provision contained in the divorce settlement, I believe they will go for it."

"Holy shit, Stuart, do you know what this means?" Stuart did not reply. "It means if the Covington project is to be saved, it comes down to me getting Shelby to trust me one last time. After all I've done? Good luck with that! It doesn't have a snowball's chance in hell."

"Shelby is a reasonable woman, Bobby. All you can do is try." Stuart wished him luck.

Here goes nothing. Bobby called the house and Oscar informed him that Shelby wasn't there, so he started to dial her cell—until he remembered it all over on the floor. He hung up. *Stupid! I need to get my shit together and stop making one goddam mistake after another.*

A second call to Stuart admitting he needed time to think, Bobby asked him to request the Fidelity Board grant a ten-day delay before axing the deal. The reason: "Mrs. Stamford is dealing with some significant medical issues at the moment." Stuart agreed to give it a shot.

The following morning, nervous to the point of having to loosen his tie, Bobby called the house. Esther answered. "In *la cocina*," she said. Evidently Shelby was there too, for he heard Esther say "*Es su esposo*." Bobby held his breath. *Get it together, Stamford.*

"What can I do for you, Bobby?" Shelby sounded all-business.

"First, accept my apology. If I were there I would get down on my knees, bum leg and all, and beg your forgiveness. I acted terribly. I'm an idiot." Silence on the other end. "Shel?"

"Yes, you did, and yes, you are, Bobby. What do you want?"

"For us to talk." He heard an intake of breath. "No, no! Not about us, Shel, I know how you feel. It's about Covington, a legal issue, routine but something we need to discuss. We could do it at home or here at the office—your choice. I would really appreciate it."

Silence, she's thinking. Bobby held the phone away from his mouth so she couldn't hear his labored breathing. "I really don't need this, Bobby, but if it's about Covington, I'm guessing it's important. I think I'd rather do it at your office. What time?"

Bobby made the sign of the cross. "Whatever is convenient for you."

"I have a 2:00 o'clock appointment today to see an apartment. How about one o'clock?"

"That's perfect. Thank you so much, Shel. See you at one." Hand shaking, he replaced the receiver gently, again overcome by emotion. As soon as he felt calm, Bobby called Stuart. "I can't believe it, Shelby agreed. We're meeting here at one o'clock. Do you want to be here?"

"Not unless you told her I was going to be there. No surprises, remember? This is a talk between husband and wife. You are going to be very calm, polite and respectful. Okay?"

"Absolutely, chief." Bobby glanced at the clock. 9:30 A.M.

He walked to his bar and downed half a glass of Chivas Regal, then sat trying to organize his thoughts. It had been one helluva week, Monday Shelby starting his day with the news she was pregnant with Ketchum's baby. That news was responsible for him getting caught in a vulnerable moment and Terri persuading him to spend the night with her.

He refused at first, but Terri won.

Terri made him forget Shelby, but then Terri could make him forget everything.

Chapter Thirty One

The intercom on Bobby's desk buzzed. "Bobby, Mrs. Stamford is here." He glanced at his watch; straight up 1:00 o'clock. He rose as Miss Telford ushered Shelby in. Seeing her brought a pang of regret strong enough to make his voice falter. "Hello... hi, Shel. I can't tell you how much I appreciate this." He pulled out a chair in front of his desk. "Please, have a seat."

"Thank you. How are you?" she said, her tone and demeanor perfunctory. Surprised how beautiful she looked, not tired and drawn like she did when she got back from Montana. She looked calm and confident, quadrupling his already glum mood.

"I'm okay, Shel. No... truthfully I'm not doing very well at all."

"Is that why you asked me here?"

"Well, that and I wanted to apologize again, in person. I am so sorry about the coffee thing and your cell phone, and...what I said. I was way out of line."

"Yes, you were. You know how I feel about divorce. I just hope this one will be civil."

"Absolutely, I want that too," he said. "There's no reason for it to be otherwise."

"Good. Maybe the lawyers can get everything completed quickly." She looked at him expectantly. "You said there was some legal thing?"

"There is, Shel, but can't we just talk first?"

"Talk about what?"

"I realize I messed up royally... Brenda and Terri. What you said in Missoula was right about me, the game and how I view things and people. I really blew it with you, didn't I?"

Shelby looked down. "You don't need to do this, Bobby, it doesn't matter anymore. You said there is a legal matter, which I assume is about the divorce, so just please tell me."

Her cutting him off hurt, at the same time driving home just how much he must have wounded her during their marriage. He took a deep breath, trying to recoup. "Yes, Shel, it is about the divorce. You know California is a community property state, which means you are a one-quarter owner of the Covington property. When Fidelity International learned the divorce had been filed, they notified Stuart they're holding up the financing on Covington. Not a dime until ownership is determined. I almost had a heart attack when Stuart told me."

The thought occurred to Bobby that he never discussed Stamford business with Shelby. *Score another screw-up, Stamford. That's what she meant about never being part of my life.*

"It is critical, Shel. Unfortunately if we can't come to some kind of agreement, Covington Square goes down the drain along with everything I've worked for in the last five years."

"Wow, that is a problem, a significant one. What can we do?"

"Well, first, Stuart asked Fidelity to hold off axing the financing for ten days to give you and me time to see if we can figure out something. It wouldn't have to be the final agreement but hopefully one you'd feel comfortable enough for Fidelity to proceed with the financing."

Bobby held his breath, remembering Stuart's advice. *No surprises. This is a talk between husband and wife. You are going be calm and polite and respectful.* Bobby fully realized his career and future were at the mercy of a woman he had cheated on and lied to. "Of course you can run everything by your lawyer, Shel. I want this to be fair."

"I've told you, Bobby, I don't want to hurt you or your family. I'm assuming the monetary value of this one-quarter interest has already been established, right?"

Jesus, she hit the nail on the head! "Yes, it has, by Fidelity the lender."

"Well," she paused, "what if I were to sign my quarter interest over to you or to Stamford Development at Fidelity's appraised value, then take back a note at the going interest rate. Either you or Stamford Development would have to make a substantial good-faith payment to seal the deal. Then I would be willing to delay monthly payments until Covington gets its first renters."

She just came up with that off-the-cuff? Bobby had to clasp his trembling hands together to cover his shock and relief. "That is a fantastic idea, Shel. Would you mind if I call Stuart and run it by him? I'll put him on speaker." She nodded and Bobby called Stuart, thankfully at his desk. "Shel is here, Stuart, and you're on speaker. How about this?" He repeated her proposal.

"That is fair, relevant, and timely—which is most critical. I sincerely thank you both."

Bobby disconnected and tried to pull himself together. "My God, Shel, I don't know what to say. Thank you doesn't begin to cover it." He rose and came around the desk, his hands held out. She rose and he took her hands in his, fighting back tears. "You could have destroyed me and everything I've worked for, but you didn't. I will always remember you, Shel, always."

The final document took five fretful days to complete. More nervous and on edge than he'd ever felt, Bobby didn't physically hold his breath for five days, instead he reasoned daily that if his heart didn't crap out over this, he just might live to reach fifty. Stuart's call came at the close of the fifth day. Shelby kept her word; she signed over her quarter interest, agreed to their million-plus down payment, and took back a note with payments to begin with the first renters. That done, Stuart called to say Fidelity agreed to proceed with the financing.

Alone in his office, Bobby broke down and sobbed.

* * *

After a restless night he arrived at the office the following morning, emotionally and physically drained. Wishing to feel excited about his project being saved didn't happen; what he felt was hollow and alone and he dreaded dealing with Terri another day. She had caught him in a distracted moment and convinced him to make the Covington project her full-time job. He agreed, trying to buy time for the detective he hired to come up with something big enough to extract Terri from Stamford Development and his life.

But Terri, interpreting the change as a promotion, was ecstatic until he said he intended to interview for a new secretary. "Not necessary, Bobby, everything is now in order. Miss Telford can handle answering the phone and simple secretarial duties." She then took the initiative to talk to her about it, and of course Miss Telford said yes. Bobby Stamford caved—temporarily.

As drained as he felt from the past six fretful days, Bobby breathed a sigh of relief when Terri greeted him with a professional air. She placed a stack of files on his desk. "You're going to love what's in these, Bobby." She sat down across from him as he glanced through several files, stunned at what he saw. "Terri, where did you get these?" The files contained copies of leases, complete with details and the termination dates on ten of Beverly Hill's best shops.

She simply smiled. "You now have the opportunity to get these leases for Covington. I can set up the appointments and you'll know exactly what to offer. What do you think?"

"That this is dynamite. But this information has to be confidential. How did you get it?"

"Oh, Bobby, I have ways of getting whatever I want. You ought to know that by now."

Oh my God, what now! After the door closed, he called Stuart. "I think Terri just handed me a bomb." Bobby read off the company names. "It's each store's lease with all the details!"

"This is beyond bad, Bobby. Terri has no idea what she's done! But first, tell me did you know she was she was going to do that? Or did you ask her to get the leases for you?"

"Hell, no! The first I knew about it was when she dropped the files on my desk."

"Then this conversation is off the record, Bobby. Terri has committed a crime. If you were to use that info, or if one of those businesses found out you even have it, Stamford Development would be buried in lawsuits or worse yet, face charges. Listen to me, Bobby. That woman is toxic. If you fire Terri, she will turn on you—guaranteed. I have a safer solution. I want you to try getting her to tell you how and when she got those files, and record it—use your digital recorder. If you get it on record, give it to me, I'll take care of it. Problem solved."

Bobby took several deep breaths, acknowledging that his play-by-the rules, everything-above-board attorney just offered to save his life and his career. Stuart was right; if he fired Terri, she would turn on him in a New York minute. *Okay, be cool. Just get it on record.* Bobby shuffled through the top desk drawer and found his Sony digital recorder. He touched the On button, spoke the date, and then placed the recorder face up in the open drawer. *I need to keep her on the other side of the desk.* Bobby buzzed Terri, then opened two of the files and pretended to be studying them.

She tapped and his office door opened. "What do you need, Bobby?"

"I don't need anything, Terri. I just wanted to tell you these files are amazing. Actually you are what is amazing." She looked pleased at his compliment. "You didn't say how you got them and I'm fascinated. I know how creative you are, but you can't keep secrets from Bobby, right? How did you ever do it?" He smiled with what he hoped was a sexy, engaging smile.

She bought it. "Well, thank you. Bobby. It's nice to know you appreciate my ingenuity and my talents." Terri's smile was dazzling; she loved praise.

"Count me as your number one fan, Terri. You have talent and ingenuity to spare."

"It was so easy, Bobby. Remember Steve Lange, the commercial real estate guy with the sailboat? He's nice, but clueless. Last Thursday he took me out for dinner and drinks."

"Last Thursday, the twelfth?" Bobby interrupted and glanced at his calendar. "So that's why you turned me down for dinner that night. I am jealous!"

"Yeah, the twelfth, and I love that you're jealous, but he's asked me out a dozen times."

"Can't blame him for that, but how did you get the files? Did he just offer them to you?"

"No, after dinner he invited me back to his office to discuss business, he said. Yeah right, I knew what he wanted. So after several more drinks and a joint, and then what I would call an intense intimate encounter, he sorta crapped out. He'd already shown me the company's prime files as he called them, trying to impress me, I'm sure. So while he snoozed, I copied—voila!"

"Very clever, Terri, you amaze me. With your talent, you could have a career as a spy."

"You bet I could." She rose, mimicked a curtsy and then breezed out of the room.

Bobby tentatively accessed the message. He had successfully identified her by name and verified the date; it was all on there and very clear. Breathing a sigh of relief, he called Stuart.

* * *

Adele accessed the internet on her cell phone and found the Dodge House Hotel. "You gotta be kidding. On Wyatt Earp Boulevard?" She called and asked to speak to Jack Ketchum. The hotel receptionist asked her to wait. When she came back to the phone she said, "We did have a Mr. Jack Ketchum registered, but you just missed him. He checked out this morning."

So relieved, Adele forgot to thank her. *Jack, you better have that damn cell phone on or I'm gonna sic the sheriff on you.* She scrolled to Jack Ketchum's name in her cell. Thankfully his phone was on, for it rang four or five times, then she heard him fumbling with the phone. "This is Jack Ketchum," he said. "Who is this?"

"Can't you see my name on your phone, you old geezer? It's Adele! You've got everybody lookin' for you except the FBI and I'm seriously thinking about turning you in to them anyway. Are you still in Dodge City, Kansas?"

"Just leaving, but how did you know where I—?"

"I'm so pissed at you, taking off without telling anyone. What's got into you?"

"Hold your horses, will ya? Tell me what's wrong."

"What's wrong is—wait, are you driving? 'Cause if you are, I'm not having this conversation. You get someplace where you can talk and call me back. Right back!" Adele paced around the café, slapping napkins down on tables, straightening chairs, trying to calm down. Jack was family and family shouldn't go off half-cocked scaring everybody. She was revving up to tell him just that when the café phone rang.

"I hope you've calmed down, Adele," Jack said.

"I'm calmer now that I know you're okay, but promise you won't be that stupid again."

"I promise. Now tell me what's got you in such a dither, that's not like you."

Adele took a deep breath, not knowing exactly where to start. "In a nutshell, you and I misread that scene on TV with Bobby holding Shelby's hand up high and them lookin' so happy. She's going to, or already has filed for divorce from Bobby, but is stayin' in L.A. because... you never told her you loved her, you didn't call her, and you didn't answer one of her dozen or more calls! What the hell's wrong with you, Jack! Shame on you. I hope it's not too late. Okay, now that you know, you old geezer, what're you gonna do about it?"

Chapter Thirty Two

Her father's call yesterday and the fact he agreed to retire was the second best news Shelby had heard; being pregnant with twins topped everything. Bobby's horrific reaction when she told him she was pregnant, she chose to erase. Negative thoughts weren't good for her babies; just the thought of them, in fact, produced an instant feeling of joy. She forced herself to think about what she needed to do. *First I need to get started finding an apartment. I guess the next thing is begin thinking about names!* That made her smile.

When she told Enrique, he was thrilled for her, as were Oscar and Esther. Like a true loving family they were happy that she was happy. She also told Enrique her plan was to extract herself from Skyline over the next few months, still continuing to do estimates and payroll and help with problem solving. But the birth of the twins would signal her permanent retirement from construction; motherhood would be the only occupation at which she intended to excel.

A dozen or more boxes of her belongings and clothes sat in the garage, waiting until she found the right apartment; she was not taking any furniture. Her father suggested she rent first before thinking of buying a home or building one. He asked her to wait on those decisions until he arrived and could help her.

Shelby found it difficult to ignore television and newspaper coverage of February 14th, Valentine's Day, "the day for lovers." She thought about what she hoped it would be, but that made her sad so she repeated her pledge. "I have no regrets. I feel nothing but joy."

Bobby had called and asked if he could take her to dinner "for one last Valentine's Day." When she politely refused, he said he would stay at his parents' for as long as she needed. He said he would phone Oscar a list of clothes and toiletries to bring to him. In the two weeks since their meeting and subsequent agreement, he had been over-the-top solicitous.

Thinking it had to be about dinner time, Shelby walked into the kitchen, a wonderful aroma forcing her to lift the lid on the pot of rustler's stew she and Esther had prepared earlier. "Gosh, that smells good." She stood at the stove and closed her eyes; she was back at the ranch the night before her father arrived. Opening her eyes, she wondered when everything she saw, smelled, or felt would quit reminding her of Montana.

Esther was on the patio dusting furniture, and Shelby saw Oscar disappear into the stables to feed the horses. Still looking outside, she was startled by the doorbell and the kitchen phone ringing at the same time. She grabbed the phone. It was Enrique wanting to speak to his mother.

"Hang on, I'll get her, but is everything alright?" Shelby knocked on the sliding glass door for Esther and then hurried to the front door as the doorbell rang a second time. "Okay, okay, I'm coming," she muttered, the kitchen phone pressed tight against her shoulder as she tried to concentrate on what Enrique was saying. Struggling to keep the phone from slipping, she opened the door, her eyes cast downward.

What she saw did not immediately register, but it didn't take long. She was staring down at two hand-tooled, tan cowboy boots, an intricate design splayed across the toe of each boot. Her eyes traveled upward, taking in familiar faded jeans, then stopping on the jacket with arms trying to balance a bedraggled bouquet of roses and a puppy wriggling to get down.

"I'll have her call you, Enrique." Shelby set the phone on the entry table, then looked up to the face above the jacket, straight into cerulean blue eyes she couldn't help but notice were the same color as the California sky. Jack thrust the roses and Shadow into her arms and took her in his, Shadow caught in the middle until he yelped and Jack had to let Shelby go.

"Jack?" Shelby backed up, still holding onto Shadow. "I can't believe... how did you... I don't understand," she said and peered around him. There in the driveway was Jack's big Ford Diesel Dually truck with a four-stall horse trailer hitched behind taking up a lengthy space of the driveway. Caught totally off-guard, she put Shadow down at her feet. He immediately took off scampering onto the grass, his rear lowered to the ground, running in ever widening circles.

"I better get him before he runs into the street." Jack hurried after Shadow, scooped him up and brought him back inside, then stood holding him. "I was in the neighborhood and thought I'd stop by to wish you Happy Valentine's Day." He turned and closed the front door.

Shelby stared at him, trying to decide whether to kiss him or deck him with a left hook. Jack put Shadow down, removed his hat and stood holding it against his chest, his expression unsure. "You're upset, right?"

Shelby stepped back. "What makes you think I would I be upset? I only tried to call you a thousand times, day and night for a month!"

"I drove fifteen hundred miles straight from Kansas to explain," he said quietly.

"I can't believe you didn't call. Not once!" Shelby lopped the flowers against his chest. Jack lowered his new Stetson out of the way and stood unflinching.

"What kind of message do you think that gave me?" Shelby felt her face flush. Jack grinned at her. Shadow was looking up at her, his head cocked, his tail wagging.

"You're riled up. I expected as much, but will you please let me explain? Please?"

"I will but..." Shelby heard the sliding door open and then close, Oscar and Esther arriving in the entryway, looking unsure. They waited expectantly, their eyes on Jack.

He offered his hand to Oscar then Esther. "Jack Ketchum. Pleased to meet you."

Esther looked up at Jack, a foot taller than she. "*Con mucho gusto, señor.*" She nodded. "We can leave for you to talk, if you wish?" Esther looked concerned that Shelby was upset.

"Yes, Esther, thank you. I'll be fine."

Shelby and Jack were still facing each other; he hadn't moved from the spot just inside the door. He was looking at her, his hand on his hat. "Well?" she said.

"I saw you on TV with Bobby, on NBC News at the Covington shindig. You and Bobby were holding hands and both smiling. Bobby looked like he'd just been elected head mouse at Disneyland. And I died right on the spot when I saw how happy you looked—I swear as happy as he did. I didn't want to hear you tell me it was over. I was certain I'd seen it for myself."

"You saw the ground-breaking ceremony on TV? That's why you didn't answer the phone at the ranch or your cell?" Shelby shook her head in disbelief.

Jack nervously fingered the crown of his hat. "I read it wrong, then I just lost it and took off. Me and Shadow drove to Kansas. I was gonna buy a couple head of cattle. Of course I should have called you and answered your calls, Shelby. It was a dumb, thoughtless thing I did."

Shadow had stopped sniffing and sat looking up at them, his tail still wagging. Jack looked down at him. "Go on, boy." Jack motioned toward the kitchen and Shadow trotted away and stretched out on the floor. "I've already kicked my butt, Shelby, all the way from Kansas."

Shelby felt her anger subsiding. Jack actually looked frightened. She'd never seen that, not when he confronted Bobby, not even when the robber had a gun pointed straight at him.

"Come on, Shelby, please forgive the unforgivable? I know I let you down," he said.

"I'm thinking about it. I just don't understand why—"

"I love you, Shelby, with all my heart," he said, staring at her with those intense blue eyes. "It took me a long time to get over Ellie. I didn't think I'd ever love another woman. Then you came along and it hurt to fall in love with you."

"What do you mean? Why would it hurt?"

"You were married and I thought you still loved Bobby. I knew you wanted a family and I didn't think I could give you children. I figured when you got back to L.A. you had time to think things over and made your decision—to stay with Bobby."

Shelby started to say something but Jack held up his finger. "I need to tell you this. When I saw you on TV with Bobby looking so happy, I was sure you had what you told me you wanted. And when I thought about it on the trip, as much as it hurt, I wanted that for you! For you to be happy and I didn't call because I thought you were." Jack's shoulders drooped. He looked at the floor, anguish on his handsome face.

"Dammit, Jack, that is so you," Shelby said, tears forming. "I can't stay mad at you."

Jack reached for her and Shelby moved into his arms, the roses crushed between them. "I am so sorry I scared you. I love you, I love you so much! That's all I can say," he said, cradling her against him as though she would break.

Shelby stepped back and looked at him; his eyes were full of tears. "Jack, are you okay?"

"I'd be better if we could sit down. All of a sudden I'm tired. I left Dodge City yesterday morning at six and been driving like a maniac, only stopping for gas and to grab a bite."

They sat down on the couch and Jack recounted Adele tracking him down the morning he left the Dodge City Hotel and calling him on his cell. "I finally decided I'd answer the damn thing. I didn't tell her I was leaving or where I was going. I just took off. When Adele got hold of me and said you called and sounded awful, I panicked." He looked and sounded exhausted. "I was afraid to call you from the road. I was sure you'd tell me to go to hell. Besides, I wanted to apologize in person and—"

"And what?" she squeezed his hand.

"Tell you I love you, ask you to marry me, and beg you to come and live with me at our ranch where there's nothing but blue skies and fresh air." There was a long silence. Staring at her, there was a glint of hope in his eyes.

Picturing the ranch house, Shelby was overcome by a feeling—it was joy. That same feeling she had standing knee-deep in the Flathead River and again seeing the golden fields with Jack on their first horseback ride. The dilemma was over. And just like her father had said, the world in which their children would be raised was decided not by reason, but by the heart.

"Yes, I will marry you—in Montana, the minute the divorce is final. I want us to raise our children where there's nothing but blue skies and fresh air."

Jack leaned forward and kissed Shelby, cupping her face in both of his hands. His eyes were closed then suddenly opened, his look questioning. "Children? Oh, Shelby, I'm not sure. Remember I told you it never happened for Ellie and me? I hope that doesn't change how—"

"I'm glad you're sitting down, Jack."

"Uh-oh, have I said or done something wrong?"

"No, no, nothing wrong, Jack, but you are mistaken." She leaned close and kissed him, a lingering kiss. "I am pregnant and you are definitely the father."

His jaw dropped and his eyes opened wide. Say again? You're pregnant and I am responsible? I'm hoping I heard that right."

"You heard right. I am pregnant. You are going to be a Daddy."

Jack's reaction touched her; he made a sign of the cross. "Oh my God, Shelby, never in my wildest dreams did I ever think I would hear that. You are sure and you're serious?"

"Absolutely sure and serious, but there's something else I'm pretty sure you'll think is great news. Come August fifth or so, Jack, you are going to be the father of twins."

Before she could say anything, Jack jumped up and hollered, "Yahoo!" He did a little cowboy jig then pulled her up into his arms. "You've made me the happiest man on this planet!"

After assuring him she and the babies were fine, they lingered over their dinner of rustler's stew, both catching up and sharing stories until she saw Jack's eyes beginning to close.

Shelby was relieved that he slept twelve hours and seemed refreshed when he woke up. After breakfast she gave him a tour of the house and barn, and introduced him to her horses. She was thrilled at his response. To Bobby they were a nuisance. Jack saw them as beautiful animals. Exiting the barn, he turned to her. "I'm hoping they are going to be part of our family, right?"

"You bet. Where I go, they go," she said, not able to stop smiling.

Jack took her hand. "Okay, beautiful lady. Tell me what's making you smile right now."

"How all this happened! You took off to Kansas in your pickup and horse trailer to buy cattle. But by some miracle, here you are in California about to haul your soon-to-be-wife and three horses! Like my dad said, how many things had to fall into place to make all this happen?"

"Faith knows no bounds, Shelby, all this—US—was meant to be." Jack's words said it all.

* * *

It took two days of meetings with her attorney to legally turn Skyline over to Enrique Flores, Contractor; it would retain the same name, just have a new owner. All that remained was the sale to Bobby of her half-interest in the house which her attorney agreed to handle for her. Bobby accepted that the transaction could be finalized by mail.

While she wrapped up the details, Jack readied the horses for their 1,300 mile trip. He bought blankets for California horses that didn't have a thick coat, shipping wraps to protect their legs in the horse trailer, lead ropes to safely secure each horse, enough hay, oats and safe "uncontaminated" water for three days. To guarantee the water, after a computer search, he found a farm supply store and returned with a new 50-gallon vertical plastic storage tank. Jack informed her they and the horses would be spending two nights of the trip at Bed 'n

Barn places. "They're nice, clean, and safe. I checked them out. And we'll be home on the third day," he said.

Looking very pleased, Jack took Shelby's hands. "Alright, beautiful lady, your horses are all set for a safe journey. So, Shelby, are you ready to go home?"

"Home! Oh, that sounds good! Yes, I am ready!"

Legal matters done, all that remained was the most difficult task— saying goodbyes. Shelby hugged Enrique and told him he and his family had a standing invitation to visit them in Montana. She called her mother in Colorado, told her about the twins, divorcing Bobby and moving to Montana to marry a cowboy named Jack Ketchum, pretty much all at once. When her mother chuckled and said she would love to visit Montana and meet her new family, it occurred to Shelby they just might be able to repair their relationship.

But Shelby simply could not fathom leaving Oscar and Esther, in her heart her closest family. "This is so hard to say goodbye. You have to know how much I want you to come and live with us in Montana and help raise your grandbabies? Would you... could you do that?"

They looked at each other with raised brows then said, "*Es posiblemente*" in unison. They gave their word they would be there for the birth of their grandchildren. Shelby pressed her BMW keys into Oscar's hand, along with the signed registration transferring the SUV to their names. They both looked so shocked she had to smile. "It's an I love you gift!"

Shelby had expected Bobby might stop by before she left but he hadn't. She wondered if he had driven by and, seeing Jack's truck and horse trailer in the driveway, chose not to stop. But after ten years, it didn't seem right not to even at least call and say goodbye. She called the office and Miss Telford transferred the call. The phone rang and rang; she was about to hang up.

"Hi, Shel. I think I know why you're calling. That's why I had a hard time answering."

"Bobby, I wanted to wish you the best with Covington, and with Terri or—"

Bobby's "Thank you," was followed by a sigh. "It thankfully won't be Terri, but please let me tell you something, Shelby. It's important to me that you know this. Terri answered our ad when I was in a terrible bind with Covington. Miss Telford had been handling everything and it was a disaster. Terri's qualifications and experience were too good not to hire her and she actually did rescue the project. But I realize now that at some point she targeted me and I was vain and stupid enough to fall for it, something I will regret the rest of my life. Thank you for letting me get this off my chest, Shelby. I truly wish you and Jack the best."

Shelby replaced the receiver, stunned by Bobby's emotional confession, an apology of sorts and, sadly, his admission of a vital lesson learned too late. *Bless you, Bobby, I do wish you well.*

After all the hugs and goodbyes, Jack Ketchum loaded Shelby's boxes into one stall of the horse trailer, her horses in the other three stalls, a certified California builder, then one puppy, and himself, the happiest man on the planet, into his big Ford pickup and headed home to Montana.

Jack called Adele and told her to expect them in three or four days. "Everything worked out better than fine, Adele." But as promised, he left Shelby's happy news for a surprise.

Their last email before leaving L.A. was to David Longren in La Orroya, Peru:

Dearest Dad, you were right. The heart has reasons which reason cannot know. Skip L.A., fly direct to Montana—your new home. We (and Adele) will be waiting for you!

Love, Shelby, Jack, Shadow—and ? ?

Also by Patti Dickinson

Kaleidoscope,
A Collection of Tantalizing Tales,
an anthology co-authored/edited

Hollywood the Hard Way,
A Cowboy's Journey

Coach Tommy Thompson and
The Boys of Sequoyah

The Indian's
Daughter

www.ingramcontent.com/pod-product-compliance
Lightning Source LLC
Chambersburg PA
CBHW050913250626
47155CB00001B/212